RED SKULL™

THE CHAOS ENGINE

BOOK 3

Author STEVEN A. ROMAN made his professional writing debut in 1993 with the publication of his comic book horror series *Lorelei.* In addition to his work on *X-Men: The Chaos Engine Trilogy,* Roman was a contributor to the prose anthologies *Untold Tales of Spider-Man* and *The Ultimate Hulk,* and was the editor of the ibooks, inc. novels *Heavy Metal: F.A.K.K.²*, *Moebius' Arzach, The Alien Factor* (by X-Men co-creator Stan Lee), and, yes, even *Britney Spears is a Three-Headed Alien.* Currently, he's working on a new *Lorelei* series, which was launched in July 2002 under his Starwarp Concepts banner (www.starwarpconcepts.com). He lives in Queens, New York.

Illustrator MARK BUCKINGHAM is presently the artist on Marvel's *Peter Parker: Spider-Man.* Before that, in the years since he became a comic book artist, he juggled his time among DC Comics' *Titans* and almost every book in the Vertigo line, including the recent series *Fables,* and Marvel's *Dr. Strange* and *Generation X.* He is also renowned for his experimental artwork for Eclipse Comics' *Miracleman.* "Bucky," as he is often known, is honorary chairman of the Comic Creators Guild, and co-organizer of the United Kingdom's National Comics Awards. He lives with his wife, Gail, and three cats in the Victorian seaside town of Clevedon, England.

BUCKY.

THE CHAOS ENGINE

BOOK 3

STEVEN A. ROMAN

FRONTISPIECE BY MARK BUCKINGHAM

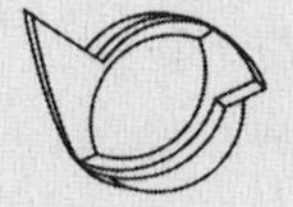

BP BOOKS, INC.

DISTRIBUTED BY SIMON & SCHUSTER, INC

An Original Publication of BP Books, Inc.

A BP Books, Inc. Book

Distributed by Simon & Schuster, Inc.
1230 Avenue of the Americas, New York, NY 10020

BP Books, Inc.
24 West 25th Street
New York, NY 10010

The BP Books World Wide Web Site Address is:
http://www.ibooks.net

ISBN 0-7434-5280-1
First BP Books, Inc. printing December 2002
10 9 8 7 6 5 4 3 2 1

Edited by Dwight Jon Zimmerman

Special thanks to C.B. Cebulski
for his editorial assistance

Cover art by Bob Larkin
Cover design by Mike Rivilis

Printed in the U.S.A.

For
The X-Fans

Thanks for your patience,
and your encouragement

X-MEN®
RED SKULL™
THE CHAOS ENGINE
BOOK 3

And Death
Grinn'd horrible a ghastly smile, to hear
His famine should be filled.

John Milton
Paradise Lost

1

HAAL'ITHOR watched in horror as the walls of the city crumbled around her.

The sky had rained death across the hiveworld for ten deenahl, bolts of multihued lightning streaking down from the heavens to obliterate all they touched. Many believed it was the work of the goddess J'raal, who had apparently decided to punish her children for some unknown transgression, though no one was able to discern exactly what that might be. And perhaps it appeared so to the most devout, for the ground trembled with the force of her mighty blows, and the air shook with the high-pitched wail of her war cry. But as a member of the High Council, Haal'ithor knew better. The "lightning" was a continual barrage of laser beams fired by warships in orbit around her world, Ishla'non; the tremors were caused by explosions when those same beams struck their targets. No, this was not the retribution of an angered storm goddess—at least with celestial beings, you had some chance of understanding the motives for their actions. An unusually dry season? More than likely the wrong beast had been sacrificed during the winter months, and the god to whom it was presented was offended. Flash floods that stripped the topsoil of nutrients?

Obviously too many offerings of nectar in thanks for a bountiful harvest—enough to heavily intoxicate even a deity like J'raal.

But what had transpired these past few days involved no matters of divine judgment—even an over-zealous high priest could see that. There was no logic to the destruction being caused, no perceptible reason for why so many of her fellow Ilon had to die. This was far worse than any punishment the Old Ones could deliver.

This was the work of *man.*

Haal'ithor shuddered. Everywhere she looked there were signs of their handiwork—in the marketplace, on the fields outside the city, in the lofty towers of jade and golden thread, their gleaming surfaces now blackened by smoke, scorched by the fires that raged out of control. The streets were littered with the bodies of young and old, their limbs bent in unnatural positions, lifeless eyes forever fixed on points in infinity. Haal'ithor's olfactory array twitched uncontrollably as the stench of burned flesh wafted up to her, more than a dozen levels above the market, carried on winds that scorched her carapace and stung her multifaceted eyes.

Behind her, the terrified wails of her three grubs echoed through the apartment, and she heard her mate scuttling across the room to ease their fears. Haal'ithor trembled slightly—they would have far more to be frightened of in the days ahead, she was certain . . . if they survived that long.

A shadow swept over her, large enough to plunge the entire city of Cle'rak into darkness. Fearfully, Haal'ithor looked up, already knowing what she would find.

It was a warship, the largest she had ever seen, more than a half-mile in length, and three city blocks wide. Hullplates bristling with weapons—all trained, no doubt, on the most populated dwellings—the cruiser hung low in the sky. Too low, in fact—its belly scraped the roofs of Cle'rak's highest towers, threatening to topple them. Haal'ithor's carapace tingled as ionized air swirled around her, the charged particles cascading from the anti-gravity engines that held the ship aloft. For a moment, an image formed in her minds' eyes: She a young grub, standing with other Ilon children beside their sac-mothers at the spaceport, watching elegant starliners and short-hop flyers landing and departing, the wash from their anti-grav beams tickling her antennae—

Haal'ithor, a voice suddenly called, startling her. *Your presence is required.* It was Geer'lak, president of the High Council, contacting her through the hivemind.

Understood, she replied, glancing upward. With a loud hiss of escaping air, a mammoth bay door opened on the cruiser, and a metal platform began a slow descent toward the council chambers on the west side of the city. A large number of figures stood on the anti-grav lift, but Haal'ithor couldn't distinguish one from the other—bipedal creatures all looked alike to her.

At a brief mental command, a pair of plates on her carapace slid open, and a set of light, ochre-colored wings unfolded. With a final glance at her family, and a silent prayer to the Old Ones that it would not be her *last* view of them, Haal'ithor pushed off from the balcony and flew away to join the other councilors.

No one could remember the last time a full assemblage of the one hundred-member High Council had been called, but everyone could agree to its necessity, given the circumstances. As she lightly touched down on the turquoise and white-tiled floor of the main gathering place and retracted her wings, Haal'ithor spotted a number of Ilon lawgivers she hadn't seen in years: El'zelius of the Southern Plains; J'laan of the Hinterlands; Kre'ssh of Ta'la'mor. Under normal conditions, there would have been time for pleasantries—how well the harvest season was going, the progress of their grubs—but with invaders apparently dedicated to destroying their world without provocation, time was the one thing the Ilon could not afford to waste.

J'laan and El'zelius scuttled over to Haal'ithor, their antennae lightly brushing in greeting. Haal'ithor was taken aback by the scarring on J'laan's carapace, and the unbalanced gait in his walk. Rumors had spread through Cle'rak of the decimation of the

Hinterlands by the offworlders, but Haal'ithor had hoped—and often prayed—they were just wild speculations. But the accuracy of such stories was now proved by J'laan's injuries, and Haal'ithor began to fear that Cle'rak would soon suffer the same fate as her sister habitation. Haal'ithor glanced back, in the direction of her dwelling, and wondered if there was still time to reach her family before the end came.

I understand the invaders are sending an envoy to meet with us, El'zelius said, matter-of-factly. *Perhaps your fears for your grubs are unfounded,* he added, clearly detecting her concerns through the hivemind.

Old Ones willing, Haal'ithor said reverently. She turned to face her old grubmates. *And it's true about the aliens. I saw them descending from their warship as I made my way here. Have they given any indication for why they've attacked?*

J'laan's antennae twitched angrily, and she held up an injured leg. *Bipeds don't* need *a reason for causing destruction. It's just their way.*

Haal'ithor and El'zelius nodded. It was a lesson most races in this sector of space had learned ever since the loathsome two-legged creatures had mastered interstellar travel: Whatever man doesn't understand, he destroys. Whatever man desires, he takes—usually by force. The Ilon had never had occasion for many contacts with such a brutal, warrior race, but Haal'ithor had heard stories of some of the atrocities perpetrated on the Lundeen, the B'tash, the Kree. If even *half* of them were based on fact—

They're here, J'laan said tensely.

Haal'ithor turned. The transport platform had landed in the courtyard, depositing what looked like a good harvest-load of aliens—all clad in gleaming black armor, all but one carrying weapons in their upper limbs. Not for the first time, Haal'ithor dimly wondered how such creatures managed to function with so few appendages.

The unarmed biped stepped from the group and approached the council. He—at least Haal'ithor *thought* it was a "he" (she'd never been good with gender classifications)—was smaller than the others, skin lightly colored, as opposed to the greenish cast of the majority of warriors surrounding him, with a closely-cropped layer of brown fur on the top of his head. He wore a metal visor over his eyes, making it impossible to see into his soul, and that set Haal'ithor on edge. It was a firm belief among the Ilon that the eyes of any living being allowed another to judge the purity of that being's life-force. To cover one's eyes was an insult—and a sign of distrust.

>*Nll r'stror g'laarnasrkklia* Sommers< the being said, pointing to himself. >*ylllrinkastral p'rol uullrekskannrrr ne oobra*<

A long silence followed the proclamation. Haal'ithor glanced around at her fellow councilors; she didn't need the connection provided by the hivemind to tell her no one had understood a single word the biped had uttered, beyond identifying himself as "Sommers." Obviously, the man attached some level of importance to the rest of his speech—the tone, if not the meaning, was unmistakable. Were it not for the unconscionable destruction he and his kind had caused, the lives they had so callously exterminated, Haal'ithor might have been amused by his efforts at communication.

The Sommers-man stared stoically at the members of the High Council, his facial muscles shifting beneath the pale skin to bend the corners of his speaking-hole downward. He grunted, then turned to the warriors behind him. >*ooll! ooll re vaes karell!*< A command of some sort, given the speed with which two of the warriors moved to carry it out. They pushed their way through the cadre of bipeds, heading for the rear of the group.

Moments later, they reappeared, dragging another small biped between them. Like the Sommers-man, the . . . woman(?) was not as physically developed as the soldiers who held her in a terribly strong grip, as though they were concerned she might try to flee. Unlike the Sommers-man, however, this creature was attired in a black, formfitting garb that completely covered her skin, leaving only her eyes and speaking-hole exposed. Manacles impeded the movements of her limbs, the short chains connecting them slowing her step enough that the warriors literally dragged her in front of the High Council. The short fur that grew from her head was a darker shade of brown, with a white streak running down the center of it. Haal'ithor wondered if this was an elder of their hive—did not white fur denote great intelligence and wisdom among the bipeds?—though the woman did not look old enough to have seen that many harvest seasons. On closer inspection, though, Haal'ithor could see the fear in the creature's eyes, hear the quick, ragged gasps she made as she drew breath through her speaking-hole. The woman was terrified, but Haal'ithor could not imagine why—was she not among her own kind?

The Sommers-man barked another order, this time at the woman. She frantically shook her head and tried to pull away from her bearers. One of them responded by jabbing her in the side with an energized baton he had taken from a clip on his armor. A sharp scream emanated from the woman as blue-white lightning crackled around and through her, and she slumped to the floor.

Barbarians, J'laan commented. *They even torture their own.*

Old Ones preserve us, El'zelius said. *Have they so little respect for life?*

Again, Haal'ithor's thoughts turned to her grubs, and she shuddered. No more than a few teek'lan into their first meeting with these creatures, and the aliens had already shown a disturbing level of intolerance for a fellow biped that had refused a command. What would they do to the Ilon if they continued to be frustrated by a simple lack of communication?

What man doesn't understand, he destroys . . . she thought darkly.

The warriors pulled the woman back onto her lower limbs, but then had to hold her upright; she appeared ready to collapse again at any moment. The Sommers-man stepped over to the group and savagely gripped the sides of her speaking-hole with one of his armored claws; the woman moaned in obvious suffering. The edges of his speaking-hole turned upward, and the biped bared his teeth, much like a wild saarlat when it was hunting. Haal'ithor started. Could it be the creature *enjoyed* inflicting pain on his own people?

Poor creature, El'zelius said. *Why doesn't he leave her alone?*

The man snarled something in his gutter-tone language, and the woman's eyes widened in terror. Then he waved a claw at the council, and the warriors began dragging the woman further into the chambers.

They're coming over here! J'laan said, panic in her voice. The thoughts she now had of suffering directly at the claws of the very invaders who had decimated her homeland not more than five deenahl ago, clearly transmitted through the hivemind, set the entirety of the council in a near-frenzy. It was a powerful sensation, detected even by the bipeds—the air was suddenly filled with the sound of safety-catches being deactivated on the weapons they held.

Order! Geer'lak shouted through the telepathic link. *There* will *be order!*

The command was strong enough to shatter the almost overwhelming feeling of dread that had taken hold of the council. Slowly, calm was restored. Even the Sommers-man motioned to his soldiers to lower their weapons.

Geer'lak scuttled forward. More than a century old, his frail legs growing steadily weaker but still able to carry him where he needed to go, the president of the High Council approached the man.

On behalf of the High Council of Ishla'non, Geer'lak said slowly and cautiously, *I welcome you to our chambers.* He paused, and Haal'ithor knew he was waiting to see if the creatures could at least understand the Ilon on a telepathic level, if not a verbal one. It had worked with other races.

The Sommers-man tilted his head to one side, as though attempting to hear Geer'lak's greeting, then shook his head. He turned to the woman and grasped one of her claws. As she struggled to pull away, he peeled off the material covering it; the dying sunlight of the day reflected off pale-white skin. With a brutish yank, he tugged her forward, slapping her bared claw against Geer'lak's antennae.

The woman screamed again; this time, her cries of anguish were joined by those of the entire High Council.

Haal'ithor reeled in pain as the biped absorbed the memories and communicative abilities of not just Geer'lak, but of *all* Ilon in the chamber—a flood of thoughts and emotions that poured through the telepathic link into a brain too small to contain it. The agony shared by all only worsened as the psychic backlash created by the intrusive mental contact tore through the hivemind. The High Council was overwhelmed with images of death and destruction projected from the woman's tortured subconscious—of planets laid to waste; of civilizations wiped from existence; of entire races enslaved. And above it all hung an immense vision of a biped's head: a giant, grinning skull, the color of dried blood.

The woman—her name was Rogue, they all now knew—groaned loudly, eyes rolling back in her head. She loosened her grip on Geer'lak and staggered back, into the arms of her guards, who quickly slipped the black material back over her exposed claw.

"No . . . no more . . . please . . ." she gasped, and Haal'ithor suddenly realized she could understand her words.

The man barked a few garbled words at her.

"Yeah, Major . . . I can . . . talk to 'em," Rogue replied, breathing hard. The biped stood uneasily on her . . . feet (?); the guards' strong hold on her upper limbs seemed to be the only thing that kept her from collapsing onto the chamber floor. "So many thoughts . . . all runnin' 'round in my head . . . too many voices . . ." An odd noise burbled out of her speaking-hole—"laughter," it was called, Haal'ithor remembered, from her brief contact with other races, though she could never recall it sounding quite so hollow. "They . . . don't know *what* . . . t'make outta y'all . . ."

She swooned then, and the guards tightened their grip as her lower limbs lost their strength. Haal'ithor couldn't help but feel pity for the creature. Obviously, she wasn't capable of handling unshielded contact with the hivemind, yet her fellow bipeds had forced her to do so. The fact that her mind hadn't been destroyed during the process was an impressive enough feat, but to realize that the woman's companions now expected her to hold a conversation without giving her time to recover from her psychic ordeal filled Haal'ithor with dread. J'laan was right—the invaders were barbarians all; the past dee'nahls' worth of planetary destruction had more than proven that observation. And if one of their own bipeds could be made to suffer so, just as a way to establish communication, there was little hope that the Ilon could simply *talk* their way out of any further unpleasantness . . .

The Sommers-man stepped forward and slapped Rogue across the face with the back of one claw; linked to her through the hivemind, the entire Council flinched from the blow. She stirred, and he leaned in close, inches from her material-encased features, muttering something that immediately brought her back to full consciousness; the rush of fear she felt while looking at her own terrified expression in the reflection of her superior's quartz visor swept through the Ilon. Geer'lak's soothing words, though, immediately brought a sense of calm to the hivemind, preventing another tense situation between invaders and inhabitants. Even Rogue began to relax, though the haunted look in her eyes never quite diminished.

She shakily regained her footing, then turned to Geer'lak. "On behalf of His Majesty Johann Schmidt, grand ruler of the *ryyl-llj'kkksrr* (another of those strange, guttural words that remained unintelligible, even through the psychic link) Empire, we demand the immediate surrender of all enemies of the Empire t'our forces." She glanced at the Sommers-man, who nodded his head once. "Y'all have one *hllrshh* (a measure of time, no doubt) t'turn them over . . . or suffer the consequences," she added, voice barely above a whisper.

A tremor of fear passed through the congregation, only to be quickly overwhelmed by even stronger feelings of anger directed toward the invaders. Haal'ithor's antennae bobbed with indignation—how *dare* these four-limbed monsters attack a peaceful civilization without warning and then issue demands upon making planetfall! Her mandibles scraped together with a sound like cutting blades being sharpened.

As always, Geer'lak was the voice of reason.

Friend Rogue, he replied evenly, *there is no need for threats. We understand the severity of the current situation, and have no desire to antagonize your people—even if you* were *the ones who struck first. But tell me: why must you communicate aloud? Through the hivemind, we can speak without words*—the irises of one multifaceted eye flickered toward the Sommers-man, then back to the woman—*or unwanted participants.*

Rogue's surprise flowed through the link; she'd never even considered that possibility. *Y'all can* hear *me?*

Indeed, Geer'lak said. He slightly inclined his head toward the other councilors. *We* all *can. As well as understand your . . . relationship with your superior officer.* The president paused. *He* enjoys *causing you pain, does he not? It was apparent in the thoughts we detected when you made your . . . unconventional method of connecting with the hivemind.*

I'd . . . rather not talk about that stuff . . . Rogue stole a glance at her superior. But with the visor covering his eyes, it was impossible to tell if he was actually watching her. *Are y'all* sure *the Major can't hear none'a this?*

Correct. Since you *were the only creature to make contact, this conversation is strictly between you and the members of the High Council. Unless you wish to translate it for the Major as we talk, that is.*

No, that's okay, Rogue said quickly. *This set-up'll do just fine. I can always fill 'im in on some'a the details later.*

The president nodded. *As you wish. Now, how may we be of service?*

Geer'lak . . . The warning tone from J'laan was unmistakable.

He rolled a stern eye toward her. *What would you have me do, J'laan? The bipeds have already laid waste to our world. If providing them with the information they seek will bring a quick end to their hostilities, then we should make every effort to be accommodating.* He turned back to the woman. *Is that not so, friend Rogue?*

I s'pose . . . she replied, though hesitantly. *I can't really speak fer Major Sommers, but I could* try *t'convince him t'lay off the attacks . . . if y'all do as he asks.*

And what would that *be?* J'laan demanded. *What could the Ilon* possibly *do for a race of starfaring miscreants like yourselves? Perhaps polish the blades of your swords before you run us through with them?*

Enough, J'laan, Geer'lak said wearily.

We're lookin' fer a terrorist faction, Rogue explained. *A bunch'a bad apples that've been causin' trouble along the edge o' the Skrull territories.* She inclined her head toward the group of green-skinned creatures standing behind her. *That's why* these *boys are here—the* ullrkk'yllon (some kind of military organization, Haal'ithor imagined) *thought havin' a squad o' Skrull warriors tramplin' through yer back yard might make y'all more willin' t'help.*

Was that decided before *or* after *your commanding officer ordered the attack from space?* El'zelius asked. *As you've no doubt noticed, we have precious little "back yard"* left *for them to "trample through" at the moment.*

Rogue shifted uncomfortably on her lower limbs and turned her gaze to the floor.

And what do these "terrorists" look like? Geer'lak asked.

They're, er . . . Rogue paused, searching for the right words, then looked up. *They're . . . bipeds like us, 'bout the Major's height, with yellow hair an' blue skin.*

They're Kree? J'laan asked, surprised. *There are Kree spies hiding on Ilon?*

That's what Skrull Intelligence says, Rogue replied. *We're hopin' y'all might be able t'tell us where we can find 'em.*

What makes you think we even knew they had arrived? Haal'ithor asked, no longer able to remain silent.

Rogue silently stared at her; then, slowly, the muscles around her speaking-hole twisted downward. *I didn't say y'all* did. *But if you folks are s'posed t'be the rulers of this planet, it's kinda* logical *t'think you'd be the ones t'ask, right?*

And you could not have done so without first laying siege to our world? Haal'ithor asked.

I ain't the one who makes policy. . . Rogue said, and looked away. It was a poor answer, a bureaucrat's answer, one apparent to all—especially to the woman who had just uttered it with more than a trace of embarrassment.

Major Sommers suddenly stepped over and grabbed her by the upper limbs. He shook her for a moment, snarling in their native dialect, apparently dissatisfied with her progress.

"I'm workin' as fast as I can, Major," Rogue said nervously, "but I had t'make our intentions clear before I could start pumpin' 'em fer information. *You* know protocol." For just a moment, the flames of defiance burned in her eyes—only to be quickly extinguished by the icy glare of her superior.

Slowly, the Major's lips drew apart in another unnerving smile. He turned to one of the Skrull warriors and growled an order. The green-skinned soldier nodded once, raised his weapon to eye level, and brought it to bear on his target.

It took Haal'ithor a moment to realize the weapon was aimed at *her*.

"NO!" screamed Rogue. She leapt forward in an attempt to stop him, only to be halted by her restraints. The butt of a plasma rifle smashed against the side of her head with a sickening *crack*, and she fell to her knees.

Closing her eyes, Haal'ithor disconnected herself from the hive-mind, to spare her fellow Ilon from sharing in her agony, and whispered a quick prayer to the Old Ones to watch over her grubs and her mate.

And then the world burst into flame around her.

* * *

"I think our intentions have been made *very* clear, Citizen Rogue," Reichsmajor Scott Sommers declared with satisfaction. He waved a hand in front of his face to dispel the scent of burning carapace that filled the chamber, irritating his sinuses. "*Ooff.* These vermin certainly make quite a stink when they're set alight, don't you agree?"

Rogue didn't respond. She lay on the tiled floor, curled up in a fetal position. Tears streamed from her eyes, mingling with the small pool of blood that had collected under her head; more continued to flow from the wound delivered by the rifle butt.

"Get up, citizen," Sommers ordered. He prodded her with the toe of his boot. "Get up and do your job, or you'll have *another* death on your conscience."

Slowly, Rogue struggled to her knees, the bulky manacles making it difficult for her to rise unassisted. She wiped her tears on the shoulders of her bodysuit, then gazed at the Ilon. The creatures had drawn back, giving her—and the smoldering corpse of their comrade—a wide berth.

The Major was pleased. With the proper display of force having been made, these vermin would now be more than willing to divulge any information they possessed about the Kree strike force. He smiled tightly. No matter where one traveled in the universe, the old saying remained true: fear *was* the great motivator—even among bugs.

"Telepathic cockroaches," Sommers muttered, shaking his head in wonder as he stared at the Ilon. "I'm sure that, somewhere in the universe, Franz Kafka must be laughing."

Beside him, the Skrull who had executed one of the bug-like things smiled broadly. Then his mouth went slack, as though he had been about to make a witty reply, only to realize he had no idea what his superior was talking about. Instead, he merely said, "Ermm, yes, Major."

Grasping Rogue by the arm, Sommers hauled her to her feet. "Talk to them, citizen. Make them understand we're only here for the Kree; once they've told us what we need to know, we'll be on our way."

"I'll . . . do my best, Major," Rogue said huskily.

Sommers patted her reassuringly on the shoulder. "I know you will." As Rogue shuffled forward to try to regain the Ilon's trust, the Major pulled aside the Skrull warrior. "I'm returning to the ship," he said quietly, then gestured toward Rogue. "Watch her, Sub-commander. If you think she's trying to make friends with another race she hopes will help her escape, kill two of them." He smiled. "I need her focused on her work."

The Skrull nodded. "Understood, Major. And when we have the location of the Kree?"

"You hunt them down, Sub-commander," he replied, as though addressing an idiot. "Your orders *are* to eliminate all enemies of the Empire, correct?" He pointed at Rogue. "And while you're doing that, have some men bring her back to the ship for a . . . *full* debriefing. Make sure they understand that under *no circumstances* are they to touch her skin." He sneered. "I don't need another Bloodstone Crater on my hands. I lost a dozen soldiers on that attempted break-out—I'll be damned if she's going to cost me any more."

"And the High Council?"

Sommers considered the question for a moment, then shrugged. "Exterminate them. The Empire doesn't need any more vermin infesting it than it already has."

Turning on his heel, the Major walked off, trying to ignore the smell of death that filled his nostrils.

Flashback

"WELL, *that* could have gone better . . ." Elisabeth Braddock commented dryly.

A groan forced its way through her lips as she struggled to sit up. It was taking considerable effort—her leg muscles felt like soft taffy, her arms appeared to have lost their strength, and her head ached as though some tremendous weight was pressing down on it.

And that, she dimly realized, was because there *was* a tremendous weight pressing down on it—a large stone block that rested on her skull, pinning it to the ground on which she lay.

How she'd gotten into this particular situation she couldn't exactly recall, but she knew it would come to her . . . eventually . . . once her head stopped throbbing . . .

Her problems began, as far as she could remember, only a few days past, when her fellow members in the mutant super hero group called the X-Men returned to Earth from a mission offworld. They'd been gone for a month, helping an old ally—Roma, Supreme Guardian of the Omniverse—with a troublesome other-dimensional tyrant named Sat-yr-nin. Short on humanity but disturbingly long on hostility, Sat-yr-nin was the dictator of the fascist Great Britain of a parallel reality, and a woman who had caused the X-Men—and Betsy, in particular—quite a bit of grief over the years. For this mission, it had been decided by Professor Charles Xavier, the leader of the X-Men, that only a handful of his students should accompany him; Betsy and their other teammates would remain behind, to watch over the Institute for Higher Learning he ran in New York's Westchester County.

Wishing the group "good luck" before they departed was the last memory she had had of the X-Men, or even the life she led with them, until their recent return. The time between the two events was a jumble of conflicting recollections and psychological digressions. All she had known was that, while she was still a purple-haired, Japanese-featured British woman in her twenties, she was no longer a mutant—no longer genetically gifted with the telepathic abilities that had made her such a formidable member of the team. Somehow, those memories had been stripped from her mind, replaced with new ones of a world without the X-Men, or even most super heroes for that matter. A world in which Victor von Doom—the armored super-villain known as "Doctor Doom"—had expanded his dictatorship of the small, Eastern European country of Latveria to encompass the entire planet, and the X-Men's greatest enemy, Magneto, had become a fugitive. How any of this had been accomplished hadn't been of concern to Betsy. In this Brave New World of thought police, mutant revolutionaries, and enforced global harmony, she had been far more focused on her career as a cabaret singer.

That was another aspect of this bizarre reality in which she had found herself: Of all the possible career choices she might have considered in her life, being a smoky-voiced chanteuse warbling love songs and show tunes for a roomful of nightclub attendees wouldn't have even made it onto her list. True, she had made an appearance or two at the Starlight Room, the midtown Manhattan hot spot owned by her boyfriend, Warren Worthington III—who, as the winged Angel, was one of the founding members of the

X-Men—but she'd never thought of pursuing it on a professional level; she preferred thinking of herself as a gifted amateur.

Still, a singer is what she had been, and it was as a singer that she was personally chosen by Arcade, von Doom's Minister of Entertainment, to perform at a Washington, D.C., gala celebrating the Emperor's tenth(!) year in power. The invitation had come as a total shock, but she hadn't hesitated in jumping at the chance to entertain a worldwide television audience that could be counted in the billions (viewing the broadcast being a mandatory requirement for all citizens of the empire).

But then she'd started hearing voices, and life didn't seem quite so rosy . . .

It wasn't a sign of mental illness, she later came to realize, but rather a slow return of her telepathic abilities—the "old" Betsy Braddock re-establishing her identity, forcing her way out of the subconscious to take control of her mind and body. Unfortunately, the process had been a painful and increasingly disturbing one—for a while, she'd begun to fear she was going mad. And yet, despite this unwanted complication in her life, she still managed to put on a performance that brought the house down—both figuratively and literally, though the latter was no fault of hers . . .

Having returned to Earth to find von Doom in charge, the X-Men formed an uneasy alliance with Magneto and launched an attack on the arts center, just as Betsy concluded her last number. In the chaos that followed, she and Warren fled the battlefield, any memories of their involvement with the team still eluding them.

That didn't mean they weren't still heroes, in their own way. Shortly after their departure, von Doom and his bride, Ororo—who, under normal circumstances, would have been fighting alongside the X-Men as the weather-controlling mutant Storm—had also exited the hall, only to be confronted by an enraged Magneto. Without pausing to consider his own safety, Warren had flown to aid his emperor, only to be cut down by the mutant overlord. His body crashed onto the grassy fields of the Washington Mall, giving

Betsy only a few last moments to comfort him before his life slipped away. He died, never knowing he'd sacrificed himself for a Doombot—a robotic replica of the dictator. The *real* von Doom had been safely holed up in a subbasement of the White House, as Betsy discovered a short time later.

Before that revelation, however, came her reunion with the X-Men, and the restoration of her memories through the aid of Jean Grey—the fiery-haired telekinetic called Phoenix. It was Jean who finally freed the real Betsy from the darkest corner of her own mind, releasing the woman warrior the X-Men knew better by the codename "Psylocke."

But the reunion turned out to be short-lived, as Betsy disappeared from the war zone, transported against her will to von Doom's sanctuary. It was there she learned of the means by which the tyrant had seized control of the planet: The Cosmic Cube.

Originally created by the scientists of the international terrorist organization A.I.M.—an acronym for Advanced Idea Mechanics—the Cube was a device no bigger than a jack-in-the-box—but what it lacked in size, it more than made up for in power. Containing the energy of a "gray hole," the Cube gave its possessor the ability to alter reality, to change the world however they wished to suit their needs. But, as was often the case—both with the original Cube, and the others that followed—the problem with using a "wish box" of infinite power was that, like the legendary "monkey's paw" of short fiction, it usually created more trouble than it was worth—sometimes with deadly results.

On "Doomworld," the problem was even greater. Having fashioned his own Cube, the tyrant had neglected to confirm the accuracy of the mathematical equations used in the creation process; thus, the final product contained a dangerous—and deadly—flaw. As the "Emperor" explained to Betsy, this Cube relied on more than just cosmic energy to power its reality-changing properties—it also drew upon the life-force of its possessor. For von Doom, that meant it had leeched years from his life, reducing one of the most feared super-villains in the world to a frail old man barely able to raise his chin from his armor-plated chest. And yet, despite the fact he knew that the Cube was slowly killing him, von Doom refused to give up his "perfect" world, refused to surrender the device—unless, he off-handedly commented, the distraught X-Man was willing to accept the terms of an unusual offer . . .

It was a simple proposition: von Doom wanted to go on living, before the Cube could strip him of his remaining years, yet also wanted his planetary empire to continue. Betsy, who had just lost the one, true love of her life, desperately wanted Warren resurrected, his deadly encounter with Magneto cast from their minds. Why not combine the two? von Doom asked. Why not take possession of the Cube and restore Worthington to full health, in exchange for becoming caretaker of the world—under the villain's direction, of course. It wouldn't last for long, though, as evidenced by his deteriorating physical condition—within a month's time, Betsy would be just as frail, just as wizened, as the Cube stole her youth, her vitality.

But for the chance to bring Warren back to life, even for one more month . . .

"Are you *willing* to make such a sacrifice, Ms. Braddock?" von Doom had asked. "Are you willing to risk your life, your world . . . for love?"

She *was,* as the tyrant had known all too well, and almost *did*—if not for the timely intervention of her teammates. Tracking Betsy telepathically, Phoenix had led the group straight to von Doom's lair, preventing Betsy from making a decision she knew in her heart she would have later come to regret.

But the danger was far from over. The X-Men explained their real reason for hurrying back to their homeworld: The Cube was not only affecting Earth—its influence was spreading across the innumerable parallel dimensions that comprised the omniverse, destabilizing the space/time continuum. If the device wasn't shut down, the barriers separating those dimensions would weaken, allowing opposing elements of one to leak into the next, ad infinitum, until all—as well as the countless billions upon billions of sentient beings living in them—were destroyed. Sent by Roma to stop this "reality-cancer" before the damage became irreparable, the X-Men closed in on von Doom to complete their mission.

And that's when Magneto and his band of revolutionaries barged onto the scene, their non-aggression pact with Professor Xavier's students dispensed with once the mutant overlord recognized the power that could be his if he seized the Cube . . .

Betsy groaned as the stone block shifted its position, pressing down harder on her left temple. The pain was excruciating; bright flashes of light strobed behind her closed eyelids, growing with such intensity she half expected her brain to explode.

And yet, despite the constant throbbing in her head, she was still able to hear the sound of one stone scraping against another—was the pile moving? Was that a good thing? For all she knew, the stones above her were about to come raining down, crushing the life from her bruised and battered body before she had an opportunity to figure out what she was doing here. Her heart began beating wildly, and she suddenly found it difficult to breath.

But then another sound reached her ears—a calm, soothing voice that whispered through the cracks and crevices around her to slow her racing heart, ease her troubled breathing.

"Hang on, Betts," the voice said. "I'll have you out of there in a minute."

She willed herself to relax, then—becoming agitated would do nothing to alleviate her situation, and that voice sounded so familiar, so reassuring—and concentrated on blocking the pain from her mind. She turned her thoughts once more to the days leading up to this predicament . . .

A short battle had followed in the White House, as the X-Men did their best to prevent Magneto's acolytes from getting to the Cube, but the outcome was never in doubt—at least to Magneto, that is. Smashing von Doom aside as the X-Men fell around him, he took hold of the Cube and activated it, rebuilding the world as *he* thought it should be.

But von Doom wasn't out of the fight just yet. Grabbing Betsy with a gauntleted hand, he activated a matter transportation circuit on his armor. With a crackle of energy, they were whisked away from the lair before the "chaos wave" generated by the Cube could restructure them to suit the needs of Magneto's self-imposed reality—to suddenly reappear within Roma's Starlight Citadel. That hadn't been part of von Doom's plans, however—he had been attempting to teleport himself and Betsy to his castle in Upstate New York, in order to make use of the time platform secreted in its subterranean levels. Once there, he intended to transport Betsy to a moment before the assault on the White House, so that she could prevent Magneto from acquiring the Cube. Of course, following through on that desperate act became a moot point once the Supreme Guardian of the Omniverse interceded—it was her technicians who diverted the transport beam to the citadel, so she could interrogate the only people to escape the world that lay at the heart of her most recent problems.

Betsy explained the situation to Roma and her lieutenant, Saturnyne—a far saner, alternate version of the villainous Sat-yr-nin, hailing from yet another Earth in the multiverse—as well as Professor Xavier, who had been devastated by the news of Warren's death. Yet, despite his anguish, Xavier had made an impassioned plea to Roma to not carry out her plans to destroy the X-Men's home dimension in order to protect the rest of the omniverse—not while there was a chance that he and Betsy could succeed where the others had failed. Much to Betsy's surprise, Roma had acquiesced. Soon enough, she found herself back on Earth, with Xavier at her side, equipped with a recall device provided by Saturnyne's technicians that would transport the two mutants back to the citadel once they had secured the Cube.

Their plan was fairly basic in its scope: find Magneto, learn the location of the Cosmic Cube, and confiscate it. However, what neither of them had taken into consideration was the possibility that Magneto might have used the Cube to *better* the world, to establish peace between the long-warring races of *Homo sapiens* and *Homo sapiens superior.* But that's exactly what had happened, and Betsy could only imagine the shock—and, perhaps, jealousy?—experienced by Xavier upon seeing the actualization of the dream he'd spent so many years struggling to bring to reality. It was a startling revelation, especially when one considered the countless attempts Magneto had made over the decades to rule the world, constantly voicing his ideals of humanity as second-class citizens—or, worse, as slaves to their mutant masters. To see that just the opposite had happened, that perhaps Magneto had come to realize just how wrong his beliefs had been, quickly turned the X-Men's task from one of saving a universe to one of destroying a potentially better one.

Not surprisingly, that wasn't the only complication Betsy and Xavier faced. It wasn't too long after their arrival on Earth that their presence was detected by their teammates—who had become devoted followers of Magneto. During a confrontation with them in a Manhattan hotel, Betsy had been forced to abandon her mentor in order to avoid capture, using her own powers of teleportation to transport her to France, the research they had conducted before the attack indicating that the mutant overlord spent most of his time living there with his family.

Unfortunately, any plans she might have been formulating for a counterstrike were soon forgotten when Warren happened to walk past her on a busy Parisian street.

It wasn't *her* Warren, of course—she knew that. The man she had loved more than any other in her life had died in her arms only the day before, so this—this imposter had to be some duplicate created by Magneto with the aid of the Cosmic Cube; for what reason that might be, Betsy couldn't even begin to fathom. What she could understand, though, was the ache she felt in her heart as she watched him go by, oblivious to her presence in that half-distracted-by-other-thoughts way of his. Yes, she knew he was some sort of imitation, a Cube-generated fantasy given form—but it didn't stop her from following him to a quaint little apartment that stood in the shadow of the Eiffel Tower . . . and then confronting him.

That turned out to be nothing short of total disaster. In this world, Elisabeth Braddock and Warren Worthington III were a happily married couple—he a much-envied multimillionaire, she the star of a popular action/adventure television series syndicated around the world. Having thought that his wife was filming an episode in New Zealand, Worthington had been stunned to see a report about her on an entertainment news channel, the story detailing an apparent tryst between Elisabeth and a bald-headed, wheelchair-bound man in a New York City flophouse. That man, of course, had been Professor Xavier, but Betsy had felt no compunction to explain the situation to an overly jealous duplicate of the soulmate she had just lost—especially when that duplicate had been created by the same monster responsible for Warren's death. Her anger got the best of her, then, and she summoned forth her psi-blade—a foot-long dagger of mental energy that she often used in battle against her opponents, capable of overloading every synapse in their brains.

Worthington had partly experienced that first-hand, as Betsy rammed the blade into his skull, forcing her way into his mind. She'd wanted answers—for why Magneto felt the need to re-create Warren, what other plans the self-imposed Master of the World might have, now that he possessed the Cube—but it quickly became apparent that Worthington knew nothing of any value.

Well . . . that wasn't *entirely* true. As she explored his subconscious, Betsy couldn't help but wonder exactly how much of this reality had been fashioned by Magneto—and how much by the Cube. The question continued to nag her as she studied Worthington's memories—they were too complete, too detailed for a simple doppelganger created out of cosmic energy. Magneto could never have known so much about Warren that he could guide the Cube in creating flawless recollections of every moment of his life from childhood on up—and why would he, for that matter? But if Magneto was incapable of that task, did that mean the Cube was therefore capable of reconstructing the thought patterns of a dead man? It was a disturbing consideration—and one she'd preferred not to dwell on for too long. Pulling herself together, she prepared to exit Worthington's mind and resume her mission—

And then Warren—*her* Warren—called out to her from the deepest recesses of Worthington's subconscious.

He was alive.

She'd wasted no time in pondering the hows and the whys of the situation before plunging into the depths of this foreign yet hauntingly familiar mind—if there was any chance that Warren's mind was trapped within the body of this Cube-construct, she would do whatever was necessary to free him.

She wasn't going to lose him again.

The journey seemed to take days, but time was subjective on the psychic plane, as Betsy well knew; based on prior experience, no more than a few minutes would have passed since she entered Worthington's mind. But no matter how long the passage of time, every moment was sheer agony for her as she tried her best to rein in her emotions, part of her almost giddy with excitement at the prospect of being reunited with her lost love, part of her fearing this might be some trick of Magneto's.

It turned out to be a combination of both. Arriving at a clearing in the jungle-decorated landscape of Worthington's subconscious, Betsy had been confronted by a representation of the Great Wall of China—or, at the very least, something close to it. After spending some time examining it, Betsy realized that the barrier must have been the method by which Magneto ensured the "cooperation" of the populace, using the Cube to enhance his limited psychic powers so that he could reconfigure his subjects' thoughts in such a way that they would never question his authority. A clever application of cosmic power—as long as Magneto possessed the Cube, humanity and mutantkind would continue to live harmoniously—but it was still wrong, no matter how well-intentioned his motives. Nevertheless, she wasn't about to let a bunch of psychic building blocks keep her from reaching Warren—not when she was so close.

Focusing her mental powers, Betsy created a sword that she used to attack the barrier, slicing away huge chunks of mortar and stone; in a short amount of time, she had carved out an opening. But before she could step through it, before she had a chance to be reunited with the man who meant so much to her she had been willing to risk her very soul for an opportunity to hold him just one more time, the blocks around her had collapsed. One struck her across the head, sending her tumbling into darkness . . .

A pinpoint of light shone through the blackness, the beam striking Betsy in the left eye. She winced and turned her head to the side—as much as the stone holding it down would allow, that is.

"Betsy?" the voice called out—and she remembered.

"Warren . . ." she whispered, suddenly afraid for some reason that, if she spoke his name too loudly, he might disappear, this time forever. Or maybe it was just that she still couldn't believe it was really him.

As more bricks were shoved aside, the pinpoint became a beam, became a widening shaft of blinding luminosity so brilliant Betsy was forced to squeeze her eyes tightly shut, her light-sensitive pupils seeking protection in the artificial darkness. And then she felt a hand brush the side of her face, fingertips delicately stroking her cheek to sweep away dust and grit and suddenly welling tears. Her skin tingled from the familiar touch, and a small, pleasurable gasp escaped her lips.

Slowly, she opened her eyes. Kneeling beside her, shoulder-length blond hair rimmed by the last rays of a tropical sunset, giving the impression that his head was wreathed in a halo, bright wings spread wide behind him, was an azure-skinned angel. He looked much the same way she remembered him from just before the world had literally turned inside-out under the influence of the Cosmic Cube: ruggedly handsome features and powerful body, attired in the dark slacks, blue polo shirt, and brown leather casual shoes he'd put on for their aborted night out at the movies. The very man whose brutal death she'd crossed time and space to avenge, risking annihilation every step along the way, only to discover—quite happily—that she'd never really lost him at all.

"Warren . . ." Betsy sighed, and an easy smile came to her lips—the first true smile she'd had in she couldn't remember how long.

"Hey, Betts," he said softly. He pointed to the destruction around them, and smiled slyly. "I always said you were good at bringing the house down."

She laughed—perhaps a bit too shrilly, but, given the circumstances, quite understandable—never before so grateful in all her life to hear one of his poor attempts at a pun.

He helped her to her feet, supporting her weight as she stepped from the mound of rubble, then led her to an uncluttered spot in the jungle clearing. Together, they sank down onto the rich soil, and Betsy threw her arms around his neck, pulling him into a deep, passionate kiss that lasted only moments but felt like an eternity, thrilling to the electricity that coursed through her body at his touch. And when at last they drew apart, Betsy silently vowed that nothing would ever separate them again—not even death . . . if it were in her power.

If it were in her power. A bold thought, she considered, as she lay on the grass, gazing at the sky. The sort of empowering statement one tended to voice when facing overwhelming odds, or vowing to avenge a death, although she tended to shy away from making such melodramatic speeches—they always sounded so disgustingly pretentious, unless they were coming from Professor Xavier. Still, she had to admit, there was some comfort in the thought that not even death could distance her from Warren ever again . . . although, when one examined the statement, it really only meant that she was willing to die beside him.

Such thoughts, however, were quickly forgotten as Betsy stared at the brilliant sky, her eyes slowly widening in surprise.

There was something wrong with the color. It was a subtle change, one that required a second glance before it became apparent that the vibrant blue that had been there a moment ago had suddenly paled. The clouds, too, seemed strange—they had thinned dramatically, the whites now tinged with a dirty gray tone.

She sat up, and gazed at the jungle around them. Here, too, the colors looked washed-out, leaves and trees and grass all spotted with the same gray tint that darkened the clouds. The bright greens and reds and purples had faded to ghostly shades, and as she watched, some of the plants began to turn an ugly brown.

The land was dying.

Lying beside her, Warren turned to face her. From the concerned expression that quickly darkened his features, it was obvious he could tell something was bothering her.

"We should go," she said before he could voice the question, and rose to her feet. "Now."

They walked quickly back through the jungle, Betsy filling Warren in as best she could, bringing him up to date on the events of Magneto's world before she had confronted his doppelganger. To say Warren was surprised by the accomplishments of Magneto the peacemaker would be an understatement, considering all the times the X-Men had almost been killed by the mutant overlord over the years. Hearing that their teammates were still alive in this new reality eased his fears considerably, but knowing that they were now dedicated followers of their greatest enemy only created new worries for him, especially when Betsy recounted her confrontation with the X-Men, and Xavier's subsequent capture.

Unfortunately, Betsy could do nothing to comfort him, for she had greater concerns at the moment—namely, watching the slow dissolution of the mental landscape in which they walked. Warren hadn't noticed it, still couldn't even after she had pointed it out to him, most likely because he lacked the sort of telepathic abilities that made her more aware of changes on the psychic plane. But *she* had no such trouble seeing the transformation, or realizing what it meant as the jungle turned ashen, the grass turned to dust, and the South Pacific horizon became an indistinct band of pale hues and muddy browns.

They needed to find a way out of the other Worthington's mind—and soon.

They found Worthington exactly where Betsy had left him before setting out on her journey to locate Warren: He was sprawled on his back, wings spread wide beneath him, laying motionless on the beach that formed the edge of the dreamscape. Just beyond the beige sands, waves gently lapped against the shoreline, while a flock of off-white gulls soared in graceful figure-eights above the gray-blue water.

Warren slowed, turning in a slow circle to admire the view. His gaze fastened on the dormant peak of a volcano rising high above the jungle from which they had just emerged. "That's Mt. Pindalayo, isn't it?"

Betsy nodded. "I imagine this is where he goes to 'get away from it all' when the pressures of the day become too great."

Warren shrugged. "Well, I can't fault the guy's tastes. It's the same place I think of when I need to relax."

"No," she replied with a frown, "but I can certainly fault him for having the temerity to snatch your . . . body . . ." Her voice trailed off as she gazed at Worthington; even at a distance, she could tell something was wrong. True, he had suffered a fair degree of psychic trauma when Betsy had bulled her way into his mind, but he should have recovered by now, should at least be sitting up instead of looking so motionless. So still.

So . . . transparent?

Without pausing to explain the situation to Warren, she charged across the beach toward his duplicate. Her progress was slowed by the loose sand, stockinged feet sinking past the ankle as she forced her way through the dreamscape. Each step sent up a small plume of beige-colored grit that stuck to her dark-blue latex outfit and lavender hair like a sprinkling of pixie dust, but eventually she reached her goal.

She dropped to her knees beside Worthington, her worst fears confirmed by the evidence before her. His eyes were wide, irises shrunken to mere pinpoints against the sclera, a fine dusting of sand turning the once-brilliant whites a dingy brown. His mouth was frozen in a silent scream, his hair a wild tangle of blond locks. But it wasn't the death mask replacing his once-handsome features that chilled her to the bone—it was the fact that she could see *through* him.

Like the landscape around them, Worthington was fading away. And once he was gone, any chance of escape would fade with him.

And she and Warren would be trapped in the mind of a dead man.

She knew, now, what must have happened. In her zeal, her blinding obsession, to free Warren from the psychic prison that had separated them for so long, she had attacked Worthington's mind with the full force of her mental abilities, without giving any thought as to what effects such an assault might have on the man. She'd broken down the barrier, yes, freed Warren, true, but more than that, she'd broken Worthington's mind.

"Oh, God . . ." she muttered.

There was a flutter of wings from above, and the sound of shoes touching down on the sand beside her. "Betts?" Warren asked. "What's wrong?"

Betsy felt numb. How could she tell him? How could she admit to him that this man—who had never done anything to harm her, who had never meant to harm her, who had simply had the misfortune to be an exact duplicate of her greatest love, thought lost forever—had been psychically ruined by her own hand?

Slowly, she rose to her feet, the words coming hard to her lips.

"He's . . . dying, Warren." She turned to him, mouth moving soundlessly for a few moments before she was able to regain her voice. "I . . . I didn't mean . . . I didn't want this to happen . . ."

He stepped forward, gently wrapping his arms around her. Betsy pressed her face tightly against his chest, finding comfort in the strength of his touch, the warmth of his body. He reached up to stroke her hair. "I know, Betts," he said soothingly. "I know . . ."

He fell silent, allowing her time to deal with her grief, letting her hot tears soak into his shirt. Of course he knew; of course he understood, she realized. They'd been through so much, both separately and together, as individuals and as X-Men, risking their lives on a daily basis. Always living with the uncertainty of whether they'd ever see each other again, dreading the day when one of them wouldn't be coming home–fearing that it might be Warren, dreading that it might be her . . .

Not so long ago, she suddenly realized, she had uttered those very sentiments to Scott Summers–the X-Men's field leader, Cyclops–when he had been willing to give up his life in order to shut down the Cosmic Cube. Betsy had pointed out that he and Jean had given so much of themselves over the years that it was about time someone else had a go at it, that someone else should take the point while they enjoyed what little time they had together between missions. In actuality, Betsy had been talking about Warren and herself, but she hadn't quite come to realize it yet–not until this very moment. Before she had joined the X-Men, she'd never thought herself capable of giving so much of herself to anyone, or of caring so much for anyone that she'd be willing to make such a sacrifice. But now . . .

Was that how Jean and Scott felt for one another? she wondered. If so, then she had finally found such a love in the person of Warren Worthington III. He knew her. Understood her. Accepted her for what she was, who she was, without question, even in her darkest moments.

How had she ever become so blessed as to have him in her life?

"Umm . . . Betts?"

"Yes . . . ?" she answered hoarsely.

"There's something I'm not quite understanding," he said. "If my double was–is–a creation of Magneto's, something he dreamed up with the Cosmic Cube, like the TV-star twin he made of you . . . well . . . how can you be sure he really existed in the first place?"

Now it was Betsy's turn to have trouble comprehending. "What do you mean?"

Warren stepped back to look into her eyes. "Well, if Worthington didn't really exist, how could you kill somebody who wasn't living to begin with?" He pressed on before she could answer. "I mean, you said it yourself: he borrowed my body. So that would lead me to believe that Magneto used the Cube to shove *me* to the back of my own mind and stick in a replacement personality that would be more in line with the world he's fashioned."

Betsy hesitated. In a way, it made sense, if she considered the hollowed-out appearance of Worthington–reestablishing Warren as the primary personality *would* cause the other to dissipate. But if that were true, then it would mean that the same psychic "overhaul" had been performed on her as well, when von Doom possessed the Cube; it would certainly account for why another set of memories–a lifetime's worth of experiences in a world controlled by Doctor Doom–were still floating around her subconscious. They were as much mental constructs as Worthington.

And then another thought struck her: If she and Warren had been "reimagined" by von Doom, then it was possible that it had been yet another duplicate who had died at Magneto's hands . . .

"And that leads to my next question," Warren said, interrupting her train of thought. "If my . . . double is dying, then his brain will die too, right?"

Betsy paused, unsure of where he was going with this. "Yes . . ." she said slowly. "Once the body dies, the brain continues to function for a short while, but eventually it shuts down as well."

Warren nodded, as though expecting that answer. He gestured

at the environment. "Well, if his brain is dying, they why are we still in his dreamscape?"

For a moment, Betsy's mind blanked; then her eyes widened in surprise. "Of course! The passage of time is subjective on the psychic plane—it feels as though we've been here for days, but in the real world, only minutes may have passed. His brain functions haven't ceased yet!" Smiling brightly, she stood on her tiptoes to plant a kiss on his cheek. "Warren, my love, I do believe you've found us a way out of here!"

"Glad to be of service, ma'am," he replied in an easy drawl. He looked past her, to the body of his duplicate, and his smile faded. "But how do we find the door?"

Betsy turned to follow his gaze. "I have an idea . . ." she said uneasily.

She again knelt beside Worthington, forcing herself to not look into those lifeless eyes. She gestured for Warren to join her, took several deep breaths to calm her nerves, then nodded to herself when she felt ready to continue. "All right, here's the plan: I'm going to 'hardwire' your consciousness to his body, allowing you to have control over it. Once that's accomplished, we'll have to reestablish a psychic connection with my body so I can get back where I belong—since I can't 'feel' myself, I'd imagine the link was broken when . . . Worthington collapsed."

"Sounds good to me," Warren replied. "How do we start?"

Betsy closed her eyes and reached deep inside herself, summoning the full strength of her mental abilities. As she opened her eyes, she channeled the power into her hands, to form a pair of rose-tinged daggers of pure psychic energy. She placed the point of one just above Worthington's forehead, then positioned the other in front of Warren's.

"Well, *this* is gonna hurt," Warren muttered.

"I know it will," Betsy said, "but we've no other options." She glanced at him. "Trust me."

A warm smile lit Warren's features, and he reached out a hand to stroke her cheek with the tips of his fingers. "No one else I'd trust more," he said gently. "Let's do it. We've got a universe to save, after all."

Betsy nodded. "Contact," she said, and plunged both daggers into their targets.

Two pair of eyes gazed out through Worthington's orbs as his body suddenly lurched into motion, arms and legs jerking spasmodically for a few moments as its new owners became acclimated to controlling its movements. With a start, the body slowly rose to a sitting position as its heart began pumping anew, warming flesh that had started to grow cold.

Inside, Betsy did her best to keep her mind at the job at hand, and not dwell on the fact that she was sharing mental and physical space with this man—a loss of concentration at this stage would more than likely result in both Warren and her becoming trapped in Worthington's mind when it finally shut down. And that would mean spending eternity in darkness, forever falling in shadow until madness claimed them both.

Kinda cramped in here, wouldn't you say, hon? Warren asked, startling her. *I mean, two minds in one brain—not exactly a lot of mental elbowroom, if you catch my drift.*

Oh. Yes. Sorry, she replied. *I'll try to be quick.*

Betsy shook his/her head, dispelling her troubling thoughts, and gazed at their surroundings. She was back in the third-floor apartment Worthington owned on the Left Bank of Paris, France, near the intersection of Rue de l'Université and Rue des Saints Peres, just a few blocks from the Seine River. Its décor was bachelor-like in its choice of furnishings—expensive "toys" like a fully stocked home entertainment center set against priceless *objets de art* that were scattered around the living room—though Worthington was, at least in this reality, married to a duplicate of Betsy. A low whistle slipped through Worthington's lips; Betsy sensed Warren's admiration for his twin's tastes—apparently, playboy millionaires were all alike across the multiverse, no matter how different their environments.

Worthington's neck muscles were stiff, but, by working in concert with Warren, she was able to turn his head enough so she could locate her own body. It was crumpled in a heap nearby, like a rag doll tossed in a corner. Again, by working together, the two X-Men were able to drag Worthington's body over to Betsy's with his hands, his legs not able to support the weight for the time being. Worthington's hand reached out to brush away the strands of purplish hair that had fallen over her face—Warren's doing.

Step Two? he asked.

Step Two. Betsy called on her psychic powers once more, and this time it was Worthington's right hand that began to glow with focused mental energy. As his hand closed into a fist, the psychic dagger formed, coming to a sharpened point inches from her head.

Contact.

"How do you feel?" Warren asked.

"Like someone just rammed a spike into my skull," Betsy replied with a groan. "Oh, wait—someone *did* just ram a spike into my skull."

He smiled. "Don't blame me. Some crazy, beautiful woman took control of my body and made me do it."

Betsy sighed. "That's the story of your life, luv—crazy, beautiful women are *always* taking control of your body. You just happen to enjoy it."

"Well, a man has his needs . . ." He reached down to help her to her feet. "The important thing, though, is that your plan worked."

She arched an eyebrow and gazed at him. "Well, not all of us are Jean Grey, but we do have our moments. How do you feel?"

Warren frowned. "Like I'm wearing another man's suit, only it's made of skin, and the fit feels kinda strange. Creepy." He shook his head. "I don't get it—this *is* my body, right?"

She gently squeezed his shoulder. "We'll have to figure it out later, luv. Right now, we need to help the profes—"

Betsy froze. Something was wrong—she could sense it; her psychic senses were screaming a warning that threatened to overload her senses. Rubbing her legs to restore the circulation, ignoring the pins-and-needles sensation that stabbed through her limbs, she staggered toward the windows.

"Betts?" Warren asked. "What's going on?"

She inhaled deeply, catching the scent of ozone that hung so heavily on the slight breeze coming off the Seine; the fine hairs on her arms stood straight up as the air filled with static electricity. Either a major storm system was brewing above the city, or . . .

But, no—it wasn't a storm; rather, it was the confirmation of her worst fear.

A curtain of brilliant energy was forming less than a mile away, the top of it lost among the gathering clouds. It hissed and crackled noisily as it began advancing through the streets, gaining speed with each passing second.

"Oh, my God . . ." Betsy whispered. "The Cube . . ."

Waves of guilt swept over her. She'd failed in her mission—too busy chasing the doppelganger of a dead lover through the alleys and avenues of Paris when she should have been trying to find the Cube and getting it to Roma so she could put things right. She'd wasted precious moments, and now time had run out—for her, for Warren, for the entire universe.

"No." A look of steely determination suddenly set on Betsy's features. "There's *still* a chance."

As Warren watched in bewilderment, Betsy raced across the room to the apartment's front door, snatching up a black canvas carryall from the floor. She ran back to him, rummaging through the bag with one hand while she held it with the other. With a cry of triumph, she pulled out a small metal box, the center of which was dominated by a very large red button.

"Saturnyne's recall device!" Betsy explained. "It'll take us back to the Starlight Citadel, and then, perhaps, Roma will be able to help us formulate another plan of attack."

Warren glanced out the window. The Cube energy was drawing closer; in a matter of seconds, they and the apartment would be consumed. "I like the plan. How does it work?"

Betsy slipped an arm around his and held up the device. "Like this." She stabbed the button.

Instantly, a bluish glow enveloped them, and they both gasped as a powerful current surged through their bodies.

"Saturnyne didn't mention anything about it feeling like *this* . . ." Betsy said through gritted teeth.

And then, with a *pop!* of displaced air, they were whisked far away from a world being remade in the image of its new master.

A world about to be shaped by the dreams of a fanatic.

2

JOHANN Schmidt had never been one for dreams.

Dreams were for the weak—pathetic fantasies designed to inspire hopes and a sense of well-being in the minds of the very louts who conceived them. But hopes for what—a better life? A world existing in harmony? An end to pain, to struggle, to hatred?

Lofty aspirations, perhaps—for those who chose to pursue them—but as delicate as bits of spun sugar in a carnival confection . . . and as easily dissolved.

Dreams were for those who lacked direction, lacked steely determination. A man might desire a better life, but how hard will he work to achieve it? He might wish for an end to misery, but what would he be willing to sacrifice in exchange for it? He might long for a better world, but what steps would he take to create it? Those were the questions that made all the difference—the ones that separated the dreamer . . . from the visionary.

It was the visionary who devised ways to end suffering, fashioned the methods by which other citizens' lives were enriched, blueprinted the architecture of a harmonious society. Direction, determination, sacrifice—these were the tools with which a man of true vision shaped a better world.

And Johann Schmidt—the man known to the world by the far more chilling name of the Red Skull—had always considered himself a visionary.

Of course, that was not entirely true, though Schmidt would never admit it. But before the "visionary," before the world-beating super-villain whose name had struck fear in the hearts of men and women everywhere for the better part of six decades, there was "Schmitty," the street urchin and petty thief, who had no place in his life for dreams or visions—unless they were dreams of power, and visions of his rivals and enemies lying dead at his feet . . .

As an orphan growing up on the streets of Hamburg, Germany, Schmidt had been an outcast among outcasts—a brooding, often violent youth who prowled the streets and back alleys of the port city in search of potential victims. Shopkeepers, artisans, sailors, even police officers—no one was safe from the crippling blows and savage kicks Schmidt administered when the lust for money—or blood—overcame him. But his most brutal attacks were reserved for the Jewish community of Hamburg. In Schmidt's mind, the Jews, more than any other ethnic or religious group in the city, deserved his ire. They had the best jobs, didn't they? They had all the money, didn't they? The fact that the targets of his anger just happened to believe in working honestly for a living, rather than accosting people on darkened streets, then running from the police, never penetrated his mind. Besides, the day would come, he was certain, when he'd be in a position above them, and then he'd spend as much time as possible rubbing it in their faces—and enjoying every moment that he did so.

And yet, despite his beliefs, despite his over-inflated sense of self-worth, Schmidt never rose above the rank of a common criminal, arrested time and again for practically every crime from theft to vagrancy—a faceless nobody destined to die in prison . . . or the gutter. The fact that he managed to survive long enough to reach adulthood should have been a sign to him that it might be possible to turn his life around—to make something of himself.

But that was too much effort for Schmidt, who firmly believed that opportunities should come to him, rather than seeking them out. It wasn't until he was in his early twenties that he finally had to face reality: he was a failure. Of course, that was no fault of *his;* the entire world had been against him since the day he was born. His parents, the police, the Jews, his fellow criminals—each in their own ways, they had all worked together to keep him from bettering his life, all plotted to deny him the power he so richly deserved.

Power—that was all Schmidt had ever truly desired. Power to take whatever he desired without consequence. Power to crush his enemies, to grind their faces into the dirt with the heel of his boot, to hear the sweet music of their death rattles as they drew their last breaths. And somewhere in the world, he knew, there was just that kind of power for the taking—power to destroy anyone who had ever crossed him, to let him finally claim what should have always been his.

Unfortunately, he lacked the motivation to go out and find it.

The passing years found him moving from town to town as he wandered across Germany, performing one menial job after another: gravedigger, floorsweeper, farmhand, manure hauler. Lacking a formal education—beyond what life on the streets had taught him—and barely able to read or write, Schmidt spent his days laboring to eke out a living and his nights, more often than not, in a jail cell.

He committed his first murder in 1935, when he was thirty.

He had been working for a Jewish shopkeeper in Magdeburg, sweeping floors and stocking shelves, angry with himself for allowing hunger and a need for shelter to force him into taking yet another low-paying position, when he spied the shopkeeper's daughter, Esther, watching him. She was a pretty girl, no more than nineteen or twenty, and it had surprised him that anyone, let alone this dark-haired angel who could have her choice of any suitor in town, would show such interest in him.

But he had mistaken her look of pity for one of desire, and, for the first time in his life, fell in love—or what he perceived to be love. Unable to properly express himself, he settled for forcing himself on her. Esther had been horrified by his savage advances and pushed him away.

Smashing her skull with a shovel had been a reflex action for Schmidt, the anger that had been building inside him for three decades at last finding its release point.

But that brutal act did more than momentarily quell his burning rage. As Schmidt stood over her body, the gore-drenched shovel held tightly in trembling hands, his face and clothes slick with her blood . . . he smiled. He had never known such ecstasy . . . such pleasure. It was intoxicating.

For the first time in is life, he suddenly realized, he knew what *real* power felt like—the power of life and death.

Still, his crime went unpunished—the victim was a Jew, so the local constabulary wasn't about to trouble itself by launching a full investigation; they quickly closed the case as "death by misadventure"—allowing Schmidt to flee Magdeburg and continue his travels without fear of prosecution . . . travels during which more than one innocent passerby expired from similar "mishaps."

Eventually, Schmidt found himself in Berlin, where he somehow managed to talk—or coerce—the manager of the most prosperous hotel in the city into offering him employment; the only position available, however, was that of bellhop. Down to his last marks, Schmidt had no choice but to accept, galling as it was to once more find himself performing menial tasks for another boorish cur—this time in an overstarched, gaudily-colored uniform that made him feel like an organ grinder's monkey, tipping his cap and forcing himself to show gratitude for the handfuls of change tossed at him by the very sort of wealthy louts and tarted-up women he'd spent his entire life despising. Here, again, he became just another faceless drone—a pack mule suitable for nothing more than carrying bags from room to room, taking the abuse doled out by short-tempered guests and his overbearing employers like any other dumb animal being disciplined by a harsh owner. What few dreams he might have possessed—if he'd ever cared to dwell on them—had long been taken from him by the cruelty of the streets during childhood, the harshness of his adult life, the constantly roaring flames of his misplaced anger.

Until that fateful day, that is.

The day he met Adolf Hitler.

Schmidt had heard stories of the man's meteoric rise to power as the leader of the *Nationalsozialistiche Deutsche Arbeiterpartei*—the National Socialist German Workers' Party—and the title of *"Der Führer"*—Leader of All Germany—that had been bestowed upon him by his followers, but hadn't paid them much attention; he'd never been one for politics, and talk of such matters bored him. Still, after Hitler attained his goal of becoming Germany's true leader in March 1933, even Schmidt had to take notice of the changes taking place around him.

The turmoil and hyperinflation collapse of the German economy following the First World War had taken an awful toll on the Weimar Republic and its citizens, both financially and spiritually. It was Hitler and his Nazi Party members who rebuilt the nation, brought pride back to its people, and re-energized business.

For the first time in his life, Schmidt had been awestruck. Here was the sort of power he had longed for, the type of respect he had always desired. He couldn't help but admire the man. To have come so far, achieved so much, in so little time, apparently! What did it matter if these changes were often brought about by brutal force? So what if others had to suffer, so long as the country was healed with their sweat and blood?

But *why* this man Hitler? he'd often wondered angrily. Why had Fate chosen a one-time beggar—someone no better than he—to lead Germany to a new Golden Age? Even *God* was against him, it seemed!

But if it was Fate that had chosen Adolf Hitler to become one of the most feared—and hated—men in history, then it was also Fate that had decided to bring together that same Fascist dictator and an embittered, nondescript bellhop in an encounter that would forever change the world . . .

Soon after Hitler and his followers had checked into the hotel, Schmidt had been ordered to deliver refreshments to their suite. He found the leader of his nation screaming in frustration at one of the higher-ranked officers in the *Geheime Staatspolizei*, or Gestapo—the Secret State Police.

"Why have I no one to turn to?" Hitler cried to the heavens, clearly upset by some failure on the part of his subordinate. "None to depend on? Must I create my *own* race of perfect Aryans?" In disgust, he had turned away from his henchman—and come face-to-face with a uniformed baggage-handler whose eyes blazed with jealousy, who did not look away as his *Führer* stared back at him.

"I could teach that *bellboy* to do a better job than you!" Hitler snapped, looking over his shoulder at his aide. A wicked smile slowly came to his lips as he turned back to Schmidt; clearly, an idea was forming. "Yes, I could . . ."

He could—and did. Hitler himself trained the former street urchin, taking this lump of clay and shaping it into something far more useful; giving it life, meaning, purpose. Teaching Schmidt to focus his anger, his burning hatred for all humanity, and use it as a weapon.

Giving him the power he'd always believed he deserved.

And when the demagogue had finished tutoring his protégé on the tenets of National Socialism, on the blueprint of his master plan for world domination, on the particulars of his "final solution" for dealing with the "Jewish problem," when he was at last satisfied with the results of his labors, this modern-day Frankenstein loosed his monster on Europe and, soon after, across the Atlantic to the United States. He even had a colorful name for this personification of evil he had created:

The Red Skull.

Wearing a bizarre mask that matched his new codename, the monster went forth to spread his master's doctrines, secure in the knowledge that he—*he*, Johann Schmidt, petty thief and vandal, brutish thug and murderer—had been chosen by the one true leader of all Germany to bring further glory to the Third Reich.

Now, at last, he had the chance to punish the world for all it had done to him. Now, at last, he would show everyone that he wasn't a failure, wasn't a nonentity. And, through his exploits, he would never let them forget his name—his *new* name.

His *true* name.

No, Johann Schmidt had never been one for dreams, but for visions. And the Red Skull had enough for them both—visions of spilt blood and torn flesh, of continents to win and worlds to conquer, of fire and smoke and the all-pervading stench of death . . .

"A glorious morning, is it not, Dietrich?" the Red Skull asked.

Standing upon the western tower of Wewelsburg Castle, an imposing stronghold that towered above the village of the same name in Germany's North Rhine Westphalia, he gazed at the peaceful countryside around him. Dawn had broken, and the Alme Valley was awash with color, the edge of the cloudless sky laced with warm pinks and lavenders, the first rays of sunlight tinting the forest with a flame-like glow that brought a faint, appreciative smile to even the Skull's lipless gash of a mouth.

And the faint wails of the damned that drifted up from the death camp at the foot of the mountain were as sweet to his ears as the cheerful twittering of the songbirds in the trees.

"Indeed, Herr Skull," his assistant replied. "A *most* glorious morning."

According to historical documents, Wewelsburg Castle had originally been constructed during the early twelfth century, eventually falling into a state of disrepair once it had been abandoned by its occupants. It was restored five hundred years later under the direction of Prince Bishop Dietrich von Furstenburg, and became the secondary residence of von Furstenburg and the prince bishops of the nearby town of Paderborn from 1603-1609. But it wasn't until 1934, when it caught the eye of Heinrich Himmler, *Reichsführer* of the *Schutzstaffel*, or *SS*—the elite guards assigned to protecting Hitler and other high-ranking Nazis—that the castle truly made its notorious mark on history, as a place of religious zealotry . . . and death. The Skull could have chosen to live anywhere in the world—England, France, even the United States, as distasteful as the notion had been—yet he had decided to settle here, in his native Germany, in what had been the mystical center of Adolf Hitler's proposed "Thousand-Year Reich."

A sense of nostalgia, he imagined. Within these walls, the plans for creating an occult Vatican were born, with Himmler and twelve "apostles" at the center of the neo-pagan religion that was to replace Christianity. It was here that the quest was initiated for mystical artifacts that the Reich could use against the Allied Forces: artifacts like the Ark of the Covenant, said to contain the stone tablets on which the Ten Commandants were carved by the hand of God, and the Holy Grail—the cup from which Jesus Christ had drunk at the Last Supper, and in which His blood had been caught during the Crucifixion. And it was here that Himmler formed his variation on King Arthur's fabled Camelot, with the SS serving as a new order of Teutonic Knights—a tribute, of sorts, to the German warriors who had fought in Palestine during the twelfth century Crusades in an attempt to reclaim the Holy Land from the Moslems.

The Skull had always considered Himmler something of a madman, attaching religious significance to the most basic troop movements, sending out memoranda listing holidays to be celebrated under the new religion. But Hitler had tolerated his *Reichsführer*'s eccentricities, even supported them, so the Skull remained silent and concentrated on more important matters.

Sixty years later, however, the Skull had to admit there might have been something to Himmler's ramblings. He could feel the power of this place—it rippled through his muscles, tingled along his bones like a mild electrical current; what caused it, he could not say. Perhaps the self-imposed high priest of the Thule Society had recognized it, too, in those prosperous years before the Reich fell. Perhaps . . .

Perhaps nothing. Himmler was dead and buried, as were his religion and his *Führer*. Their dreams for a global empire, for an end to all religions but one? Dissolved like so much discarded cotton candy in a rainstorm.

Now there was only the Red Skull, and his own plans for the world.

He glanced at his aide. In his late thirties, head and face shaved clean to indicate his unquestioning loyalty to his death-masked master, Dietrich had, for a time, served as the Skull's right-hand man, always at his side, always ready to defend him from his greatest enemies—and his closest allies. Standing smartly at attention, his dark gray uniform crackling with a heavy application of starch, its buttons and decorations gleaming brightly in the morning sunlight, Dietrich had always been everything the Skull expected in a Nazi: devoted, determined, willing to sacrifice everything to help the Reich rise again. Had it not been for his untimely demise at the hands of Nick Fury, the one-eyed, gravelly-voiced leader of the law enforcement agency S.H.I.E.L.D.—an acronym for Strategic Hazard Intervention, Espionage, and Logistics Directive—Dietrich would have continued to serve his master's interests, and the Skull would not have had to look elsewhere for followers.

But Dietrich *had* died, and the Skull *had* sought followers. He found them among the sullen, self-absorbed youth that seemed to be everywhere these days—so-called "loners" who kept to themselves, relying on computer chatrooms and Internet web sites for companionship rather than the teenaged classmates who scoffed at them, shunned them, berated them because they were "different." Youths obsessed with death, with hatred, and, in many cases, with the vision of a charismatic German leader long dead before they had even been conceived—a vision that gave them direction, and purpose, and a way to empower themselves, and encouragement to strike out at anyone they perceived as an enemy. At anyone who had ever laughed at them. At anyone who had ever treated them as a nonentity.

And deep within the mind of the Red Skull, just behind the flames that burned so hotly within the eyes of one of mankind's greatest enemies, Johann Schmidt knew that he had found others of his kind.

Here was clay to be molded, clay to be fired in the kilns of a revived National Socialist movement, clay upon which a foundation could be built—the foundation of a new Reich. All it needed was an artisan to give form to it—a gifted sculptor who could transform these disaffected young men and women into warriors dedicated to his cause.

Was the Red Skull that skillful? True, he might be a patron of the arts—he had learned to appreciate them during his sessions with his beloved *Führer*, who was a failed painter himself. And he was an aficionado of classical music—although somewhere along the way he had developed an unhealthy obsession with Chopin's "Funeral March." But an artisan who could shape young minds and inspire them to create the "perfect" world he and his former master had once envisioned?

Of course. There was none better for the task . . . at least in his opinion.

The goal he set for himself had not been an easily attainable one, but he knew from the outset that it would take time to achieve it. The first step had been the development of a web site that would appeal to today's youthful outcasts; this was accomplished through the use of skilled twentysomething technicians who were part of the Skull's worldwide network of neo-Nazi and other White Supremacist organizations—the source of his seemingly-limitless supply of muscle during his many attempts to take control of the planet, though that supply had begun to thin out over the past few years. There had been some setbacks along the way—most recently involving encounters with his arch-nemesis, Captain America, and the group of mutant super heroes called the X-Men—but the Skull never lost track of the progress of his plan, never allowed those he left in charge during his absences to deviate from it.

And when he finally revealed his part in this drama, when he at last stepped from the shadows to welcome these wayward children into the movement, he felt like a proud parent—or what he imagined a proud parent felt like, considering he had only brought one child into the world, and a daughter at that. Of course, there had been some dissension among his initiates when they realized who their leader was—it was to be expected, given the headstrong nature of children and their resistance to authority figures—but those who objected were never seen again. The world is full of missing teenaged runaways, after all . . .

As for those who remained—the ones dedicated to the vision of a world under his rule, who would sacrifice all, destroy all, to make it a reality—they and a handpicked group of the Skull's most devoted followers retreated to a base their "Controller" maintained on the far side of the Moon. There the Red Skull sat and waited, biding his time until the proper moment presented itself for him to strike at his enemies; considering the growing racial tensions in America and Europe, the escalation of hostilities in the Middle East, and the schism among United Nations member countries over granting the Jewish mutant Magneto—the self-proclaimed "Master of Magnetism"—control of the mutant-ridden island of Genosha, he didn't expect to wait too long for a sign.

He was still waiting, just beginning to lose his patience, when a powerful flare of the purest energy exploded from the vicinity of Latveria, the postage stamp-sized, Eastern European country ruled by Victor von Doom—an armored dictator better known to the people of the world by a far more ominous name: Doctor Doom. As the Skull watched, the image transmitted to his base from a number of satellites orbiting the Earth, the energy rapidly spread out from the epicenter to envelop the globe. And when it finally subsided, a new world had been born—one in which von Doom had become its master.

The Skull knew instantly what had happened, for only one device could have been capable of transforming the Earth into von

Doom's private playground within seconds; a device that he, himself, had held on a number of occasions. It was a wish box of limitless energy, a scientific Philosopher's Stone that gave its possessor the ability to transmute, not just base elements, but reality itself—to change the entire planet, as well as its population, into whatever—whomever—they desired.

An object called the Cosmic Cube.

The Skull knew all about the Cube, for he had been the first to tap into its power; the first to know what it meant to be a god, holding the power of Creation in his gauntleted hands . . .

It had been an accident of birth, this cosmic genie fashioned by the renegade scientists of A.I.M., the result of the organization's attempts to pierce the fabric of space-time in an ongoing pursuit to devise a weapon that would finally allow them to rule the world. After much trial and error, they had succeeded in forming a meta-singularity—a "gray hole," in layman's terms—that produced an element never before known on Earth. Through the use of overlapping forcefields, the rogue scientists trapped the element in the perfect form of a cube and began to run a seemingly inexhaustible series of tests, hoping to uncover the nature of what they had discovered.

They never were able to reach a satisfying conclusion, for their tests were interrupted when the Cube was . . . acquired by the Skull, with whom A.I.M had made a decidedly unwise alliance. But the Skull's dreams of a star-spanning Fourth Reich were quickly shattered by the intervention of Captain America, who tricked the death-masked war criminal into relinquishing possession of the Cube.

There were other Cubes, though, over the years, other opportunities for the Skull to mold the world to his liking. And he took advantage of each of them. But it always ended in frustration, his dreams perhaps too large for the Cube's abilities, his enemies too quick in taking advantage of a lapse he might have made in concentration.

After all, not even "God" is perfect.

But when he saw what von Doom had created in fashioning a Cube of his own, when he looked down upon the world from his safehouse on the dark side of the Moon and realized how limited his armored rival's scope of vision had been—why rule just one planet when you could make the entire universe your own?—he knew this Cube, too, must be his.

However, before he could formulate a plan for obtaining it, the Cube changed hands, falling under the control of one of von Doom's greatest enemies: Erik Magnus Lensherr—the mutant overlord known as Magneto. That, more than anything von Doom had done during his short reign as emperor, angered the Skull the most, sending him into such fits of rage that his followers feared for their very lives. To think that a . . . a *Jew* should possess such power! And what did he do with it? Squander it on wasteful fantasies of a peaceful, beauty-enriched world!

It was an action that the Skull had to admit even puzzled him, given the records he had gathered detailing Magneto's background. As a youth, Lensherr had been an inmate of Poland's Auschwitz concentration camp during World War II; had watched as his parents were marched off to the gas chambers; had seen the worst humanity had to offer—or so he thought. And yet, in spite of the daily horrors he faced, he managed to survive long enough to reach that day in 1944 when Allied forces liberated the camp. After that, the accounts of Lensherr's activities were spotty, until, decades later, the gaudily costumed villain Magneto made his first public appearance, espousing his philosophy that mutantkind should become the dominant species on the planet, and that humanity should be harshly punished for decades of alleged mistreatments—a philosophy that quickly rallied other mutates to his cause. With such a background, with such a passionate hatred expressed toward all *Homo sapiens*, the Skull had expected Lensherr to create a veritable hell on Earth for the non-powered population, using the Cube's energies to form internment camps, slave auction houses, possibly even extermination centers.

Instead, he created a veritable paradise in which humans and others of Lensherr's kind—the genus he had dubbed *Homo sapiens superior*—lived in harmony . . . under his benevolent rule.

It had turned the Skull's stomach.

The taint of Magneto's dream had even pervaded the Skull's stronghold, as the Cube's energies swept outward from the Earth, adapting his once-loyal staff to fit this new reality. It was only by releasing a deadly gas through the air-processing units of the base that the Skull was able to keep the men and women who had served under him from betraying his presence to their new master. Only one lackey survived the purge: a blond-haired youth named Leonard, who served as the Skull's personal aide. He had been safe inside "The Controller's" office, avoiding death behind foot-thick walls and sealed entrances, while his peers collapsed at their stations, lungs boiling, drowning in their own blood. Leonard's continued existence had not been part of the Skull's plan, but he wasn't about to open the door to throw the youth out, only to subject himself to the poisoned air.

Besides, there was no point—no real pleasure—in gloating about one's genius in having a plan in place for an emergency such as this if there was no one around to agree with him.

As for why the Cube had had no effect on him or his assistant, the Skull attributed that to his contact with, and mastery of, previous Cubes—in particular, his most recent encounter with one, in which he had absorbed the wish box's energies and used them to change the world . . . momentarily. Again, as always, it was Captain America who found a way to defeat him, in spite of the near-godlike status the Skull had attained. Nevertheless, though he had lost in the end, the grotesque villain managed to retain some of the Cube's power—not enough to rule, or even to alter reality, but enough to prevent him and his aide from becoming wall-eyed followers of Magneto's.

Soon after, he and Leonard teleported to Earth to seek out the Cube. They found it in Paris, in Lensherr's private apartments. Claiming the prize hadn't taken too much effort: merely stabbing Lensherr with an obsidian blade with a plastic handle—a weapon designed to prevent the mutant overlord from using his magnetically-derived powers to destroy it—and then beating to a pulp some bald-headed imbecile who tried to come to Lensherr's aid. With one enemy unconscious and the other bleeding to death, there had been no one to stop the Skull from seizing the Cube—and making some much-needed changes to the world . . .

Dietrich softly cleared his throat to get his master's attention. The Skull started, then shook his head to clear his thoughts. Letting his mind wander was a bad habit, one he'd never been able to break despite his best efforts; had he still any enemies, they might have seen such woolgathering as a sign of weakness. Slowly, he turned around to face his aide. "I imagine you are here for a reason . . ."

"Your knights have gathered in the North Tower," Dietrich replied, "and—"

"And you have come to tell me they are eager for my participation." The Skull glanced at him from the corner of his eye. "I am a poor host, am I not, Dietrich—to make my guests wait until I am ready to make an appearance?"

The blood drained from Dietrich's face as he fumbled for an answer that would not sound insulting to his master. Say the wrong thing, and he would bear the scars of the Skull's volatile response for the rest of his days—were he allowed to live that long. Eyes wide with fear, lower lip trembling, he had the appearance of a doomed soul waiting to be cast into the pits, knowing he had been judged by an angry god—and found wanting.

The Skull knew that look well—practically the entire global population wore it on a daily basis; a look of horror shared by every inhabitant on every world his star-sweeping armies had conquered. Knowing that he had served as its inspiration brought him a feeling of . . . elation.

The corners of the Skull's lipless mouth curled upward in a hideous fashion—the closest approximation of a smile he could manage, given the fact that, years ago, an accidental exposure to a chemical agent had turned his features into a flesh-and-blood replica of the mask he had worn for decades. He reached out to place a hand on his assistant's shoulder—and chuckled as the man drew back.

"Calm your fears, Dietrich," he said. "It was a rhetorical question; I expected no answer." His eyes narrowed. "Still, the next time a question is put to you, I expect an answer—immediately."

"Y-yes, Herr Skull," Dietrich stammered.

The Skull nodded, then brushed past his aide and started down a carpeted hallway. "Inform the knights and my advisors that we will convene in ten minutes' time," he called back. "The empire continues to grow with each day, and I must know that it runs efficiently. For without order, there can be only chaos—but only if the Red Skull commands it!"

"I shall notify them at once, Herr Skull!" Dietrich replied, but his master had already rounded a corner.

As he strode through the hallways, boot heels ringing sharply against the marble tiles, a satisfied grin contorted the Skull's grotesque features. Here, at last, was the world he had always envisioned. One of order and fear, of unquestioned discipline and swift punishment, of immeasurable power and one man's iron will.

A perfect world. But not a perfect universe.

Not yet.

But with the Cosmic Cube his to control, with his armies sweeping across the stars like armored locust, the Red Skull was certain it soon would be. If not, he reflected darkly, he could always wipe it from existence and start over.

3

IF there ever came a time when someone invented a way to wipe all dirt from existence so she could maintain a sparkling clean household, Jean Sommers would be the first on line at the store to purchase it.

Dirt, grime, dust bunnies—there were days when she felt she'd been waging guerilla warfare with the filth invading her home, battling it from room to room, winning the bathroom but losing the kitchen, seizing the kitchen only to lose possession of the master bedroom. It was maddening and frustrating and repetitive and . . . well . . . so damnably *boring*. But it wasn't a sentiment she could express to anyone—not her parents, not her friends, and *especially* not her husband. As a highly decorated commanding officer in the Reich's space force, Scott Sommers was the poster boy for obedient National Socialists, ready, willing, and able to give his all in the name of their glorious leader, the Emperor Schmidt. His face was plastered on recruitment banners from Times Square to Moscow to Mars Station. His exploits were reported on news broadcasts. For the wife of one of the Party's most respected and admired warriors to whine to friends or family about the dullness of her life—true though it might be—would have been considered scandalous—and an embarrassment.

Still, it wouldn't kill Scott to pay for a maid. He certainly made enough money as a commissioned officer . . .

Sighing, Jean brushed a loose strand of bright red hair away from her face, tucking it back under the green kerchief that covered the top of her head, and gazed around her latest war zone: the library. As beachheads went, it wasn't the hardest to defend—that honor was reserved for the living room of their split-level apartment on Manhattan's Upper East Side, mainly because its colorful indigo-and-red Persian carpeting was so tempting to their two miniature dachshunds, Sturm and Drang, they of the bottomless stomachs and overactive bladders. Still, the library presented enough problems of its own, since the mahogany bookcases and leather-bound editions acted as magnets for every dust particle on the lower floor, and the shelving ran from floor to ceiling, as well as along the length of the room. As for the liquid plasma television set mounted on the northern wall, it had already accumulated a fine coating of motes on its thirty-six-inch screen after this morning's wipedown. So many nooks and crannies for dirt to gain a foothold in her stronghold . . . It also smelled of the cigars Scott and his fellow officers often indulged in after a hearty meal when they entertained, in spite of Jean's numerous attempts to scrub the odor from the carpet and drapes, or the fact that Scott hadn't been home in almost two months.

But Jean wasn't the sort of person to give in so easily. Dressed in her traditional combat gear of one of Scott's old T-shirts—this one emblazoned with the washed-out logo of Beer Hall Putsch, one of his favorite East German rock bands back in his college days—knotted just above her bared midriff, faded blue Capri pants, and low-topped sneakers, armed with an assortment of cleaning products and the most powerful vacuum cleaner in five boroughs, she stepped forward, prepared to launch a first strike against her archenemy—

—and came to an abrupt halt.

Slowly, she gazed around the room—at the towering bookcases, piled high with volumes; at the antique desk, its surface covered with congratulatory telegrams from Scott's admirers and paperwork from the Ministry of Space to be addressed upon his return; at the plaques and framed medals and autographed photos—shots of him standing beside some of the most respected members of the Party. There was nothing of her in this place, she realized with a start. No evidence that Reichsmajor Scott Sommers had a wife; no sign of any sort that she even existed. This was a shrine to his world, his life—the accomplishments he had achieved, the victories he had won, the glories bestowed upon him.

Jean looked down and stared at the yellow rubber gloves covering her hands, the fingers of one oversized mitt grasping the vacuum cleaner hose, the others clasped around a red plastic bucket brimming over with polishes and sprays and paper towels. A tremor ran through her body, and the bucket and hose slipped from her hands, to clatter mutely on the thick carpeting, as the reality of her situation finally struck home. Cooking. Cleaning. Trying to make babies. Following the commands of her husband without question. Doing everything expected of the good housewife, as outlined by the tenets of the Nazi League of German Women—principles created almost six decades ago, but still in effect today. Giving everything she had, without question, without hesitation, until there was nothing left of herself to keep *for* herself.

This was *her* world, then. *Her* life.

A wave of depression suddenly swept over her, and she allowed its undercurrent to pull her down, not even bothering to put up a token struggle against the black thoughts that now flooded her mind. When she eventually opened her eyes, she discovered that the tide had cast her upon the leather couch in the center of the room.

Jean stared at the darkened television screen across from her, and at the fiery-haired young woman with the dour expression who looked back at her from the glass. There was a sadness in that woman's eyes, a haunted expression that marred her otherwise beautiful features; you could see it in the way her lips bowed, in the dull gleam of light on once-bright green pupils, in the sag of her shoulders. Here was someone without direction, without meaning being given to her listless days and solitary nights, without hope. A woman to be pitied.

Jean hated that woman.

It wasn't her—never should have *been* her. The Jean Grey who existed long before she ever heard of Scott Sommers had been an energetic woman, eager to do her part for the Reich as a science teacher at the prestigious Frost *Akademie*, located just outside Boston, Massachusetts. It was one of a baker's dozen of such Political Institutes of Education scattered across North America, though this facility differed from most in that it focused on shaping the minds of the *Jungmaedel*, or "young maidens," of the Reich. Like the girls she instructed, Jean had spent her formative years in such a school, learning all she could from her teachers and military instructors, then spending a year working on a farm as part of the Labor Service, followed by a Household Year, in which she provided domestic service for one of the Empire's more prosperous families. And all the time, it was made clear to her that it was her duty—both morally and as a patriot—to marry and bear children for the Empire. It was a lesson she carried into adulthood, as she so often reminded her students: serve the Reich to the best of your ability—whether you're a housewife or a warrior, all are doing their part for the Empire, and their Emperor.

And when Scott Sommers entered her life, it seemed as if she'd at last have her chance to do hers. Unfortunately, she hadn't taken into consideration the very real possibility that, in order for her to serve her Emperor well, she would have to abandon the life she had once so happily led.

Now, five years later, her hopes and dreams—her very life—had apparently reached a dead end. Oh, there was no doubt in her mind—or heart—that she truly loved Scott, and that he felt the same toward her. She enjoyed every moment of their time together, made even more precious because of his frequent trips to the front line, as the Empire continued to expand its boundaries. And she understood his commitments and responsibilities to the

Reich and his Emperor; she just wished there was more time for themselves. The longer Scott spent away from Earth, the more distant they had started to become as a couple—first, the love letters he used to sent via hypermail had dwindled to nothing, then the daily conversations they used to have at the end of his watch—brief to begin with, so the transmissions couldn't be used by enemy vessels to track the movements of his fleet—became weekly, became. . . . She hadn't heard from him in almost a month now, and, not for the first time, she'd started to wonder if she'd made the right choice in putting her life on hold indefinitely in order to show support for Scott while his military career took centerstage.

Maybe if they'd a child by now, she often thought, there wouldn't be such a sense of division between them. They'd tried—Woden knew they'd tried often enough—but nothing seemed to work, no matter how passionate their lovemaking, no matter how many specialists they had seen. As far as the Reich was concerned, the problem lay not with Scott—he was a virile, able-bodied warrior, after all—but with Jean. Obviously, it was decided—from doctors on down to her own parents—that something must be wrong with her. No one had thought to consider Scott's background, for that was one of the darker secrets of the Empire, one that only Jean seemed to be aware of: that Reichsmajor Scott Sommers, the poster boy of the space fleet, the living embodiment of the "true German," was a *mutant*—a filthy, bottomfeeding aberration. A freak of nature, unfit to live among the genetically pure—or so press releases from the Ministry of Science often stated in newscasts, in the papers, on billboards and the Internet.

Perhaps it had something to do with the amounts of radiation his parents had absorbed while working in the Chicago munitions factories, preparing weapons for the Empire's starships—the same radiation that gave him the ability to project force beams from his eyes; an uncontrollable ability, however, which was why he was forced to wear ruby quartz lenses in order to harness the destructive power. But it wasn't something Jean could ever discuss with *anyone*—not unless she wanted to risk both of them facing an execution squad for what would certainly be considered an embarrassment for Emperor Schmidt. And so, for both their sakes, she had no choice but to quietly live with the stigma of having failed her husband and her Reich—a useless trophy wife suited for nothing better than dusting bookshelves and mopping floors . . .

Jean sighed, feeling the strength drain from her limbs, and flopped bonelessly against the couch cushions, letting her head roll back and forth across the metal support bar. She gazed up at the ceiling, noticing for the first time a spider's web that had formed across one corner. Idly, she wondered if the step ladder in the kitchen would provide enough height for her to reach it with a broom . . .

Her eyes snapped shut, and she moaned softly. Couldn't she even stare into space anymore without having thoughts of housekeeping fill her mind?

Opening her eyes, she immediately turned her head downward, before the dust particles collecting on the TV screen drew her attention, and spotted the glossy cover of a magazine laying on the teak end table beside the couch. It was last week's *Der Television Guide*, its cover story an interview with Elisabeth Braddock, an Asian actress who starred in one of the Reich's more popular programs: *Kwannon, Bushido Mistress*. Then again, *any* program that showed the Empire cannily destroying its enemies in a display of gaudy, cheaply-produced special effects could be considered popular. Jean wrinkled her nose; she'd never been one for fantasy shows, especially when there were far better reality-based ones to watch, like *The West Brandenburg Gate* and *Crime and Punishment: Blitzkrieg Unit.*

And yet, there was something about the photograph of Braddock on the cover that held her attention. The deep-blue latex costume, the so-obviously dyed lavender hair, the strange, blood-red-colored symbol that ran along the left side of her face, from just above her eyebrow down to her cheekbone—there was something . . . familiar about them. She couldn't put her finger on just why that might be—she'd never given any mindfulness to the show, never seen more than a few seconds of any episode beyond what she caught while switching channels—but she was suddenly struck with the sense of having seen them, and Braddock, too, in a different setting. In person.

Jean frowned. She hated when something like this happened—now she'd probably spend the rest of the day driving herself crazy, trying to remember where she'd seen them before. It was almost as bad as getting a lyric from a particularly bad song stuck in her head, having it repeat over and over again; it'd taken her the better part of a week to get the words to Gilbert O'Sullivan's "Alone Again . . . Naturally" out of her thoughts the last time this annoying little problem cropped up. Had she ever met Elisabeth Braddock? A possibility. Maybe at one of the functions Scott was always dragging her to, when the Reich was eager to congratulate its most photogenic officer on yet another victory. When exactly that might have occurred she couldn't say—they'd been to three such extravaganzas in the past year, and so many people were in attendance it was difficult to keep track of them all. Or maybe it was at one of those youth rallies the *Akademie* often held while she was teaching—those usually drew a number of celebrities as guest speakers, their words meant to bolster the spirits of the students, preparing them for a bright future as productive members of the Empire. Or . . .

Jean exhaled sharply. No, it was no good. She just couldn't recall where she'd seen Braddock before, and trying to force herself to remember wasn't going to help. She'd have to let the question linger in the back of her mind; the answer would probably pop up when she least expected it—usually when she was distracted by something else.

Unconsciously, her eyes drifted back toward the ceiling—and the spider's web hanging in the corner. It taunted her, nagged at her, whisper-thin strands swaying hypnotically in the slight breeze that billowed from the vents of the building's central air conditioning unit.

With a groan, Jean rose from the couch and headed for the

kitchen to retrieve the step ladder. Any potential memories of an encounter with Elisabeth Braddock were soon forgotten as another thought loomed large in her mind: whether anyone's life could be as incredibly, frustratingly dull as her own. . . .

Dust.

Dust and sand and grit as far as the eye could see, covering everything. It was a view Ororo Munroe had grown so tired of gazing upon she'd often wondered why, every morning, as she dragged herself from bed, she still managed to have hope that something—anything—of even minor interest might appear to divert her attention from the wearying monotony of her days, and the endless wastes that surrounded her.

Taking residence in Araouane, a village in the West African state of Mali, had not been her idea—Ororo had always been, for all intents and purposes, a city girl at heart, born in a New York hospital, raised among the manmade cliffs and valleys of that hectic metropolis for the first six years of her life, then moving to Cairo, Egypt, with her parents—her father, a photojournalist named David Munroe; her mother, N'Dare, an African princess. For a six-year-old child, the thought of living in a two-room, mud-brick shanty on the edge of the Sahara Desert, like the ones that comprised the village, might have sounded like a great adventure—for a time—but the initial excitement would have quickly faded, once it was made evident that there was really nothing to *do* there. However, for a twentysomething woman used to commanding weather patterns across the globe and soaring through the skies, borne aloft on winds she controlled—a woman who had been worshipped as a *goddess* for a few short years—the thought of such "adventure" wouldn't have even been a consideration, not when there was an entire world to explore.

Unfortunately, being black on a world for which racial equality usually meant having the same white skin, blond hair, and blue eyes of your neighbor, the notion of traveling freely *anywhere* was out of the question, especially once the *Schutzstaffel* Race and

Resettlement Bureau had begun forcibly instituting its policy of "repatriating" most of the planet's black population to Africa during the 1980s—"the better to keep an eye on them, having them all in one place," as the Emperor Schmidt had commented at the time. Being a black woman had its own complications, especially since the female population was seen as nothing more than property to be bought and sold by the Empire's wealthiest families—or to be used as mistresses for some of the Reich's more lascivious powerbrokers. And, of course, as Ororo had learned over the years, having been born a mutant was the greatest sin of all: a genetic defect no better than the "untouchables" of Hindu beliefs, whose very touch was considered a form of pollution—although, based on the "evolutionary chain" once devised by the Reichminister of Health, Arnim Zola, and his assistant, Dr. Henry McCoy, in order to give students a clearer understanding of the tenets of "genetic purity," even *that* lower caste ranked higher than Ororo and her kind.

No, settling in Araouane hadn't been her idea; it was where the SS had forced her to go after they had stripped her of her powers, to keep her from "infecting" any large centers of population. Why they hadn't just killed her was a question that still haunted her from time to time. Was she to be part of some Nazi plan to be implemented in the future? Was she considered too valuable to eliminate?

Or was it that she just hadn't been worth the effort of killing?

The memories of her fall from godhood still tore at Ororo's heart: the betrayal by worshippers she'd come to think of as friends; the blast of sonic power emitted by the villain Klaw that had knocked her from the sky, and into the hands of the SS; the pain of the surgery she'd had to endure—performed without anesthesia—that had forever stolen the skies from her. Unconsciously, she placed a hand at the small of her back, feeling the ever-present, gumball-sized lump of the neural inhibitor that had been welded to the base of her spine. Small it might be, but it was powerful enough to shut down her element-controlling abilities—and it couldn't be removed without killing her.

Would that be so bad, though—to die at least in trying to free herself before this sand-washed purgatory could finally claim her soul? She couldn't help but wonder. She had felt empty enough when she'd lost her powers of the storm, but when she'd been robbed of her gift of flight . . . For someone who had soared with the birds, played tag with the clouds, chased the moon through nights ablaze with the light of billions of stars, being confined to the ground was the worst sort of punishment imaginable. There were days when the sense of loss became almost too much to bear. Days when her heart ached as she watched the lowly vultures spinning in lazy circles through skies so blue it seemed as though the Bright Lady herself must have painted them. Days when the slightest of breezes gently ruffled her waist-length hair and she heard the winds softly call her name, the clouds urging her to come play with them . . .

Ororo shook her head, angered by allowing herself to fall into yet another pitiable bout of useless reverie. Yes, she missed the freedom she'd once taken for granted, the powers she'd possessed, but pining for their return was a waste of time. This was her life now, and she had never been the sort who gave in to bouts of depression for long. She tightened the sash of her once-white robes and held her head high, determined not to lapse into any further periods of morbid daydreaming.

"A good day, is it not, my lady?" asked a pleasant female voice.

Ororo turned. Standing beside her was a tall, narrow-waisted African woman in her thirties, wrapped in a blanket emblazoned with yellow, blue, and green patterns set on a red field. Her face alight with an infectious smile, she ran a hand through her short, dark hair, shaking loose the particles of sand that had settled in it, carried by the humid breeze; in her other hand she held an oversized bowl.

Ororo smiled. "And what makes you say that, Abena Metou?"

Her companion gestured at their surroundings. "A blue sky, a light wind, a desert at rest, allowing me to spend time with my family." Her smile widened. "Is that not proof enough that the Bright Lady blesses us?"

Ororo slowly nodded. "Indeed . . ."

Abena Metou had been a resident of Araouane long before Ororo had arrived and—so far as the former goddess could tell—had apparently never set foot outside its boundaries. For her, the world was a sand-covered oasis no more than a mile in circumference, in which life was lived through an endless progression of stiflingly hot days and chillingly frigid nights, where having pantries stocked with sufficient amounts of water and food for one's family was considered far more important than amassing wealth, and where the only sort of war that mattered to its inhabitants was fought between the slowly advancing dunes of the Sahara and a handful of women armed with nothing more than large bowls to sweep them away—primitive weapons, to be sure, but more than effective in holding the line. And yet, Abena accepted this existence without protest, happy enough that, no matter how frustrating her daily skirmishes with the desert might become, she would still receive small payments of rice and sugar from the other villagers for her efforts—enough for her family to live on.

With a slight bow, Abena turned and headed back toward her home. Before she reached it, the door opened, and her four-year-old daughter, Jnanbarka, came racing out. The child galloped across the sand, barefooted, and began dancing in a wide circle around her mother, who made playful attempts to grab her, but the girl always remained just out of reach. Then, as Abena spun to one side, Jnanbarka ran in and grabbed the bowl from her hand, turning it upside-down and placing it at a jaunty angle on her head. Proud of her pottery-hat, Jnanbarka marched ahead of her mother, chin up, leading her back inside the house.

Ororo laughed softly. Abena was right: it *was* a good day—one to enjoy, not waste moping. Smiling brightly, she began walking back to her own home, eager to get on with her activities. Perhaps, she reflected, her life *wasn't* as bad, wasn't as boring, as some other's might be. . . .

He stood on the bridge of the battlecruiser *Valkyrie*, narrowed eyes locked on those of his Kree counterpart, whose azure-hued features filled the main screen.

"For the last time, Captain," the Kree warned, "drop your shields and surrender your ship, or prepare to make peace with whatever god you worship."

The Captain merely smiled and slowly shook his head in exasperation. No matter where he and his crew traveled among the stars, it seemed that one Kree commanding officer was as ignorant as the last he'd encountered, and more than likely as the next he'd run into. Hadn't any of these fools heard of his victory over the N'garai on Goering's World? How he'd broken through the Goa'uld blockade of Andromeda, allowing a hundred-odd worlds the honor of joining the Empire? Of the destruction of the Shi'ar munitions factory on Arkonides?

Didn't these blue-skinned idiots realize who they were messing with?

"What say you, Captain?" the Kree demanded. "I assure you, if you surrender peacefully, we will treat your crew with the utmost care." A wolfish grin twisted his upper lip, revealing yellowed teeth. "Especially your women."

The Captain snarled, and glanced around the bridge, noting how expectantly his crewmembers sat at their stations, looking to him for guidance, relying on him to find a way to beat the great odds against them, as he had done on countless other missions. His gaze drifted to his yeoman, standing close by as always, ready to support her captain in whatever decisions he might make, no matter how perilous the situation in which they might find themselves.

Of all the women he'd loved on dozens of worlds, Sharon Carter was still the most beautiful in the galaxy—the sort of plucky, desirable girl with whom any starfaring officer worth his spacedust wouldn't hesitate to settle down and raise a family. Unfortunately, there was another love in the Captain's life, one that received his full attention at all times, one not even the most ravishing female in twelve parsecs could compete with: his ship. Amazingly, though, Sharon understood, and was more than willing to settle for second-best in his heart. There were times when he thought he didn't deserve to have someone that special in his life—and then immediately cast aside such a preposterous notion. *Of course* he deserved someone like that—he was the Captain, wasn't he?

And yet, he couldn't help but feel sorry for her, as she trembled under the lustful gaze of his enemy, nervous fingers pulling at the hem and plunging neckline of her micro-miniskirted uniform. It was clear she knew she was being mentally undressed by a barbaric member of a notoriously degenerate race. He'd have to put an end to that quickly—no mongrel-raced alien filth ogled *his* crew!

Sharon turned to him, eyes full of pleading. "Oh, Captain," she whispered.

He reached out to brush away a tear that rolled down one perfect cheek, then gently ran his fingers through her golden, shoulder-length hair.

"Ev'rythin' will be all right . . . *petite*," he said softly.

Doe-like blue eyes grew wider, and a warm smile lit her delicate features. He'd always enjoyed that smile.

"I know it will," she sighed, pressing her cheek against the palm of his hand.

With a wry grin, the Captain turned to his weapons officer, Lieutenant Sean Cassidy. "Quantum phase-shifters at maximum," the red-haired officer said quietly, so as not to be overheard by their opponent. His voice was tinged with a brogue born of the Irish countryside. "Standin' by."

"Engage," the Captain said.

One moment, the viewscreen had been filled with an image of the Kree warship's bridge, its captain clearly running out of patience; the next, it showed the flank of the enemy vessel. In the blink of an eye, the quantum phase-shifters had teleported the

Valkyrie away from its position under the Kree gun emplacements to a spot just over two kilometers *behind* them.

"Fire," the Captain said.

Cassidy's fingers flew across his console with the dexterity of a concert pianist, and death in all its various manmade forms—lasers, guided missiles, nuclear torpedoes—leapt from the *Valkyrie*'s weapons batteries to tear apart its target. In less than a minute, the battle was won.

The crew cheered its victory, and the Captain swept Yeoman Carter into his arms. The kiss they shared was long and passionate, and left her gasping for air when he finally released her.

"Oh, *Captain* . . ." she purred, lips pursed and eyes half-closed in a seductive expression he knew all too well. She threw her arms around his neck. "Take me, Captain! There's nothing I'd like more in the entire universe than for you to—

"WAKE UP, LEBEAU!"

The high-pitched shriek that rattled Remy Lebeau's eardrums wasn't half as painful as the slap across his face that accompanied it a moment later—the hefty ring worn around one finger struck his jaw with the force of a small club.

With a groan, Remy slowly opened his eyes—to find himself looking at the most beautiful woman in twelve parsecs. He grinned, still half asleep. "Sharon . . ." he sighed.

The delicate fingers that had been poised to gently stroke the Captain's rugged face now closed around the lapels of Remy's uniform jacket and roughly hauled him from the chair in which he'd been "resting his eyes." A quick twist of the wrists, and he was flying over his desk, scattering folders, reports, packs of playing cards, and various and sundry office supplies around the broom closet-like space that served as his inner sanctum. He crashed against the far wall, between a battered file cabinet and a plant of some kind that had seen neither sunshine nor water in a dog's age, and slid to the floor in a contorted heap amid the stacks of faded pulp magazines and weathered paperback novels that served as inspiration for his fanciful daydreams. From his sprawled position on the warped wooden floorboards, Remy pushed away leafs of multicolored papers that had settled over his face and glanced sheepishly at the hardened features of his superior officer.

As *Obergruppenführer* of Ernst Kaltenbrunner Spaceport—a facility based in Queens, New York, named after the late head of the *Reichssischerheitsamt*, the Reich Security Office, during World War II—Sharon Carter might well be one of the most desirable women in the empire, but she was hardly the sort who could be described as "plucky." Her blond hair tied back in a ponytail so severe it made her eyes bulge from their sockets—a look made even more disturbing by the way her blood-red-colored lips were pulled back in what seemed to be a perpetual snarl—Carter looked every bit the "she-wolf" the staff at Kaltenbrunner had dubbed her . . . behind her back, of course. She was dressed in a leather jumpsuit so tight it appeared as though it had been spray-painted on her, covering every inch of her body from neckline to toe. It was complemented by highly polished leather boots and a gunbelt worn low on her hips; the pistol grip of a Luger protruded from the holster strapped to her right thigh. Remy took note of the way her right hand hovered above the weapon—clearly, she was deciding on whether to reprimand him for napping without permission . . . or shoot him.

"Err . . . *Gutten tag, Herren Obergruppenführer,*" Remy muttered in an easy drawl born of the Louisiana bayous. "I didn't hear you come in."

"Of *course* you didn't, Lebeau," she snapped. "You were too busy dreaming your pathetic little dreams again to notice when an officer entered the room." She flashed a lipless smile that made Remy think of a shark opening its jaws, preparing to take a bite out of its prey. "Were you fantasizing about *me* this time, Lebeau?"

Remy felt his cheeks reddening and quickly cast his gaze to the floor. "No, *Obergruppenführer.* 'Course not. Dat'd be 'gainst regulations."

Carter snapped off a laugh—one that sounded like a short burst of gunfire. "Well, I'm pleased you know *some* of the laws governing this facility, Lebeau," she said icily. "But perhaps it's slipped your tiny Cajun mind that sleeping on the job is *also* against regulations." Her eyes narrowed. "Need I remind you of the punishment for dereliction of one's duties?"

"I'm *real* sorry 'bout dat, ma'am," Remy said. "I won' let it happen again. I promise." He started to pick himself up off the floor, but a stiletto-heeled boot jabbed him in the chest, forcing him back.

"Did I give you permission to get up, pig?" Carter growled.

"Umm . . . no, ma'am," Remy said quietly. "You'll . . . uh . . . lemme know when I *can,* d'ough, right?" He flashed his winningest smile at her, hoping to defuse the situation with charm before he got into worse trouble. It always worked in his dreams . . .

Carter's upper lip curled, and she grunted in disgust. "You're a sad little man, Lebeau. When you first joined my staff as a clerk two years ago, I thought you had potential . . . but I see now that I misjudged you. You're lazy, you're irresponsible, and you lack discipline." She grabbed one of the dog-earred paperback books he'd landed on, sneered as she glanced at the gaudy cover, and flung it at him. *Perry Rhodan: Death Waits in Semispace*—one of the better books in the series, Remy noted. "You sit in this sty all day, reading garbage that brings a note of excitement to your otherwise meaningless existence, while avoiding your duties as much as possible. Asking you to perform the simplest task is like making demands of a wall—but at least the wall has an excuse for not following through on the assignment." She pointed an accusatory finger at him. "I bet you haven't even looked into who's behind those recent thefts of office supplies."

Remy cleared his throat and looked at the floor again, finding it hard to look her in the eye. "Well, findin' de t'ief ain't all dat simple a task, ma'—"

She ground her boot heel into his chest, grinning at Remy's

painfully sharp intake of breath. "You're a piece of offal, Lebeau—a pile of excrement stinking up my spaceport. And if you're not careful—" she dragged her foot sharply across his torso, and he yelped "—I'll scrape you off on the curb. Do you understand?"

"Yes, *Obergruppenführer.*" Remy rubbed a hand across his sore flesh, trying to ease the pain. He was somewhat grateful she hadn't drawn any blood—she might have punished him for wearing a dirty uniform.

Her nostrils flared angrily. "And didn't I tell you to get a haircut?"

Remy's other hand unconsciously slid to the back of his neck. He'd been letting his dark brown hair grow far beyond the parameters of the regulation crewcut for the past three months, despite two previous warnings from Carter about the "shabby" appearance he was cultivating. The ends now reached just past his collar. "Yes, ma'am."

"Then do so at once. I won't tolerate anyone under my command looking like . . . like some gypsy! You're an officer of the Reich—start acting like one!" Without waiting for a response, Carter turned on her heel and stormed out of the office.

Remy waited until he heard the door to the outer hallway slam shut before he dragged himself to his feet. His chest still burned where Carter's boot had scraped it, and he had a bump on the back of his head the size of a golf ball, courtesy of the wall he'd slammed against when she tossed him across the room. Not such a bad start for a Wednesday morning, considering he was still feeling the bite of her riding crop on his legs and back from the week before. He limped around the desk and collapsed into his chair.

A small smile came to his lips as he gazed at the door, and he sighed. "Dat *fille* . . . she crazy 'bout ol' Remy—she just playin' hard-t'get . . ." The smile froze, then slowly melted into an embarrassed frown. " 'Least dat what I *wish* it was . . ."

Leaning back in his chair, Remy closed his eyes and let his

thoughts carry him away—back to the depths of space, where the kind of power and respect he so sorely lacked in reality could be found simply by wrapping his strong arms around the shapely waist of the most beautiful woman in twelve parsecs. . . .

4

IF this is what it was like to rule infinity—sitting idly by, deep within a city-sized construct that floated at the center of Time and Space, waiting for something to do—then Victor von Doom was sorely disappointed.

Slouching on the ornate throne previously occupied by Roma, she who was now the *former* Supreme Guardian of the Omniverse, von Doom rested the chin of the metal helmet that encased his head on a gauntleted fist and gazed at the voluminous interior of Roma's private quarters. Designed in the style of a gothic cathedral, the throne room was a marvel of sweeping arches, polished stone, delicate wooden fixtures, and a ceiling so high it was lost in shadow. On the far side of the transept, tucked away in a corner, was a small wading pool, its cool waters provided by a fall that flowed from somewhere above; von Doom hadn't been interested enough in it to determine the source. Most of the lighting came from hundreds of candles set in tall, elaborately designed holders spaced about the area around the throne and crossing, which meant that most of the sanctum was bathed in darkness—and within the depths of that black curtain, *something moved*. What it might be, von Doom wasn't certain; he could only see it from the corners of his eyes, since gazing at it straight-on proved ineffective. Presumably it was some kind of defensive system Roma might have unleashed on him, if he hadn't struck her down before she could activate it. Without its mistress to command it, the creature—creatures?—remained in shadow, apparently content to leave von Doom alone with his thoughts.

In one way, with its brooding architecture and Olde Worlde charm and potential deathtraps, the throne room reminded the armored tyrant of his own castle, in his native Latveria—a stronghold from which he ruled his tiny nation with a just, but fair, hand. In another, it reminded him of a prison—for, though it had not taken a great deal of effort to secure this place, he had soon realized that he couldn't leave its environs.

An annoyed frown twisted the scarred features hidden beneath the armor. Yes, it was a prison, von Doom reflected darkly, and he its sole inmate.

There was nothing that actually kept him there—no powerful forcefield to restrain him, no fail-safe mechanism that might have been created by Roma to trap an invader on the chance that someone might succeed in taking control of the Starlight Citadel; if he wanted to leave, all he had to do was step through the main doors and into the adjoining hallway. But it wasn't as simple as that, as von Doom well knew. For before he had barged in here and overpowered the Guardian with a makeshift technological weapon, the citadel had been placed on high alert after it had been discovered that he was running loose through its corridors. That alert was still in effect and, although von Doom feared no one, he knew his enemies' strength lay in their numbers—a dozen foes he could deal with, perhaps more, but there were hundreds of sentient beings living in the citadel, as well as the legions of superpowered warriors that comprised the Captain Britain Corps. Not even von Doom was foolish enough to think he could beat those kinds of odds.

That wasn't to say, however, that he was simply willing to sit comfortably in the shadows, trembling with concern that his presence here might be detected, when there was ultimate power for the taking.

Of course, it was his search for ultimate power that had led him to this maddeningly dull situation in the first place . . .

The scientists in his employ had never planned to create a Cosmic Cube; it had been a happy accident—if one could consider stumbling across the means to fashion a Jack-in-the-Box-sized device that would allow its possessor to rule the world a joyous occasion. Much like the specialists of Advanced Idea Mechanics, they had tapped into a "gray" hole during an experiment, though this one involved penetrating the Negative Zone: an anti-matter universe first discovered years before by von Doom's rival—and arch-nemesis—Reed Richards, the leader of the cosmic ray-powered super hero group called the Fantastic Four.

Once the scientists realized what they had discovered, the project leader, Dr. Nils Browder, wasted no time in informing their employer. The news had pleased the dictator: After all the times the Red Skull had made use of such a device to transform the world into numerous recreations of the Third Reich—the limitations of the man's mind were almost beyond belief!—only to have his dreams shattered by Captain America or some other brightly-costumed do-gooder, it should only be right that Victor von Doom be the one to show Schmidt, and every other pathetic, superpowered, would-be emperor grasping for power, what a true visionary could do with the Cosmic Cube.

All other projects were put on hold, as von Doom's subordinates threw themselves into attaining their goal—especially when the risk of failure on their part brought with it a death sentence. Forgotten were plans for the tyrant's latest strike against the accursed Richards and his team—at least temporarily. Work was suspended on the mind-control gas meant to enshroud London; strategies were postponed for the invasion of Washington, D.C.; halted were batches of a deadly neurotoxin to be released above the undersea realm of Atlantis—an act of revenge against his former ally, Prince Namor, the Sub-Mariner, for opposing him once too often. For von Doom, crafting the Cube became his overriding ambition—nothing would deny him the opportunity to create a world of his own.

Unfortunately, all the ambition in the universe wasn't enough to prevent what happened next.

It was during the creation of the cube-shaped container that the trouble began. Not a true, physical box, the container was, instead, formed through a combination of forcefields, the overlapping of their diverse energies calibrated in such a precise manner that there could be no room for error; the slightest miscalculation could result in the "gray" hole's power spilling out of the cube, contaminating the laboratory with unknown levels of radiation. Such a warning meant nothing to von Doom—he was paying his staff handsomely; they should be honored to sacrifice themselves in his name. Browder, however, cautioned that the danger might be even greater than that—who could say that the radiation wasn't powerful enough to spread out across the planet? The scientists at A.I.M. might have known, but the original research team had been murdered by their leader, shortly after the first Cube had been fashioned—and then the Red Skull had stolen it before anyone could properly monitor it. Perhaps, Browder suggested, they should slow their efforts, make certain that all precautions were taken; given enough time, maybe four to six months, they would be able to create a flawless container, one that would properly—

When the high-pitched whine of von Doom's gauntlet-mounted laser projectors finally died down, there wasn't enough of Browder left to sweep up from the laboratory floor.

The rest of the team finished the work ahead of schedule.

On the day von Doom took the Cube in hand, he knew his destiny had arrived: to be lord of the planet. To become Emperor.

To become a god.

And as he listened, the Cube sang to him—of worlds to be shaped, masses to be led, dreams to come true. A wondrous song, full of pomp and grandeur, that told the awe-inspiring story of a Gypsy youth, an orphan, who fought and clawed and struggled against insurmountable odds to become the ruler of a great nation, then moved on to make his mark on the world as a man to be respected, to be admired.

To be feared.

But there was more to the song than the mere recounting of a marvelous life lived. There were promises of infinite power, of empires to be built, of future generations of charismatic leaders who would proudly carry the name of von Doom across the stars.

And all it would take to make them reality was the simplest of wishes.

So von Doom wished—for power, for glory, for a family to share his triumphs. He wanted his ruined face restored to its former beauty; wanted a monarchy where his rule was unchallenged by any of his former allies or enemies; wanted a strong, beautiful woman at his side, one who would bear him children worthy of their father's name. And in a burst of light, the Cube responded, bringing him everything he desired . . .

Well . . . *almost* everything. When the light faded, Emperor von Doom ruled a world in which his enemies and allies were either dead or loyally serving him. He had two healthy children and a strong, beautiful wife: Ororo Munroe, the white-haired, weather-controlling, African-American member of the mutant hero group the X-Men—a woman he had always found attractive, both in mind and body. But when it came to the tyrant's vanity-driven wish, something went terribly, horribly wrong.

He had awoken in a body ravaged by age, lungs straining to draw breath, heart beating weakly against the withered, almost translucent skin of his chest. His eyesight had grown dim, and his limbs had barely been able to support his own weight, let alone the three-hundred-pound armor he wore. And yet, his thought processes were as sharp as ever; at least he hadn't lost control of his faculties. Still, his was the mind of a man in his forties, trapped in the flesh of an octogenarian.

The realization of his predicament had almost driven him mad.

Nevertheless, he persevered—he *was* von Doom, after all—and eventually he found ways to make peace with his situation:

transferring part of his consciousness into the body of an android Doombot so that he could enjoy some measure of this world he had created; using Erik Magnus Lensherr—the villainous mutant Magneto—as a pawn in a global game of hide-and-seek with the Emperor's armed forces, in order to pass the time; preparing himself for the day he would die, when he would make one last wish with the Cube: to destroy the world before it returned to normal, rather than allow anyone else to rule it.

It was while he was making those plans that he at last figured out what had gone wrong with the Cube: Somehow, one of his scientists had botched the calculations, and that mathematical error had caused a breakdown in the cube-construct's integrity. The Cube had worked, true, but it was flawed—damaged enough to give him a world of his choosing, only to seal him inside a dying body with no means of escape.

Von Doom, of course, overlooked the fact that it was *he* who had provided the final round of computations before the Cube was activated, not trusting such an important task to a roomful of lackeys—even though all were world-renowned experts in their field. To anyone who knew his background, it would have appeared to be a case of history repeating itself, for the last time he had ignored someone's advice about mathematical errors had been decades before, while he was attending an American college. Back then, he had been experimenting with matter transmutation and dimensional warps, in an attempt to contact his late mother's spirit in the afterlife. Despite the warnings given by fellow student Reed Richards, von Doom proceeded with his work, only to cause an explosion that wrecked a sizeable portion of the dormitory—and permanently scarred his face. One would have thought, perhaps, that he might have learned from his costly mistake . . . but Victor von Doom never *made* mistakes . . .

And so, although the errors were different, the results were fairly the same: von Doom received the brunt of the backlash.

Worse still, as the newly-appointed Emperor came to deduce, the reason why his body was failing could be traced directly to the

Cube: It was drawing upon his life-force in order to stabilize the faux reality. At the rate at which he was deteriorating, he estimated that he had no more than a month to live, unless he could find someone to take his place—someone willing to sacrifice their own life in exchange for maintaining von Doom's world. He thought he had found such a prospect in Elisabeth Braddock, who had been pining away for her lost love after his brutal death, but her fellow mutant miscreants had interceded before they could come to an agreement.

And then that imbecile Magneto and his mindless followers had barged in, quickly overpowering the X-Men so that there would be no one to stop the mutant overlord from claiming the Cube for himself.

A low, feral growl spilled from the armored dictator's lips as the unpleasant memory filled his dark thoughts. To think that a genetic inferior would dare to touch the royal personage of Doom—to have the temerity to strike him down with the back of his hand, as though he were some disobedient child! But, at the time, von Doom could do nothing more than moan in pain and collapse bonelessly to the floor, too weak to prevent Magneto from wrapping his hands around the Emperor's prize possession—and ordering it to recreate the world in *his* image.

Yet, despite his loss, von Doom was not defeated; not while he had other options available to him. True, having his teleportation beam intercepted by Roma and her minions had not been part of his plans, but he had always been able to make the best of any situation—especially when the alien technology of the Starlight Citadel at last freed him from his elderly prison. Much to his surprise, it turned out that the Cube had not really aged him; rather, it had apparently placed his consciousness, and his soul, in the body of another Doctor Doom: the true dictator of an already existing world that von Doom thought he had fashioned with his wish box. A replicant who told him all he knew of the citadel and its god-like mistress, encouraging his younger self to make use of the information before they were both imprisoned.

Von Doom rewarded the old man by making his death a swift—though not altogether painless—one.

And then, by making use of a self-aggrandizing physician named Stanton—a pathetic little man with an axe to grind against the Supreme Guardian—von Doom was able to escape the medical ward and secure an ally: the dictator Sat-yr-nin, who was being held in stasis until Roma had passed sentence on her for numerous crimes perpetrated against the citizens of an alternate Earth. By capturing Sat-yr-nin's alternate—an annoyingly haughty young woman who acted as Roma's second-in-command—and placing her in the stasis chamber, no one, not even the Guardian, was aware that the coolly efficient Saturnyne had been replaced by an equally coldhearted madwoman.

It was that last bit of subterfuge that ultimately led to Roma's downfall, and von Doom's rise to power, for Sat-yr-nin had been able to get close enough to the Guardian to attack her. Apparently unused to physical combat, Roma had been distracted long enough by the unexpected assault to fall prey to the armored tyrant's improvised weapon: a variation on the same multiphasic crystal accelerator that had been used to separate him from the wizened Doctor Doom. In this case, though, the device was used for a far more sinister purpose, stripping layer after layer from the Supreme Guardian, weakening her as a number of alternate versions of herself were peeled away by the scalding radiation. Apparently, Roma derived her considerable power from being a collective of sorts, her physical form housing every variation of herself that was possible, from an infinitude of parallel dimensions, all combined to create a single celestial being.

Roma was, truly, the sum of her parts, as von Doom had wryly commented, watching with some degree of amusement as she and her "sisters" writhed in intolerable pain at his feet. But now, with some of her parts amputated, if she wished to avoid further "surgery," then she would have to prove her usefulness to the self-appointed Master of the Omniverse—or join his elder self in oblivion . . .

* * *

Von Doom rose to his feet and stepped down from the apse on which the throne stood. The time for introspection had passed—now was the moment to take action. Although he might be confined to the throne room until he was prepared to face his enemies, that didn't mean there weren't matters that needed his attention.

Like learning all the secrets of the Starlight Citadel and its mistress.

Striding purposefully, he began walking across the transept, pausing only long enough to glance at a platform, and the pulpit-like stand upon it. Protruding from the latter were an infinite number of crystal shards; from what his elder counterpart had told him, during the brief time their minds had been linked while they shared the same body, each six-inch-wide shard contained the life-force of an entire dimension. How, exactly, the older von Doom had known this was something he would never understand—perhaps if he hadn't acted so rashly by brutally ending his life before he could impart all his knowledge . . .

But, no. Victor von Doom needed no one's help; in time, he was certain, he would come to learn everything the old man had—and take full advantage of the information. He had already come to understand the reasons for Roma's concern about the effects of his Cosmic Cube on the omniverse simply by accessing the citadel's computers . . . although that had been accomplished with Stanton's aid, now that he remembered it. Still, he would have eventually located the terminal on his own, disguised though it was as a series of stained-glass tableaus along one wall, the half-dozen panels depicting some of the accomplishments of Roma's father, Merlyn, over the centuries. And he would find a way to walk the corridors of this magnificent stronghold unmolested . . . even though he had to rely on Sat-yr-nin's intelligence reports for the time being, since no one had yet realized her true identity; it gave her a degree of freedom to roam the citadel temporarily denied her ally.

Turning from the crystal-lined pulpit, von Doom walked

around and behind the apse, to enter a small, semi-circular corridor hidden within the shadows behind the throne. At the center of the passageway was an elegantly-carved oaken door; he pushed it open and stepped into a large chamber—what would, he imagined, be considered Roma's private quarters. Like the throne room, her chambers were of a gothic design, with sweeping stone arches and dark-toned wood paneling and the somber lighting of hundreds of candles. The air was tinged with the perfume of jasmine and incense, the tiled floor adorned with colorful Persian rugs and oversized cushions. A large, four-poster bed—its framework hung with silken draperies of such varying hues that the cloth appeared to continually change colors as he stared at it—stood at the far end, its blankets and top sheet turned down in anticipation of its mistress' use, though von Doom doubted a celestial being would truly have need for rest. And, all about the room, ten-foot-high tapestries and elaborate woodcuts half that size hung from thick chains on the walls. Von Doom noted with some surprise that Roma's likeness appeared in most of the artworks—he had not thought the woman vain enough to collect images of herself. But then, all women were driven by vanity, he considered; unlike Doom, they were unable to rise above pursuing such trivial obsessions as immortalizing their beauty.

Unconsciously, he touched a hand to his mask—and the scarred features hidden behind the cool metal.

He found two men waiting for him, both seated near the door in large, white, egg-shaped chairs that were completely at odds with the rest of the chamber's furnishings; a personal touch of decorating by the Supreme Guardian, no doubt. One was a tall, broad-shouldered man with bright-red hair tied in a ponytail, dressed in ceremonial garb: golden armor, sky-blue tunic, and a white, ankle-length cape; a sword hung loosely from the wide, golden belt that held his tunic in place. The other man was only a few inches shorter than his companion, but seemed like a child in height by comparison. He was also much thinner, and possessed far less hair. His attire consisted of green surgical scrubs, a white laboratory coat, and a pair of wingtip shoes.

The former was Alecto, the top officer of Roma's handpicked personal bodyguards, whose primary occupation was ensuring that no one bothered the Supreme Guardian unless she wished to see them—a job von Doom had now made obsolete. The latter was Dr. Henry P. Stanton, one of the many physicians stationed on the citadel, now von Doom's highly-strung lackey. There was a nervous look in Stanton's eyes, but the armored tyrant ignored it—there *always* seemed to be a nervous look in the man's eyes. Alecto, on the other hand, merely stared blankly at his new master—the result of a small mind-control device implanted on the back of his neck, one von Doom had easily fashioned from his battlesuit's spare parts. The other members of Roma's elite guard wore similar mechanisms, and had been ordered back to their posts at the entrance to the throne room so that he could remain undisturbed by the citadel's other residents.

"How fares your patient, physician?" von Doom asked.

Stanton rose quickly. "I was just waiting for you to arrive, Mr.—" He froze, recognizing the fire that suddenly blazed in the dictator's eyes. *"Lord.* Lord Doom," he quickly recovered. "I . . . apologize for the error." The fire burned low behind the mask, but did not go out. "I—I thought you'd rather see for yourself."

Von Doom nodded, pleased by his lackey's groveling. He allowed Stanton to lead him a side door that, on first glance, appeared to be for a closet. The physician opened the portal and quickly stepped aside, so that his master could enter first. As the dictator crossed the threshold, he felt a mild tingling, even through his armor, that forced his lips to curl. Before he could question what was happening, or, better yet, wring the neck of the doctor for leading him into a trap, he was suddenly through the electrical field, coming to a halt in a void of the brightest white.

It took a moment or two for his senses to stabilize, for his eyes to regain their focus so that he could see that he was standing in another room, whose depths were impossible to discern as floor, walls, and ceiling all blended into a continuous field; the color of the room and the even lighting–which seemed to come from all around–made it difficult to tell where one ended and the other began. It had to be a room, hadn't it? he thought. What else could it be?

"What is this place?" he asked slowly.

Stanton suddenly appeared beside him, his stern features twisted into a grimace; apparently, he disliked the electrical field as much as his master. "This is Merlyn's personal chamber–although it hasn't been used since his last departure for parts unknown," he replied, and sniffed. "Not much of a taste for decorating, wouldn't you agree? But then, he preferred spending his time wandering the omniverse–he never really stayed here for very long." He motioned back the way they had come, though von Doom couldn't find any indication of a door; the wall was as smooth as the others. "From what I understand–and I'm no physicist, mind you–this is a pocket dimension of some kind, where he could test out some of his more . . . hazardous experiments without accidentally blowing up a few hundred realities." His voice dropped to a whisper. "Perhaps you should try that next time."

Von Doom ignored the comment and eyed him warily. "And how do you know of this place?"

Stanton sneered. "Before Roma sweet-talked her father into hiring that annoying little Scot as the citadel's Chief Physician," he said, in reference to the man who had been his superior in the Medical Wing, "Merlyn had offered the position to *me*. The two of us got along quite well, and he let me in on one or two of his secrets. Obviously, he understood my–"

A gauntleted hand suddenly snapped out, grasping Stanton by the throat. As he struggled to breathe, fingers slipping helplessly along the polished metal in a futile attempt to free himself, von Doom pulled him close, until the doctor's face was pressed against his mask.

"Then you must *also* know how to exit this 'pocket dimension,' physician," von Doom said heatedly. "Is that not so?"

Stanton bobbed his head frantically. "The . . . electrical field we . . . passed through . . . registered our bio-data. All you have to . . . do is . . . walk in the direction . . . of the field—the . . . stronger the . . . tingling gets . . . the closer to . . . the doorway . . . you are. It will . . . open . . . automatically . . . when you're . . . close enough . . ."

The armored despot tightened his grip, cutting short Stanton's labored response. "What *other* 'secrets' have you been withholding from Doom, you miserable cur?" he growled.

"Not . . . many . . ." Stanton wheezed. "Nothing . . . of importance . . ." His eyes were beginning to bulge from their sockets, his face turning a bright shade of crimson. "I . . . I *did* say . . . only one . . . or . . . two . . . remember . . . ?" The veins in his forehead were pulsing strongly, pushing against the reddened skin as though trying to force their way out. "Do you . . . really think . . . Merlyn . . . would have . . . trusted *me* . . . with anything . . . of value . . . ?"

With a grunt of disgust, von Doom tossed the gasping physician on the floor. He stood impassively as Stanton lay in a heap, massaging his injured throat while doubled over in a fit of coughing that lasted for some time. Finally, the spasm subsided, and Stanton shakily raised himself to his hands and knees.

"Remember this moment well, you pathetic wretch," the armored tyrant warned, a metal-encased index finger pointed at Stanton. "Each moment you continue to draw breath, every second your heart continues to beat, passes only because Doom wills it. Conceal any further information from me, and that privilege will come to a swift—and brutal—end. Do you understand?"

"Y . . . yes, L-Lord Doom," Stanton wheezed. He wiped his spittle-covered lips against the right cuff of his lab coat, then used the other to absorb the tears that filled his eyes. "I'll . . . let you know . . . if any more . . . come to mind . . ."

Von Doom nodded. "A wise decision. Now, take me to the woman."

Stanton pushed himself to his feet, staggered for a step or two, then regained his balance. Still rubbing his throat, he pointed in a direction away from where they stood, although it was difficult to have any sense of direction in this seemingly endless void. "The Guardian is . . . right this way. If you'll . . . follow me . . ."

As they started on their journey, von Doom looked back, to the point from which he and Stanton had entered. This time, however, he wasn't trying to locate the entrance; rather, he was pondering what might be happening beyond the boundaries of this pocket dimension—specifically, what actions Sat-yr-nin might take, should she learn of his absence from the throne room. Would she risk discovery, and use her masquerade as Roma's second-in-command to rally the Captain Britain Corps behind her? Would she stage a coup, destined though it might be to failure? There were too many possibilities to consider, too many variables to take into account, and von Doom cared for none of them—yet was concerned by *all* of them.

For him, though, there were no other choices. He had to obtain Roma's power, strip her of her control over the forces of Time and Space. And once that power was his to command, his alliance with Sat-yr-nin—as well as the madwoman herself—would be terminated soon enough.

Pleased with his decision, von Doom quickened his pace, heading deeper into the void.

Toward his destiny.

5

EVER since childhood, Opul Lun Sat-yr-nin had been a great believer in destiny—that she was fated to become a powerful figure, a great leader, possibly even Mastrex of the Empire of True Briton. And once her mind had been made up, even at such a young age, she was determined that nothing was going to keep her from reaching that goal. Ultimately, nothing could.

Mother and Father would have been so proud to see their baby realize her potential—if their precious little girl hadn't killed them when she turned eighteen.

She'd developed a taste for death long before then, of course—all murderers have to start someplace, after all—but she'd become tired of the puppies and parakeets, the kittens and gerbils and bunnies and tropical fish and . . . Looking back, she'd never been able to understand why Mother had ignored her disturbing inability to keep a pet for very long. Maybe she had thought it was just a childhood phase, one her daughter would eventually outgrow when something new attracted her attention. Maybe she had been too embarrassed to address the issue, for fear of others learning of her little girl's macabre hobby—imagine, the eldest child of one of the most well-respected families in the Empire an animal killer! What would their friends in high society say?

Or maybe she had simply been terrified that, if she openly confronted Sat-yr-nin about the matter, her child's interests might turn from household pets . . . to larger prey.

How was she to know that had already happened?

Mother and Father were the first to fall by her hand, but they were certainly not the last—there were all those bothersome siblings to dispense with, for one thing. And then, as she climbed the political ladder, first making use of Father's government connections, then building her own, the Lady Sat-yr-nin never failed to leave at least one or two rivals literally broken and bleeding on the rungs beneath her. Within five years, she had become one of the most respected—and genuinely feared—politicians in the Empire, her swift ascent through the ranks catching even the eye of the Emperor. Recognizing her talent, he made Sat-yr-nin the head of the Office of Imperial Security, where she would command the Warwomen, an army of Amazonian soldiers dedicated to protecting the boundaries of the Empire against its dwindling number of enemies. It didn't take long, however, for Sat-yr-nin to become bored with all the death and destruction her troops caused, primarily because she wasn't able to take an active part in the carnage she created. But if she wasn't happy enough with her current position—one of the highest in the Empire—then what more could she possibly want?

Well, there was always that childhood dream of becoming empress . . .

The coup didn't take all that long—less than a year, actually. It might have taken longer, if she hadn't already been provided with the finest warriors in the Empire—warriors who'd been willing to do whatever she commanded, even lay down their lives for her as she directed the final assault on the palace. Seeing all the blood and gore staining the marble halls, the blasted flesh and broken bones scattered around the carpeted chambers, Sat-yr-nin had become so giddy that she couldn't help herself from joining in on the fun. With a single cut, she separated the Emperor's head from his shoulders, using the same sword he'd presented her with when assigning her the very position that ultimately led to his downfall.

The Emperor was dead—long live Opul Lun Sat-yr-nin, Mastrex of Briton!

It was the sort of moment that might have brought a tear to her eyes if she hadn't been otherwise preoccupied, dancing about the throne room with the Emperor's head in one hand and her sword in the other, her hysterical laugh echoing throughout the palace.

Thus began a new chapter in the history of the Empire of True Briton.

The Mastrex's reign, however, would not be without its complications . . .

Her troubles began a few years later, with the arrival of a man named Brian Braddock on her world. On an alternate Earth, he was a costumed superhero named Captain Britain; as it turned out, he was also the spitting image of Byron Bra-dhok, her Royal Konsort. When the two exchanged places—without her knowledge—and Braddock wound up in her bedchamber, Sat-yr-nin soon discovered just how different the two men were: he'd actually led a revolt against her! And as she watched her empire begin to crumble, as she realized that the fates had turned their backs on her for reasons she couldn't even begin to fathom, Sat-yr-nin's mind took the final step into madness.

Much to her surprise, she found the sensation . . . comforting.

But the onset of insanity didn't make her any less dangerous; in fact, it made her more so. She became far more cunning, far more ruthless, than she had ever been, her thoughts of empire replaced with an overwhelming obsession to destroy Captain Britain and everyone he held dear. She had come close to succeeding a time or two, but her plans had always fallen apart before she could deliver the killing blow. Eventually, she had tired of such games and returned to her homeworld to rebuild her powerbase. The task was simpler to achieve than she'd first thought, mainly due to the efforts of loyal supporters who'd been appointed to the new government and the ineffectiveness of the interim Mastrex, who hadn't known how to respond to the sudden reappearance of her predecessor—beyond dying after being shot in the head, that is.

At last, Sat-yr-nin was back in power, and she had quite a few plans for the future of the Empire. Maybe, with all those myriad realities out there in the omniverse, it was time for True Briton to start expanding its boundaries . . .

But then the X-Men had popped up outside the palace, courtesy of Roma, accompanied by row upon row of members of the Captain Britain Corps, and she had found herself right back where she had started from—deposed, debased, and detained. Facing a possible eternity locked away in stasis, while Roma decided on what to do with her. But how the tables had turned once von Doom had freed her! Now, it was the Supreme Guardian who was the prisoner, and Sat-yr-nin the one free—to plot, to plan, to rule . . . after her armor-clad ally had been dealt with, of course.

After all, it only made sense that a woman destined to rule an empire should now turn her thoughts to ruling all of creation . . .

Sat-yr-nin strode through the halls of the Starlight Citadel, noting with pleasure the manner in which its citizens either scattered to get out of her way, or hurriedly bowed their heads in respect, muttering worthless compliments about the stylish cut of her shoulder-length white hair, the smartness of her wardrobe choices—a white satin, floor-length gown with matching fur-trimmed cape that trailed behind her; one among dozens of similar outfits hanging in the closets of her dimensional twin, Opal Luna Saturnyne—or wishing her a good morrow when temporal measurements of night and day were useless on an edifice floating at the center of Time. Pathetically transparent attempts to stay on her good side—or, to be more accurate, the good side of her smarmy doppelganger. Not that either of them truly had a *good* side, per se—just rare moments when they were willing to tolerate the imbeciles with whom they had to interact. At least they had *that* much in common.

Well, that, and an overwhelming desire for power.

Of course, no matter how much satisfaction she might derive from all the bowing and scraping and fear-driven scampering going on around her, Sat-yr-nin's current position was far from what she considered a powerful one. She was the deposed leader of a world-spanning empire, locked away in a suspension tube to keep her from causing Roma any more trouble, only to be released so she could play at being Omniversal Majestrix and take orders from a tin-suited dictator from another Earth who had the infuriating habit of referring to himself in the third person. If Sat-yr-nin had her druthers, she wouldn't hesitate to find the nearest available gun and use it to punch very large holes in her ungrateful ally's armor, and then seat herself upon the throne as the new Supreme Guardian. Unfortunately, there were no energy or projectile weapons at her disposal, due to the citadel's "state of grace": an all-encompassing field that rendered such munitions ineffective. True, she might have no trouble in obtaining a sword or battleaxe—at least *those* would still work in this environment—but they'd more than likely shatter against von Doom's metal encasement.

Her assessment wasn't entirely accurate, though, she had to admit upon further reflection. There was *one* energy weapon that still functioned aboard the citadel and, naturally enough, it was in the possession of von Doom, which was the only reason Sat-yr-nin was willing to put up with his commands. Having seen what sort of lash-up the dictator could assemble with just a soldering iron and a few parts from a multiphasic crystal accelerator, and the effect the beam it emitted had on Roma—slicing off cosmic layers of the Supreme Guardian like so much meat in a butcher shop—she had no desire to wind up being similarly turned inside-out after making an ill-conceived attempt to seize the throne. She might be mad, as so many of her opponents had accused her of being over the years—in their last moments, just before she had them executed—but she certainly wasn't stupid.

Perhaps what she really needed wasn't a weapon, but an

alliance—with someone, *anyone,* other than von Doom. Not Stanton, certainly—the man was spineless and lazy, doing just enough to make himself useful to his new master, but no more. He might agree to help her, but once he sensed that von Doom might gain the upper hand—even for a moment—he'd cut her loose and side with the good doctor. And she couldn't turn to the Captain Britain Corps, not without risking the chance that one or more of the costumed do-gooders might tumble on to her charade. Roma? Saturnyne? Not bloody likely. They'd caused her enough strife over the years; she wasn't about to give them another opportunity, no matter how badly she wanted von Doom out of the way. Besides, any pain they were currently suffering paled in comparison to what she'd had to go through at their hands whenever they felt the need to single her out for punishment. No, it had to be someone she could control, who could be used just as effectively against him as a gun, who—whether willingly or unwillingly—could take the brunt of von Doom's counterassault, giving her the opportunity to steal behind him and stick a blade through one of the unprotected areas in his armor. Sat-yr-nin's blue-colored lips grew back in a rictus-like grin as she imagined von Doom's anguished howls when the point of her dagger slipped through the eyeholes in his mask and punctured the soft corneas that lay just beyond the metal . . .

It took a few moments for her to realize that the sound she heard was coming, not from von Doom's tortured vocal chords, but from the miniature communications set built into the teardrop-shaped bauble dangling from her right ear. Slowly, her grin settled into a snarl of annoyance. She'd never liked it when someone interrupted her in the middle of a daydream, especially one that made her feel so . . . tingly inside.

She came to a halt and tapped the end of the comm set with a sculpted fingernail. "Yes?" she snapped.

"Your Whyness," came the response from a hesitant male voice. The title was used to acknowledge the real Saturnyne's station as Omniversal Majestrix, a job that required her to maintain order throughout the infinite dimensions. "This is Supervisor Troughton of the Dimensional Development Court. I apologize for disturbing you, but our four-dimensional scanners have detected movement in the vortex."

Sat-yr-nin frowned. "And why should that be of concern to *me?* I would imagine there's always *something* flitting about between dimensions."

"Umm . . . yes," Troughton mumbled. There was a tone in his voice that made it clear to Sat-yr-nin that the flippancy of her response was not one he would have expected from Roma's lieutenant; she'd have to be careful about that, before she gave herself away. "Yes, that's very true, Your Whyness, but the temporal signature of the traveler is consistent with that of the recall device we provided for the humans from Earth 616. It appears to have been activated."

Sat-yr-nin paused. Earth 616—that was von Doom's world . . . and the X-Men's. And now someone else from that bothersome dimensional plane was coming here, it seemed. It wouldn't surprise her if it was that dunce Captain Britain, come to spoil von Doom's party.

"Your Whyness? Are you there?"

"Yes, Supervisor Troughton," Sat-yr-nin replied drolly, putting just enough of a bored tone in her voice to make him dismiss any thoughts he might have that she wasn't who she was supposed to be. "Have you any indications of who might be using the recall device?"

"None so far, m'lady," Troughton said. "But I *can* say that there are *two* beings in transit. They should be arriving at the debarkation suite shortly."

"Good work, Supervisor," Sat-yr-nin commented. "I shall meet with them once materialization is complete."

"Shall I have some officers from the Corps report there as well?" Troughton asked.

Sat-yr-nin bit down on her lower lip before she could say "no." Bad enough the Corps had been blocked from seeing Roma with reports that she wished to remain undisturbed; denying their presence at the debarkation suite would only further any suspicions they might have that something was wrong with the Guardian. She'd just have to bluff her way through the situation. Not a terribly difficult task when she thought about it, since most members of the Captain Britain Corps had a tendency to think with their fists, not their brains. They probably wouldn't even notice any differences in the Majestrix's behavior that might pop up if she momentarily slipped out of character.

"Well, of *course* you should, Troughton," she said, with more than a trace of annoyance. "You don't expect me to stroll into a meeting with unknown sentients without *some* sort of protection, do you?"

"Certainly not, Your Whyness!" Troughton replied quickly. "I shall inform the Corps at once!"

Sat-yr-nin grunted and switched off the comm-set before the man could continue his bothersome chattering. She needed time to think.

Two beings from von Doom's world, equipped with a recall device fashioned by Saturnyne's technicians: An emergency matter transporter that no doubt came with instructions that it should only be used in the direst of situations. But that would mean the travelers originated from the citadel. If so, to whom would Roma have given such a device?

"The X-Men . . ." Sat-yr-nin whispered. It made sense: They had come to Roma's aid when she asked them to lead a strikeforce on Sat-yr-nin's world. But now it appeared there were troubles on their own Earth, and two of them were hurrying back to report to Roma. She couldn't help but wonder if von Doom was aware of this, then dismissed the thought. He was locked up in the throne room—how could he be aware of *anything* occurring outside its walls? And if he knew nothing about the travelers—

About her new *allies,* she thought darkly.

Sat-yr-nin smiled. It could only be destiny that would deliver two of the X-Men—the very group that had robbed her of an empire—into her hands, so that she could use them to create a new one.

What else could it be . . . ?

For Betsy, this was the second time in less than a week that she'd found herself shooting across infinity on a transmat beam; she didn't find this trip any more pleasurable than the first.

She could sense Warren's thoughts through the mental link she'd established a moment before they'd left Earth, and was amused to discover he didn't care much either for their unusual mode of transportation. That surprised her—after all the adventures he'd had as a founding member of the X-Men, one would think he'd become used to such forms of travel.

Just because I've done something a lot, hon, doesn't mean it gets any easier over time, he commented.

I . . . float corrected, Betsy replied as the omniverse went whipping past them like so many multicolored ribbons—ribbons that, as she watched with growing horror, began to turn a mottled brown along some of their lengths; a few had even turned black. Was *that* the effect the Cosmic Cube was having on the other dimensions? Seeing it in this manner, Betsy began to understand Roma's fears . . . and Saturnyne's insistence that the Guardian destroy the source of the "reality-cancer" before its taint became incurable.

But there had to be a cure for this bizarre disease; she was certain of it. If the Cube-virus was man-made, there was a chance that something could be created to counteract it; perhaps von Doom could even be coerced into working on it, despite the fact that he had no idea what had gone wrong in the first place—beyond the faulty mathematics involved in the construction of the Cube, that is. And yet, as disgusted as she had been when she'd forced her way into his mind to get at the truth after they'd arrived on the citadel, Betsy wouldn't hesitate to do it again, if that's what was required to force him to help. All she needed was Roma's permission.

What, though, if the "cancer" *wasn't* man-made? What if it was a result of the gray hole energy contained within the device—something for which there was no apparent "cure" . . . ?

Don't think like that, Betts, Warren said. *We have to remain positive about this situation, otherwise we might just as well give up once we get to the citadel. As long as there are even* two *X-Men free to act, the Earth still has a fighting chance. And if Doom's not the answer to the problem, then there must be* somebody *out there in all these dimensions who might be able to point us in the right direction.*

Betsy couldn't help but smile. *Warren, luv, what would I—*

"—ever do without you?"

Betsy blinked. The vortex was gone, replaced with gleaming white walls, floor, and ceiling—so white, it was difficult to see where one ended and the other began. She'd been here before, or in a room very much like it, when she and von Doom had been plucked from the space between the dimensions by Roma's technicians. Apparently it was meant to be a debarkation suite of some sort; a cosmic version of an airport lounge where travelers were shunted after a dizzying flight through eternity. It also meant that they'd just have to wait until someone came to greet them, since there was nothing resembling a doorway that she could find.

Her attention turned to Warren, who was laying beside her, wings spread out beneath him. He glanced at her and flashed a boyish grin. "I think we've arrived."

Betsy smiled. "You always *were* a master of the obvious."

"Just one of my many abilities," Warren replied, sitting up. He tapped an index finger against the corner of one eye. "When you've hung around the X-Men as long as I have, one of the things you pick up is the power of keen observation."

Betsy raised an eyebrow. "And that would explain your uncanny knack for losing five sets of apartment keys in three months in *what* way . . . ?"

Warren grinned sheepishly. "I said the power of keen observation, *not* the power of long-term memory. *That's* the one you get when you hang around the Fantastic Four."

"Does that mean, then, I should have your tailor sew little '4s' on your clothing in order to better focus your attention on the contents of your pockets, or just have him attach the next key ring to the cuff of your jacket?"

Before Warren could come back with a witty response, a small hiss of escaping air cut short their conversation, and an oval-shaped portal suddenly appeared in one of the walls. Through it stepped a quartet of Captain Britains—two men, two women—looking ready for action in their Union Jack-themed costumes. Behind them trailed Saturnyne, who looked somewhat surprised when she caught sight of the two arrivals.

"The sister . . ." she heard the Majestrix mumble.

It was an odd response, considering she had seen Betsy and Professor Xavier off when Roma had sent the two X-Men back to Earth; she had even provided the recall device that lay smoking and twisted on the floor beside Betsy, its circuits overloaded by the trip, its single function now at an end. For a moment, suspicion gnawed at Betsy's mind—what sort of game was Saturnyne up to?—but then she quickly dismissed the notion. With the omniverse facing total destruction, it was perfectly understandable for Saturnyne's thoughts to be focused elsewhere, and then for her to be a trifle confused by Betsy and Warren returning to the citadel; most likely, she had been expecting Professor Xavier to be with her—along with the Cosmic Cube.

Betsy jumped to her feet, Warren beside her. "Saturnyne, I need to speak with Roma immediately."

The Majestrix shook her head. "Out of the question. The Supreme Guardian has sealed herself in the throne room and left instructions that, under no circumstances, is she to be disturbed. For *any* reason."

" 'Any reason'?" Betsy was stunned. How could Roma lock herself away at a time like this? "But what about the Earth? The threat to the omniverse? She needs to know what's happened—"

"When she is ready," Saturnyne snapped, emphasizing each syllable. She flashed a smile that tried to appear friendly, but it was too wide, too false, to be anything less than mildly disturbing. "In the meantime, you can relate anything you would have to say to her to me. Should m'lady be willing to allow me access to the throne room, I will then take your information to her and ask for a decision."

Nonplused, uncertain how to respond, Betsy slowly turned toward Warren. He shook his head violently. "This is crazy. From what Betsy has told me, Roma is counting on every scrap of information she can get, since her equipment is on the fritz."

Saturnyne raised an eyebrow and looked down her nose at him. " 'On the–' "

"The scrying glass," he explained curtly. "That device she uses to observe worlds. Betsy said it stopped working when von Doom's Cosmic Cube transformed the Earth."

The one visible eye–the left–that could be seen beyond the sweep of Saturnyne's Veronica Lake-styled hair widened in obvious surprise. "The . . . Cosmic Cube . . ." she said haltingly. "Yes . . ."

She suddenly turned on her heel and began hurriedly walking away. "I will speak with the Supreme Guardian," she called back. She glanced over her shoulder and gestured to the costumed guards. "Escort them to one of the suites. I will be along shortly to debrief them." Before either Betsy or Warren could call her back, the Majestrix had turned the corner.

Warren turned to Betsy. "Well, *that* certainly got her moving."

Betsy frowned. "Yes . . ." she said slowly. "But something feels very wrong around here. I'd hate to disobey a directive from Roma, but–"

A polite cough interrupted her thoughts. She glanced over at one of the male officers, who smiled sheepishly and gestured toward the doorway. "If you'll just accomp'ny us, miss, we'll take you an' yer gennelmen-friend t'one o' the guest suites, jus' like the Majestrix ordered. I'm sure she'll get this all sorted out soon enough."

Betsy sighed. "Very well." She gazed at Warren, the corners of her mouth twisting downward with concern. "I just hope Saturnyne has some good news for us when she finally comes down from the mountaintop . . ."

"That . . . that toad! That miserable little armored subhuman!"

Sat-yr-nin stormed through the corridors of the citadel, ignoring everything and everyone around her as she muttered softly to herself. So, *that's* why Roma had been so preoccupied when she and von Doom had attacked her in the throne room! *That* was why she'd allowed her guard to drop! Somehow, von Doom had created a device that could alter reality—a detail he'd neglected to mention when he'd suggested that they form an alliance. It was also one she'd failed to focus on when von Doom and Roma openly discussed it in the moments before the Guardian had been overwhelmed by their two-pronged assault, simply because no such device had ever existed on Sat-yr-nin's world. But if what Braddock's sister and her lover had said was true—and what reason would they have to lie to their dear, trusted friend, Saturnyne?—then this "cube" contained power enough to potentially destroy not just a planet, but the omniverse itself!

On the one hand, Sat-yr-nin wasn't all that surprised that von Doom had withheld such information—if their positions had been reversed, she wouldn't have told him, either. On the other, though, she was incensed by his lack of trust; just because she wouldn't hesitate to slit his throat if the opportunity presented itself was no reason to keep her in the dark about such an important matter!

And yet, one thing was clear to her: von Doom no longer possessed the Cube. It was the only explanation she could conceive of that would account for his desire to seize the throne and gain a new powerbase. It also meant that someone else now controlled the Cube. Someone equally as dangerous, no doubt, otherwise Braddock wouldn't have come to the citadel, begging to see Roma.

Sat-yr-nin smiled, her fevered pace slowing. Perhaps she'd been looking in the wrong direction for an ally—why bother with freaks of nature like the X-Men when there was someone out there in the omniverse who'd already shown they were capable of putting von Doom in his place? Who now held ultimate power in their hands? She slowly nodded, pleased with her assessment of the situation.

But before she could put any plan into action, she needed to know more about the Cube—how it functioned, what it was capable of doing, how it could be controlled. And there was only one handy source of such information, though she would have to be careful in her inquiries so as not to tip her hand.

A Cheshire Cat-like grin twisting her features, Sat-yr-nin resumed her pace, heading for the throne room. She would get the answers she sought, and then, perhaps, she would be able to show the infamous "Doctor Doom" just how the Mastrex of the Empire of True Briton rewarded her allies for their efforts.

INTERLUDE V

THE rifle butt came down in a sweeping arc, and Prisoner #937881 howled in agony as his left cheekbone shattered. For a few moments, he thought he had been struck blind as well by the blow, his vision suddenly plunged into total darkness, the inky blackness occasionally broken by kaleidoscopic flashes of color that shot across the void. Slowly, though, his sight began to return. He heard the thin fabric of his workclothes tear at the knees as he collapsed to the hardpacked ground, felt the warm stickiness of blood gush from the abraded skin. Somewhere off in the distance—or so it seemed to his ringing ears—a gruff voice taunted him for his weakness. It was hard to think clearly, even harder to form words to respond. He tried to open his mouth to speak, only to hear an unaccustomed moan issue from his bruised lips. It was quickly followed by a ragged gasp as a razor-sharp piece of bone sliced across the lining of his mouth.

Why? he thought bitterly. *Why won't they let me die . . . ?*

Standing above the prisoner, the two guards who had been escorting him across the compound roared with laughter. They watched with amusement as blood spilled from his mouth, to be hungrily absorbed by the eternally parched soil.

"What's wrong, Jew?" one of them hissed. "I thought you were supposed to be powerful. Why, you can't even make it across the yard without tripping and injuring yourself!"

The other guard chuckled. "Better watch out, Carl," he warned, voice dripping with sarcasm. "This one could tear you in half."

Carl looked surprised. "What–this one?" He lashed out with a booted foot, delivering a savage kick to the man's ribs; an evil grin split his lips as he heard one snap beneath his heel. The prisoner tried to cry out, but his lacerated mouth could only produce a soft whimper. "No, Wilhelm. You must be thinking of someone else."

The second guard rubbed his chin, as though deep in thought. "No, no, I'm certain this is the one." He reached down to grasp one of the prisoner's wrists, which was tattooed with an identification bar code. He unclipped a laser-scanner from his belt and swept it across the small black bars, then glanced at the readout. He nodded in satisfaction. "It's him, all right."

Carl clucked his tongue. "Amazing." He sighed melodramatically and slowly shook his head. "How the mighty have fallen." He bent down, leaning close enough to place his mouth beside one of the inmate's bloodied ears. "I guess that's what happens when you wrong the Emperor, isn't it?"

Wilhelm glanced at his watch. "We'd better get him to the infirmary, have that cheek and rib repaired. He's no good to the facility if he's unable to work." He looked up to exchange malicious smiles with his partner. "Besides, we can always pick up where we left off. He's not going anywhere."

"That's why I enjoy working with you, Wilhelm," Carl said, beaming. "Always thinking of the big picture."

"Makes the day go faster," the other guard replied. "You should try it sometime."

Carl shook his head, his oversized ears waggling slightly. "Not my style. You know me–live for the moment, get what pleasures you can while you can get them." As if to emphasize his point, he jabbed the toe of his boot into the prisoner's side, and smiled as the man coughed up blood-flecked spittle.

The guards grabbed their charge by the arms and roughly hauled him to his knees. The prisoner moaned again as he was dragged through the dirt, leaving behind a bloody trail.

"Don't worry, freak," Wilhelm said. "We'll have you back on your feet soon enough . . . just in time for our *next* session."

The trio set off for the medical center, weaving through the throngs of prisoners clustered in the main yard.

"You know, I was just wondering," Carl said in a conversational tone, lips twisted in a savage sneer. "When we see you again, how would you like us to address you? 'Jew'? 'Freak'?" The sneer quickly transformed into an animalistic snarl, and he practically spat out his next words. "Or do you prefer . . . 'Magneto'?"

Head lolling against his chest, blood continuing to seep from his pulped features, Inmate #937881—the mutant overlord who once went by the name Erik Magnus Lensherr—mercifully slipped into unconsciousness before he could hear their cruel laughter.

The pain kept him from sleeping.

Lying on a worn, rusted metal bunk, Lensherr stared at the ceiling, his gaze drifting along the hairline cracks that ran through the cheap plaster. Beside him, his bunkmate—a half-starved, scar-covered younger man named Jean-Paul Beaubier—shifted around in his sleep, pulling more of the thin blanket they shared over himself. For a moment, Lensherr considered reclaiming his half of the covering, then decided not to—if wrapping himself in a makeshift cocoon brought some comfort to the hideously thin mutant in his final days, then let him enjoy it; Lensherr would have it all to himself soon enough.

Gingerly, he touched his reconstructed cheek with the tips of his fingers, and winced. The medics had told him the pain would linger for days, but he had refused medication—partly because he had no use for drugs, but mainly because he wasn't going to give his tormentors an opportunity to make him dependent on narcotics.

One of the broken slats in the bedframe shifted under his weight and dug into the small of his back . . . and the sizeable lump just under the skin there. Lensherr grunted. Like most nights, the neural inhibitor hardwired to his spinal cord was making him more than a little uncomfortable, though the pain it gave him was nowhere near as great as that caused by his current injuries. Not for the first time since his arrival in this hellhole, an unnamed concentration camp deep in the Canadian woods, he wished that he could find some way to remove the cursed thing that kept him from using his mutant powers, but he had already learned first-hand what would happen if he tried to disconnect the device without a proper medical procedure: It took him an entire day to regain the use of his paralyzed limbs—agonizing hours during which he was unable to walk, or eat without assistance, or speak clearly. The inhibitor had shut down most of his motor functions, leaving him a crippled, drooling idiot confined to his bed, unable to shut out the derisive comments hurled at him by the camp's guards.

For the first time in his life, he had prayed for death, to a god he had turned his back on when he was a teenager, after his parents had been killed by the Nazis. But, Lensherr knew, the Red Skull would not allow him such escape—not after he had used the Cosmic Cube to reanimate him, moments after the Nazi had sunk the obsidian blade of a special combat knife deep into his heart . . .

He had just turned over possession of the Cosmic Cube to his one-time friend, and long-time enemy, Professor Charles Xavier. In the moments before he did so, Lensherr had made an impassioned plea to the X-Men's leader to save one tiny piece of the world he had created: the life of his daughter, Anya.

Xavier had said no.

It was a crushing blow to Lensherr. In the "real" world, before he had ever held the Cube, before the Red Skull had used the device to turn the planet into a living hell, Anya had been the first child that Erik and his wife, Magda, had conceived during the years that followed their escape from Poland's notorious Nazi concentration camp, Auschwitz. But though the war had ended a short time later, humanity's hatred for, and fear of, anything different never completely went away, and not even a ten-year-old girl was immune from their effects. The fire that took her life could have been prevented, had not the people of the town in which the Lensherrs had settled turned against the family, delaying Erik from reaching Anya before it was too late. As he watched his daughter's fire-consumed corpse tumble from their apartment window to land at his feet, Lensherr had felt his mind switch off as he slipped into madness. When he finally recovered, it was to find everyone around him dead, the air heavy with the stench of static electricity and burned flesh.

That had been the night Magneto—and his relentless quest to punish humanity, no matter the cost—was born.

But with the aid of the Cube, Lensherr had been able to reunite with Anya and Magda, to heal the wound in his soul that had lain festering for so long. All he wanted was a chance to keep what little goodness he had managed to create.

Xavier had clearly been torn by the unusual plea, considering all the times his old friend had tried to kill him. And yet, though his heart obviously went out to Lensherr, he had to reject it, explaining that, with the Cube threatening the existence of multiple dimensions, nothing of Magneto's world could remain if order was to be restored.

Lensherr hadn't known what to say in response. Instead, he had directed Xavier to take the Cube, then set off to be with his family in the last moments they would have together before the Professor changed everything back to normal.

But then a dagger had pierced his chest, and the Red Skull pushed past him to steal the Cube. Xavier had come to his aid, but Lensherr was more concerned with what might happen to Anya in a world overrun with Nazi butchers. He begged Xavier to protect his daughter, and, as consciousness began to fade, he dimly heard his friend agree. Secure in the belief that Charles would honor his pledge, Lensherr ceased struggling against the chill that was spreading through his body. The world went dark—and yet he did not die. When he again opened his eyes, it was to discover that he was, astonishingly, still alive . . . and in a far worse situation than he could have ever imagined.

One that was horrifyingly familiar.

One that made the grave seem preferable to having to relive a nightmare from which he had barely escaped the first time . . .

But death was a luxury denied him. For all the beatings he received, for all the cuts, bruises, and broken bones he suffered, the guards were under the strictest orders to not deliver the fatal blow that would free the mutant overlord from his punishment. No matter the severity of his injuries—including the occasion just the day before, when his skull had been split open by a shovel wielded by another prisoner—he would always find himself back at the medical center, being tended to by sadists and drunkards whose pathetic ministrative skills had landed them here because they were more hindrance than help to the Empire's soldiers. And yet, such poor performance meant nothing at this camp—if a Jew or a gypsy or a mutant died at their clumsy hands, what did it matter?

Nor was he spared the memories of what had come before the Skull had shattered his dreams of a peaceful world. Under the control of its previous owners, Doctor Doom and Magneto, the Cube had altered the minds of every man, woman, and child on the planet, modifying them so that the population never questioned how such infamous super-villains could become their exalted monarchs; they simply accepted them as benevolent dictators and went on with their lives. But for what must have been purely personal reasons, the Skull had apparently decided to allow Lensherr use of his full faculties. No doubt it was his way of constantly reminding an old enemy of all he had lost when the world changed—friends, family . . .

"Anya . . ." Lensherr whispered, blinking away tears that had suddenly formed. "I'm sorry."

He swung his legs onto the floor to sit, hunched over, on the edge of the bed. Slowly, he stood up, ignoring the slight crackle of electricity along his spine that the inhibitor spat out whenever he moved. The soles of his wooden shoes scuffling against the equally worn wooden paneling, he stepped over and around the men curled up on the floor—a difficult task, given that there were 400 people crammed into a room meant to hold, perhaps, no more than sixty or seventy—and made his way to one of the small windows built into a far wall.

Through the wire mesh, he could see that the yard was empty, the remainder of the camp's 15,000 inmates having long since been hustled into the surrounding barracks to settle into troubled sleep. In the pale moonlight, guards moved along the watchtowers, their silhouettes occasionally merging with those of the structures as they walked a circuit around their stations. Straining his hearing, he could just make out some of their words as they passed the time conversing—mostly talk about the Empire's latest campaign, or thoughts of home, or vulgar and explicit comments about one of the female prisoners.

Lensherr sneered. He'd heard similar talk before, at another concentration camp in which he'd been locked away more than six decades ago. The guards here were no different than those at Auschwitz, or from any other jackbooted thug he'd ever encountered in his life; the only thing that separated them was the passage of time.

Time. If what Xavier had told him about the Cube was true, time was something that was swiftly running out for the universe. He didn't know how much was left, but he was certain it couldn't be a great deal. If he remembered correctly, the world run by von Doom had existed for at least a month; his own, less than a week. The Skull's Nazi paradise couldn't be more than a few days old, though, under the Cube's influence, it felt as though it had existed for decades. Which left—what? Days? Hours? Minutes, perhaps?

And where was Anya in all of this? Or Magda? Or his other children, Wanda and Pietro? Had they been scattered across the globe as the Cube took the world apart and restructured it to fit the needs of its new master? Could they have been transformed, too?

Or were they dead?

Lensherr shook his head. No. He couldn't believe that, *refused* to believe that. He had had much taken away from him over the years—his powers, his freedom, trusted allies and devoted followers—and had come to accept it as part of life; over time, they could be replaced or restored. But to have finally reclaimed the missing pieces of his heart, his soul, only to possibly lose them forever . . .

"I *will* escape from here and find you, Anya," he vowed, gazing at the stars that filled the night sky. "We *will* be reunited, though the gates of hell might be thrown wide open and every demon set upon me." His lips twisted in a sinister smile. "And then the Red Skull will discover just how much pain Magneto, Master of Magnetism, can inflict—before I tear him limb from limb . . ."

Lensherr turned from the window, made his circuitous way back to the cot, and sat down. He huffed out a mighty breath, only to tremble spasmodically as racking coughs punched their way out from his lungs. Slowly, the coughs subsided, and he spat out a thick wad of yellow-tinged mucus; he noticed traces of blood in the phlegm. With a grunt, he roughly wiped his mouth with the cuff of his black-and-white striped prisoner uniform.

"This was *not* how I expected my retirement years to pass . . ." he muttered.

6

IT was the sight of the invaders, more than the staggering numbers of them, that shook Phoenix with uncontrollable fear.

From a distance, they looked like giant insects, their dark-green, chitinous bodies propelled by a half-dozen segmented legs, each of which ended in a deadly, pointed barb. It was only as they drew closer that it became evident they were far more than oversized cockroaches—the death's-head grin naturally formed by their horrifyingly large, razor-sharp teeth, and the malevolent gleam in their multifaceted eyes, were proof enough of that.

They were members of an alien race called the Brood—and they were all heading in her direction.

From her vantage point on a small hill, Phoenix could see thousands upon thousands of the invaders as they advanced; they covered the ground as far back as the horizon, possibly even beyond that.

A hand gently touched her shoulder, and she almost jumped out of her skin. She turned to find her husband, Scott Summers, standing just behind her, a grim smile etched on his rugged features, looking handsome and determined in his blue-and-yellow costume. With his eyes hidden behind the single-piece ruby quartz visor that kept his destructive forcebeams under control, it was easy to understand why he went by the codename "Cyclops."

"Don't worry, hon," he said reassuringly. "We've been in tougher scraps than this. All we have to do is hold off the Brood until the rest of the X-Men can get here."

Phoenix tried to return the smile, to put on a brave face in the shadow of overwhelming odds, but could only manage a sickly grimace. She cast a furtive gaze at the swarm that was bearing down on them, then turned back to her husband. "Nothing *too* demanding, right?" she replied.

Cyclops nodded. "A walk in the park." He reached out to brush away a few strands of her bright-red hair that had fallen across her equally bright green eyes, then kissed her lightly on the forehead.

"You lovebirds just about done?" asked a gruff voice nearby.

Phoenix pivoted, then tilted her head downward, to make eye contact with a man a few inches shorter than she. Like Cyclops, he wore a costume of blue and yellow spandex, but the sleeves of the yellow tunic were missing, exposing thickly-muscled arms covered with an equally thick matting of dark hair, and the mask covering the top half of his face sported two unusual protrusions that resembled bat-like ears. He stood in a half-crouch, as though that was his normal stance, lips pulled back in a permanent snarl, head cocked to one side, apparently listening to some sound only he could hear; it all reminded Phoenix of a wild animal, ready to spring to the attack.

She frowned. "Is there a problem, Wolverine?"

The snarl flowed into a smile that was obviously meant to look friendly, but Wolverine's sharpened canine teeth only made his expression look more threatening. "Nah, Jeannie," he replied in a rough-edged voice. "Just makin' sure you an' Scottie are focused on the job."

"Don't worry about us, Logan," Cyclops shot back. "We'll be fine." He flashed a quick smile. "But you'll let me know the minute *you* need any help, right?"

Wolverine clenched his fists, and a half-dozen, foot-long spikes suddenly protruded from the backs of his hands. He scraped the edges of the deadly bio-weapons against each other, with a sound like that of a sword being drawn from its scabbard. "*That'll* be the day."

"They're getting closer," said a woman standing near Wolverine, each syllable wrapped in a cultured British accent. She was Asian, possibly of Japanese origin, in her twenties, and she stood as tall as Phoenix, dressed in what appeared to be a dark blue latex swimsuit with matching stockings and fingerless, full-length gloves. Lavender-hued hair tumbled down to her waist, and her supermodel features bore an unusual, j-shaped tattoo that covered part of the left side of her face.

"Den let 'em come, Psylocke," replied a handsome, brown-haired man in a black-and-maroon outfit and brown leather duster. His eyes glowed as brightly as the playing cards he held between the thumbs and index fingers of both hands. "Ol' Gambit, he an expert when it come t'killin' bugs."

"You *oughtta* be, considerin' that pigsty of an apartment you keep in New Orleans," quipped the woman beside him. She wore a green-and-yellow spandex bodysuit, accented with yellow leather kid gloves and knee-high boots; a black "X" adorned the left breast of the bodysuit, as well as the buckle of the loose-fitting belt that rested on her hips. A battered, brown leather aviator's jacket, its sleeves pushed up past her elbows, completed the outfit. Her hair was a lush brown and fell past her waist, with a white streak that ran down the center, starting from her forehead and ending at the tips.

"Dat's cold, Rogue," the one calling himself Gambit said. He sighed melodramatically. "An' here I always t'ought o' dat as our special place . . ."

A sharp gust of wind brought a quick end to the discussion before Rogue had a chance to comment. Phoenix looked up, to see a dark-skinned, white-haired woman descending from the pink-and-purple-tinted sky. Her black leather outfit was highlighted by a large cape that swept outward like a great pair of wings, allowing her to navigate effortlessly through the weather systems that were hers to command. She lightly touched down in the center of the group.

"Nice'a ya t'join us, Storm," Wolverine said. "Thought the flamin' party was gonna get started without ya."

Storm flashed a warm smile. "I had left my invitation in my other costume, Wolverine. I did not think I would be able to attend the gathering without it."

Wolverine laughed—a sharp, barking note. "Always room fer one more, darlin', with or without an invite." He nodded toward Cyclops. "Right, Scottie?"

Cyclops grunted in reply. He pointed at the advancing lines of invaders. The Brood was picking up speed, the tread of millions of legs sending a tremor through the blasted and burned earth that set Phoenix's teeth to chattering.

"Here they come!" Cyclops yelled. "Get ready!"

Phoenix drew in a deep breath, held it for a few seconds, then slowly released it, forcing herself to calm down. Lose your head during combat, she knew, and you stood a very good chance of losing your life. Her gaze drifted down from the battlefield, and for the first time she realized that, like her teammates, she was also attired in a colorful costume: a green spandex bodysuit, accessorized with gold opera-length gloves, thigh-high boots, and a sash that trailed around her ankles, the latter held together by a bird-shaped clasp. The emblem adorning her chest represented her namesake: a mythological creature always fated to die in fire, only to be reborn in order to start the cycle anew.

What an odd choice of clothing to wear to my death, she suddenly thought.

And then the Brood swept over her, their war cry filling the air like the wails of the damned as they burst out of the gates of hell . . .

Jean Sommers awoke with a start, a scream caught in her throat. Eyes wide, breathing hard, she looked at her surroundings in a blind panic, head whipping from side to side, waiting for the monsters that lurked in the darkness to claim her. Eventually, when no attack came, she realized that she was no longer on a battlefield but in her bed, safe from the claws and teeth that had been trying to rend her flesh.

Slowly, her labored gasps subsided, her racing heart eased to a normal pace, and she sat up. Ignoring her chattering teeth, she used the heels of her hands to wipe away the tears that had streamed down her cheeks, then smoothed back her sweat-drenched hair, away from her face. A tremor ran through her body, and she pulled the bed sheets tighter around herself, seeking some comfort from the soft touch of the silken layers.

The dream—the nightmare—was still fresh in her mind, and she knew it would be some time before she was able to get back to sleep. She pounded the bed with a fist—why was it always the *bad* dreams that had to be the ones that lingered, the ones that could be remembered with crystal clarity even hours later, when the cloying darkness had been replaced with bright sunshine?

But where had *this* particular nightmare come from? she had to wonder. What would make her conjure up such grotesqueries as that . . . "Brood," was it? And those ridiculous clothes she and Scott had been wearing! They weren't regulation combat uniforms—at least none she had ever seen during her brief visits to the military bases at which Scott had been stationed; they looked more like fanciful costumes from a newspaper scientifiction comic strip. Despite the heart-pounding fear she'd just experienced, she had to laugh at the vision of herself dressed in an outfit so scandalous it left little to the imagination, fighting alongside her husband, who wore his own like a second skin, even though the color scheme was nothing like what he normally wore—mostly blacks and browns and dark grays. She had to admit, though, that it made him look quite sexy . . .

That woman had been there, too, she suddenly realized; that Asian actress from the cover of *Der Television Guide.* Elisabeth Braddock, she remembered. But that name had she gone by in the dream—

Psylocke, a small voice whispered from the back of her mind.

Jean shook her head. It was a name that meant nothing to her, and yet . . .

And yet, somehow, she felt that it should. Exactly *why* that might be was as much a mystery to her as the source of the bizarre images—and individuals—that had populated the dream. Wolverine? Storm? Rogue? They sounded like characters from a children's story, but something in the depths of her mind insisted that they were familiar names, *important* names, as important to her as her own.

Phoenix, said the voice.

"Ridiculous," she muttered, and kicked the sheets aside. Ignoring her slippers, she stepped from the bed and walked to the bathroom, enjoying the cool feel of the plush carpeting between her toes. She flicked on the vanity lights lining the mirror, wincing as the oversized bulbs filled the room with blazing fluorescence, then ran cold water in the marble sink while she tied back her hair with a large scrunchie. She splashed her face a few times, hoping to wash away the last remnants of the nightmare along with the sleep-crust stuck to her eyelashes, and dried herself on a black cotton towel hanging from the shower curtain. As she lowered the towel, she caught sight of her reflection in the mirror.

She was still young, still attractive—no denying that. But there was an emptiness in her eyes, as though the life had been drained from them.

And that was when the apparition appeared in the mirror.

It wasn't a real apparition, not some ghost that suddenly popped up in the silvered glass, its dead hands reaching out to grasp her. No, this was a strangely alternate reflection of her own features: one of a vibrant-looking woman with a mane of fiery hair, eyes filled with a pale-green light that glowed as warmly as the smile that dimpled her cheeks. It was her, and yet it wasn't. She knew this woman, she suddenly realized—it was the Jean Grey she'd once aspired to be, full of life, ready to take on the world.

It still could *be,* her reflection said. *If you're willing to take a chance.*

Jean raised her hands, intending to rub her eyes so she could make certain that she was actually seeing this, to convince herself that she wasn't still asleep and possibly entering another layer of the nightmare. But she stopped short when she saw that her reflection was wearing golden, opera-length gloves . . . and a bright-green costume.

She screamed, and stumbled back, her right elbow glancing off the towel rack before she finally came to rest in an awkward sitting position on the clothes hamper. She moaned loudly and rubbed the funny bone, gritting her teeth as waves of pain traveled up and down her arm.

Are you all right? asked the voice in her head.

Jean clasped her hands over her ears, though she knew that would do nothing to block the sound, and screwed her eyes tightly shut. Maybe if she didn't look at the mirror, she considered, then the strange vision would fade away. Better yet, maybe she should just walk out of the bathroom . . .

She rose unsteadily and cautiously opened her eyes, training her sight on a framed movie poster hanging on the far side of the bedroom: *The Cabinet of Dr. Caligari*—one of her favorite German Expressionist films of the early twentieth century. By focusing her attention on the painted image of the stern-faced "somnambulist," she was able to ignore the growing urge to look at her reflection—or, rather, the costumed duplicate who now lived in the glass.

Jean, please, the voice said. *We need to talk.*

"*No!*" she cried, and bolted from the room. She slammed the door behind her, then threw herself into a reading chair that stood near the foot of the bed. She sat in darkness, hands still pressed to her ears, rocking back and forth on the edge of the seat, wondering why this was happening to her.

She'd never displayed any signs of mental illness—at least, none that she could ever recall. She didn't talk out loud to herself, didn't think anyone was out to "get" her, didn't hear hidden messages in songs playing on the radio. Oh, there was the occasional bout of depression—what housefrau *didn't* suffer from them? When your life was an endless succession of boring days and—in her case—lonely nights, when the colorful fantasies you'd once dreamed of becoming *somebody* in the world degenerated into finding ways to better serve your husband's dreams instead, who *wouldn't* get depressed?

But to hear voices? To see things that weren't there?

It was madness.

No, it's not, *Jean. You're* not *mad—you're fine. If you'd just let me explain—*

"A nervous breakdown," she whispered. "That must be it. I'm having a nervous breakdown."

A tremor of fear ran through her body, and she ran shaky hands through her hair. She couldn't begin to fathom why it might have happened, or what could have caused it. Was her life *that* terrible? Was her mind *that* desperate for escape from crushing boredom? Tears formed in the corners of her eyes, obscuring her vision, but that was all right—it meant she couldn't see the costumed woman who had suddenly appeared in the poster frame.

Jean—listen to me! You're not *going crazy—I'm really here, in your mind. I don't know* how *it happened, but you have to help me! At the sake of sounding overly dramatic, there are literally* billions *of people depending on it!*

Jean laughed, a slightly hysterical note she didn't even try to control. "What about your friends in the . . . 'X-Men,' is it? Why not ask 'Storm' or 'Gambit' or—"

Scott, Phoenix said. *What about Scott, Jean? Should I ask* him?

Jean froze, an image of her husband popping into her thoughts. She missed him so much, right now. "Scott . . ."

That's right, Jean, Phoenix said gently. *There's a Scott Summers where I come from, too. You saw him in the dream.*

"My dream . . ."

My memory, *actually,* the reflection said. *One you unconsciously tapped into while you were sleeping.* She shivered, and hugged her shoulders. *A replay of a particularly unpleasant moment in my life—one I never would have survived if I didn't have a man I love more than life itself, and who loves me just as much. The* only *man I've ever felt that way about. I'd do anything, sacrifice everything, for him, without hesitation.* She paused. *You know that sort of feeling, don't you?*

"Y-yes . . ." Jean said slowly, wiping the tears from her eyes. "Yes, I do."

He's out there, somewhere, Jean, Phoenix said. *Possibly even trapped inside* your *Scott's subconscious, as I am here. I want to free him; I want to free* all *my friends, before time runs out for everyone on the planet. But I can't do that without your help.*

Jean drew in a shuddering breath, then released it. "Why me?"

You're the only person I can speak with. No one else can hear me because . . . well, because I've become a part of you.

Jean blinked. "You're . . . me?"

Phoenix waggled a gloved hand at chest height. *Not exactly. More of a . . .* She glanced upward, as though she could see the picture frame, then shrugged. *Well, more of a* reflection *of you than actually* being *you. An alternate Jean Grey from a different reality.*

"And how did you get inside my head?" she asked after a few moments.

It's kind of complicated, Phoenix explained. She tapped the side of her head with an index finger. *Let's just say that I got trapped in your subconscious. It's taken a while for me to free myself and get your attention.*

"Uh-huh. And *that* doesn't sound crazy to you?" Jean asked sarcastically.

Phoenix opened her mouth to reply, then paused. *I see your point. But I* swear *to you,* she added hurriedly, you're not *going insane. Just hear me out, all right?*

"If I help you," Jean replied, with a considerable amount of hesitation, "then what?"

Her glamorous twin smiled. *Well, if it all goes correctly, and my friends and I are able to put things back the way they should be, you won't even remember I was here. It'll be as if I never existed.*

"And my Scott?"

The same for him. With luck, we'll be out of your . . . hair before you even know it. The smile broadened. *What do you say? Helping save the Earth sounds a lot better than chasing dust bunnies and cobwebs, doesn't it?*

Jean paused. "I won't have to wear anything . . . scandalous, will I?"

Phoenix chuckled. *I thought you* liked *this outfit.*

"In the privacy of my bedroom, perhaps," Jean replied with a small smile, her cheeks reddening considerably. "But it's nothing I'd care to be seen wearing in public."

Jean stared quietly at the woman in the glass. It would be so easy to turn and walk away and pretend none of this conversation had ever occurred. Well, not so easy, she considered; if Phoenix really *was* taking up space in her mind, it would mean she'd still have her buzzing like an annoying fly in her thoughts, insisting she be heard. Still, what the woman said *felt* sincere . . . and true.

Is *this* how madness begins? Jean wondered. With a belief that something so totally outrageous is undeniably true? If so, she decided, better to suffer a madness borne of pursuing a crazy dream of saving the world, than spend the rest of her mundane life wondering what might have happened if she'd only *listened.*

It was certainly better than formulating plans for assaulting the plaque buildup on the shower tiles in the morning . . .

"What do you need me to do?" she asked.

"If it were up to *me,* I would turn this craft around and return to England."

Kurt Wagner folded blue-skinned arms across his chest and glanced around the cramped cabin at his fellow travelers, almost daring them to respond to his complaint. Beside him, the blond-haired shapeshifter known simply as "Meggan" grunted in disgust and pulled her swastika-adorned headband down over her eyes. Wagner smiled, flashing sharpened fangs, admiring—not for the first time—the manner in which her skintight uniform hugged her exquisite curves, the eagle-like emblem of the shoulderless top displaying a copious amount of cleavage. Wagner sighed. If only she wasn't so enamored of her thuggish boyfriend . . .

"For the tenth—and last—time, Nightcrawler, shut your mouth," ordered the hulking brute of a man seated in front of him, as if on cue. "Whether or not we continue this mission is not *your* decision to make, we are *not* returning to England until we have completed it, and I am tired of your constant whining." He gazed over his shoulder at Wagner, lips drawn back to bare his teeth, blue eyes narrowed beneath the black-and-white headband that matched Meggan's. "And if you continue leering at my woman, *freak,* I will have no other recourse than to crush your thick skull and toss your carcass from this ship. You may be of true German descent, unlike the rest of us, but it will be a cold day in Hades before I allow a genetic mishap like *you* the opportunity to sully a warrior maiden of the Reich with your foul touch." With that, Hauptmann Englande, one of the Empire's premiere superpowered heroes and Wagner's commanding officer in the team codenamed "Lightning Force," turned back to the controls of the V-winged jet he was piloting. Apparently, he considered the discussion over; wisely, Wagner decided to agree with him.

Chin resting on a three-fingered balled-up fist, he gazed out one of the observation ports in the craft's hull, his frown deepening as he watched the endless wastes of the Sahara Desert streak by below. Even though the jet's cabin was air conditioned, he was certain he could feel the waves of heat rising from the sands, and this was supposed to be one of the *cooler* days in the region. He wasn't looking forward to stepping into such a blast furnace when he and his teammates arrived at their destination.

He shifted a bit in his seat, taking some weight off the three-foot-long prehensile tail that protruded from just above his buttocks; sitting too long like this often caused it to cramp, and he was uncomfortable enough in the small cabin as it was without suffering from muscle spasms. But changing position caused the high, starched collar of his blood-red-colored uniform to bite into his neck; twisting around to fix that problem resulted in his knocking off his mirrored sunglasses, exposing his light-sensitive, pupilless yellow eyes to the harsh desert glare. Retrieving his glasses from the floor, Wagner sat back in a huff—on his tail.

A soft chuckle reached his pointed ears, and he turned to find Meggan gazing at him, a gloved hand holding up an edge of the headband so she could watch him with her right eye. A small, wicked smile played at the corners of her mouth, and she glanced at the back of her boyfriend's head, then back to Wagner. For just an instant, her body shimmered, like the heat waves outside the jet—she had activated her shapeshifting abilities. When the effect ended, her skin was as deep a blue as Nightcrawler's, her eye just as yellow, her waist-length hair just as black; the tip of a pointed tail flexed sinuously behind her as she playfully stretched, arching her back.

Wagner felt his heart pound within his chest, unable to hide his attraction for her, even at the risk of sending his commander into a murderous rage . . . should he become aware of what was happening behind his back. Smiling broadly, encouraged by the come-hither gesture of Meggan's now three-fingered hand, he reached out to place his own on her thigh—and was rewarded with a slap across the face by her tail. He reached up to touch his burning cheek, and was surprised to find blood on his white glove.

"What is going on back there?" demanded Hauptmann Englande.

"Nothing, my Captain," purred Meggan. Wagner noted with

surprise how quickly she had shifted back to her normal appearance. "Kurt was merely . . . stretching his tail."

Englande grunted. "Well, keep it in your pants, Wagner," he said with a snarl. "I don't need that damnable thing strangling me because you can't control it."

"I will . . . endeavor to do so, Captain," Wagner said glumly. He cast a heated glance at Meggan, who laughed silently and pulled the headband back down over her eyes. Once again, she had played him for a fool, and he had willingly allowed his overactive libido to put him in harm's way.

Wagner folded his arms across his chest and sneered at the blond-haired vixen. One day that blasted tease was going to get him killed . . .

The V-wing touched down less than a half-hour later, settling onto the hot sands with a burst of Vertical Take-Off and Landing jets. Wagner stared out through the windshield, repulsed by the ramshackle appearance of the village just ahead—what sort of barbarians would choose to live in such a manner, withering away on the edge of a vast desert, when the Reich offered so much in more civilized locations? But then he saw the dark skin of the village's inhabitants as they came out to greet the new arrivals, and he quickly understood. They were blacks—genetic inferiors in relation to the pure Aryan makeup, exiled to their "mother country" so the Empire could keep them all in one place. The realization sent an involuntary shudder through him. The situation reminded him of Lightning Force's last visit to Genosha, the island-nation just to the east of the African coast that served as the dumping ground for most of the world's mutant population—and the prime source of Reichsminister Arnim Zola's material for genetic experimentation.

"What is this place?" he asked.

"It is called Araouane," Englande explained, rifling through the contents of the mission pouch he held.

"And *this* is where the Ministry of Health wanted us to go?"

Wagner said incredulously. "What could they possibly want from such a worthless ruin? And why should the Empire's most celebrated strikeforce be wasted on a task that could be carried out by some lowly errand boy?"

Englande glared at him. "I do not know, Nightcrawler. Perhaps you can ask Reichsminister Zola yourself when we meet with him later."

"M-meet with him . . . ?" Wagner stammered, unable to keep the fear from his voice.

Meggan suddenly wrapped her arms around his shoulders and playfully hugged him. "What's wrong, little elf?" she whispered in his ear.

"Nothing," Wagner snapped, a little too forcefully.

Meggan laughed, and roughly tousled his closely trimmed hair. "*I* think the Reichsminister *frightens* you, little elf," she chided. "Why *is* that, I wonder?" She smiled brightly. "Perhaps you fear he might take an interest in you, make you the focus of one of his . . . research projects?" She stroked his cheek, reopening the cut with a quick slice of a fingernail.

"*Enough,* Meggan," Englande snarled. "We're wasting time." He turned in his seat and pointed toward a door at the rear of the cabin. "Go retrieve the little Jew from her cell and meet us outside. There's work to be done, and we may have use for her talents, although I doubt there will be any trouble."

Meggan pouted, bringing a small, satisfied smile to Wagner's lips. "All right, Brian. You don't have to be so brusque."

"Go," Englande said.

She sniffed derisively and headed for the cargo bay, slamming the door behind her as she left the cabin.

Wagner flashed an uneven grin at Englande, hoping his friendly act would distract his commander from focusing on the attention he had paid to the fluid motions of Meggan's exit. "Women, eh?"

Hauptmann Englande sneered at him. "Shut up, freak." He

shoved Wagner aside and headed for the cabin door that led outside.

Luckily for the blue-skinned mutant, the stream of German invectives he muttered as Englande climbed from the jet apparently went unheard.

The group reassembled a few minutes later in the shadow of the V-wing, Wagner's dark coloration making him almost invisible as he clung to the cool underbelly of the craft.

The trio had been joined by the remaining member of Lightning Force: a gaunt, frightened-looking young woman named Katheryne Pryde. She was usually addressed only by the codename "Shadowcat" by her teammates, if for no other reason than it kept her at an emotional distance from them; calling her by name, even allowing her to sit in the cabin rather than in the tiny room she occupied in the back of the jet, would mean they considered her one of them, and that wasn't about to happen. For although she might be a mutant like Wagner, she would never be treated as his equal—he was a German, at least, a proud warrior of the Fatherland; she was a Jewess, her left wrist tattooed with an identification bar code, head shaved bare, forehead emblazoned with a six-pointed Star of David. She wore a light-blue shift with billowing sleeves and a hood that served to hide the haunted look that constantly filled her brown, doe-like eyes. At a glance, from the way she hovered a few inches above the ground, her body almost transparent in the brutal sunlight, one might think she was a ghost—and, in fact, that is exactly what she was: a woman forever trapped between life and death, between light and shadow. A victim of her own mutant power to phase through solid objects, gone horribly, fatally, wrong, courtesy of experiments conducted by the Ministry of Health.

Hands on hips, Hauptmann Englande looked every bit the posturing *übermensch*, every bit the epitome of Aryan superiority, and Wagner was certain he knew it, too. His skintight uniform—the bottom half white, the top half red, decorated with a representation of an eagle—swelled as he puffed out his chest, the better to make an impression on the villagers as they drew closer. Sunlight glinted along the edges of black leather boots and gauntlets shined to a brilliant polish. A coarse desert breeze ruffled the top of his closely cropped blond hair. No man—no warrior—could look better.

A man in his late sixties or early seventies, skin toughened to dark leather by decades spent under the powerful rays of the sun, hunched his way over to them, his weight supported by a thick, gnarled staff; Wagner couldn't help but wonder where he could have obtained the wood from which to fashion it in this endless dune sea. Presumably, this was a village elder, sent to greet the quartet, although the fear that shone in his eyes was all too evident.

"Good day, my friends," he said in halting German, stopping directly in front of Englande. He smiled, revealing a wide gap where the right-side row of his upper teeth should have been. "How may we of Araouane be of service to you?"

"First off, old man," Englande said, his anger barely contained, "we are *not* your friends, and I will turn what few teeth you have left to a fine powder if you insult us with such unwanted familiarities again."

Hidden in the shadow of the V-wing, Wagner rolled his eyes. *Hauptmann Englande—as* always, *the master of tact . . .* he thought sarcastically.

"Secondly," the costumed warrior said, gesturing at his companions, "we are Lightning Force, the Empire's greatest band of decorated agents, here on a mission for Reichsminister of Health Arnim Zola himself." He gazed past the elder, at the crowd of villagers who were standing well back from the jet. "We have come for the mutant—the one called Ororo Munroe!" he bellowed.

A loud murmur ran through the crowd as the citizens of Araouane talked amongst themselves. And yet, when the garbled conversation died down, none of them made a move to either point out the mission's target, or move aside to allow her passage.

Englande frowned, and turned to the elder. "Tell her to step forward, old man, or we will be forced to find her ourselves . . . in the rubble of your village."

"There is no need for threats, Captain," said a strong female voice from within the crowd. "These kind people merely sought to keep me from harm."

The congregation parted, and a lithe, white-haired woman moved forward. She held her head high as she walked toward the team, as though she were royalty, or the goddess she had pretended to be for a time. Wagner had heard reports about this Ororo Munroe, and the mutant powers she had once wielded, but none of them had ever mentioned the obvious strength of her will . . . or her incredible beauty.

"And what sort of harm might that be, girl?" quipped Meggan. "You should feel honored that the Reichsminister has requested your presence." It was clear to Nightcrawler from both her attitude and body language as she stepped closer to Englande that Meggan had been expecting to find a wizened hag instead of this dark-skinned lovely; now, she felt threatened. After all, Nightcrawler wasn't the only one in Lightning Force with an eye for the ladies . . .

"I have already experienced Zola's . . . hospitality on one occasion," Munroe replied, "and hoped never to do so again." She gestured at the small of her back, where Nightcrawler knew a neural inhibitor had been surgically attached. "He has already crippled me—what more could he possibly want?"

"It is not my place to ask such questions, mutant," Englande said curtly. "Nor is it yours." He jerked a thumb at the V-wing. "Get in the craft before I lose my patience."

As Munroe approached the ladder that led up to the flight cabin, Wagner released his grip on the hull, executing a perfect three-toed landing. Ignoring the heat of the sand as it permeated through his leather boots, he stepped from the shadows to greet her, adjusting his sunglasses so they rested midway down his nose. He wanted the best possible view of her as she drew close.

The sight of a yellow-eyed demon materializing from beneath

the plane obviously took her by surprise. Munroe gasped and stepped back, losing her balance as the sand shifted under her foot. Wagner's tail flicked out, encircling her waist and pulling her into his arms.

"*Gutten tag,* Fräulein Munroe," he said, gaining some pleasure from her touch, even though she was trying to push him away. Her skin was smooth, not yet weathered by the sun and sand, and he detected a hint of jasmine in the locks of her flowing mane. She really *was* an exquisite creature, even if she was—

He froze suddenly, then pulled her closer, until their noses were almost touching. He stared into her pupilless eyes, studied the curve of her cheekbones, the fullness of her lips, the cut of her hair. There was something about her, something familiar . . .

"Do I *know* you, Fräulein?" he asked.

"Of *course* you know her, Wagner," Englande said, his voice dripping with sarcasm. "She's a *freak*—like you. Your kind *always* recognizes each other. You're much like the Jews in that—" he quickly rounded on the wraith-like Pryde "—isn't that so, Shadowcat?"

The spectral woman flinched. "Y . . . yes . . . Hauptmann Englande . . ." she said quietly. "That is so . . ." She acted as though afraid that the hulking brute might strike her, as impossible as that would have been, given her constant state of intangibility.

Wagner released their prisoner and took a step back. He shook his head, unable to make sense of the thoughts now racing through his head. "Strange as it may seem, Fräulein, I somehow feel as though I should know you. Have we met before—Tangiers, perhaps? Or Cairo?"

Munroe shook her head. "And yet I feel the same," she said with a mixture of surprise and confusion. "But why should that be?"

Before Wagner could reply, Meggan stepped forward and gave the white-haired mutant a brutal shove between the shoulder blades, sending her bouncing off the armored plating of the V-wing. The woman turned to face her attacker, but wisely made no attempt to retaliate.

"I am certain we will have plenty of time to discuss it on our way to Genosha, as fascinating a topic as it may be," Meggan said caustically. "But the Reichsminister is a very busy, very important man, and should not be kept waiting, Nightcrawler—" she pointed an accusatory finger at him "—while you try to determine in which port of call you may have picked up this African trollop." She gave Munroe another shove, and pointed at the ladder. "Now, get into the *verdamnt* plane, cow, before I finish the job of 'crippling' you that the Ministry started!"

Wordlessly, Munroe clambered up the rungs, Meggan close behind. Not needing to be told what to do, Shadowcat quietly floated upward, phasing through the V-wing's hull on her way back to her cramped quarters, apparently eager to put some distance between herself and their volatile leader.

Wagner turned to face him. "What about the others?" he asked, pointing toward the villagers.

Englande shrugged. "My orders say nothing about razing this sty, or exterminating the filth living within its walls. No doubt the Emperor has some use for these dregs, astounding as it seems."

"And what that might be—"

"Is none of our business."

Wagner nodded. "I thought as much."

The sound of Meggan barking orders at their prisoner caused both men to look at the cabin's hatchway, as though expecting one or both of the women to come tumbling out of the craft, locked in combat. There was a loud *crack*, as from someone being brutally slapped across the face, followed by a throaty chuckle.

Englande smiled. "I believe Meggan has matters well in hand," he commented. "Women, eh?" he added with a wink.

The smile that had started to form on Wagner's face was wiped away as his superior officer pushed him aside and began climbing the ladder.

Sitting on his tail on the hot sand, feeling the coarse grains working their way into his uniform, Wagner vented his frustrations by pounding the ground with his fists. Aware that the villagers were watching him with a degree of amusement, he stood up and adjusted his clothing, only to scrape his jaw along the starched collar. He grunted angrily, turning his back to the crowd, and made his way up the ladder.

"If it were up to *me,* I would turn this craft around and return to England . . ." he muttered.

7

SHE was burning.

Flames licked at her body, her face, scorching her hair and flesh, filling the air with the pungent odor of overcooked meat. She rolled across the tiled floor, beating at the fire with her hands, trying to extinguish it as it charred her skin, melting the leather bodysuit until it was welded to her, the metal zippers branding her with small serrated patterns as they bonded with bubbling flesh through torrents of blood. She pulled frantically at the material, shrieking in agony as each piece she tore came away with another layer of blackened skin, a small part of her mind begging, praying, for the torment to end.

Her ears filled with blood, her eyes began to boil away. And yet she could still hear the laughs of the green-skinned monsters standing around her, still see the oversized weapons they carried—the bringers of flames, of death.

And then the fire roared higher, brighter, hotter, consuming all she was, all she had been . . .

Rogue sat up on the cold deck where she had collapsed, her screams still echoing along the smooth metal walls of the small chamber. Her breath caught in her throat—the nauseating smell of burnt flesh still clung to her clothes, her hair, still filled her nostrils—and she coughed raggedly. She spat black-flecked phlegm into a corner, the taste of bile thick on her tongue, then yanked at the leather hood encasing her head until the zipper finally gave.

Her face was dirty and streaked with tears, her eyes thoroughly bloodshot; she hadn't stopped crying until fatigue had gently, finally, wrapped her in darkness soon after she'd been returned to the battlecruiser.

She'd failed them: the High Council of Ishla'non. Watched in horror as the Skrull warriors butchered them, using flamethrowers to exterminate the pacifistic creatures instead of the powerful sidearms they wore strapped to their thighs—all the better to prolong their victims' pain . . . and the Skrulls' pleasure. She had still been linked to the hivemind when the one called Geer'lak was set alight; theirs had been a shared agony, one that continued to build with frightening intensity until it consumed every member of the Ilon assembled in the council chamber.

And then the slaughter began . . .

Rogue shivered, rising uneasily to her feet, using a wall to support her. She had experienced every one of their deaths, unable to disengage herself from the psychic connection until the last councilor had succumbed to the terrible flames, leaving her once again broken in mind and spirit. But the pain hadn't ended there, for the images continued to replay again and again in her thoughts until her mind had finally shut down. She couldn't even remember how or when she'd been returned to her cell.

She stumbled over to her bunk—a small metal platform bolted to another wall, its furnishings nothing more than a tattered mattress, a lumpy pillow, and a threadbare sheet—and sat on its edge, waiting for the tremors running through her body to come to an end. She rubbed her sweat-drenched face with leather-wrapped hands, grateful that at least one of the brutish Skrulls had taken a moment to put back the glove Reichsmajor Sommers had removed when he forced her to have direct contact with the Ilon. Without it, she would have spent every moment fearful of making even the most casual of contacts with anyone on the ship—human, Skrull, or mutant. And after her nightmarish experience on Ishla'non, she could never handle accessing someone else's mind—not right now. She'd go irrevocably mad; she was sure of it.

"Contacts with anyone." She almost had to laugh. Here she was, locked away on the lowest level of the starship *Nuremburg*, allowed to step outside the confines of her cell on the rare occasion when she was needed for a mission—and only under the heaviest of guard—and she was worried about accidentally touching someone and leeching both their memories and their strength. The chances of that under normal circumstances were pretty much nil: the humans treated her like she carried a plague, while the Skrulls looked upon her with contempt, so neither were about to come anywhere close to her unless ordered to do so. And, following the events on Bloodstone Crater six months ago, when her last escape attempt had almost succeeded, the life-forces of twelve Skrull warriors coursing through her supercharged body, even the few mutants among the crew had taken to giving her a wide berth.

A freak even t'my own kind . . . she thought darkly. *If it wasn't so outright pathetic, it'd almost be funny—in a mean-spirited sorta way.*

Rogue sighed and lay back across the bunk, staring at the ceiling, listening to the hum of the hyperdrive engines three decks below. Ordinarily, the sound lulled to her to dreamless sleep, providing her with some peace of mind. Now, though, each pulse of the warp system was like the roar of a Skrull flamethrower to her ears, each squeal of the deckplates like the anguished cries of a hundred Ilon as death claimed each of them. Sounds that would be with her for the rest of her life.

Placing her hands over her ears, Rogue curled up on the bed and screwed her eyes tightly shut, wishing, hoping, for it all to just go away.

It did nothing to clear away the awful smell that lingered in her nostrils—or ease the screams that echoed and re-echoed in her mind . . .

* * *

Reichsmajor Scott Sommers reclined on the bed in his quarters, pillows propped up behind his head, and studied a copy of the latest mission report—his idea of light reading before turning in for the night.

He had exchanged his battle visor for a far more comfortable pair of glasses fitted with ruby quartz lenses, though the lighter spectacles did nothing to alleviate the dull ache in his eyes that was always present during his waking hours—a constant reminder of the terrible power that lay just behind the corneas. The only times he no longer felt the nagging pressure of the extradimensional energy that sought release whenever he opened his eyes were when he slept, and when his thoughts were focused on other matters—like a mission gone well.

The one on Ishla'non, as the report indicated, had gone exceedingly well: the Kree spies had been hunted down and executed, the High Council exterminated like the bugs they so grotesquely resembled, the planet secured as the latest colony of the ever-expanding Empire. And with the task of setting up a new government left to the warships of the Ministry of Imperial Bureaucracy, Sommers and his crew had been rewarded for their latest victory with an early shore leave—back home on Earth.

Sommers closed the report cover and tossed the folder on his desk, pleased with the summation of the mission; if there was one thing his yeoman, Gwendolyn Stacy, was good at, it was finding just the right dramatic tone for mission statements that were guaranteed to impress his superiors. He swung his feet onto the deck, stood, and stretched, smiling as his vertebrae popped back into place. He should be resting, he knew; the voyage home, even at maximum hyperspatial speeds, would still take more than a day to complete. The problem was, he didn't feel tired; in fact, he felt just the opposite. But that was to be expected—as with any successful mission, the hours afterward were never spent sleeping, but in finding ways to burn off the adrenaline still coursing through his system.

He considered his options. He could turn off the cabin lights and lie down, try to fall asleep, but he knew he'd only wind up either staring at the ceiling or, should he remove his glasses, watching the bursts of energy that exploded like fireworks within his closed eyelids. He could dress and go up to the bridge, but then he'd start hanging over his officers' shoulders, checking their readings, adjusting courses—generally getting in the way; not that he cared how they felt about the intrusion, but it would only show the men how restless he was, and a fidgety commander runs the risk of losing his crew's respect. He could go to the gymnasium on E-Deck, to challenge Security Chief Horst Buckholz to a game of racquetball, or perhaps get a good rubdown from masseuse Wanda Maximoff—the woman might be a gypsy, but she *was* a lovely creature, he had to admit; her touch would certainly help him to relax!

Or he could call Jean.

Sommers smiled—now *that* was an idea! A glass of schnapps, a bit of conversation with his wife to discuss the day's efforts . . . If hers was anything like the last time they'd spoken, she'd probably lull him to sleep with some boring tale of what dresses she'd bought and the conversations she'd had with her girlfriends while buying them, or how she spent hours scrubbing the kitchen and they really should hire a maid . . . Why, he could almost feel himself nodding off already!

He glanced at the ship's chronometer: It should just be after eight A.M. in New York; Jean would have been up for at least an hour by this point.

Sommers opened the mini-bar that was bolted to the wall on the far side of his cabin, and withdrew a glass snifter and a small bottle of mint schnapps. He poured himself a liberal dollop of the liquor, then locked up the decanter and settled into the plush leather chair situated before his desk.

Pressing a small stud built into the mahogany surface, he activated a ten-inch-wide screen that rose from the desk. As it hummed to life, he used a built-in keypad to enter his personal identification code, making certain the signal would be scrambled so no one would be able to eavesdrop on his conversation. With that accomplished, he punched in the transmission coordinates that would connect him with the communications set in the apartment, then hit SEND.

It took some time for the call to go through; longer than he would have imagined, since Jean was usually so prompt in answering the signal. He drummed his fingers on the desk, gazing at the screen through narrowed eyes, as though daring it to remain blank. It wasn't that he felt any sort of concern over her lack of response—after all who would be foolish enough to attack the wife of a high-ranking Imperial officer? Besides, where would that silly woman go to put herself in any danger? She hardly ever left the apartment when he wasn't there! No, he wasn't concerned for her safety; rather, he was angry for being kept waiting.

Finally, though, there was a small spark of light within the depths of the screen, and an image began to take form, growing larger as it sharpened, until it filled the frame. Jean stood just to the left of the picture, the camera mounted on the bureau in their bedroom; behind her, through the open windows, he could see the sun rising above the Manhattan skyline. Her face was hidden by her bright-red hair as she bent over to put on an open-toed, high-heeled shoe.

"Just a minute," she muttered, adjusting the ankle strap. That done, she snapped her head back, allowing the hair to billow around her face as it settled onto her shoulders. Sommers noted the high-collared white blouse and black leather skirt she was wearing—she looked as though she were getting ready to go out.

"Yes?" she said, picking up a small diamond earring from the bureau and pinning it to her right lobe. When no answer was forthcoming, she stopped primping and leaned forward, until her face was mere inches from the camera. Her eyes widened in surprise. "Scott?"

"Of *course* it's Scott, you imbecile!" he snapped. "Who *else* would it be, calling at this hour?"

She stepped back from the camera, as though she'd been slapped. "I . . . I . . ." she stammered. Then her eyes narrowed, suddenly filled with a fire he'd never seen before, and she leaned forward again. "Who the *hell* do you think you're talking to?" she demanded.

Now it was Sommers' turn to recoil. His mouth hung open, midway to giving a response, yet unable to believe what had just happened. Had she really said what he thought he'd heard? Was she actually *talking back* to him?

His lips pulled back in a snarl. "What did you just—"

"If all you're going to do is sit there and chastise me for not picking up the call on the first ring, Scott," Jean interjected, "then don't bother. I have things to do today, and I'm already running late." She paused, obviously waiting for an answer, but he was still trying to figure out exactly when she might have developed a backbone. Then: "Was there something you wanted to talk about?"

"Yes," he replied, using his anger to focus on the situation before it completely slipped from his control. "I'm on my way home. We should be making planetfall by tomorrow evening."

Her turn to look surprised again. "Tomorrow?"

He nodded, pleased by the look of fear that momentarily flashed in her eyes. "And when I get there, I think you and I should sit down and discuss this new attitude you're suddenly displaying towards your *husband*—and what you're doing that is so important you're running out of the apartment this early in the morning."

Jean's mouth worked silently for a few moments, then she swallowed. Loudly. "I . . . look forward to it," she said quietly.

"As do I," he said the coolly. "I'll see you tomorrow night, then." He reached out to touch the screen, ran an index finger down it, as though stroking her cheek. "Count the moments until then, my love. I'll be with you before too long."

He stabbed the DISCONNECT button before she could reply, then sat back in his chair, elbows resting on the arms, fingers steepled in front of his face. He stared at the blank screen for a number of seconds, then punched another number on the keypad.

Almost immediately, an image formed of a wizened, white-haired frau in her seventies or eighties, the angle of her sunken cheeks almost as severe as the hawk-like nose down which she stared at him. She wore a dark-colored shawl, one that almost gave the appearance that her head was disconnected from her body, so well did the material blend in with the black velvet curtains that hung behind her. She gently stroked the back of a large black cat that lay across her lap.

"You have reached the League of German Women," she said, with just a trace of the dramatic in her intonation. "I am Frau Harkness. How may I be of—" Her dark eyes, hidden within the depths of swollen eyelids, suddenly opened wide; obviously, she recognized the caller. She smiled. "Reichsmajor Sommers! To what do I owe this pleasure?"

Sommers frowned. "I wish I *could* consider this a pleasure, Frau Harkness, but I'm calling on a matter of some urgency."

She nodded sagely, as though already aware of his problem. "Your wife," she said.

An eyebrow rose behind ruby quartz lenses. How could the woman know that? He shook his head slightly, dismissing the flash of suspicion that ran through his mind. It didn't take a scientist to figure out how that could be—he was contacting the League of German Women; who *else* would he be calling about, if not his wife?

"She's acting strangely . . ." he began.

Again, a nod. "You desire to know why that is." She smiled frostily, and scratched the cat behind its ears; the creature purred happily. "Fear not, brave Major—the full services of the League are at your disposal. We shall find the answers you seek—with or without your lovely wife's permission . . ."

"Damn it!" Jean Grey barked, staring at the blank screen. She hadn't meant to lose her temper like that, but she wouldn't have taken that kind of garbage from *her* Scott Summers, even before the Cosmic Cube turned the world upside-down. She certainly

wasn't going to accept it from some fascist counterpart intent on putting her in her place.

Unfortunately, she probably just gave herself away with that display of anger, she quickly came to realize. The Jean Sommers of this world would never have acted in such a defiant manner, especially with her husband.

She sighed. It had all seemed simple enough, when the woman codenamed Phoenix had formulated her plan hours ago: Convince her alternate to allow her control of this body, then set out to locate the remaining X-Men who had accompanied her to von Doom's world: Rogue, Nightcrawler, Wolverine—and Scott. Unfortunately, the sixth member of the team, a Cajun thief named Remy Lebeau—Gambit—had died during that mission, sacrificing himself so his teammates would be able to escape the facility in which the armored dictator's flunkies had imprisoned them. The loss had been especially hard on Rogue—she and Remy had been as close as lovers. There would be time for mourning his tragic death later—if the world, and the universe, had any time left, she thought glumly. And there was still a team to reassemble.

Of course, getting to the point where Jean Sommers would even listen to her hadn't been the easiest task to accomplish. Not long ago, Phoenix had been trapped in the subconscious of yet another version of herself: a Jean Grey fanatically devoted to following the X-Men's old enemy, Magneto, as he used the Cosmic Cube to reshape the world into one in which humanity and mutantkind lived in harmony—under his rule, that is. Phoenix had found herself locked away in the deepest levels of Grey's psyche, unable to break through the many barriers that stood between the two telepaths. She had made a number of efforts to contact her alternate's conscious mind, but hadn't been able to accomplish anything more than giving her a slight headache.

That situation changed, however, when the Cube apparently switched hands yet again, this time winding up in the possession of the Red Skull, as she had been able to gather from the thoughts of this latest surrogate. Gone was Phoenix's villainous counterpart, replaced by a kinder, gentler Jean Sommers—one lacking telepathic abilities, or psychic defenses to overcome.

It hadn't taken too much effort to get Jean to accept the idea—after easing her fears that seeing a costumed woman in her mirror wasn't a sure sign of oncoming insanity, of course—but the last thing Phoenix expected was for Nazi-Scott (she couldn't really think of him as anything else; he certainly didn't act like *her* husband!) to call out of the blue, then snap at her for not answering fast enough. He should have been pleased that she took the call in the first place; if it wasn't for the other Jean guiding her along, she never would have found the blasted communications set hidden in the bureau. But then, when he called her an "imbecile," yelled at her in a way meant to intimidate the woman he thought was his wife . . .

The nerve of that pig! If she didn't know better, she never would have imagined the "real" Scott Summers could be trapped somewhere in the depths of that bully's subconscious. But having experienced it first-hand on two occasions herself, it wasn't so hard to believe—just frustrating.

Jean angrily snatched a purse from a table in the foyer and stomped her way to the door, throwing on a short black jacket as she went. She unlocked the door and pulled it open—to find a stern-looking young woman standing in the hallway, one hand raised as though she had been about to knock. She was in her mid-twenties, give or take a year or two, but the frown that twisted her features and the crow's feet that creased the corners of her eyes—apparently she spent a great deal of time glowering at people, Jean imagined—made her look ten years older. Her light-brown hair was cut in a pageboy style, bangs framing the tops of pencilled eyebrows, ends just brushing her shoulders. The severe cut of her black suit—tight jacket with wide lapels, equally tight, knee-length skirt—made it clear she wasn't here to sell her some appliance.

"Frau Sommers?" the woman asked.

"Yes . . . ?" Jean replied slowly.

She reached into a black leather handbag, withdrew an identification badge. She held it up so Jean could read it. "I am Fräulein Jennifer Walters, of the League of German Women."

Jean smiled, trying to act polite. "What can I do for you, Fräulein Walters?" she asked pleasantly. But a quick psi-scan of the woman's mind told her all she needed to know: Scott had reported her to the League. The realization took Jean by surprise—just how quickly did the secret police move on this world? She'd only spoken to him no more than five minutes ago!

Walters also smiled, but it looked as though it was taking a great deal of effort to force her facial muscles to curve upwards. "Your presence has been requested at League Headquarters," she said. "Frau Harkness herself would like to speak with you."

Jean nodded, willing to play along—at least for a few moments. "In regard to . . . ?"

The smile faltered a little—obviously, the muscles weren't used to maintaining the façade for too long. "She thought that, although your husband is often lauded by the Reich for his accomplishments, perhaps his significant other should also be recognized for her own work. After all, 'behind every good man there is an equally good woman'—don't you think so?" She nodded, either pleased with her logic or just used to agreeing with herself. "Frau Harkness was contemplating a dinner in your honor, and wished to discuss the details."

Jean shook her head, beginning to lose her patience, but careful not to have another caustic outburst. "Perhaps on another occasion. But right now, I really must be going, Fräulein Walters." She moved to step around her unwanted visitor. "Please give my thanks, though, to Frau Harkness."

The woman would not be denied, though, placing herself directly in Jean's path again. "You can give them to her *yourself,* Frau Sommers," Walters snapped, the smile having at last collapsed under its own weight. "If I haven't made myself clear, let me do so now: You *will* accompany me to League Headquarters."

"For what reason?" Jean demanded.

"Your husband has expressed some . . . concern about your recent behavior." Walters reached into her purse, coming up with a small handgun clenched tightly in her fist. "This is *not* a request."

Jean glared at her, and snarled. "I don't have time for this." Her eyes glowed with a bright-green light. "And I *especially* don't like it when people point guns at me."

Walters took a step back, her usually dour expression suddenly replaced by one of fear. "What–" she began.

And then she collapsed at Jean's feet. The gun slipped from her hand and bounced into the apartment, landing with a clatter on the hardwood floor of the foyer.

Jean glanced up and down the hallway; thankfully, there was no one around to witness her telepathic display. Having to shut down any other minds would have just complicated matters–one was more than enough.

Making use of her telekinetic abilities, Jean scooped up Walters from the floor and levitated her into the apartment, placing her gently on the living room couch. The gun and handbag went into a foyer closet, next to a pair of yellow galoshes her faux-husband hadn't worn in years.

With a final glance at her unconscious guest, Jean closed the apartment door and headed for the fire stairs–her previous sweep of Walters' mind had revealed the presence of three other League agents in the lobby, all lurking near the elevators. As she hurried down the steps, heading for the delivery entrance on the other side of the building, Jean reached into her handbag and pulled out a page she'd printed out using Sommers' computer. It was from an online edition of a Westchester County phonebook she'd accessed when she began the search for her teammates. The familiar listing made her heart beat a little faster:

XAVIER, CHARLES
15 GRAYMALKIN DRIVE
SALEM CENTER, N.Y.

I hope you'll be happy to see a familiar face, Professor, Jean thought. *Otherwise, considering Scott's suspicions and the group of overzealous femiNazis he's sent chasing after me, I might find myself in* deeper *trouble—if that's even possible. . . .*

8

"AND when Alexander saw the breadth of his domain, he wept, for there were no more worlds to conquer . . .' "

As he strolled through the German countryside, the Red Skull couldn't help but be reminded of the old saying—never before had it seemed so appropriate than right at this moment. Granted, it wasn't entirely accurate—not with an entire universe to conquer, and untold hundreds of thousands of planets still to be offered the full attention of the Empire's resources. But the thrill of the hunt, the satisfaction he once felt when he held the life of an enemy in his hands, saw the terror on their eyes, smelled the fear that clung to them like the sweetest perfume—those days were long past, much to his regret. Replaced by thoughts of strategies and campaigns, of paperwork and electronic reports, of countless speeches and endless meetings.

The Cube hadn't made him a god. It had made him a bureaucrat.

The Skull snarled, disgusted with himself. When he had seized the Cube from Magneto, he'd thought ultimate power had finally been within his grasp, never to be taken from him. He had learned from the mistakes that developed with previous versions of the device, made certain he avoided repeating them. True, there were still superpowered men and women in his world, but they were under his complete control, as loyal to him now as dogs were to their master. Old enemies had been eliminated with just a thought—here one second, gone the next, all memory of them erased from the minds of his subjects. There was no one to oppose him.

Perhaps that's what he missed most of all. There were no more challenges—no need to be concerned with attempted assassinations by secret agents, or power plays enacted by some costumed buffoon looking to make his mark in history by calling himself a "villain" without having any real understanding of the term, or struggles against a colorfully-garbed do-gooder while explosions tore apart the ground under their feet. He had beaten them all, kicked their faces into the dirt of their graves with the heel of his boot, seized everything he had ever desired—all without ever having to dirty his hands.

But now, there were no more worlds to conquer . . .

"Your Majesty . . . ?"

The Skull looked up, surprised to see where his wanderings had taken him: He was standing before the metal gates of the concentration camp that stood in the shadow of Wewelsburg Castle. Back during the war, Niederhagen had been a small but productive facility, the 3,900 prisoners housed within its barbed wire fences used by the *Reichsarbeitsdienst*—the Reich Labor Service—as construction workers during the castle's renovations in 1939; their efforts were rewarded with barbaric living conditions, undernourishment, and death. American soldiers eventually liberated the camp in 1945, but by then more than 1,285 of the inmates, among them a large number of Soviets and Jehovah's Witnesses, had died.

To the Red Skull, seeing the camp restored to its former glory, its barracks packed with the lowest of the low, its gas chambers and ovens working at peak efficiency when required, was like stepping into his past.

Like coming home again.

The man who had addressed him stepped forward, a welcoming

smile lighting his features. He was tall and broad-shouldered, blonde hair cut short, yet stylishly, blue eyes sparkling with obvious joy at seeing his Emperor. In appearance and demeanor, from the gleam of polished leather and pewter on his crisp black uniform to the swagger of his step, he was everything an Aryan should be—yet his roots were in the East Coast of America. A tragic mishap of geography, really—despite his intense hatred for him, even the Skull had to admit that the man made an excellent Nazi . . .

"Commandant Rogers . . ." the Skull said evenly.

Here, at least, was something from which the Skull could take a measure of enjoyment. For decades, Steve Rogers had been a thorn in his side, constantly interfering with his plans for world domination—no, that wasn't true; it wasn't Rogers who had been the problem, but his costumed alter ego: the American flag-draped super hero known far and wide as Captain America. "The Sentinel of Liberty," he had been called, a shining example of everything that was good and decent and patriotic about his country, everything the Skull was not. A living legend who had fought for the Allies in World War II, and then again, many years later, alongside some of Earth's mightiest heroes. A man who had fought for peace, for democracy, for harmony, no matter how staggering the odds he faced, even at the cost of his very life.

Who better, then, to be the commanding officer of a death camp?

The irony of the situation had been too delicious for the Skull to pass up. How Rogers' soul must be screaming in anguish as it watched the horrors of the prison through eyes grown cold with hate! Even now, the thought of it brought a smile to what remained of the Skull's lips . . .

Rogers looked mildly flustered by the sudden appearance of the Emperor at his gates, but tried to hide it by broadening his smile. "Your Majesty, had I known you were coming for an inspection—"

The Skull shook his head. "There is no inspection, Commandant; I merely wished to be alone with my thoughts. My arrival here was unplanned." He glanced past Rogers, toward a pair of brick smokestacks that towered above the far end of the camp. Smoke billowed from the structures, the black clouds thick with the pungent odor of burnt flesh and powdered bone. "Perhaps I was drawn here by the pull of old memories . . ."

For a moment, a flash of nervousness glittered in Rogers' eyes. "Then, I apologize for . . . disturbing you, Your Majesty. If I've offended you . . ."

The Skull waved him to silence. He studied the man for a few moments, not quite certain why he didn't feel some sense of satisfaction at having finally bested his old enemy. Was it because Rogers didn't remember their numerous clashes in the past? Was it because he was *too* subservient—programmed to obey too well? Or was it simply because he wasn't dressed in that gaudy, red-white-and-blue uniform the Skull was so used to seeing him in, sunlight gleaming off the tiny links of chainmail that protected his upper body, right hand gripping the straps of the large, round shield that was his only weapon, its center decorated with an oversized star?

Yes, the Skull thought. That was *exactly* the problem.

Captain America had been the one constant in his life—ever vigilant, ever strongwilled, ever standing between the Skull and his destiny. He could always be counted on to make an unwanted appearance, just as victory was within the Skull's grasp; was always able to rise, phoenix-like, from the ashes of defeat to win the day. But the accursed shield-slinger was gone now, replaced by an obedient servant who presented no opposition—no challenge—to him . . . and *that* was what kept the Skull from gaining complete pleasure from the situation.

For a few seconds, he considered calling upon the Cube's cosmic power, using it to restore Rogers to the man he had once been—just for a little while, at least. A momentary diversion, to chase away the sense of ennui that had overcome the Skull of late. But then he dismissed the notion, recalling that a similar train of thought years ago, with another Cube, had caused him to resurrect his foe in order to crow about how he was now Captain America's master. He'd ended up losing four teeth and the Cube, and stumbling off the edge of a cliff as he tried to make his escape.

Some things, he reflected, were better left alone . . .

"Well, as long as you're here, Your Majesty," Rogers said, "would you and your aide care to tour the facility?"

"My . . . ?" The Skull looked back, over his shoulder, expecting to see Dietrich standing beside him.

It was Leonard he spotted, however, standing ten yards away, skulking as always in the shadow of his master. He'd forgotten the boy had accompanied him on his stroll through the countryside; then again, it wasn't too difficult for that to have happened, given the youth's quiet, fearful nature. Perhaps the boy should have trained as a Ninja assassin, rather than as a National Socialist—his talent for stealth would have served him better.

"Come along, boy!" the Skull barked. "I have no patience for dawdlers!"

"Yes, Your Majesty!" Leonard trotted over obediently, coming to a halt beside the Emperor.

The Skull nodded, pleased that his former aide was still capable of responding to a command, but uncertain as to why he should have ordered the boy to accompany him, rather than Dietrich. He supposed it didn't really matter—one lackey was as good as the next. With a mental shrug, he turned to Rogers, and gestured toward the camp.

"After you, Your Majesty," Rogers said pleasantly. "I think you'll be quite pleased with what you see."

"*I* shall be the judge of that, Commandant," the Skull growled. "Remember that as we proceed."

Rogers nodded quickly and moved aside, to allow his master access to the main yard. The Skull brushed past him, angered by the way Rogers fought to keep his bottom lip from trembling.

Weakling, he thought heatedly.

Perhaps his world *was* better off without Captain America . . .

* * *

When he first saw the gates of the camp through the tree line, Leonard had felt a lead weight settle in his stomach. Ever since the Skull had changed the world, using the Cube to transport them both to the Fatherland so he could set up his power base, Leonard had done his best to avoid having to see any of the horrors his master had created; the camp had been high on his list of places to steer clear of. He'd also tried to remain quietly in the background—after all, now that the Skull had reached his ultimate goal, what need did he have of lackeys?

He knew the Skull detested him, considered him unfit to be called a Nazi. But what he couldn't figure out was, if the grotesque villain hated him so, why did he keep him around? With the Cosmic Cube in his possession, the Skull could have anyone he wanted as his right-hand man; he'd demonstrated just that by resurrecting his previous aide, Dietrich. And with that task accomplished, Leonard's role had been rendered obsolete; if the Skull wished it, he could be wiped from existence, never to be seen again—or even remembered.

Maybe the Skull needed someone to gloat to, he considered. With all his enemies defeated or dead, there was no one to acknowledge the power he now possessed. Maybe he needed someone who knew how the world had been just over a month ago, before the Cosmic Cube and its trio of owners had each torn it apart and rebuilt it to their specifications. Someone who could appreciate the accomplishments he'd achieved, and who could respond with the right amount of awe. Well, there was Magneto, but Leonard couldn't see any reason why the Skull would even bother—the super-villain was so far beneath his notice, it had apparently skipped his mind that he'd allowed an enemy to live, locked away as he was in the depths of the Canadian wilderness.

Maybe he'd just forgotten all about his former assistant, as well; Leonard certainly hoped that was the explanation. And by keeping to the old adage of "out of sight, out of mind," he had managed to keep the Skull from focusing on him for too long, perhaps even from reaching a decision that Leonard dreaded he would make one day: that he no longer needed anyone around to remind him of the "old days" . . .

His life had never seemed this complicated—certainly had never been filled with such perils—during his childhood in Chicago, long before the Red Skull entered it.

No, that wasn't entirely true. His parents had tried to impress upon him the dangers that existed in the world as he was growing up, but Leonard Mathias Jackson had been a typical kid back then, unwilling to take the advice of adults, secure in the belief that he was invincible. The only dangers he had to face were avoiding old Mrs. Mendelbaum next door when he and his friends played on her stoop, or getting his butt kicked by some of the older kids at school. He knew about super heroes and super-villains like the Fantastic Four and Doctor Doom—those costumed types were pretty cool!—but wasn't interested in hearing about boring stuff like job security and "affirmative action" (whatever that was) and how minorities were stealing positions that should be filled by honest (white) Americans. Unfortunately, it was all his old man ever seemed to talk about during Leonard's pre-teen years, which made it difficult to block it out entirely, and which only widened the gap between father and son—not that they had ever really been close to begin with. Eventually, though, Nathaniel's hate-filled diatribes began to sink in, and Leonard began to listen. There was some truth in his father's words, he realized, once you got past the heat of the message. But it wasn't until Nathaniel was passed over for a promotion, and the position was given to a black man who had worked under him, making him Nathaniel's supervisor, that Leonard began to wonder if his father might have been right all along . . .

It was about that time that he learned of Adolf Hitler and the Third Reich.

It was part of his high school history lessons: an examination of World War II. It was meant to impress upon the students the horrors of war, and the monstrous actions a society could enact on its citizens only because they were different—actions directed by a single individual on an insane quest to dominate the world. Most of the kids in his class were only interested in the exploits of the costumed superpowered men and women who'd fought on behalf of the Allied Forces: Captain America and the Invaders. Miss America and the All-Winners Squad. The Destroyer, The Patriot, and dozens of others.

But it was the villains who caught Leonard's eye. Master Man. Baron Blood. The Red Skull. Bad guys were always cooler, because they were willing to take the sort of risks good guys were afraid to. They would go anywhere, do anything, destroy anyone who got in their way. And it was because they were so "cool" that Leonard began doing his own research on them, and their cause—the Internet was full of web sites dedicated to both, with links to even more URLs. Gradually, he even began to join in on the chat rooms for some of the sites, which led to connections with people his own age—people whose philosophies he eventually made his own.

He went to Auschwitz, once, just after he'd turned twenty-one. His parents, oblivious to the kinds of friends he'd acquired, had paid for the trip to Europe as a late graduation present; Poland was just one of the stops on the tour. The concentration camp had been nothing more than a curiosity to him—a tourist attraction where guides somberly spoke of the more than one million Jews, gypsies, Poles, and Russians who had been put to death within its fences. The number was just too big to get his head around it, but his friends certainly found the figure impressive. "A good start," he'd heard Kevin Boyer mutter. They'd all had a good laugh over that.

And then they went dancing.

The club in which they'd partied the night away was as unusual—and disturbing—a location as one could possibly conceive. It stood in the nearby town of Oswiecim, in a building that had been used by the Nazis to sort the hair taken from Jewish prisoners after extermination—hair used for, among other things, stuffing mattresses and insulating the boots of U-boat crews. But he hadn't known about that when they burst through the doors, nor would he have cared—he was there to have fun, and that's exactly what he found. The heavy-metal music had gotten his pulse racing, the vodka had loosened him up, and the women had been incredibly beautiful . . . and amazingly accommodating.

It was there he first learned of "The Controller" and his plans for re-establishing the supremacy of the white race. Not that Leonard was interested in hearing recruitment speeches—far from it—but it was apparently the price one had to pay for enjoying the charms of their hostesses. So he sat and listened, and the words he heard made sense to him. More than made sense—they sounded true, accurate. Whites *were* losing power in the world—he had only to look at his father to see proof of that. Given enough time, they would find themselves in the minority—and that could not be allowed to happen. Not, as it was so clearly explained by him, and the others in that noisy, smoke-filled club, when there was a man ready to lead them against their enemies. A man who knew how the world could be, *should* be, if they were willing to follow his lead.

A man with a vision . . .

Now, as he walked in the shadow of his master, Leonard could only stare in horror at what that man, that vision, had wrought.

Death was all around him. He could see it in the terrified expressions of the prisoners as they huddled together, forced into small groups by the guards; could smell it in the air; could feel it settling into his bones like a winter chill. Waves of despair roiled across the yard to break against him, threatening to drown his soul in a tide of darkness. A tremor ran through his legs, but he remained standing, hoping his master hadn't seen that moment of weakness. And as he screwed his eyes shut to block out the sights and sounds and smells, he began to understand why it was that the Skull treated him with such scorn.

He felt sorry for his enemies.

He knew he shouldn't; in fact, he should have been feeling

elated. Here were prime examples of the very minorities he had come to hate, who had tried to destroy his country from the inside, like a cancer. He should be laughing in their faces, taking pleasure in their fear. And yet . . . and yet, he could only feel pity—and shame.

Gazing at the hollowed eyes and gaunt faces of the women behind the fences, he suddenly found himself thinking of Kate Ashbrook, the computer hacker he had once dated when they'd first begun working for the man they came to know as The Controller. She'd given her life for the Skull's dream, hadn't she? She and all the others whose skeletons would continue to circle the Earth until they eventually crumbled to dust. Dead people on a dead planetoid—orbiting a dead world?

That, more than anything else, was what deeply troubled Leonard: the thought that, if the Skull grew tired of his new world—as he was starting to show signs of, by his recent bouts of melancholy—he might destroy it on a whim. If the Cube made him so powerful that he didn't even need to hold the wish box to call upon its cosmic energies—as Leonard had seen with his own eyes after the planet had been reshaped—if he could mold reality to fit his needs with just the force of his own mind, then he was virtually a god. And even a god could become weary of his creations . . .

A small gasping sound pulled him from his reverie. A few feet ahead, the Skull and Commandant Rogers had come to a stop near the administrative offices; they stood beside a frail-looking woman who cowered in their presence. Leonard hurried to join them before his absence was discovered.

". . . this is Anya Lensherr, the lead violinist of our orchestra, Your Majesty," Rogers was saying with a note of pride as Leonard quietly approached the Skull.

"Yes . . . I have heard their talentless assaults on the classics each day, from the castle," the Skull commented, fixing the woman with a hard stare. He turned to the commandant, his expression the same. "You were not planning to assail my ears with an off-key rendition of the 'Funeral March,' were you, Rogers?" His eyes narrowed. "It would be a grave error, to insult your emperor in such a fashion."

Rogers blanched. "Of course not, Your Majesty!" he responded immediately, snapping to attention. "I merely thought—"

The back of a gloved hand whipped forward, striking Rogers across the face. Remarkably, the man managed to take the blow without either flinching or stumbling backward.

"You thought *nothing!*" the Skull barked. "*I* am the one who does the thinking *for* you—for *all* the pathetic sheep of this world! The one who guides your worthless lives, gives them meaning. Who allows you to *continue* living only because I wish it! Before me, there was nothing; after me—" He paused. "After me . . ."

A chill running up his spine, Leonard watched as a disturbing gleam lit the Skull's eyes. This is it, he thought. This is where he ends it all . . .

"After me . . ." the Skull said slowly, ". . . there is only oblivion. For without me, nothing would exist—not this world, not this universe. It is only by the strength of my indomitable will that the forces von Doom has foolishly unleashed are kept at bay." He looked skyward, and Leonard followed the direction of his gaze, expecting to see whatever it was his master was observing. But there was only brilliant sunlight and clear blue skies above them; if the Skull saw anything else, it was beyond Leonard's ability to perceive it.

"No," the Skull finally said. "I have labored too hard, created too much, for my vision to be torn apart because of the ill-conceived planning of some gypsy filth. *I* control the Cube now, and only one who has known its true powers, who has touched the face of Eternity itself, could hold together a cosmos that strains to tear itself apart. *ONLY THE RED SKULL!*" he bellowed, shaking a fist at the heavens. "I have sterilized your virus, von Doom, corrected the flaws your bungling scientists had made! Your failsafe device has been rendered inoperative! This Cube—this universe—is *mine,* now and forevermore!"

And as he watched his emperor Leonard couldn't be sure if he should feel relieved that the Skull had apparently abandoned thoughts of destroying the planet on a whim—or dread what he might do with it now. . . .

9

THE taxicab dropped Jean off before the padlocked wrought iron gates of Xavier's estate. As the yellow-and-black vehicle roared away, she made a telepathic sweep of the area, just to make certain there were no Nazi Women's League members lurking in the bushes.

Satisfied that she was alone, Jean took one last glance up and down the well-paved country road, then telekinetically raised herself into the air, floated over the gates, and gently landed on the estate grounds. Gazing at her surroundings, Jean couldn't help but feel depressed. The driveway that wound from the road to the mansion's front door was pitted and potholed, and the acres of well-mown lawns hadn't seen a groundskeeper's touch in a dog's age—the grass was almost at eye level, patches of it turned a hideous shade of brown. The air was thick with flies and mosquitoes, the former drawn to the trash scattered around the gates—rotting food, half-empty plastic containers and greasy boxes from take-out joints, discarded bottles and cans of soft drinks and alcoholic beverages—while the latter had taken residence in puddles of stagnant water somewhere in the overgrowth; Jean couldn't see the fetid pools, but she could certainly smell them. With a sigh, she set off down the driveway, dreading what she would find at the end of the road.

Given the poor conditions of the grounds, she wasn't all that surprised by the sight that greeted her minutes later, when she pushed her way through the last rows of weeds, wildflowers, and mottled grass. And yet, as she stared in dismay at the crumbling, weather-beaten edifice standing before her, she was suddenly struck by the notion that there was no hope to be found in this place.

The facade was as pitted as the driveway, the plaster cracked and crumbling, revealing the bare brickface just underneath. Most of the windows on the first floor, and more on the second, were broken, the splintered frames holding nothing more than jagged shards of glass. A number of spray-painted messages covered the walls and front door, the words blazing in red, orange, and green Day-Glo letters:

DIE FREEK!
MUTEE SKUM!
NAZI SYMPATHIZER BURN IN HELL!

A flutter of wings caught her attention, and Jean watched as a trio of pigeons flew inside, quickly disappearing in the darkness of what had once been the library; apparently, the once prestigious mansion had turned into an aviary over the years.

But those were phantom years, Jean knew. Time that had only passed in the minds of the people inhabiting this world—people living fictitious lives, as she and the other X-Men were leading; as they had on the Earth of Magneto's making. Not to mention those members of the group who had fallen prey to Doctor Doom's tyrannical visions. Members like Psylocke, or Archangel.

Jean frowned. Betsy and Warren. Where were *they* in this madness? Could Betsy—or at least her duplicate—really now be the star of some adventure series, as that television magazine had reported? She shrugged. Anything was possible when the Cosmic

Cube was involved—she was still finding it hard to believe her previous alternate had been a staunch supporter of Magneto's twisted philosophies.

And there was another concept that took some getting used to. It was odd to think of a different yet similar Jean Grey in such terms: "alternate," "duplicate," "doppelganger." The Jean Grey of Erik Lensherr's domain was every bit as real as the woman who called herself Phoenix. Jean knew that all too well—she could feel her . . . double still lurking in the corners of her mind, enraged that she was as much a prisoner in the depths of this Nazi-born body, as Jean had been in hers. If it hadn't been for Phoenix's greater mental abilities, she might have been trapped in Sommers' subconscious, instead of being able to push herself out and lock her evil twin behind her.

There has *to be a way to put an end to all these overlapping personalities,* Jean thought with a grim smile. *I'm not sure there's any room left for more me's in this brain . . .*

Well, if anyone could help her find a solution, there was no one better than Professor Charles Xavier . . . at least, she *hoped* that would be the case.

She'd felt Xavier's mind brush hers back on Magneto's world, when her alternate had psychically interrogated him. At first, Jean had been surprised to realize that the Professor was on Earth—she and the X-Men had left him back on Roma's Starlight Citadel, while they traveled to von Doom's reality; Xavier had known the group would be better able to gather intelligence without having to worry about their wheelchair-bound mentor. Obviously, he had taken matters into his own hands when his students failed in their mission, but he must have known the trouble he'd get into once Magneto's followers became aware he was on Earth. Still, Jean had been comforted by his presence; just knowing he was there had given her enough hope that the X-Men would ultimately succeed. She hadn't been able to contact him, to let him know that she could telepathically "hear" him, but the desire to do so gave her the strength to overcome a good deal of her alternate's mental defenses as she fought her way to the front of the brain, determined to wrest control of what she had thought was her own body from the usurper who had stolen it from her. Given enough time, she might have succeeded—but then all hell had broken loose once more, and she'd awoken on another Earth, trapped in another version of herself. No doubt the same had happened to her teammates, and Xavier as well; like her alternate, they would all be followers of the Red Skull now, their personalities submerged in the depths of their counterparts' minds.

Would Xavier help her to free them—for that matter, would she be able to help him free *himself?* Or would he turn against her, maybe even notify her hunters, who were probably scouring every inch of Manhattan to locate her at this very moment?

Good questions, all, but she would never find any answers . . . if she didn't ring the doorbell first.

Hesitantly, she stepped through the weeds that sprouted across the cracked asphalt, the toes of her shoes occasionally jarring the stem of a dandelion, or scraping the top of a wildflower. And then, before she knew it, she was at the door, index finger pressing against the rusted button to the left of the frame.

Nothing.

No clanging of chimes, no grating buzz—just silence.

Well, I can't say I'm all that surprised, Jean thought. *There's probably not an electrician in Westchester County who'd be willing to navigate that jungle back there just to fix a doorbell.*

She stepped back and considered her options. She could try climbing through the library's shattered windows, but the tight fit of her knee-length skirt ruled that out; she'd never be able to lift her legs high enough to clamber over the molding wood. She could use her mental powers to lift herself up to the second floor, but someone passing by on the road might see her.

Or I could just give the door a good telekinetic shove. Given the state of this place, what's a little more property damage . . . ?

She braced herself, feeling the power build within her mind—

And then the door opened.

It swung in on well-oiled hinges—quickly, silently. And standing on the other side of the threshold, one hand holding the edge of the door, was an attractive woman in her twenties. She wore a black, knee-length dress, with a wide leather belt cinched tightly at the waist, making her look like a human hourglass. High-heeled shoes—and a formidable-looking handgun—completed her ensemble. Her shoulder-length blond hair hung loosely, parted on the left side of her head to flow over the right side of her face, in a style like that adopted by 1940s movie star Veronica Lake. And although Jean couldn't see the woman's right eye clearly, its icy-blue pupil more than likely matched the heated gaze that shone brightly from the left eye.

But it wasn't the sudden appearance of someone at the door that took Jean by surprise—it was the fact that she *knew* this woman.

"Carol Danvers?" she exclaimed.

To say it was a shock seeing her old friend would have been an understatement. The last time Jean and Carol had been together was on von Doom's world, where Danvers had been one of countless political prisoners held in work camps around the planet because their views differed from that of the much-exalted emperor. The difference, however, was that this particular camp had been built on the very grounds upon which Jean now stood—the location of the Xavier Institute for Higher Learning. As an enemy of the state, Carol was facing a life of hard labor and harsher abuse, at the hands of both camp guards and other inmates. The X-Men had put an end to those barbaric conditions, though, when they liberated the camp, and Carol had elected to join them on their mission to locate other superpowered men and women who could aid them in overthrowing von Doom's regime. The group reached New York without any problems, but once Jean had started psi-scanning for possible allies, her efforts had somehow been detected, and the X-Men suddenly found themselves facing off against a team of super-villains who worked for one of von Doom's security agencies. In the midst of the battle that erupted on Fifth Avenue and Forty-second Street, Jean had lost track of Carol, then forgotten all about her in the chaotic events that followed.

But now, here she stood, staring at Jean as though she were a stranger—and looking none too happy about having an unexpected visitor.

Of course *she wouldn't recognize me,* Jean realized. *To her, I'm just another citizen of the Reich . . . one trespassing on private property.* Her glance momentarily moved to the gun in Danvers' hand, its barrel pointing at her chest. She didn't doubt for an instant that this woman was as deadly a marksman as her friend—not that she'd give her any chance to prove it if the time came . . .

Danvers frowned. "What is it you want?" she demanded.

Jean's smile evaporated under her heated glare. "I'd . . . like to see Professor Xavier."

The frown became a teeth-baring sneer. "No."

And with that, she slammed the door—or, at least, tried to do so. Unwilling to be stopped this early in her quest, Jean caught it in a telekinetic grip and shoved—hard. The door flew back, catching Danvers across the temple and knocking her to the floor. As the gun flew from her hand, Jean caught that, too, with a mental snare, and tossed it deep into the weeds behind her.

Smiling sweetly, she stepped around the stunned Danvers. "Don't get up—I know my way around." Not waiting for a reply, she proceeded down the main hallway.

The interior of the manor house was only slightly less depressing than its exterior. The main hall alone was an interior decorator's nightmare: paint faded and chipped, blue-and-gold runner beneath Jean's feet dirty and threadbare, furnishings coated with a thick layer of dust; she could only imagine what the rest of the house looked like. From within the recesses of her subconscious, Jean felt her Skull-world alternate practically quiver with the urge to shriek in horror and run for the nearest vacuum.

Well, I think it's safe to assume that whatever job Carol has here, it certainly doesn't involve housework, Jean thought, fighting a sudden urge to sneeze as dust particles swirled around her.

She continued down the hall until she came to a familiar door—one that, on her world, she had walked through a thousand times. This was the portal to the calm eye of the storm of prejudice and intolerance that had constantly threatened to destroy every mutant on the planet, in the years before von Doom had activated his Cosmic Cube. A place of refuge for those seeking to understand what they had become, why they were so hated; a place of security, protecting those same lost souls against the forces that hunted them down like wild animals. The very spot from which a dream had been born: of humanity and mutantkind living in harmony, their differences forgotten, their hatreds banished.

A birthing chamber Jean knew better as the private study of Professor Charles Xavier.

Swallowing hard, she reached out and lightly knocked on the door.

"Yes?" replied a coarse, tired voice.

Slowly, Jean opened the door and stepped inside the room. And immediately wished she hadn't.

"Oh, my God . . ." she croaked.

Her breath caught in her throat as she glanced around—at the mountainous piles of yellowed news journals and scraps of paper; at the half-eaten meals, around which flies buzzed; at the chipped cups and cracked glasses crusted over with the thick film of various beverages, long since evaporated. The air was thick with the stench of decay, the noxious odor a jarring counterpoint to the gentle ballet of dust motes that danced across shafts of morning sunlight spilling through the torn velvet curtains that hung over the windows.

But it was the sight of the man sitting behind the mold-encrusted mahogany desk on the other side of the room that almost brought Jean to her knees in despair.

He was scrawny and thin-limbed, his bald head looking

immense in comparison to his body. His scalp and hands were dotted with liver spots, his cheeks and eyes so sunken as to resemble a death-mask, rather than the sharp, hawkish features of the great leader he had once been. A charcoal-gray suit now a size too big for him hung on his frame, its dark color broken by a once-white dress shirt, frayed at the collar, and a bright red tie. He sat slumped in his wheelchair, hands folded on the blanket covering his legs, staring blankly through the grime-covered window that faced the weed-covered grounds and, beyond that, the deserted stretch of Graymalkin Drive outside the main gates.

"Professor Xavier . . . ?" Jean said softly.

"I felt you coming," Xavier said. He turned to face her, tapped the side of his head with a gnarled index finger. "In my mind. You're a mutant." A wizened smile split his creased features. "Have you come to kill me?"

The question took Jean aback. "N-no . . ." she stammered.

Xavier's smile brightened. "Why not?" he purred. There was something about the sudden gleam in his eyes that made Jean take a step back; something about the way his lips pulled back to bare his teeth . . .

She cleared her throat. "Professor, I'm here because I need your help."

"My . . . ?" Xavier stared at her for a moment, then suddenly burst out laughing; the sound reminded Jean of a worn bellows expelling a puff of air. She stared at her hands, feeling extremely uncomfortable as the laugh degenerated into a brief coughing spell. Eventually, the coughing subsided, and the professor chuckled mildly. "You want *my* help. Are you absolutely *certain* of that, Frau Sommers?" He smiled as her eyes widened in surprise. "Oh, yes, I'm well aware of your identity. I try to keep up-to-date on current events." He waved a hand at the newspapers around him; some of the piles looked dangerously close to crashing down on him. "Perhaps you should have done a bit of reading yourself," he said, the smile fading, "before you wasted your time coming here."

"I . . . I don't understand," Jean said.

Xavier sneered. "Not a student of history, Frau Sommers?" Gripping the tires of his wheelchair, the professor rolled himself out from behind the desk and maneuvered his way through the debris, coming to a halt before his visitor. He studied her for a moment. "You *really* have no idea who I am, do you?" When Jean found herself unable to mouth an answer, he shook his head in disgust. "Then allow me to enlighten you."

The assault on her mind was sudden—and brutal. Without warning, Xavier forced his way into her thoughts, ripping through her psychic defenses as though they were tissue paper. The room swayed, blurred, disappeared, to be replaced by a flood of sound and images: smoke filled her lungs, heat reddened her skin. Her eardrums vibrated with the wails of the dying and the damned.

She was standing in the middle of a street littered with waste, the asphalt cracked and discolored, the air heavy with the stench of rotting garbage and stagnant water. It was late at night, but the sky was awash in hues of red and gold, cinder and ash, making it appear more like twilight. Thick plumes of black smoke obscured the stars, and the full moon that shone high above was painted a hazy, burnt orange.

With a start, Jean realized that the tenement buildings around her were burning out of control. She glanced up the block to see a group of men and women clad in black leather uniforms and thick-soled boots, all moving in her direction. Each was equipped with a long-nozzled flamethrower, which they triggered seemingly at random, igniting the buildings on both sides of the street.

She knew that she was standing in the midst of a psychic projection—she'd been in similar memory-created environments countless times during her life with the X-Men—but she couldn't remember the last occasion when she had been in one so tangible, so . . . real. Her throat burned from the acrid smoke; she couldn't keep her eyes from watering. Not even "her" Charles Xavier was capable of creating such a powerful mental landscape . . . at least not to her knowledge.

A sharp cry of anguish caught her attention, and she wheeled around. Behind her were gathered the residents of the block: hundreds of people surrounded by armed guards attired in the same type of uniform worn by the flamethrower brigade. And behind the soldiers, towering over the scene so high that Jean had momentarily thought they were office buildings, were two gigantic humanoid constructs, their metal-plated chests emblazoned with huge, black swastikas.

Jean gasped. "Sentinels . . ."

On her world, Jean—and just about every mutant on the planet—knew of the robotic monsters. Originally created by a man named Bolivar Trask, the Sentinels' duty was to protect humanity from the growing "mutant threat" by either capturing or exterminating the members of *Homo sapiens superior*—no matter how young or old their targets, no matter how weak or harmless their victims' powers might be. To see that such emotionless hunter/killers had been incorporated into the Red Skull's empire sent a chill through Jean; she wondered if mutants were *all* these Sentinels had been constructed to persecute . . .

She looked back to the crowd, and saw the fear etched into the features of the residents, all rousted from their homes in the middle of the night and forced to watch as lifetimes' worth of memories were destroyed. They were all mutants in one form or another, most possessing the appearance of "normal" humans, though there were also quite a few unusual-looking individuals scattered amongst the hundreds huddling together. As she gazed at the haunted expressions of these frightened members of her race, Jean suddenly realized why there was such a high concentration of them in one place.

She was in a ghetto—a neighborhood into which mutants had been herded so a watchful eye could be kept on them. From the memories of her Skull-world counterpart, Jean saw that the same had been done with other races—at least those for which the Empire still had a use. It was a policy applied to the Jewish community, initiated under Adolf Hitler in World War II; apparently, the Red Skull had widened its parameters when he became emperor.

The roar of an approaching engine from behind made Jean glance over her shoulder. Down the street, the flamethrower brigade had stepped aside to allow passage to an armored transport, the manned cannon on its roof aimed directly at the crowd. The vehicle ground to a halt, and one side of it rolled back to reveal a metal platform, which slid out to reveal two passengers. One was a horrific little man whose face appeared on a viewing screen in the middle of his chest, rather than on a head he apparently didn't possess; Jean had no idea who he was. The man's companion, however, she knew all too well. He was a few years younger, handsome, arrogant in his bearing. Moonlight played across the top of his clean-shaven head.

Professor Charles Xavier stared at the frightened crowd, nodded in satisfaction, and leaned in close to the little man. He muttered something, and the abomination laughed loudly. A shared joke, perhaps. The professor gestured at the residents. "Your men work quickly, Minister Zola. I expected it would take them at least until morning to gather everyone together."

Zola smiled—a grotesque twisting of facial muscles made even more disturbing by its appearance behind the glass screen. "Fear can be a great motivator, Herr Professor—especially when one's home is burning down. It tends to add wings to one's feet." The smile slowly drained away. "Now, then: Where is this 'special' freak you pulled me from my laboratories to see? The one you detected with that mutant-location computer of yours?"

"Cerebro," Xavier corrected politely. "It first detected her powers in the American southeast, but she fled her home before she could be picked up for questioning. The delay was a temporary one, however; nothing remains hidden from Cerebro for long—not even when the subject tries to hide like the proverbial needle in a haystack of mutants." He nodded toward the residents, who were moving aside to let someone through. "I believe your men have found her . . ."

A pair of soldiers marched past Jean, dragging a semi-conscious women between them. She couldn't be older than seventeen or eighteen, bundled up in layers of clothing even though it was a warm summer night. A chill played along Jean's spine as the light of the burning buildings highlighted the white streak that ran through the girl's dark-brown hair.

"Minister Zola," Xavier said, "allow me to introduce you to . . . er . . . Rogue."

" 'Rogue'?" Zola said with a snarl. "What kind of insipid name is that?"

Xavier shrugged. "Who can understand the ways of today's youth, Minister? I have long since given up trying."

The soldiers dropped the girl on the ground, then stepped back to cover her with their weapons.

"From what you told me, Herr Professor, I thought she would be more . . . animated," Zola commented.

"She put up a struggle, sir," one of the soldiers replied. "We had to sedate her."

"It doesn't matter," Xavier said with a wave of his hand. "What we're interested in is the extent of her powers." He pointed to the soldier who had addressed Zola. "You. Barton. Remove one of your gloves."

Jean could tell the man was surprised—and worried—by the ease with which Xavier had plucked the name from his mind. He turned to Zola. "Sir?"

Zola chuckled. "Do as he says, Sergeant. The Professor might be a mutant, but he likes to think of himself as one of the higher-born. Humor him."

Barton pulled off one of his gauntlets and tucked it into his belt.

"Now, touch the girl's face," Xavier ordered.

"NO!" Jean cried, though she knew she would go unheard. She was a phantom here, out of synch with the dreamscape around her,

unable to alter the course of events being played before her—events that had transpired years past. That didn't stop her, however, from racing to the girl's side.

Barton knelt beside Rogue and rolled her onto her back. Hesitantly, he reached down, pausing only long enough to register the stern look he was getting from Zola before brushing his fingertips against her cheek.

The reaction was instantaneous. Both Rogue and Barton screamed in agony as she leeched his thoughts, his strength, his very essence into herself. But while the woman Jean considered a teammate and close friend would have been able to break contact with the soldier, this girl was still years away from controlling her powers. The air crackled with static electricity as the transfer continued, the process causing Barton's body to slowly dry up, to shrivel away, until there was nothing left but a desiccated corpse in a baggy leather uniform.

"Oh, Rogue . . ." Jean whispered.

And then, with startling speed, the girl was on her feet, scooping up Barton's weapon before anyone could stop her. The muzzle flashed with a staccato rhythm, and soldiers around her collapsed in a hail of bullets. She spun around, to level the rifle directly at Zola's faceplate. Her finger tightened around the trigger—

—but nothing happened.

"I think that's enough of a demonstration," Xavier said dryly. He turned to Zola. "As you can see, Minister, the subject has absorbed the strength of the late Sergeant Barton—which accounts for her ability to throw off the effects of the drugs in her system—as well as his martial prowess. It is only because I have seized control of her mind that she is unable to fulfill her desire for slaying you."

Zola grunted. "And the point of all this, Xavier?"

"Imagine, if you will, Minister: An agent capable of stealing away knowledge, strength, identity from any given target; absorbing language, information, with just a touch."

Zola nodded, although it required the movement of his entire armored body. "Such a mutant *would* have their uses."

"I thought you would agree." Xavier's eyes closed for a moment, and Rogue suddenly collapsed; he'd "switched off" her mind, rendering her unconscious. He watched as some members of the flamethrower brigade moved in to collect her. "Yes, I expect some great things from our Rogue . . ."

The feral smile that Xavier suddenly leveled at her sent Jean fleeing into the darkness, in spite of herself.

Zola was right—fear *did* add wings to one's feet.

Wrong—it was all so horribly wrong; Jean knew that now, as she finally managed to break free of Xavier's mindscape. Wrong of her to come here, to expect Xavier to help her, to venture all this way on a fool's errand when time was running out for countless dimensions. Wrong to think that the decent, caring visionary she loved as much as her parents could possibly exist in such a hate-driven, fearful world as this. She withdrew from his mind, sickened by it all, wondering where she could turn for help now—

And then something exploded against the base of her skull, and she crashed to the floor.

Groggily, Jean turned her head to see Danvers standing over her, a leather-encased blackjack in one hand. She attempted to rise, but Danvers bent down beside her, driving her knee into the small of Jean's back. She then grabbed a handful of her prey's fiery mane and pressed her head to the moldy carpeting.

"Try any other tricks like the one with the front door, Frau Sommers," she warned, "and I will not hesitate to snap your neck. It wouldn't do for the wife of such an esteemed Reichsmajor to be accidentally killed while running from a simple interrogation."

"No fear of that, Fräulein Danvers," Xavier said quietly. "Frau Sommers won't be doing *anything* unless *I* will it."

Jean gasped, feeling psychic talons dig deeply into her mind—and close tightly. She hovered on the edge of consciousness, her eyes rolling back in her head, unable to do little beyond whimper softly as Xavier forced his way through her memories with all the subtlety of one of the Skull's stormtroopers. He was rooting around for information–learning who she was, where she came from, why she had come to him.

And there was nothing she could do to stop him.

"You surprise me, Herr Professor," she heard Danvers say. "I didn't think you capable of subduing her."

"Lucky for you that I did, Danvers!" Xavier snapped. "She might have killed me at any moment, and *then* what would your leaders have said about your efficiency as an agent? What the devil *kept* you?"

"I would appreciate it if you kept your tiresome barking to a minimum, Herr Professor," Danvers replied evenly. "Nattering on so makes you sound like an old woman. *And* it gives me a headache."

Jean heard a tiny *pop* just above her ear, as though the covering was being removed from a small container. "What . . . ?" she began to say, only to yelp as a needle penetrated her neck. She moaned softly as a powerful sedative raced through her veins, turning her muscles to rubber. Dimly, she became aware that Danvers and Xavier had released her. From the sound of the woman's voice, she was back on her feet and heading for the door.

"Now, if you will excuse me, Herr Professor," Danvers said, "I must inform the League of Frau Sommers' capture."

"Perhaps we should inform the Ministry of Health as well, Fräulein Danvers," Xavier commented. "Apparently, we have an unregistered mutant on our hands . . ."

The scream building in Jean's throat forced its way through her numbed lips as a hoarse rattle–one that only she could hear. And then the drug took full effect, pulling her into darkness.

10

ARNIM Zola lived in a box.

Literally.

Oh, he might possess arms and legs like any other man, but there was no head to be found resting between his shoulders—only a small, rectangular, metal box packed with miniature electronics. He had a face, but if you wanted to gaze upon it, to stare into the cold, hazel eyes of a monster who had sent millions of innocent men, women, and children to their deaths, you had to look through the glass screen housing it—the one framed by the metal box that served as his torso.

He hadn't always looked like that. Once, he had been a normal human being—quiet, unassuming, rather plain in appearance, rather unremarkable in personality, but far from the glass, metal, and plastic construct that continued to use his name, seven decades later. A lifetime ago, he had been human, but that was before his interest in genetics became an all-consuming obsession, ultimately leading him to experiment with dark forces that man was truly never meant to know . . .

Locked away in his Swiss castle, Zola shunned contact with other humans unless absolutely necessary, preferring instead the company of test tubes and Bunsen burners, microscopes and Petri dishes . . . and the grotesque creatures to which he gave life. Creatures that roared and mewled, crawled and shrieked—in fear, in anger, in despair over the humanity that had been stripped from them at the hands of a soulless monster.

He regarded them as his children; over time, they came to call him "father."

Arnim Zola, you see, was quite mad. But just *how* mad no one could have ever suspected—until the day a power-hungry German warlord took his first steps toward conquering the world . . .

When Germany launched its first attacks in 1939, refugees flooded across the Swiss border, many of them begging Zola for shelter from the Nazi war machine—and he suddenly found an inexhaustible supply of genetic material to use in his studies. Material that enabled his experiments to become far grander in scale, more hideous in design, until even the Führer himself was made aware of his work, and set him to work alongside another notorious butcher: Dr. Josef Mengele.

They learned much from each other, Auschwitz's "Angel of Death" and his "bio-fanatic," and the fruits of their labors helped their master conquer half a world.

And years later, when the atom had been split, and Germany had harnessed its power in a bomb used to decimate Washington, D.C., thus winning the war, there were new opportunities for Arnim Zola to explore. The effects of atomic radiation had gone relatively unexplored during the decade-long conflict—Hitler was more interested in the power of the explosion being unleashed, rather than any lingering genetic calamities its power source might cause in years to come. But in the 1950s, stories began spreading of bizarre-looking freaks—mutations—wandering the blasted streets of America's former capital. It was while investigating these claims that Zola himself contracted radiation poisoning; his only cure lay in constructing a new body, one that would have none of his weaknesses, and more than enough strength to last for a hundred years or more.

Thus it was that Arnim Zola finally became the monster

outwardly that he had always been within—a hideous body to match the diseased soul it contained . . .

Zola was immersed in his latest experiment when the visi-phone call came in. For a time he tried to ignore its nagging bleating—its discordant tone interfered with the melodic strains of the death rattle that was forcing its way through the tracheal tube of the young mutant strapped to his worktable. Eventually, though, he had to turn his attention to answering it, if for no other reason than to silence the infernal sound.

He punched the RECEIVE button on the control panel, and was greeted by the sallow-skinned visage of a man whose existence he hadn't even thought about in the past year or two. "Charles Xavier! What a pleasant surprise this is!" he bellowed, his electronically enhanced voice dripping with false sincerity. He winked slyly, as though sharing an old joke—one from which only he still found some degree of humor. "How is my favorite collaborator?"

"As well as can be expected, Minister," Xavier said gruffly, "given the circumstances."

Zola flashed one of his grotesque smiles. "Is Fräulein Danvers giving you any trouble? You know she is only there to protect you from the more . . . outspoken members of your race."

"And a pitiful job she's been doing of it!" Xavier snapped. "A young woman barged in here today, could have used her powers against me if I hadn't taken steps to prevent it."

Zola frowned. "And so you have called upon me to register a *complaint?*" He waved a hand in a dismissive gesture. "Contact the League of German Women, then—I am certain they will give you a new referral."

Xavier shook his head. "No, that is *not* why I am calling, Minister." A sly grin inched its way across his features. "Aren't you curious as to the *identity* of my would-be assailant?"

Zola huffed. "I have neither the time nor the patience for games, Herr Professor. Kindly get to the—"

"Jean Sommers."

Zola paused. "Sommers. Are you referring to the wife of . . ."

Xavier nodded. "Indeed. Reichsmajor Scott Sommers. The woman is a mutant."

The Minister frowned. "Impossible. I examined her personally, before she was even allowed to start dating Sommers. There was no trace of the x-factor detected in her genetic structure then, or in subsequent examinations. She is a pure-bred German maiden."

"Then you should have your machines recalibrated, Minister, because something, somehow, has triggered the gene in Frau Sommers," Xavier replied. "She now possesses psychic abilities that might even be on a par with my own."

"I must see her—immediately."

"I thought as much, which is the reason Fräulein Danvers and I are already en route to New York City. I was hoping you would be able to arrange passage for us on the first available flight from there to Genosha." Xavier paused. "But there is more to this situation than just a case of latent mutagenic growth, Minister. From what I have been able to gleam from scanning Frau Sommers' mind, she is on a mission that might spell disaster for the Reich . . . and the Emperor. And she is not working alone."

Intrigued, Zola leaned closer to the screen. "Tell me more, Charles . . ."

Ororo sat beside one of the jet's windows, gazing enviously at the clouds that drifted by.

She'd made no attempt to escape, or shown any sign of resistance since peacefully surrendering to Lightning Force, but that, apparently, meant nothing to the team member named Meggan. The blond-haired shapeshifter had taken an almost perverse amount of pleasure in shackling her prisoner to the seat, securing the ankle and wrist clamps tightly enough to make Ororo gasp. From the heated stare she directed at the back of Hauptmann Englande's head, then toward Ororo, it was obvious she felt extremely territorial where her lover was concerned. Not that it mattered in the least to Ororo—just the thought of possibly being attracted to a pompous, overbearing fascist made her stomach turn.

A small motion at the corner of her eye caught her attention. She turned her head—as much as the metal collar would allow—to look at the blue-skinned mutant sitting across the aisle; Nightcrawler, she remembered. For someone who vaguely resembled a demon, she wouldn't have thought him to be so fidgety—and yet, ever since the jet had departed Araouane, there hardly seemed to be a moment when he wasn't squirming in his seat. Ororo mentally shrugged. Maybe he just didn't enjoy air travel. Or maybe it wasn't the flight that upset him . . . as much as the destination.

Genosha.

Just *thinking* the name sent shivers down her spine. The memories were still too fresh, the nightmares still too raw, for her to maintain her normally cool demeanor, even in the face of her enemies. The fact that Nightcrawler was so visibly shaken did nothing to calm her fears.

Why was it, she wondered, did she think she knew this man . . . ?

He twisted in his seat again, becoming aware that she was staring at him. He smiled weakly, apparently more to put himself at ease than his prisoner; it didn't work. "Enjoying the trip, Fräulein?" he asked.

Ororo frowned. "Not particularly."

He nodded, as though in understanding. "I would imagine not."

"Nor are you, I take it." She gestured toward his feet; one was tapping the floor to a nervous rhythm only his tensing leg muscles could detect.

Another sickly smile. A shrug. "I have had more pleasant ones, I must admit."

She sneered. "And why is that? I thought you would look forward to showing off your prize to your master."

A look of unease flashed in Nightcrawler's eyes. He stole a

quick glance at the cockpit, where Meggan had joined Englande at the controls. They appeared to be deep in conversation.

"Zola is not my master," he whispered hoarsely. "But he is our–" his lips curled in disgust "–genetic superior. He, as well as the rest of humanity, must be treated with all the respect due their evolutionary station."

Ororo sniffed derisively. "He is *your* superior, perhaps. But never mine."

Nightcrawler grinned. "Defiant to the last, eh?"

"No. Simply unwilling to play the part of the faithful mutant lapdog. Unwilling to spout Party doggerel in a pathetic and futile attempt to fit in better with the hatemongers that call themselves our betters." Ororo ignored the warning growl issuing from Nightcrawler's lips, and leaned toward him. "You will *never* be accepted by the humans; you *must* realize that. To them, mutants like ourselves are to be hated and feared–never to be their equals, always to be treated as an inferior race. We are the monsters they warn their children about–perversions of the evolutionary chain whose very touch is as deadly as any virus." She shook her head sadly. "You are no valued member of this team, Nightcrawler. You are a mascot–an oddity to be paraded around to delude mutants into thinking they have a place in the Empire." She sighed. "And I think the one person fooled the most by this reprehensible tactic . . . is you."

A white-gloved hand flashed across the aisle, catching Ororo across the mouth.

"And *I* think you had best keep your opinions to yourself, Fräulein," Nightcrawler growled, "else I shall be forced to muzzle you."

Ororo used the tip of her tongue to wipe away the blood that trickled from the corner of her mouth. She studied the way Nightcrawler shifted around in his seat, preparing to deliver another blow should she make any further comment. He relished the opportunity to do so–she could see it in the set of his jaw, the tension in his arms, the tightness of his clenched fists. She'd struck a nerve, though he would never admit it; all he needed was an excuse to vent the anger building within him.

She refused to give him the satisfaction. Sniffing haughtily, she turned away and returned her attention to the clouds that streaked past her window—and the island that lay below.

Even from the air, Genosha looked like the devil's playground. The south end of the island was a jumble of dilapidated buildings and weatherworn tent cities: housing for the unfortunate mutant population that had been gathered from all corners of the world. "Unfortunate" because the housing was only meant to be temporary—none of its occupants were expected to live for too long after passing through the electrified fencing that separated the two hemispheres of the island. Anyone who tried to convince themselves otherwise had only to glance toward the southernmost tip, and the red brick smokestacks that rose high above the internment center. The stench of burning fat that hung thick in the air and the minute pieces of bones scattered across the ground—ones not consumed by the blast furnaces at the bases of the towers—were constant reminders to all of the ultimate fate of Arnim Zola's playthings.

To the north lay Hammer Bay, the island's capital—a collection of gleaming marble buildings that served as both headquarters for the administrative offices of the Ministry of Health and medical research facility for Reichsminister Zola and his staff of gengineers. "Medical research," however, didn't quite accurately describe the sort of work performed within the antiseptic-white walls and polished glass; "experimentation" might be a better word.

Or even "butchery," as Ororo knew first-hand. For it was here that Zola and his acolytes continued the sort of horrendous operations and biological tests begun by Mengele in the darkest days of World War II, and developed further in the decades following the notorious doctor's passing by his most talented disciple. And it was also here that her mutant powers had been stripped away, at the brutal hands of human monsters that dared call themselves physicians. Ororo clamped her teeth together as a chill ran through her body, images of scalpels and clamps, demonic smiles and blood—*Bright Lady, so much blood!*—flashing before her eyes. It was a miracle she had survived the surgery, let alone the callous treatment of the guards and nurses as they bundled her weakened, scarred body aboard the last shuttle bound for the Sahara.

And now she was returning—for reasons she could not fathom, for tortures she had no doubt she would soon experience . . .

The jet touched down a few minutes later, on one of the landing pads that jutted out from the sides of the Ministry's main building. A coterie of armed guards rushed out to meet the Lightning Force members—and their unwilling passenger—and stood at attention on both sides of the team, forming a corridor that led from the plane to a door at the far end of the platform. Ororo noticed how Nightcrawler tensed up as the guards approached—no doubt he momentarily feared that they were coming for him.

"The Minister is waiting for you in his apartments, Hauptmann Englande," one of the soldiers said.

"Then, let us not keep him waiting a minute longer!" Englande replied. He nodded toward Ororo. "Bring the prisoner." Without waiting to see if his command was obeyed—more likely confident that it would be—he set off for the end of the landing area, boot heels ringing against the metal surface.

Meggan attached a length of chain to Ororo's collar, and gave it a sharp tug. The white-haired former skyrider stumbled forward, almost colliding with her captor, and fell to her knees. Meggan snarled, eyes shifting from pale blue to blood red, and yanked harder.

"Up, pig!" she roared. *"Get up and walk!"*

For the first time in her life, Ororo wondered what it might be like to kill someone, to have some measure of revenge against all those who had ever wronged her, all those who had treated her as filth, as a pariah, from the day she had been born right up to this moment. And given the situation, there seemed no better target for her anger, for her blinding hatred, than the blond-haired witch happily trying to strangle her.

She repressed the urge to find out, though—this was neither the time nor the place for an attack; not with so many guns that could be leveled at her if she made the wrong move. There *would* be a time, however; Ororo was certain of that. All she had to do was wait long enough, and the Bright Lady would provide . . .

As she struggled to her feet and shuffled after Meggan, Ororo had to bite back a tiny laugh that threatened to bubble past her lips. Just a day ago, she had been consumed with thoughts of suicide, pining away for her lost powers. And yet, here, now, she had become focused on staying alive . . . at least long enough to strike back at her captors.

Tilting her head down so her ghostly mane would hide her smile, Ororo followed Meggan into the building, making a mental list of all the possible ways in which the haughty shapeshifter could die by her hand.

She'd thought of more than twenty by the time they passed through the doorway.

The Mastrex was in a similar mood when she barged into the throne room of the Starlight Citadel. She was so consumed with rage, in fact, that she ignored protocol, shoving aside the guard standing watch in the hall when he moved to intercept her. Allowing von Doom the satisfaction of making her wait until he was ready to receive her was not on her agenda of things to do.

Wringing answers from him, however, was at the top of the list.

"Von Doom!" she roared, stomping up the main aisle. She noticed the throne was vacant of his slouching figure. "Where are you hiding? We need to talk!"

Her strident voice echoed around the immense chamber, the only reply a chittering laugh from the darkness around her; apparently, Roma's little shadow-pets found her outburst amusing.

Given half a chance—and a Level-12 phosphorgun—she would have demonstrated to them in great, fiery detail that the Mastrex of the Empire of True Briton lacked a sense of humor.

A deep frown tugging at her features, Sat-yr-nin continued across the transept and came to a halt at the base of the steps leading to the throne. The lack of response puzzled her: given von Doom's inflated sense of ego, he should have reacted immediately to her unannounced arrival—threatened her, tried to strike her, even ignored her in a bid to reestablish his superiority, to remind her of "her place." Not that a small part of Sat-yr-nin wasn't grateful he didn't answer her challenge—while his armor still possessed circuitry from the medical wing's multiphasic crystal accelerators, open displays of hostility toward the super-villain would probably be handled by a quick burst of lethal energy from his gauntlets.

And those gauntlets were the *only* functioning weapons in the entire citadel, Sat-yr-nin reminded herself, given the "state of grace" that enveloped this fortress, rendering all other devices useless. Perhaps, she considered, it was for the best that von Doom apparently wasn't around to hear her outburst . . .

But where could he have wandered off to, then? It was unlikely he'd grown tired of sitting around the throne room and gone stalking the corridors outside; she would have been alerted to his activities by the security forces who thought she was the "real" Saturnyne, instead of her more . . . foul-tempered counterpart. So, if he hadn't left the throne room, then he must be somewhere in its depths; it wouldn't surprise Sat-yr-nin to learn there were hidden rooms behind the walls, with passages leading to all points in the citadel. It was the sort of tactic she would have expected from Roma's secretive father, Merlyn; she had done the same thing in the stronghold on her world. His offspring, however, would never have been so duplicitous—or so clever.

Sat-yr-nin turned in a slow circle, then set off toward a pulpit-like structure near the throne. As she moved across the chamber, a large chessboard floated out of the shadows to join her. Sat-yr-nin halted, and the board did likewise, hovering at chest height.

"Lost without your mistress, little toy?" she addressed it with a snarl. She didn't expect an answer. From what she knew of Roma's machinations, and Merlyn's before her, the chessboard was primarily used by the Supreme Guardian to direct the lives of sentients at crucial junctures in the space/time continuum—games played by a pair of celestial beings who imagined themselves gods. The board fashioned pieces that resembled the unsuspecting "pawns," and play began once father and daughter had chosen sides.

Not many pawns usually survived long enough to learn who had won the match.

The Mastrex studied the ivory and black onyx squares, and the few pieces standing on them. There were representations of Braddock and her winged lover, Worthington, in white, at one end of the board; at the other, black pieces that matched the features and costumes of the X-Men who had invaded her world and carted her away as their prisoner. She could have sworn there had been another piece in place of Worthington's when she'd first entered Roma's chamber, before von Doom attacked: a baldheaded man in a wheelchair. But it wasn't there now, and Sat-yr-nin couldn't be bothered with trying to work out how the board could have made such a substitution without direction.

Turning from the chessboard, she climbed the short set of steps, her gaze drawn to the almost hypnotic fashion in which the light of the hundreds of scented candles decorating the platform glinted off polished crystal. This, in a way, was the true source of Roma's—and, ultimately, von Doom's—power: the life-forces of countless parallel universes, contained within slivers of quartz. Billions of worlds, countless billions upon billions of inhabitants, each just slightly out of synch with its counterpart so as to keep realities from literally colliding, each separated by a thin vibratory curtain that prevented two bodies, or two planets, from occupying the same position in Time and Space.

At least, that was what was supposed to be happening, to Sat-yr-nin's understanding. But, based on a quick review of her alternate's computer records, the harmonic curtains were now apparently decaying, the spaces between parallel worlds growing smaller with each passing hour. And von Doom himself was the cause of it all—or, rather, the Cosmic Cube he had cobbled together.

Her attention was drawn to one crystal in particular. Unlike those surrounding it, the surface of this sliver was darkened, as though covered with a thick layer of soot—from the inside. A fair number of its neighbors were showing similar discoloration. It didn't take a Supreme Guardian to realize that the blackened quartz must be the source of the trouble—the "threat to the omniverse," as Braddock had put it.

Earth 616. Home to von Doom, the X-Men, Captain Britain, and hundreds of other superpowered beings who, if they hadn't already caused Sat-yr-nin grief at some point in the past, might very well do so in the future. But not if she ended the threat in a simple, direct manner . . .

Sat-yr-nin ran a shapely finger along the polished sliver, an unexpected smile lighting her features as a mild charge of electricity ran through her. Then, giggling softly, she plucked the crystal from its setting, and held it delicately between thumb and index finger.

"All it would take is a slight accident—" she released the crystal, then quickly caught it in her other hand, and laughed "—and the 'threat' would end . . . along with so many bothersome lives . . ."

She took a step back from the pulpit, attention focused on the darkened sliver—and suddenly lost her balance.

As she thudded to the floor, cursing the proverbial blue streak (a most un-Mastrex-like display of profanities), the crystal slipped from her hands and went skidding across the pulpit. Sat-yr-nin watched as the container for Universe 616 slid underneath a decorative iron grating, and into the darkness beyond.

In frustration, she pounded the floor, and yelped as her hand struck a piece of ivory—the very thing that had upset her balance. She picked it up and stared at its features: they were those of a man in a long coat and form-fitting costume, with unruly, shoulder-length hair. In one hand, he held a long staff; the other grasped a playing card between two fingers. Sat-yr-nin remembered the man it was based on quite well—he had used a similar playing card to detonate her stronghold's armory during the X-Men's final assault.

"Gambit," he had called himself, in that annoying way that some costumed fools—von Doom among them—had of referring to themselves in the third person.

With a start, Sat-yr-nin glanced up to find the chessboard hovering beside her. Did the damnable thing follow *Roma* around this closely?

"Here!" she said, and slammed the figurine down on the board. "Now you have a third white piece. Why don't you go somewhere and play a game against yourself?"

Rising to her feet, Sat-yr-nin dusted herself off and headed down the steps, renewing her search for her partner.

She never saw the blue-white crackle of electricity that surrounded the restored chess piece.

Remy Lebeau was just closing up his office for the night when the change came upon him.

He'd managed to survive another day without any further run-ins with *Obergruppenführer* Sharon Carter, had even succeeded in looking like he was actually doing work whenever she or one of her lackeys passed by. The search for the supply room pilferer was still an ongoing investigation, he assured her; it was only a matter of time before the thief was caught. It was the best he could offer, under the circumstances—surrendering himself and confessing that the missing items (staplers, paper hole-punchers, pens, pencils, note pads, even two laptop computers) could be found in the basement of his apartment building was not an option. Nor would he be able to explain just *why* he had felt compelled to "acquire" the supplies during the past few weeks—it was as much a mystery to him as it would be to any potential interrogator. Except Remy wouldn't have to beat himself about the head and body to arrive at that answer.

All in all, then, it had been one of his better days—slow, dull, meaningless, but still better than having Carter slap him around while venting her frustrations about his slacker mentality. Maybe now he'd even work up the nerve to knock on the door of his neighbor across the hall, ask her out for drinks, or a cup of coffee.

Remy smiled awkwardly and shook his head—now he was going *too* far. Susan Storm was a beautiful woman, too good for a lowly spaceport clerk; she must have dozens of suitors lined up at her door every night. No, better to avoid the situation, rather than run the risk of rejection. Maybe some other night . . .

And then . . . *it* happened.

There was nothing subtle about it—no trembling of limbs, no pounding of his head or heart, no sense that something was about to befall him. One moment, he was reaching for the light switch by the door; the next, he was facedown on the linoleum tiles, groaning as consciousness slowly returned. He rolled onto his back, and opened his eyes.

Fluorescent lighting glinted off pupils so black they looked more like glassy portals than eyes—but then, it has long been said that the eyes are the windows to the soul.

In this case, they were the windows to one *very special* soul.

With some effort, Remy sat up. There was something different about him, though, beyond the unusual coloration of his eyes—a slyness in the way he looked around the room. An almost cat-like grace as he leapt to his feet. An almost comical expression as he came to an abrupt halt, confused by his surroundings.

"*Dis* sure don' look like Heaven," he muttered. "So, where d'hell did ol' Gambit wind up *dis* time . . . ?"

INTERLUDE VI

HE was in hell. He knew that now, for nothing else could explain the nightmare in which he was living.

It was the stench of burning flesh that finally brought him to his knees as he stumbled through the woods, the bile forcing its way up from his stomach and past his lips. In all his years since Auschwitz, Erik Lensherr had never forgotten the smell, or the crackling tone of the flames, or the ear-piercing screams that assailed his ears as the fire consumed the last of those still alive in the pit.

No, he had never forgotten them, but he had often prayed—if such an unrepentant terrorist as the man he had been before he touched the Cube had any right to call upon a deity for help—that, for a time, he could at least block the memories. Shut out the smells and sights and the sounds, if only for a little time.

Shut them out, just as he was praying he could do right now . . .

He had been assigned to a work detail at the crack of dawn, rousted from bed along with the one hundred or so other inmates he joined as they stumbled from the barracks. Marching in twos, they were prodded toward the farthest part of the camp, where an assortment of shovels, picks, and hammers had been assembled, then directed to proceed outside, beyond the fences.

The procession moved through the gates, under the watchful eye of the tower guards. Lensherr paid them no attention—his attention was focused on the wasteland that lay just past the confines of the camp.

What had once been a lush forest that towered over the rear of the camp had, over time, been bulldozed flat and transformed into a scarred, dead No Man's Land, containing acre upon acre of irregularly shaped hillocks—too many to count. There was life to be found here, though: numerous displays of wildflowers that sprouted in clumps on and around some of the larger earthen bumps—colorful splashes of violet and red, blue and gold, that broke up the browns and grays and blacks of this manmade canvas.

On the edge of the forest, about two miles from the camp, they were told to start digging. Lensherr's stomach had turned over, then, for he knew exactly what the purpose of their task was.

They were digging their own grave. Adding yet another hillock to the twisted landscape, as other groups of inmates had done before them.

He could tell by the expressions on the faces of the prisoners immediately around him that only some realized what they were doing; the rest were either too broken in spirit or too exhausted by their labors from the day before to give the work any consideration. It was an order, and they were there to simply carry it out.

A woman in her sixties had begun wailing, then, only to have the man beside her—her husband, perhaps—quietly beg her to fall silent before the situation grew worse. How that might be possible not even Lensherr could imagine, but he said nothing. What *was* there to say, after all? There could be no words of comfort here, no soothing phrases that sprung to mind that might ease their fears. They were going to die, and waxing poetic before it happened would be a waste of breath—a departure from old habits for someone like Magneto, who had never been short on words, but then much had changed since the Cosmic Cube came into his life. Maybe he was becoming wiser with age. An ironic situation, he considered, that such wisdom should come to him just as he was about to face Death.

And he had no doubt that this would be the final time. The mutant overlord had had many appointments scheduled with her since beginning his crusade to make *Homo superior* the dominant species on the planet, yet he had been lucky enough—or clever enough, in his opinion—to miss all of them. After a while, it had become almost standard operating procedure for him to find her waiting nearby as he battled the X-Men, or the Avengers, or countless other heroes and villains, all of whom would have cheered—privately, of course—if he hadn't escaped from that exploding island stronghold, or avoided that solar eruption, or pried himself loose from some deathtrap or other; he felt the same way about them. But he had no mutant powers on this world to call upon to avoid her this time, only the strength of a body well into its seventies. And no matter how well-sculpted his musculature might be for someone his age, no matter how sharp his mind might still be, without his powers he was only a man.

Only a *human.*

Another irony, he thought glumly. *All those years of fighting, of struggling for a dream, and I face the end of my life on the same level of those I sought to subjugate. How the mighty have fallen, indeed . . .*

The work started immediately, Lensherr angrily stabbing at the hard soil with the point of his shovel as others fumbled with the tools. He kept to himself; the last thing he wanted before Death claimed him was to get to know any of these people. Occasionally, the sound of sobbing could be heard over the digging, but he was able to tune it out by focusing on the task—and on his own thoughts. It was difficult, though. Humility has a way of opening the mind, of making one more aware of how their actions affect those around them. And between Doctor Doom and the Red Skull, the great Magneto had learned a good deal from being humbled . . .

His thoughts turned back to the village of Araouane, in Africa, on von Doom's version of Earth. It was there he had met a woman named Abena Matou, one of the "sandwomen" who fought daily to keep the edge of the Sahara Desert from enveloping what few homes remained. He had been surprised by her buoyant spirit, even more so by her unflinching dedication to what he considered a useless exercise–eventually, despite her efforts, the desert *would* win. And yet, still she battled, moving the sand from one place to another, day after day, comforted by the fact that her work put food on the table for her family. To see that even a lowly human could give so much of herself for a thankless task, not to mention the genuine warmth she had shown him when he joined the village, made even Magneto begin to reconsider his harshness toward her kind. So much so, apparently, that when he gained possession of the Cube, one of his first acts–after laying claim to the planet under his leadership, of course–was to transform the desert around Araouane into a paradise, and to restore the village to its former glory. It was an act he was still bewildered by, given his unbridled hatred for humanity in general, but one he soon stopped questioning as he focused on running the empire he had built. In the back of his mind, though, he knew why he had never used the Cube to create internment camps, and force the humans to live–and die–in them, as so many of them wanted mutantkind to do: It was because it would have made him no better than the Nazis–the same monsters who had murdered his parents. And having seen what such a world might have been like, as it was now under the reign of the Red Skull, Erik Lensherr had begun to wonder how he could have fallen so far from grace in pursuit of a dream . . .

The hours passed quickly. As the pit widened, whispered explanations of what they were really doing began to spread among the prisoners. Some suggested fighting against their captors; others simply resigned themselves to their fate. Lensherr knew it would be a hopeless battle, if it came to that—the guards would cut them to pieces with their weapons once the first fist was raised in defiance. An odd belief, coming as it did from someone from who had not only survived, but escaped from, Auschwitz. Yet that escape had only come about near the end of the war, because American G.I.s were in the midst of liberating the camp, fully occupying the guards' attention so he and another prisoner—later his wife—Magda could slip away. Had it been attempted any other time, he had known even then, neither of them would have survived.

But there would be no distractions this time, no last-minute rescues that might mean salvation for prisoners for whom the Nazis apparently no longer had a use. There would only be the chill of the grave, and then blessed oblivion . . .

The pit was completed all too soon. It wasn't very deep—no more than four or five feet—due to the hardness of the ground; to go any deeper would have required earth-moving machinery. More guards arrived, and the prisoners were lined up along the edge of the shallow grave—all except for Lensherr, much to his surprise. Instead of joining the ranks, he was hustled off to one side by Carl and Wilhelm, his tormentors from the yard, who had accompanied the other soldiers.

"Don't worry, freak," Wilhelm muttered to him. "You're not scheduled for extermination—yet. But you'll come to wish you had been, soon enough." As if providing a preview of things to come, he punched him in the stomach, driving the air from his lungs. Lensherr collapsed at his feet, gasping for breath—

And then the shooting began. Bursts of gunfire that seemed to go on forever, loud enough to rattle his teeth, but not enough to drown out the screams that pierced his eardrums. Then came the impact of the last bodies as they tumbled into the pit, on top of those already fallen. It was a wet sound, of boneless flesh squelching onto pools of blood and bits of brain, and not even covering his ears with his hands prevented him from hearing it. And when the shooting was over, one of the camp's officers called for the flamethrowers.

"A waste of fuel," the man commented to one of his subordinates, "but we've had some trouble with animals these past few weeks." He chuckled hollowly, and gestured at the fresh corpses. "I guess even *these* wretches might be good for a meal or two . . . if the creatures are that desperate."

"Or the Wendigo," the soldier replied.

The officer glared at him. "Listening to old wives' tales, corporal? I wouldn't think a soldier of the Empire would pay any attention to a bunch of backwoods talk from rabble such as this." He waved a dismissive hand at the bodies clustered beneath them. "There aren't any 'cannibal men' stalking the Canadian wilderness, corporal. And if I hear you've been perpetuating this ridiculous myth among the prisoners, you can join the next group out here. *In the pit.*" He leaned in close and bared his teeth. "Understood?"

"Y-yessir," the corporal stuttered.

It was at that moment that the moaning began.

Weakly, Lensherr dragged himself to his feet so he could look over the lip of the grave. There, trapped under the weight of two corpses, was a young woman—she couldn't have been older than nineteen or twenty; somehow, she had survived the slaughter. She was struggling to get free.

The clatter of footsteps drew Lensherr's attention to the guards. A quintet of men dressed in fireproof gear had arrived, each of them carrying a large flamethrower. In horror, he looked from them to the girl, then back again. A blue-white jet of fire sparked at the end of each nozzle.

"God, no," he said. *"NO!"*

He leapt forward, only to be beaten to the ground by his captors. Unable to rise, he could only stare mutely as sheets of flame erupted from the devices, setting alight everything—and everyone—in the pit.

The girl shrieked as her hair and clothing caught fire, as her flesh began to sizzle. And then she turned her head, and Lensherr suddenly found himself staring into her eyes. They were so bright, so light brown in color; so like Anya's.

Anya.

The memory of her tore at his soul. Like this girl, he had had to stand by and watch as his daughter burned, kept from aiding her by barbarians who feared what they could not understand. Had to watch as she tumbled from the apartment window, her cries of pain melting his heart. Had to watch as she died in his arms . . .

"NO!" he roared. *"NOT AGAIN!"*

And then he was on his feet, lashing out at his two tormentors, snatching the weapons from their hands and bludgeoning them to death. There would be no more punishments at their hands.

As the other guards rushed forward to attack, Lensherr felt his anger building, *building,* until it demanded release. He snarled, calling upon the power that was his to command, ignoring the crackle of electricity that shot through his body as the neural inhibitor acted to override his nervous system. The pain was unbearable, and he fought the urge to stop this foolish act before the device killed him.

The guards halted mere feet from him, clearly uncertain of what to do as tendrils of electrical energy spun away from his body, growing more intense with each second. At the center of the storm, Lensherr forced himself to remain on his feet, to remain conscious, refusing to allow anything to keep him from taking his measure of revenge.

He felt one final stab of agony from the inhibitor, one that almost caused him to black out—and then the pain ended.

He was free.

A slow, feral smile came to his lips as he raised his hands, reveling in the familiar way his fingers tingled as the power built in his hands, seeking release. He glanced up, to find the guards staring at him, their faces chiseled with blood-drained expressions of terror. His smile widened.

"Die," Magneto said.

* * *

"THERE HE IS!"

Lensherr looked over his shoulder. In the bright moonlight, he could see the surviving guards from the camp charging through the woods, rifles and flashlights clutched tightly in their hands. The man who had spotted him was a bumpkin named Faust, a rotund sergeant with a bushy mustache who was always nosing around the prisoners, looking for troublemakers; his dark gray uniform was stretched tightly across a belly that was intimately familiar with all the meat-and-potato pleasures of German cuisine.

Using the back of his hand to wipe away the last traces of bile on his chin, Lensherr staggered to his feet and lurched deeper into the woods. He breathed sharply through clenched teeth, rubbing the base of his spine, where the lump of the neural inhibitor reminded him of its presence. Although he had shorted it out, he was still feeling some lingering effects of the damnable device: He was too exhausted to fight now, too weak to tap into the severely depleted reserves of his mutant abilities. The release of all that pent-up magnetic energy at the gravesite had placed too great a strain on his tortured body. He would need time to recover–time the guards were not about to give him as they closed in. But, he had to admit, exterminating their fellow vermin before the chase began had been worth the effort. Watching their bodies writhe as his magnetic powers tore them apart had felt so natural, so . . . *exhilarating*.

He flinched as a bullet tore into a tree trunk, at a point level with his head. They were shooting to kill, then; whether or not it was being done with the Skull's permission, however, wasn't a subject he wished to discuss with them.

More bullets, and even a few particle beams, began exploding around him, and suddenly the once-peaceful area was transformed into a war zone. Bushes around him burst into flame, and the ground was torn up by rifle fire. He zigged and zagged, ducked and jumped, pushing his body to the limit.

For a man who had resigned himself to dying, he thought with a grim smile, *I certainly seem to be putting up quite a struggle to do otherwise . . .*

He vaulted over a fallen tree, then cried out in surprise as he saw there was no ground on the other side—just an embankment, which he slid and tumbled down, until coming to rest in a clump of bushes. Bruised and bloodied, he fought his way out of the thick vegetation . . . to find himself facing a quartet of soldiers. All of them were pointing rifles at his head.

"Damn it . . ." Lensherr muttered. For a short while there, he had even convinced himself that he might succeed in escaping. It was depressing to think he'd been right about his fate all along.

The rest of the guards made their way down the embankment to join their comrades, Faust huffing and puffing as he brought up the rear. They formed a rough firing squad, standing in a semicircle around Lensherr. He glared at the men, then at their metal weapons. Had he been able to call upon his overtaxed magnetic powers, he thought darkly, he would have shown these scum exactly what he thought of their guns and rifles—and what *he* was capable of doing with them. But there *were* no powers to call upon, no strength to fight back left in his pain-wracked body—and no chance of escape.

"Have you anything to say, Jew, before the men fire?" Faust asked after he'd managed to regain his breath.

Lensherr sneered. "Not to any of you pigs."

"A man of few words, eh?" Faust smiled. "*Sehr güt.* I hope you will be as equally accommodating, and have the courtesy to die quickly after you've been shot." He turned to his men and nodded. A dozen weapons were leveled at the mutant overlord—

—and then all hell broke loose.

A . . . thing leapt down from the trees, landing in the middle of the group and lashing out with thick fists—and something metallic. Lensherr dove for cover as the soldiers fired wildly, seeking to hit their attacker, but succeeding in only cutting down their comrades.

Was this the "Wendigo" he had heard other prisoners talking about? Lensherr wondered. If so, he was surprised—from the descriptions he'd been given, he had expected the flesh-eating monstrosity to be well over seven feet tall, and covered with thick, white hair. The man-like animal he saw before him didn't seem nearly that tall, and there wasn't a trace of white hair to be found on its body. Still, it certainly growled and roared and cut men to pieces with its claws well enough to possibly be related to the legendary "cannibal man," if it wasn't the actual beast.

The fight was over in seconds, the last of the guards grasping his throat to try and staunch the blood that was flowing from the brutal gash across his neck. His efforts didn't last for long.

Slowly, Lensherr rose to his feet to face the assailant. With widening eyes, he watched as the creature stepped from the shadows and into the full light of the moon.

He was not a large man, barely just over five feet in height. His dark hair and sideburns were overgrown and unkempt, as though he hadn't seen a comb or brush in years, and there was an almost animalistic look to his features—the sharp angle of his nose, the wild gleam in his eyes, the feral snarl that showed abnormally long incisors. He wore combat fatigues and boots—both black, both obviously tended to with pride. But it was the weapons he had used to dispatch the soldiers that caught Lensherr's attention: a half-dozen, foot-long metal spikes that jutted out from the backs of the man's hands. If he were truly as close to being an animal as he seemed, one could almost consider them his claws.

"Logan . . . ?" said Lensherr.

The man stepped closer, raised his head slightly, and sniffed the air. "This ain't the time or place fer jawin', bub," he growled in English. "More soldier-boys're on their way." The claws retracted into his hands with a sharp *snik!*, and he pointed down a thin footpath. "Got a safehouse a few miles down this way—we can yak all ya want when we get there." He glared at Lensherr, and frowned. "An' then ya can tell me how it is ya know my real name. 'Specially since I ain't gone by it in almost forty years."

"No?" Lensherr asked. "How are you addressed, then?"

He gestured toward the corpses scattered around him, and flashed a chilling smile. "Most of 'em—least the ones who manage t'survive long enough t'mention their run-ins with me—call me 'the Wendigo.'

"But *you* can call me 'Wolverine.' "

11

THIS is ridiculous," Warren complained loudly, not for the first time in the past three hours or so. "You'd think with the kind of crisis we're facing, Roma would drop whatever it is she's doing and have us rushed in for an emergency meeting." He flapped his wings sharply in frustration. "Damned inefficient way to run an omniverse."

Draped across the cushions of a mahogany settee, Betsy couldn't help but grunt in agreement. Since being escorted to one of the many suites dotted throughout the Starlight Citadel, neither X-Man had been allowed to leave. Their numerous requests for an audience with the Supreme Guardian, more often than not, had been met with a noncommittal shrug or an uncomfortable shuffling of feet as their guards muttered excuses for why they couldn't do anything to help. Generally, their responses fell into three categories: "I'm just doing my job, Sir/Madame"; "I wouldn't know anything about that, Sir/Madame"; "If you'd care for a swim, there's a pool in the room behind the master bedroom." That last one was aimed at Betsy, whom the trio of male Captain Britains concluded was wearing a bathing suit, rather than the (admittedly scant) working clothes of a former Ninja assassin.

She'd picked up their thoughts about it the last time she'd stuck her head out the door to ask for (what seemed) the hundredth time about Roma's availability.

She let out a sharp breath. "Maybe Saturnyne is debating with her again over the merits of destroying our dimension before the Cube's reality-cancer spreads further. It seems to be a favorite topic of hers these days."

Warren gazed at her in alarm. "Are you serious?" Betsy nodded grimly. "Wait a minute—I thought she was supposed to be our ally! Is that the *best* solution she could come up with?"

"Well," Betsy replied, "given the severity of the situation, and the limited time we have left to reverse the Cube's effects . . . yes."

Warren frowned. "Not very big on putting a research group on the problem, or having her techs run simulations to devise some alternate plans, is she?"

Betsy shrugged. "Well, not everyone has your business acumen, luv. Most of us have to get by on our instincts—and Saturnyne's are telling her that eliminating the problem at the source is a great deal easier, and far less time-consuming, than trying to fix it."

"Not very practical, though," Warren commented. He paused for a moment, eyes narrowing as he tried to work out the problem.

A small smile tugged at the corners of Betsy's mouth as she watched him gently pull at his lower lip—an unconscious habit of his, one reserved for only his most serious thinking sessions. He stared into space while he considered potential options, frowning occasionally as he discarded those less likely to succeed. She didn't need her telepathic abilities to tell her what was going on inside his mind—his body language alone spoke volumes.

Eventually, Warren's eyes widened, a broad smile lighting his features. He pointed at Betsy. "How about this? Roma isolates our dimension until we've found a solution, then we—"

Betsy shook her head. "It's too late for that—the infection has already spread to other realities. So, either we find some way to repair it, or . . ."

"Or we get a front row seat to the death of the multiverse."

Warren blew out a sharp breath, then rubbed the back of his neck. "Sounds so weird when you say it out loud, you know? It's just so . . . big a concept, it's hard to get your head around it."

"That's putting it mildly. And it's not going to get any smaller unless we do something to prevent it." Betsy rose from the couch. "I don't know about you, luv, but I think we've been more than respectful of Saturnyne's request that we wait until Roma calls for us."

Warren grinned slyly. "And . . . ?"

"And I think we've waited long enough—so long, in fact, that I can't help but worry about what Roma and Saturnyne might be up to right now."

The grin quickly dissolved. "You don't think they destroyed the crystal while they stuck us in here, do you?"

"I'd like to think Roma's above that sort of duplicitous behavior, but Saturnyne . . ." Betsy frowned, then waved a hand in a dismissive gesture. "Regardless of my suspicions, though, this situation has become positively ridiculous, as you've said. Roma might want nothing more than to seal herself up in the throne room and brood about all the destruction being caused by the Cube, but *we* still have a job to do—and I, for one, am eager to get back to it." She nodded sharply. "She's *going* to hear what we have to say, and that's all there is to it."

Warren gestured toward the door. "What about getting past the Three Stooges outside?"

Betsy grinned. "They won't even know we're gone."

"How so?"

She walked over to join him, then took his hand in hers. A gray haze flowed across her eyes, and tendrils of black energy suddenly began streaming from her pores, to collect on the floor. The pool of darkness spread outward in a perfect circle, then stopped when it had surrounded the area around both X-Men. It was not a natural ability of hers, this power to open portals that led to whatever destination she desired; rather, it was a byproduct of an adventure that had nearly cost her her life. Some time ago, Betsy had been kidnapped by the minions of a creature named Kuragari, who wished to make her one of his "undercloaks"—servants dedicated to carrying out the orders of Kuragari, and the master he, in turn, answered to: the Crimson Dawn. With Warren's help—and at the risk of his soul—she had managed to break free of the conditioning she had undergone, and ultimately defeat Kuragari. The victory, however, had come with an unexpected benefit: she retained her undercloak's powers, among them the ability to teleport across distances. It had come in handy on more than one occasion since then.

"Decided to zip us over to the throne room?" Warren asked. "So, why didn't you just do this *before* I started wearing a hole in the carpet with all my pacing?"

"Well, for one thing," Betsy replied, "I was trying to abide by Roma's wishes. Just popping into her chambers uninvited might have only put her in a cross mood—" She cut him off with a gesture before he could say anything. "Yes, I know we're facing a crisis, and circumstances being what they are, following protocol seems like a waste of time. But I've had a little more experience with Supreme Guardians than you or the rest of the X-Men—especially since my father was one of Merlyn's personal guards. And if there's one thing I've come to learn, it's that celestial beings like Roma and her father resent people barging in when they're . . ." she shrugged ". . . doing whatever it is that celestial beings do. It makes them feel as though they're not in control."

Warren grunted. "Yeah, I can imagine having lower lifeforms running in all the time with *real* problems to solve can put a real crimp in your chess games."

Betsy chuckled. "You're beginning to sound like Wolverine."

"I guess that would be why I have this sudden urge for Canadian bacon and a bottle of Molson's." He shivered melodramatically. "I'll never be welcomed in a country club again."

As they spoke, they slowly began sinking into the black pool, the icy touch of the magical energy sending a pleasurable chill through Betsy's body. Beside her, Warren simply smiled, and tightened his grip on her hand.

"Hope we don't pop in while Roma's in the shower or something," he said.

Betsy laughed. "You wish."

"Hey, a guy can dream, can't he?" Warren sighed. "Oh. You said respecting Roma's wishes was *one* reason for not jumping there sooner. What's the other?"

Betsy smiled. "Well, you just look so *cute* when you're fuming. It brings out the color in your eyes . . ."

And then the darkness swallowed them, and they were on their way.

They materialized moments later in the center of the throne room, rising up through a pool of shadow near the pulpit containing the omniversal crystals.

Warren glanced around. "Looks like nobody's home."

Betsy nodded, frowning. "How strange . . ." Her eyes were drawn to the pulpit, and before she knew it, she was climbing the steps.

Warren trailed behind her. "What's up?"

"I want to check on something . . ." Her voice suddenly trailed off as she reached the top step, and she came to a halt, eyes widening in shock. "Oh, God, no . . ." she whispered hoarsely. "It's gone."

"What is?" warren asked.

"The crystal . . ." Betsy muttered.

"What crystal? *Our* crystal? The one holding our dimension?" Warren couldn't keep his voice from creeping up an octave or two as he joined her at the edge of the platform. He followed her line of sight, and immediately spotted the gap among the quartz slivers. Gently, he eased Betsy aside so he could inspect it more closely. "This is where Roma kept it? You're sure?"

Betsy nodded dumbly, suddenly unable to speak. To have gone through all the heartaches, the terrors, the torments, only to discover it was all for nothing . . . "We failed," she said, her voice drained of emotion.

"Now, let's not get ahead of ourselves, Betts," Warren said. "Jumping to conclusions is only going to drive you nuts." He looked over the spot where the crystal had been, ran a hand along the edge of the setting, then felt around inside it. He stepped back, and glanced at the floor, then bent down on one knee and looked under the collection of slivers. With an interested "Hmmm . . ." he rose to his feet and turned to her.

"What are you looking for?" she asked.

"The crystal."

She shook her head. "I just told you: If it's not there, then—"

"Then it's just not here," he interjected. "That doesn't mean it's been destroyed." He held up a hand to silence her before she could argue the point. "Look, Betts, you said the easiest way to stop the Cube's infection from spreading was to smash the crystal—at least in Saturnyne's opinion, right?" She nodded. "All right, then." He gestured at the area around him. "Well, I didn't see any broken shards or specs of quartz, either in the setting or on the floor; that, to me, indicates the crystal's still intact."

"Maybe she had it taken somewhere else and had her people destroy it," Betsy said. "Or used her powers to disintegrate it. Roma's not the most physical person, you know."

"Not when the hired help can get their hands dirty instead?" Warren shook his head. "You really think she'd turn over a job like that to just anyone, with the lives of billions of people at stake? I don't think she'd even allow Saturnyne to do it. It's *her* responsibility as Supreme Guardian, and hers alone."

"You're right," Betsy had to agree.

"One of the disadvantages of being the boss," Warren commented. "You have to take the blame for the disasters, as well as the praise for the successes. And this is one hell of a disaster she's got to balance on her shoulders. And as for zapping it with her powers . . . Didn't you say something about she'd given her word to the professor that she wouldn't do anything to the crystal until the X-Men had used up all the time they had to fix the problem?"

Betsy nodded. "Yeeess . . ."

"And have you ever known Roma to go back on her word?"

"No."

"And how much time do we have left?"

Betsy paused. She'd lost track of time with all the hopping between Earth and the Starlight Citadel she'd been doing, and the currents of the temporal stream moved differently here—sometimes slower, sometimes faster. "I . . . I'm not sure. A day? Less?"

"Well, however long it is, I'd rather play it safe and say she's still honoring her agreement than focus on the possibility she was jerking our chains. For all we know, she stashed it somewhere to keep Saturnyne from 'accidentally' dropping it on the floor when her back was turned."

"And where might that be?"

Warren shrugged. "Hey, *you're* the one with all the experience with Supreme Guardians, remember? Does Roma have an apartment, or does one of the walls in here swing out into a Murphy bed?"

"I'm not even certain she *sleeps,*" Betsy replied. "And I've never seen any indication of living quarters during my previous visits."

"Well, she has to have *someplace* to hang her robes." Warren gazed into the shadowy depths of the chamber. "Wouldn't surprise me a bit to find out she's got a *mansion* tucked away in a closet somewhere. With a full staff." He shrugged. "Well, we're not going to find it standing around here. Start looking for a door or a hatch or a secret panel. Let's just hope we don't catch her in the middle of a nap or something . . ."

Roma awoke slowly, her head throbbing dully. A soft moan escaped her lips—a decidedly un-Guardian-like sound to make, she thought hazily.

"She's conscious, Lord Doom," she heard someone say. The

voice was familiar, but her head ached too much for her to focus her thoughts.

"Perhaps *this* time she will be wise enough to provide the information Doom seeks," replied a deep, electronically enhanced voice near her. A voice that sent unaccustomed shivers along her spine.

She forced her eyes to open, then groaned as brilliant, white light assaulted her pupils. She tried to raise a hand to shade her eyes, only to discover it was restrained—as was her other hand, as well as both feet. Tilting her head to one side, she opened them again, though no more than narrow slits this time, giving her vision time to acclimate itself to the lighting conditions. The process was a slow one, but eventually she was able to see clearly—although what she saw when that happened made her consider shutting them.

There was a multiphasic crystal accelerator pointed at her. And standing beside it, arms folded across his broad, armored chest, was the invader who had forced his way into the throne room, who had used a variation of the technology in the medical device to strike her down, with the help of his mad ally, Sat-yr-nin.

An invader who called himself "Doctor Doom."

"I trust you slept well, Guardian?" he asked, though the tone in his voice made her title sound more like a distasteful curse than a sign of respect.

Roma pulled at her restraints, noticing that she had been secured to an upright metal platform—one of the surgical tables from the medical wing's operating theater. "What have you done?" she demanded.

"Seek not to question your better, woman," von Doom replied coolly. "Focus, rather, on the ways in which you might serve him."

"Serve *you*?" Roma snapped. She laughed sharply. "I'd sooner leap into the vortex and allow the time stream to tear me apart than even *consider* recognizing a . . . a *human* as my superior."

Apparently, that wasn't the sort of answer von Doom was expecting. With a low, electronic growl, he stabbed at a button on the accelerator's controls. The tip of the pressure tube glowed brightly, and an emerald beam shot forth, stabbing into Roma's chest. She howled as she felt her molecules being pulled apart, felt her life-force depleting—

—and then an alternate version of herself peeled away and collapsed to the floor.

She was a willowy thing, with gray-green skin and short tufts of dark hair along her arms and legs, and a fairly equine look to her features. This was how she appeared to the sentients of Earth 5127: the goddess Dallentré of the House of Fallon, who offered compassion and wisdom in times of need. One more aspect of herself, savagely torn away by a metal-adorned creature that imagined itself an enlightened being.

The accelerator powered down, and Roma slumped back against the table.

Through a haze, she watched as a pair of her once-loyal guards carried away her unconscious alternate—to where, she knew not.

The clang of metal boots drew her attention back to her tormentor. Von Doom was standing beside her, staring coolly at her. Though she could only see his dark brown eyes through the slits in his mask, she knew that he was smiling in triumph.

"I trust there will be no need for another lesson in manners," he said evenly. "When one invites a guest into one's home, it is expected that the hostess will make every effort to make her guest feel welcome." His gaze hardened. "You are not fulfilling your obligations, Guardian."

"If by doing so, you mean that I should open every door in the citadel to you," Roma said through clenched teeth, "then you are sorely mistaken. I may have allowed you to remain here, when I could—and, perhaps, should—have annihilated you for the destruction you are causing, but I will never allow you to control the citadel, or to use its powers to rule your world."

Now it was the armored monarch's turn to laugh. "For a child of the cosmos, Roma, you are staggeringly naïve. Why would Doom be interested in ruling one world . . . when he could become master of them all?"

It took a moment for the words to sink in, but when they did, Roma's eyes widened in shock. "You seek to possess the omniverse?" Her lips pulled back in a sneer. "Ignorant mortal!"

Von Doom reached out, seizing her face in one gauntleted hand. Roma didn't know what was worse—the pain he inflicted as he squeezed, or the revulsion she felt at the physical contact.

"We shall see which of us is ignorant, woman," he hissed, "when Doom claims his destiny."

"And . . . which destiny . . . would . . . that be?" she managed to ask, though it was an effort to move her lips between his tightening fingers.

He leaned in closer, voice dropping to a whisper. "Why, to become the *new* Supreme Guardian, of course . . ."

It was Betsy who finally located the entrance to Roma's apartment, behind the apse of the throne room. She'd been surprised to find it—she'd always thought Supreme Guardians lived on a higher plane of existence, or at least in another dimension. Knowing that they actually had a need for living quarters seemed so . . . so disappointing. And yet, it was probably necessary

Betsy hesitated for a moment, feeling rather awkward at the thought of bothering the Guardian in her private chambers, then rapped sharply on the oaken door with her knuckles; when no answer came, she knocked again.

Still nothing.

Betsy drew a deep breath, and sighed. "Well, old girl, 'in for a penny, in for a pound' . . ." she muttered, and pushed open the door.

The first thing that caught her attention when she stepped inside wasn't the opulence of the furnishings, but rather the hulking, red-headed man sitting in an egg-faced chair—Roma's Captain of the Guard, Alecto. He was facing the door, staring blankly at her, a rather formidable-looking sword resting on his lap.

The second thing that caught her attention was Saturnyne, lying in a heap in the middle of the room. From the rise and fall of her chest, Betsy could tell she was still alive, but the large bump on her left temple showed she had been unconscious for some time . . . which, to the lavender-haired X-Man, explained why Her Whyness had never returned to fetch her guests.

Betsy took two steps toward the Majestrix, and Alecto was suddenly on his feet, gripping the sword in both hands.

"No one enters these chambers," he said, though the tone of his voice was devoid of emotion.

"I just want to check on Saturnyne," Betsy said slowly, moving in an arc that would keep her out of any sword thrusts.

"She refused to obey me," Alecto said hollowly. "No one enters these chambers."

"Yes," Betsy agreed. "You've mentioned that." She kept walking to one side, maintaining eye contact with the guard—if he decided to attack, she'd see signs of it there, before he made any move. "I imagine you're going to be in quite a bit of trouble when she wakes up, though."

"She should have heeded my warning. No one—"

" '—enters these chambers.' Yes, I know," Betsy said. "You know, Alecto, you've always been something of a boor, but I've never known you to be so . . . short on conversational skills. Is everything all right?"

Alecto stepped toward her, sweeping the air near her throat with the sword; if she hadn't hopped back, he might have cut off her head.

Betsy glared at him. "All right—that's enough of that." She eased into a combat-ready stance, feet apart, hands at chest level, balancing on the balls of her toes. "I'll give you one chance to drop that oversized representation of your manhood—before I take it from you."

The guard lumbered forward, holding the sword above his head to deliver a killing blow.

She easily avoided the downward arc of the blade, then stepped inside Alecto's attack to deliver a quick series of jabs and chops to his arms and neck, seeking the pressure points that would cut off the flow of blood to his limbs and brain. But the armor worn by the burly guard deflected most of the blows, and a brutal elbow smash to the side of her head sent her stumbling away from him, and into a dressing table. She yelped as a corner of the burnished wood dug into her back, then instinctively jumped forward—and into a meaty fist that caught her across the jaw.

Another blow exploded into her stomach, driving the air from her lungs, and a boot heel caught her in the ribs. The impact sent her airborne, to crash heavily into one of the woodcuts hanging on the walls. Splintered oak and bruised Ninja rained onto the oversized cushions scattered about the room.

Betsy forced herself onto her knees, clutching her aching stomach as she sought to regain control of her breathing. The inhalations were short at first, but soon she was able to draw deeply on the candle-scented air. She looked up to find Alecto bearing down on her, holding the hilt of the sword in both hands; for some reason, his form reminded her of a rugby player, winding up to deliver a smash to a pitched ball. In this instance, though, his follow-through would result in her head being separated from her shoulders.

She rolled out of the way, the blade cutting through the air where she'd been a moment ago, though she didn't escape completely unscathed—a few strands of lavender hair floated to the floor. The dark-clad X-Man, however, had more important matters on her mind to pay it any attention. As Alecto spun around on the balls of his toes to renew his attack, she lashed out with a stockinged leg, catching him behind the left knee; the sweeping kick took him off-balance, and he stumbled into one of the stone columns supporting the ceiling. Betsy smiled as his head rebounded off the unyielding rock, and he staggered drunkenly around the room, apparently unable to focus his vision long enough to locate his target.

She used the opportunity to get behind him. "I'm over here," she said in a stage whisper.

Alecto lurched around to confront her, but she blocked his

sword arm with a wrist strike delivered with her left hand; the heel of her right hand, at the same moment, connected with his nose, breaking it at an odd angle. The guard's first instinct was to staunch the blood that gushed down his face, and she moved in quickly to disarm him; the sword went spinning across the room, impaling the headboard of Roma's four-poster bed. Before Alecto could respond, Betsy followed through by igniting her psi-blade and ramming its glowing point into his skull. With a loud groan, he staggered back, eyes rolling around in his head, and crashed, face-down, to the floor.

"Well . . ." Betsy said as she stopped to catch her breath. "Now I can understand why Brian never liked you."

A glint of candle light on metal caught her attention, and she bent down beside the unconscious guard to inspect the back of his neck. Some sort of device had been grafted to the skin, at the base of the skull; exactly what its purpose might have been she couldn't say, for the psychic dagger had fried its miniature circuitry. Still, based on Alecto's bizarre behavior, and his single-tracked insistence that he had to keep her out of the chamber, she had a fairly good idea that it had been controlling his mind. But as for who might have implanted it, well, that truly was a mystery to her. Roma seemed out of the question—she'd never been the type to rely on mechanical constructs like mind-control chips, not when she possessed the powers she did. Saturnyne? Perhaps, but the Majestrix wouldn't have used something that could malfunction in such a way that it would cause her own pawn to turn on her.

But if not them, then who . . . ?

"Betts!"

Betsy looked to the front door. Warren was standing just inside the room, grasping a long metal candle stand in both hands like a staff. He looked from her to Alecto, then to Saturnyne, then back to her. His eyebrows rose.

She pointed to the insensate Majestrix. "I had *nothing* to do with that."

"Didn't say you did, hon." Warren placed the stand in a corner and glanced at the damage around him. "But forgive me for thinking this was all your handiwork."

Betsy sniffed haughtily. "And I suppose *you've* never trashed a room or two in your time."

"Well, never on my own. But, then, I don't have your talents." Warren moved across the room to kneel beside Saturnyne. He placed the tips of his right-hand index and middle fingers against the carotid artery in her neck. "Her pulse seems pretty strong, but she's gonna have a helluva headache when she wakes up."

Betsy gestured toward Alecto. "Not as bad as the one *he's* going to have, I imagine." She pointed to the mind-control device, and explained her suspicions.

"So, who else might be a sus—"

"Von Doom!" Betsy interjected. "If there's anyone in the citadel capable of doing this kind of work, it's that tin-covered worm." She paused, scratched her chin with bright-red nails. "But he should be confined to the medical wing . . ."

"Then, I guess that's our next destination," Warren said as he joined her. "We can turn your playmates over to the doctors there."

Betsy shook her head. "No. For some reason, Alecto was determined to keep out any and all intruders, including Saturnyne; I want to know what that reason is. It might explain where Roma has gotten to."

"All right," Warren said. "But I don't think we're going to get any answers from him anytime soon." He glanced at the smoking metal patch. "Psi-blade?"

Betsy nodded. "Psi-blade."

"Well, that'll keep him napping for a couple of hours." He stared at the unconscious warrior, sprawled across a trio of floor pillows, then shrugged and ran a hand through his blond hair. "Too bad."

Betsy shrugged, too. "Couldn't be helped, luv. It was either that, or give him a chance to cut off my head." She paused, waiting for a response, then frowned when none was forthcoming. "Now you're supposed to say, 'Well, I'm glad he didn't *get* that chance, Betts. I like your head just where it is.' Or something like that."

"Uh, sure, hon," Warren said, his thoughts clearly elsewhere. He was looking across the room, at a door on the far side.

"Find something of interest?" She playfully tapped him on the side of the head. "Don't make me come in there again to learn what it is."

"I was just thinking," Warren replied. "If Sleeping Beauty here was left to guard something, then it stands to reason it must be that door. It's the only other way out of this room, and the only place Roma could have gone if she passed through here. And if Doctor Doom was controlling him—"

"—then Roma must be with von Doom," Betsy concluded. "And I rather doubt it was by her choice."

"If that's true, we've got some catching-up to do," Warren said. "But first . . ." He walked over to Saturnyne, picked her up, and carried her to Roma's bed. "Might as well make her comfortable while we're gone. Not that I think it'll do anything to improve her opinion of us when she wakes up."

Betsy smiled. "Ever the gentleman, eh?"

He walked over and placed his hands on her shoulders. "Well, if there's one thing we Worthingtons know, it's how to treat a lady—even an acid-tongued one."

"I hope you're referring to Saturnyne . . ." she said playfully.

"Sure," Warren replied quickly. "Of course, I am. Who *else* would I be talking about?" He nodded toward the door. "So . . . you ready?"

Betsy bent down and picked up Alecto's sword. She took a few practice swings, spun it with one hand a few times, then nodded in approval of the weapon's balance and heft. "Now I am."

Walking side-by-side, they headed for the portal—not certain what might lie on the other side, but more than willing to face it together.

12

THE first indication Reichsmajor Sommers had that something was wrong came just after the *Nuremberg* touched down at Kaltenbrunner Spaceport. Instead of the standard honor guard sent to greet the crew as it disembarked, Sommers and his people were met by close to one hundred armed soldiers—and a Sentinel.

An armored jeep roared up the runway from the control tower and screeched to a halt at the bottom of the ship's ramp. As Sommers and his second-in-command, Lieutenant Johan Ledyard, came down to meet it, the passenger door on the vehicle opened, and Sharon Carter stepped out.

"Good evening, *Obergruppenführer*," Sommers said, warily eyeing the giant robot. "Would you care to ex—"

The gun was in her hand and leveled at his head before his mind had even registered her movement for it.

"Down on the ground!" she commanded. *"Schnell!"*

Behind the ruby quartz lens of his visor, Sommers' eyes narrowed in anger. "What is the meaning of this?" he demanded.

A bullet was her reply; it *ping*ed off the hull of the ship. Close to his head.

"Do as I say, Major," Carter warned, walking up the ramp, "or the *next* shot will be the *last* you ever hear."

As if in response to an unspoken command, the soldiers trained their weapons on him. The air was filled with the click of rounds being chambered, and the hum of pulse rifles building a charge.

Sommers glared at her, but bent forward anyway, as though to sit on the ramp. "Very well, Carter. But there had better be a *damn* good reason for this embarrassment, or I will see to it *personally* that you wind up scrubbing toilets on some backwater planet near the Kree border." As he spoke, one hand hovered near a hidden stud on the left side of the visor; he felt the power he always fought to control increase in intensity, straining for release. Given the circumstances, he couldn't think of a better time to do so . . .

And that was when the Sentinel spoke.

WARNING, it stated loudly through amplifiers built into its humanoid head. PRESENCE OF MUTANT BIO-ENERGY FORCE DETECTED.

It stepped forward, the ground vibrating with each footfall, and came to a halt beside the jeep. Sommers' hand immediately dropped away from the visor as the robot pointed its own mammoth hand at him; its palm glowed with a buildup of energy that signaled the activation of a repulsor beam projector the size of a bank vault door. If it were fired, there wouldn't be enough left of the Major to sweep into a dustpan.

This was it, then, he suddenly realized. His dirty little secret had finally been exposed. They all knew now—knew he was nothing but a lowly mutant, masquerading as a human. He could tell by the expressions on the faces of Carter and her men: some were angry; others, disappointed. Most, though, wanted him dead—he could see it in their eyes.

Slowly, Sommers sat down and placed his hands on the back of his head. Resistance at this point would have been futile; discounting the Sentinel, he was still outnumbered by a factor of 100:1. He fought the urge to leap up and attack, to force them to kill him before news of his "secret identity" became public knowledge; at least that way he'd be spared suffering through the humiliation. But, no—despite the exposure of his true nature, despite his embarrassment, he was still, first and foremost, an officer of the Reich, and would act accordingly. And no self-respecting officer of the Reich would ever consider suicide a solution to his problems.

Carter turned to a group of soldiers clad head to toe in body armor. "You men—find the other one: Rogue. She should be in a cell near the engineering section. And take all precautions—she's a power-leech. If she attempts to make contact with your skin, shoot her immediately, or she'll drain you like a battery."

The men nodded their understanding and hustled up the ramp. They pushed aside the members of the *Nuremberg*'s crew that had gathered at the entry portal—men and women clearly stunned by the revelation that their commanding officer wasn't human—and disappeared inside the ship.

"Of what *possible* interest could that blubbering sack of meat be to you, Carter?" Sommers asked. "Woden knows she's been more hindrance than help ever since she was foisted upon me at Farpoint Station."

"Silence, *freak,"* she snapped. "Playing the wide-eyed innocent at this stage will only earn you a private interrogation session with my security officers." She flashed a toothy, shark-like grin. "I was never told what condition you had to be in for the transfer—only that you had to be ready." The grin widened. "I'll make sure they leave enough blood in your broken body to keep your heart beating."

Much to her apparent surprise, he returned the smile. "And people say you lack compassion, *Obergrüppenfuhrer,*" he said sarcastically.

She sneered. "Abomination," she hissed. "Were it in my power, I would see to it that you and all the other freaks onboard your ship were lined up and shot."

"Then I am grateful that it's *not* in your power, Carter," Sommers replied. "Although, I must confess, being shot *would* be preferable to listening one moment longer to that harpy-like shriek you call a voice."

Carter bit back whatever reply she'd been about to give—it wouldn't have been a wise move, to lose control of her temper in front of the troops. She settled, instead, for rapping him across the jaw with the butt of her gun, then turning on her heel and stomping down the ramp, back to her vehicle. She barked an order to one of the soldiers to keep an eye on the prisoner.

Chuckling softly, Sommers rubbed his bruised chin and turned his head to face Ledyard, who had been quietly standing beside him the entire time. "Two sides of the same coin," the Major had once referred to them—Sommers, dark and brooding; Ledyard, easygoing and full of life. They worked well side-by-side, complemented one another, serving their Emperor to the best of their abilities as they conquered new worlds and annihilated his enemies. And in facing death numerous times over the years, in adventures that had become legendary throughout the Reich, they had become fairly close—as close as Sommers dared ever let anyone get, that is. But as the Major watched him now, it was obvious by the lieutenant's horrified expression that their friendship had come to a swift end. The distance he was giving his commanding officer was proof of that.

Sommers raised an eyebrow, flashed what he considered a warm smile. "Come now, Johan—I don't bite."

Ledyard stared at him, wide-eyed, but made no move to approach him. "I—I'm sorry, Major. It's just that—"

"Ah," he said sagely. "The 'mutant virus.' " He shook his head despondently, and sighed. "You know that's just an old wives' tale, Johan."

Ledyard nodded, but his bottom lip was trembling. "I have . . . heard that. It's just . . . I have two children—"

"Franz and Greta," Sommers said coldly. "And a beautiful wife, as well." He sneered at his officer, angered by this betrayal, from someone he considered a friend. "I *know*, Lieutenant; I have met them—on many occasions. Held them in my arms—on many occasions."

A thin sheen of sweat suddenly appeared on Ledyard's forehead, just below the hairline. "*Gott in himmel* . . ." he whispered. "You held them . . ."

"On *many* occasions." A vicious smile twisted Sommers' features. He couldn't help himself—it was a small measure of payback for the indignity he was experiencing. "You'll be certain to give each of the children a kiss from Uncle Scott when you see them later tonight—won't you?"

His callous laugh was cut short by the heavy tread of boots vibrating through the ramp. He turned around to see that Carter's men had carried out their errand: Rogue stood in the center of the group, her mask once more covering her face, the chains she was often fitted with again impeding her movements. Head bowed, she marched down the ramp, not even sparing a glance at her former commanding officer.

An armored transport vehicle rolled up to the base of the ramp, and Rogue was shoved into the rear. The soldiers followed, closing the door behind them. The transport roared off as another came to take its place.

Carter stepped from her jeep and approached Sommers. "Your turn, freak. And if you try anything, my men have orders to shoot to kill." She shrugged. "It's entirely up to you."

Hands still on his head, Sommers rose to his feet and silently walked down the ramp. A quintet of soldiers followed, rifles brought to bear on him, while another opened the rear hatch.

Sommers paused in the doorway, and turned to the spaceport commander. "Exactly when do you plan on telling my wife what's happened to me, Carter? She and I were supposed to have a little talk—"

"About the League of German Maidens?" She laughed sharply. "Why, she already *knows* about your predicament, Major." She leaned forward, her voice dropping to a conspiratorial whisper. "You see, *she* was the one who told us all about you . . ."

* * *

"Well, *dis* don' look too good . . ." Gambit muttered.

Standing on the roof of the spaceport's administration building, he watched the circus-like goings-on around the *Nuremberg* through macrobinoculars he'd found in a desk drawer. As for what they'd been doing in his doppelganger's office when the man had had no prior use for them . . . well, only a thief knew the forces that propelled him to "acquire" things he didn't need. Gambit knew *that* all too well.

He adjusted the magnification by running a thumb along a grooved wheel on one side of the viewer, and zoomed in for a better look. He saw someone who looked like his team leader, Cyclops, start down the ramp, only to be met by a veritable army, accompanied by a Sentinel. When the big robot had passed the main building on its way toward the starship just moments before, Gambit had ducked back down the stairwell, then breathed a sigh of relief as he realized its sensors hadn't detected him.

He ducked again, though, when the Sentinel went into protection mode, and stepped toward the ship. But it was Cyclops the robot was after, not him—or, at least, the guy who *looked* like the man he knew as Scott Summers. It was all hellishly confusing, and Remy hadn't a clue as to exactly what was going on around here.

The last thing he remembered was the explosion—one that had leveled Psi Division Headquarters, just outside Washington, D.C. It was a facility that used powerful telepaths to scan the globe, seeking any negative thoughts anyone might have toward the armored tyrant who ran the world—the notorious Doctor Doom—and then reporting them to the proper authorities. The X-Men had been brought there for interrogation, after their capture by von Doom's agents in New York—a battle that had resulted in Remy being infected with a deadly technovirus. An infection that, bit by bit, transformed his flesh and bone into circuits and wires. It was a slow death sentence—one from which there would be no last-minute reprieve.

What had scared him more than watching his body turn to metal, though, was working up the nerve to finally come right out and say how he'd always felt for Rogue, while there was still time to say it. He'd never been so honest with anyone in his life, not even with himself, and it had torn him apart to see how deeply his heartfelt sentiments affected her.

And then they'd had to say good-bye.

As Nightcrawler, aided by some of Magneto's followers, teleported the X-Men from the facility, Remy stayed behind. He was no good to the team now—the pathogen racing through his system made him too infectious for anyone to touch, especially Rogue—but he was still able to provide them with enough time to escape. All it took was using his biokinetic mutant energy to detonate the metal parts of his body, and blow up the building. There was a flash of light and heat—

And he'd suddenly found himself sprawled on the floor of a broom closet-sized office, wearing another man's uniform—and, apparently, his body, as well.

It took a while for him to come to the conclusion that this place wasn't Heaven, Hell, *or* Purgatory—although the idea that he might be a desk-bound bureaucrat in this reality made him reconsider the Hell part. But the truth of it was, he was alive; the why and the how of it he was willing to leave to the experts. Maybe Roma could explain it to him when the mission was completed.

The mission. He couldn't be sure, but he had a sinking feeling that, if the world had changed as much as it apparently had, then the X-Men had failed to save the day. He ignored the thought that popped into his head that, if that were the case, then his sacrifice had been for nothing. But it *hadn't* been for nothing, he sternly reminded himself—by destroying Psi Division Headquarters, he'd at least given back to his teammates their freedom; given them another chance to try and reverse whatever it was Doctor Doom had done to the planet.

Now, it was *his* turn.

He'd spent the next few hours becoming acclimated to this new world, using his alternate's computer to get a handle on things. Or as much a handle on things as one could manage, when they wake up to discover they're on an Earth where the Nazis won World War II, and the Red Skull is now its king. He was just grateful that he'd somehow absorbed enough knowledge from his twin to understand German, since there didn't seem to be a whole lot of people around who still spoke English—or French. Through the computer, and its Internet access, he'd tried to locate the other X-Men, but the task was made impossible to accomplish because of variations in the spelling of surnames he typed in—too many for him to wade through—and the fact that most government agencies regarded their files as classified information, and thus were inaccessible.

It was only when he tried "Rogue" that his luck changed. There was only one listed, and that was in the listing of crews for the Empire's spacefleet. And when he saw that her ship, the *Nuremberg,* was scheduled to make planetfall later that day, he knew the cards were in his favor. Even better, the ship's commander was named Scott Sommers—too close a coincidence to be anyone but the X-Men's leader, under a similar name.

But any plans he'd had of trying to contact either of them had just been trashed, courtesy of the port's she-wolfish commander.

He watched as someone—a woman, by her figure—was led in chains from the ship, and something told him it was Rogue. Perhaps it was the style of her outfit that alerted him—no one else he knew would have every inch of skin covered to avoid making contact with the people around her. Or perhaps it was just that streak of white hair poking out of the top of her mask. His heart sank when he saw how cruelly the soldiers were treating her as they bundled her into the back of an armored car. Yet he held his anger in check, forced himself to remain where he was, and not go foolishly rushing headlong into danger. It would do neither of them any good if he got himself killed coming out of the gate.

A wry smile turned up the corners of his mouth. He'd always known hanging around the X-Men might be good for something—he just hadn't expected it to be for gaining wisdom. Well, he surmised, even a street-smart thief could learn a trick or two from those around him—if he was willing to listen.

The transport pulled away from the *Nuremberg*, and headed for one of the exit gates.

"Damn," he muttered. "Dey're splittin' 'em up." Now, he had a decision to make: Go after Rogue, or wait for Cyclops' transport and follow that instead.

It wasn't that difficult a choice.

"Sorry, Cyclops," he muttered. "But dere's a certain *fille* needin' a helpin' hand right 'bout now, an' Gambit . . . well, he's always had a soft spot fo' de ladies. Hope you understan'."

Tucking the macrobinoculars into one of the deep pockets of the black trenchcoat he'd appropriated from another office, Remy paused to watch the direction in which Rogue's vehicle was heading—west, toward Manhattan. Then he sprinted for the stairs, and the employee parking garage.

Jean Grey was getting awfully tired of waking up with a headache.

She never used to have them with such frequency, but then, before she joined the X-Men, she never had to worry about blows to the back of her skull, or psychic attacks on her mind, or being injected with powerful sedatives. It was getting so she was starting to forget what it felt like to sleep normally, without outside influence.

On von Doom's world, she'd been struck in the head with a paving stone wielded by one of his super-villainous government agents; it had left her with a mild concussion. When she was shunted into Magneto's reality, though, she'd been too engrossed in freeing herself from her duplicate's mind to worry about being knocked unconscious. But now, on the Red Skull's Earth, it seemed she was making up for lost time: first, Xavier's unexpected mental assault; then, the drugs Carol Danvers had injected her with. Her condition had been made even worse by Xavier's ransacking of her thoughts and memories; her mind was now a confusing jumble of sights and sounds, all scattered across the floor of her subconscious during his brutal search for information. It was difficult for her to think clearly, even more so for her to remain awake, but she wasn't willing to give in to the cool, inviting waters of the dark tide that washed over her mind.

"She is conscious, Commander," she heard someone say, and dimly recognized the voice as Xavier's.

Slowly, Jean opened her eyes, and found herself gazing into the cold, dark orbs of someone she'd hoped never to see again. "Lady Viper . . ." she whispered hoarsely.

The last time Jean and the beautiful—and very deadly—femme fatale had met was on von Doom's world, shortly after the X-Men's capture. There, the former leader of the international terrorist organization Hydra (in the real world) had been assigned the task of running "Emperor" von Doom's high security agency S.H.I.E.L.D., and Jean was just another prisoner to be interrogated. The electroshock therapy Jean had undergone at her hands wasn't something the X-Man was going to forget anytime soon. However, she didn't expect Viper to remember that encounter—the world *had* undergone a change or two since then, courtesy of the Cosmic Cube.

Yes, the world might have changed, but Viper certainly hadn't. She was still clad in a bright green latex catsuit that accentuated every curve, still wore the same garish lipstick and eye shadow, still styled her shoulder-length hair—also tinted green (did the woman only know of *one* color in the spectrum?)—in a Veronica Lake fashion. Her Asian features were as striking as ever, and her lips bore the same perpetual snarl her counterpart had displayed. She regarded Jean quietly for a moment, then turned to the side. "Is she—"

"Going to cause any trouble?" Xavier replied. "Not at all."

Jean raised her head to glance at her surroundings, but it was taking all her strength. It felt as though a large weight had been placed on her head.

Not a weight, child, Xavier's voice suddenly echoed in her thoughts. *Just a few psychic barriers to keep you in check. If you try to break them, I'm afraid you'll only wind up crippling your mind. Permanently.*

The pressure eased a bit, and she was able to lift her head. There was an Art Deco influence to the design of the office, one she never would have expected to fit Viper's style, given the woman's obvious tastes for all things rubber and leather. Beyond a massive mahogany desk covered with paperwork and some of the commander's personal "toys" was a trio of soaring windows. On the other side of the glass, city lights sparkled brightly against the night sky, and her attention was drawn to a familiar skyscraper in the southwest that stood high above the others: the Empire State Building.

I . . . think we're in . . . the Chrysler Building, she realized, with some effort; it still hurt to focus her thoughts. *So that means . . . we're back in . . . midtown Manhattan. But . . . why? And . . . what happens . . . next . . . ?*

She tried to turn in her seat, only to discover she was held fast by a number of broad leather straps that confined her to the wheelchair she was sitting in: her wrists were secured to the arms of the chair, her legs to the hangar brackets supporting the footrests, her torso to the stiff wooden back. She tilted her head to the right, and saw Carol Danvers seated on a leather couch nearby, glaring back at her. The blow to the left temple she'd received when Jean telekinetically shoved open the front door at the mansion had turned into an ugly bruise; the black-and-blue coloration did wonders for bringing out the anger in her eyes.

To the left sat Xavier, who was deep in conversation with Viper. That didn't mean, however, that he wasn't aware of her watching him.

"When do you expect to hear from Minister Zola, Commander?" he asked. "I would have expected him to have us flown to Genosha on the first possible transport."

"The Minister moves at his own pace, Herr Professor, and for his own reasons," Viper replied. "It is my understanding that we are waiting for a prisoner transfer before we begin the trip."

Xavier chuckled. "Ah. Some of Frau Sommers' colorfully named friends, I imagine. Well, given the information she's provided—" he flashed a satisfied smile at Jean "—it shouldn't be too difficult to round up the rest of them." He frowned. "I must admit, however, that I was surprised by some of their identities."

"As was Berlin, when I informed the Ministry of Security." Viper sneered. "Perhaps mutants have outlived their usefulness, if we have to start worrying about revolutionaries in our midst."

Xavier started—Jean could feel waves of fear radiating from his mind—but he quickly recovered. "Nonsense, Commander," he said with a forced smile. "I have no doubt that, once Frau Sommers' fellow conspirators have been rounded up, things will return to normal." He waved a hand in a dismissive gesture. " 'Cyclops.' 'Rogue.' 'Wolverine.' 'Storm.' 'Psylocke.' 'Archangel.' " He huffed mightily. "In time, each and every one of these rogue mutants will be brought to justice."

Jean glanced at him. *I notice . . . you've left* yourself . . . *off the list . . . "Professor X" . . .*

The pressure on her mind suddenly increased. *Indeed, Frau Sommers. And if you wish to avoid becoming a mindless, drooling idiot, you will keep such information just between us.*

Her eyes narrowed, and she coaxed her lips to form a sly smile. *What's wrong, Professor—afraid of being exposed as a "conspirator"?*

A cruel smile contorted his features.

She knew it was coming, then, but could do nothing to stop it. Jean screamed and twisted in her seat as a psychic pulse raced through the link, shattering her consciousness.

And then her mind went blank.

"Is there a problem, Herr Professor?" Viper asked.

Xavier smiled beatifically. "None at all, Commander. Why do you ask?"

Viper stepped forward and grasped Jean's chin in a gloved hand, then tilted back her head. The redheaded mutant's eyes had rolled upward, showing only the whites. A thin line of spittle oozed from a corner of her gaping mouth. "Well, it's just that I usually don't see prisoners react in such a manner until *after* I've completed my questioning."

"A mild seizure, no doubt caused by the stress induced by her current situation." Xavier shrugged. "Nothing more."

Viper frowned, and let Jean's head fall back on her chest. "Such a condition isn't listed in her medical records."

"Neither is any mention of psychic powers," he commented.

She paused to mull that over. "True. But . . ."

"Please, Commander, don't worry so!" Xavier said pleasantly. He motioned toward Jean. "You see? She's recovering already."

It was the closest she'd been to death in . . . she couldn't remember how long. And it had been accomplished with all the ease of flicking a light switch.

Jean shuddered. Was there *nothing* of the real Charles Xavier left in this monster? Or had his Nazi twin "switched" him off permanently, as he had almost done with her?

Feeling better, child? Xavier asked, startling her.

I . . . got the message . . . Professor, she said, her heart pounding in her chest. *There was . . . no reason for . . . a demonstration . . .*

I believe in teaching by example, Frau Sommers, he replied. *It often eliminates the need for me to repeat myself.* He turned to face Viper, who was talking on a cell phone that had been clipped to her belt. "Any news from Minister Zola, Commander?"

She ended her conversation and nodded. "Not yet. But I was just speaking with the commander of Kaltenbrunner Spaceport. Two of the other conspirators are on their way, via armored car." She raised an eyebrow, and glanced at Jean. "One of them is Reichsmajor Sommers."

Xavier turned to Jean and patted her reassuringly on the knee. "There—you see how helpful you've been to the Empire, Frau Sommers? If you hadn't revealed your powers to me, no one would have suspected that one of the spacefleet's most respected officers was actually the ringleader of an underground mutant revolution.

And once we have all the other key members of your rebellion, the citizens of the Empire will be able to breathe a little easier, knowing such rabble are off their streets." He smiled wolfishly. "I'm sure the Major and you will have much to discuss when he gets here."

"Oh, yes," Jean muttered sarcastically. "It'll be one big, happy family reunion . . ."

13

WELL, now *this* is what I call a pretty big hall," Warren commented as he and Betsy walked through the limitless depths of the pocket dimension. "Bet you could throw one hell of an X-Men reunion in here, and still have room for the Avengers and the FF . . . and the entire Shi'ar Empire . . . and a hundred-piece orchestra or five . . ."

"I wouldn't want to be responsible for the catering bill," Betsy added.

They'd been exploring this unusual side chamber for what felt like hours, guided only by an inner compass that Betsy seemed to possess—part of her birthright, apparently, as the daughter of one of Merlyn's former guards. It would explain, she'd commented to Warren, why she never got lost whenever she visited the citadel. Still, no matter how well developed her sense of direction might be, they'd seen no evidence of the Supreme Guardian—or her unwanted guest, for that matter.

Warren came to a halt. "Okay—stop." He looked around at the endless white field, then turned to Betsy. "Hon, there has *got* to be a better way to do this. I mean, we could wander around this place for a hundred years and never find Roma—not unless we come across a signpost pointing the way."

Betsy flashed a small smile. "Your next stop: *The Twilight Zone.*"

He shrugged. "Hey, at least then we'd know we were *going* somewhere."

She nodded, then fell silent. Her brow furrowed, and she started tossing Alecto's sword from one hand to the other, then put the point of the blade on the ground and idly twirled the weapon.

"I can hear the gears turning in your head, Betts," Warren said. "Anything coming to mind?"

"Maybe," she replied. "I was thinking of my teleport ability. Unlike our friend, Nightcrawler, I don't necessarily have to know the exact location I want to go to in order to get there. So, perhaps, if I just focus on finding Roma, instead of where she might be—"

"We might be able to jump right to her." Warren smiled. "Have I ever mentioned how much I admire you for your brain?"

"For my *brain?* No," she replied sarcastically. "You're usually too focused on my other . . . winning attributes."

"Oh." He shrugged. "Well, I'll make a mental note to do it more in the future."

"If we *have* a future . . ." she noted darkly. She took him by the hand, and a portal formed beneath them.

They emerged, seconds later, in the center of a medical nightmare.

A dozen glass-and-metal cylinders towered in a circle around them, each connected to a control unit that monitored the vital signs of the female figures locked inside. The women floated in a thick, blue-colored liquid—a fluid so cold Betsy could feel its chill from six feet away. Some of them had serene expressions on their faces, while others stared at the X-Men in wide-eyed horror.

"I think they're frozen," Betsy said with a shudder. "Some kind of suspended animation."

"I feel like I just walked into the middle of a Robin Cook thriller," Warren said, "and some crazy doctor's started harvesting organs from unwilling donors." He stepped toward one of the cylinders, and looked closely at its occupant. "Is that Roma?"

Betsy joined him. Yes, it was, but a vastly different version of the woman she knew as the Supreme Guardian. Her dark hair was short, and frosted a bright pink color at the ends, and the robes Roma normally wore had been replaced with black leather pants tucked into black boots, and a white T-shirt emblazoned with the logo for the heavy metal band Megadeth. Her left earlobe and nostril were pierced by a number of small metal studs. All in all, the woman looked more like a resident of New York's St. Mark's Place than a cosmically aware goddess.

With a growing sense of unease, Betsy moved on to the next cylinder. Here, too, was another Roma, blond-haired and elfin in appearance, dressed in what looked like a collection of tree bark, twigs, and leaves. Slowly, she gazed at the cylinders, then turned back to Warren.

"They're *all* Roma," she concluded.

"How can *that* be?" He gestured at the cylinders. "Are you saying they're clones, or replacement bodies, or something like that?"

She shook her head. "No. I'm saying they're all *her*—parts of her, at least." She saw the confusion on his face. "And before you ask, no, I don't know how I could know that. It's just a . . . feeling."

"Like knowing your way around the citadel?" Warren nodded. "Well, your feelings are usually right, so I'll take your word for it. Question is, if these are just parts, then where's the actual body?"

"Away from any of your possible meddling, mutant," replied an all too familiar, electronically enhanced voice.

"Looks like somebody tripped a silent alarm," Warren muttered.

Betsy sighed. "Yes. I wonder who those 'somebodies' might be . . ."

They slowly turned around. Standing behind them was three more guards—all dressed similarly to their now unconscious captain, Alecto, all brandishing swords. Behind them, arms folded across his armored chest, was the very tyrant the X-Men been looking for—and unconsciously hoping not to find.

"What have you done, von Doom?" Betsy demanded, gesturing at the cylinders. "And where's Roma?"

"Doom answers to no one, mutant," the dictator replied. "Least of all to genetic inferiors like you and your lover."

"And here I'd always been under the impression you were too intelligent to be a racist," Warren said heatedly. "Guess you're not as smart as you think."

Von Doom ignored the jibe. "Dispose of them," he ordered the guards, "*without* damaging the equipment, or your lives will be forfeit. Then toss their corpses into the vortex. Doom has more important matters to which he must attend."

And with that, he turned and walked away. He soon disappeared from sight over what appeared to be an artificial horizon, although Betsy was fairly certain it was just an optical illusion.

"Why, that arrogant—" Warren began, but she cut him off.

"Warren, luv, I think it would be best if you concentrated on the matter at hand," she suggested, just before the guards rushed forward.

She parried the first attack from the guard closest to her—Gorka, if she remembered his name correctly. He was a heavyset man in his thirties, with dark hair and a pencil-thin mustache, and he used his sword as though it was a natural extension of his arm. Betsy, on the other hand, was more comfortable with a Japanese *katana*, a weapon much lighter than the two-handed broadsword she'd appropriated from Alecto. This blade took greater strength to control, which meant she spent more time blocking Gorka's attack than she did in pressing her own.

Stumbling back as she just managed to avoid a thrust aimed at her throat, Betsy caught a glimpse of Warren. The other two guards were concentrating on him, one feinting a charge while the other circled around.

It sounds rather strange, but I don't know if I should feel grateful that I have only one of these idiots to fight, Betsy reflected as she blocked another strike, *or insulted that they apparently consider me the weaker of the two . . .*

Chauvinism aside, however, it was clear by the force of Gorka's assault that he didn't care whether she was a man, a woman, or the incredible Hulk—all he was focused on was killing his opponent to please his master. Not exactly her sentiments—she was more interested in incapacitating von Doom's drone than decapitating him—but she could understand his mind-controlled point of view.

"Warren!" she cried. "Behind you!"

He glimpsed over his shoulder, saw the second guard running at him, and took to the air. As the armored duo passed beneath him, he lashed out and kicked them both in the head. The men lost their balance, crashed to the floor, and then immediately rolled back onto their feet, looking for their target.

But Warren had used the time to get behind them. He swooped down low, almost skimming the floor, and slammed into their legs, like a football player throwing a low tackle. The men cartwheeled through the air, then bounced hard off the floor; their swords went spinning away. Wings flapping, Warren dove in for another pass.

Gorka's sword cleaved the air where Betsy had been standing a moment before, and she spun on the balls of her toes, inside his attack, to deliver an elbow strike to his ribcage, at a point where the front and back halves of his chestplate were joined by thin leather straps. He grunted and staggered back, and she followed through with a high heel kick that caught him below the left eye, then slammed the flat of her blade against his skull. As he tried to remain standing, she swung in low and delivered a scissors kick to his legs that toppled him like a redwood. He crumpled to the floor in a heap and lay still.

Dropping her sword, Betsy turned and launched herself toward Warren's attackers. As she vaulted into the air, she summoned forth her psychic dagger, and then plunged it into the back of one guard's head as she landed on his back. He moaned loudly and collapsed, smoke trailing from the mind-control device attached to his neck.

Using the distraction created by Betsy's attack, Warren delivered a haymaker to his opponent's jaw, followed by a combination of blows to the man's face and ribs that quickly put him down for the count. As the guard fell bonelessly onto the floor, the winged mutant glanced at Betsy, who stood over her prey, smiling.

"Hey," he said, pointing at the man and trying to sound hurt, "I *was* gonna take care of that."

She smiled. "Never said you couldn't, luv, but time waits for no one."

"True," he agreed. His eyes narrowed. "So, now that we're finished with the preliminary bouts, I'd say it's time for the main event—and I'm just in the mood to make Doom tell us everything he's been up to since he got here."

"Yes. And if we're *very* lucky," she added coolly, "he'll even tell us how to free these other Romas—*before* I'm forced to tear that knowledge from his mind . . ."

It wasn't the first time Gambit had ever freed anyone from a jail cell—but for the life of him, he couldn't remember trying it at 60 mph, on a crowded highway.

Following the armored car containing Rogue hadn't been too difficult, considering every other car on the road gave it a wide berth. But following it and catching up to it without drawing attention to himself were two different things, and Remy had never learned to be much of a conservative driver when he was growing up. Of course, that was usually because the cars he'd driven then had been "boosted" from parking lots and curbside spaces so he could go joyriding through the streets of New Orleans. He'd always considered courteous driving and speed limits as things created for cowards and blue-haired old ladies, to keep everyone behind them as they slogged along on the interstate for ten miles or more, with the left turn-signal blinking the whole time. For him, there were two ways of driving: fast, and airborne; the latter only came into play when he was cresting a hill, with his foot crushing the accelerator to the floor—or when he lost control while negotiating a bad turn on a country road (he'd learned to stop doing *that* over time; keeping his hands on the wheel helped).

Unfortunately, possessing all that questionable driving experience wasn't doing him any good, under the current circumstances—his LeMans approach only alerted the driver of the transport to his presence.

And when the shooting started, Remy wasn't all that surprised—but he *was* annoyed that such a fine-looking ride was being torn apart by automatic fire.

Sure glad dis ain't my *car,* he thought with a wry grin. *Den I'd* really *be in a bad mood . . .*

Any other thoughts were shelved for the moment—he needed to concentrate on driving.

He roared across two lanes, swerved around a Sports Utility Vehicle, then stomped on the gas. His best bet was to get close to the transport, away from the gun ports that had opened on the rear of the car. After that . . . well, he'd figure out something; if there was one thing Remy Lebeau was good at, it was thinking on the fly. He knew better than to try ramming it, of course—the vehicle's armored plating would tear apart his borrowed sportscar on first contact.

With a sharp twist of the wheel, he swerved back toward the transport, grimacing as he heard brakes locking behind him, followed by the squeal of tires and the impact of metal against metal. He glanced over his shoulder, and breathed a little easier when he saw that no serious accidents had occurred—there were a lot of bent fenders, but no injuries.

Turning his attention back to the transport, it took him a moment to realize that, while he'd been averse to sideswiping the armored car, its driver had no such reluctance.

"Aw, damn . . ." he muttered.

The front left-side tire banged off the edge of the sportscar's bumper, and Remy found himself fighting the wheel to keep from slamming into an eighteen-wheeled semi passing on his other side. He regained control—just as the transport swerved over again.

This time, the car *did* bounce off the semi, too close to the cab's right-side fuel tank for Remy's comfort. He gulped as the front bumper was stripped away by one of the oversized tires, to be flattened by the ones behind it. The left headlight shattered, spraying glass at him; idly, he wished he hadn't put down the sportscar's retractable roof before setting out on his rescue mission.

He spun the wheel, and smashed the convertible against the transport's side—not trying to overturn it, but just to give him some breathing room. The armored vehicle shuddered, then slid over a hair, and Remy stomped on the brake, making the transport overshoot him on its next pass. It collided with the semi, its bumper punching a hole in the truck's fuel tank, then screeched back into its lane. But not before the momentarily entwined metal scraped against each other—and created a spark.

"Merde!" Remy shouted, as a wall of flame suddenly erupted in the middle of the road.

Spinning the wheel, he stomped on the gas and swung the sportscar toward the transport's right side—just as the semi's cab and remaining fuel tank exploded. The trailer it had been hauling spun high on its rear tires, then crashed down, across the width of the highway, and detonated as well. The fireball it created could probably be seen from Manhattan.

"How'd I know *dat* would happen?" Remy asked himself with a smile. "Now, all Gambit needs is Sandra Bullock, an' we got ourselves an action/'venture movie."

More bullets *ping*ed off the car, smashing through the windshield, and he ducked below the dashboard for cover. Steering with one hand, he felt in his pockets of his trenchcoat for anything that he might be able to use as a weapon.

But not something to shoot. Something to *throw*.

His hand settled on a hard plastic case, and he pulled out the macrobinoculars he'd used at the spaceport.

"Yeah, dese'll do jus' fine," he said. "Bet dey was 'spensive, too."

Falling silent, he concentrated on summoning forth the

kinetic energy his body's cells were constantly generating. First his hand, then the binoculars, began to glow with a pinkish-white light—one that grew stronger with each passing moment. When it had reached a certain level of intensity, he glanced at the transport.

"Rogue!" he called out. "Don' know if you can hear me, *chere*—but *DUCK!*"

And with that, he hit the brakes and flung the binoculars at the transport's rear doors as it passed.

The kinetically-charged explosive detonated on contact, blowing both doors off their hinges and sending the guards inside flying through the air as though shot from a cannon. It also sent the vehicle skidding across three lanes before the driver managed to regain control—perhaps, Remy considered, he'd made the charge a little too strong. But when the smoke cleared, he knew he had done all right, for he saw only one figure huddled on the floor—one with the most beautiful streak of white running through her hair he'd ever seen. He pounded the steering wheel and laughed uproariously as he saw her slowly pick herself up and look back at him. He knew that look of hers all too well—she thought she was dealing with a lunatic.

He pushed the convertible to its limits, bringing the edge of its hood as close to the blown-out rear of the transport as possible. "Rogue! You have to jump!"

She pulled off her mask and stared at him in disbelief. "Are you *crazy?*" she shouted back, and gestured to her chains. "I can't do *anything* with these on!"

The wail of sirens in the near distance caught his attention. Looking to the right, he saw the familiar flash of red and blue lights just above the top of the highway's concrete sound barrier. Glancing ahead, he realized that they were coming to an on-ramp; in a few moments, the road would be filled with police and armed forces vehicles.

"*Chere*, you gotta jump!" he demanded. *"NOW!"*

She glanced at the approaching lights, and he could tell she knew she had to do it, no matter how insane a stunt it might be. She looked skyward and muttered something—a prayer, probably, if he knew Rogue—and then she leapt from the transport.

He caught her with one hand as she bounced off the hood, then hauled her in. Once she was settled in the passenger seat, he hit the brakes, swung the car around, and tromped the accelerator. The sportscar bounced over the lane divider, then roared across the five east-bound lanes, away from Manhattan. In its wake were left one of the largest traffic jams in the city's history—and a pursuit force now unable to catch up with the escaping felons.

Maneuvering the convertible through the streets of Queens a short time later, Remy grinned broadly at Rogue. "Now, *dat's* what I call a jailbreak, eh, *chere*?"

She nodded noncommittally. "I s'pose."

His smile faded as he took a closer look at her. She looked as though she'd been through all the tortures of hell, and was still suffering their aftereffects. When they stopped at a red light, he reached out to place a consoling hand on her arm. She pulled away from him so quickly, it took him by surprise.

"Hey, now, *chere*," he said soothingly. "No need t'get all jumpy. Gambit didn't mean no harm."

"I . . . I just don't like t'be touched," she said hoarsely.

He smiled warmly, and nodded. "I know, *fille*. Sorry."

The light changed, and he guided the car down another street.

"Better ditch dis thing, 'fore we wind up gettin' into any more trouble," he said. "By now, de police've pro'bly got a good description of it from 'bout half de drivers in de state." He pulled into a darkened alley between two factories, then hopped out, and motioned for her to do the same.

"Ain't y'all forgettin' somethin'?" she asked, her voice a bit stronger, and held up her chains.

"Oh, right." He scratched his chin for a moment, thinking of a solution, then: "Can ya open de glove compartment? Might be sometin' in dere I can use t'open de locks."

Rogue popped open the small hatch and rooted around for a few seconds. She tossed the contents on the driver's seat. There wasn't much.

Remy picked up a slip of paper and opened it—a statement of ownership. He whistled when he saw the signature at the bottom. "Commander Carter's gonna be mighty angry when she hears 'bout dis . . ." He shook his head sadly. "An' it'd just rolled outta de factory, too."

He tossed the paper aside, then retrieved a small packet of thin, curved metal rods from the collection of items on the seat. "Bobby pins?" he asked. "T'ought *filles* didn't use dese t'ings anymore."

"'Course, they do," Rogue countered. "Jus' like garter belts an' silk stockin's—" she sniffed derisively "—if yer inta those sorta things."

Remy's eyes sparkled, and he flashed a wolfish smile. "You ever meet a man who's not, *chere*?" He awkwardly cleared his throat when she glared at him, and held up the packet. "Uh . . . dese'll do de trick jus' fine."

The work went quickly, and Rogue was soon rubbing the circulation back into her wrists and ankles. Remy tossed the chains onto the back seat and pocketed the bobby pins. He walked to the alley entrance, looked up and down the street to make certain no one was around, then nodded to Rogue. She hurried to join him.

Remy shrugged out of his trenchcoat and held it out to her. "I t'ink it'll draw less attention den dat outfit o' yours, *chere*," he explained. She hesitated, then accepted the offering and draped it over her shoulders.

They walked slowly down the street, trying to act nonchalant, though neither of them could resist occasionally glancing around to make sure they weren't being followed.

"Some night, eh?" Remy commented, smiling.

Rogue nodded solemnly, but a hint of a smile was pulling at the corners of her mouth. "Never had one like it, that's fer sure," she said.

"Bet you never t'ought you'd see ol' Gambit again, eh, *chere*?"

He chuckled. "Tell ya de truth, *ol' Gambit* never t'ought he'd see ol' Gambit again." He gazed at her, and saw the confused expression that was furrowing her brow. "Bet you got a lotta questions on yer mind, huh?"

"Jus' one," Rogue said. "Who the hell *are* you . . . ?"

INTERLUDE VII

SO, the name Erik Magnus Lensherr means nothing to you."

Wolverine shrugged. "Didn't the first time ya said it, when we were runnin' through the woods. Still don't." He raised an eyebrow in an inquisitive fashion. "Is it s'posed ta? You some big-time Jewish leader I shoulda heard of that got locked up 'cause ya honked off the 'Emperor'?" He gestured at the few furnishings of the cabin in which they stood. "If ya ain't noticed already, I ain't exactly got a radio or one'a them television sets everybody else has t'keep up with world events."

"I gathered as much," Lensherr replied.

He gazed at their surroundings. It was an old, one-room log cabin that Wolverine used as his sanctuary, one he had crafted by hand, as he'd explained when they arrived. The furnishings were, indeed, sparse: some chairs—including a musty-smelling, weather-beaten easy chair that must have been thrown out with the camp's refuse—a long table, a bookcase with a number of military titles on its shelves, and a bed. The kitchen consisted of a pot-bellied stove, a sink, and some cabinets attached to a wall. Water came from a nearby spring. As for the lack of a bathroom, Logan's only comment was, "Y'know where a bear does his business . . . ?"

"So . . . you've been living here since the end of World War II?" Lenshberr asked.

Wolverine nodded. "Built it *before* the war, but—yeah. After D.C. got hit with the bomb, it was pretty clear the fightin' was over. An' then the squad I was with got butchered in Poland; we were tryin' t'liberate one'a the big camps there."

"Auschwitz," Lensherr said hollowly.

"That's the one. 'Cause o' my healin' factor, I was the only one who survived, an' then I was stuck behind enemy lines. Hadda take the long way 'round t'get back t'Canada—through Russia, 'cross the Bering Strait into Alaska, then through the Yukon."

"I imagine it took you some time to complete the journey."

" 'Bout a year or so. Spent most of 'em dodging patrols when Hitler an' his bullyboys started expandin' the Reich's borders, even in Siberia. They were everywhere—like cockroaches." He grunted in frustration. "I finally make it back t'home sweet home, and y'know what happens 'bout ten years later?"

"They started building the camp."

"Practically right at my flamin' front door!" He sneered. "Turned my stomach when I saw the first bunch'a prisoners bein' brought in. I'd seen what those Nazi thugs were capable o' doin' . . ." His voice went flat, the heat slowly dying in his eyes. "But what could *I* do 'bout it? Didn't have no troops t'back me up, no weapons—" he held up his hands "—other than these pitchforks I'm carryin' 'round from the 'Super Soldier' experiments back in '43. I'da only wound up gettin' everybody in there killed."

"So you didn't even try to free them."

Wolverine shook his head. "Nope. Don't even get too close t'the place 'less there's somethin' big goin' on—like some crazy fool blowin' up part o' the burial grounds."

"So, then, there is no truth to the rumors that you—"

"What, dig up an' eat the prisoners after they're buried? Hell, no! I'm a hunter, bub, not a flamin' cannibal. I want meat, I can always bring down a buck or two for venison." A sly smile lit his features. "But I've heard the stories—all that talk 'bout 'the

Wendigo.' 'Long as it keeps those creeps from venturin' too far into these woods, I can be any boogeyman they want me t'be."

Lensherr raised an eyebrow. "I thought you didn't get too close to the camp anymore."

Wolverine grunted. " 'Sides, I think those poor devils back there go through *enough* sufferin' while they're livin'—no reason to go desecratin' their graves once they've finally escaped that hellhole."

Lensherr started. "You consider cold-blooded murder a form of 'escape'?"

"I consider *anything* that puts an end t'the kind o' inhuman treatment those prisoners get at the hands of those Nazi buzzards an 'escape.' Climbin' over the fences or bein' cut down by a firing squad—if it means yer sufferin's at an end, it's all'a same t'me."

"So, if you are so concerned about the mistreatment of the prisoners, why have you done nothing to stop it?"

Wolverine shook his head. "I done my share o' fightin', a long time ago, bub. Didn't do no good back then, wouldn't do no good now."

Lensherr sneered. "You disgust me, Wolverine. The man *I* knew would have waded into that camp without hesitation. *He* wouldn't have allowed any of those humans to endure such tortures."

"Yeah? Then mebbe ya oughtta track down yer ol' pal, an' get *him* t'help ya out." Wolverine's eyes narrowed as he stared hard at his guest. " 'Humans,' huh? What's that make you—a mutant?" His lips curled back in a feral snarl. "I *knew* there was somethin' different about you; just couldn't figure out what it was."

Lensherr stood tall, looking down his nose at his host. "You act as though being a member of *Homo superior* is something to be ashamed of."

" *'Homo su'*—is *that* what you people go callin' yerselves these days?" He snorted. "Well, it don't matter what kinda fancy names you go throwin' around t'make yerself feel better, bub—yer still bottom o' the food chain in *this* world."

"Yes. My point exactly," Lensherr replied. " 'This world' shouldn't exist at all. It's a fabrication of the Red Skull's. An actualization of his mad desire to create a Thousand-Year Reich."

"So you were sayin' on the way here." Wolverine grunted. "Feels pretty flamin' real enough t'me."

"Because you were made a part of it, Logan, as was I. As were your teammates when the Skull took power."

"An' what 'teammates' would those be? 'Case y'hadn't noticed, there ain't too many clubhouses in these woods."

"The . . . X-Men," Lensherr explained, although he found it somewhat distasteful to utter the name.

" 'X-Men.' " Wolverine paused, then shook his head. "Nope. Never heard o' 'em. They friends o' yers?"

He *just* managed to stop his upper lip from curling. "Not . . . quite. But they *are* friends of *yours.*"

"On this other Earth, right?" Wolverine replied. "This 'real' world you keep mentionin'. Which is how ya know my real name."

"Exactly." Lensherr mentally sighed. It seemed that, no matter which version of Earth he might be on, one feral mutant was as dense as the other.

"An' what're *we* in the 'real' world?" Wolverine asked, eyeing him warily. "We buddies, too?"

Lensherr paused. "Let us say we possess enough . . . dissimilar beliefs for our relationship to transcend the limitations of friendship."

"Mortal enemies, huh?" A throaty chuckle issued from Wolverine's throat, and he flopped down into the easy chair. A cloud of dust rose from the faded leather as he settled in. "Figgered as much. Yer too highbrowed fer us t'ever get along." A sinister smile came to his lips. "I ever try t'kill ya?"

Lensherr frowned. "I've lost count of the attempts you've made on my life," he said dryly. "But, then, you could probably say the same about me."

"Anytime y'wanna get froggy, bub, just say, 'Jump,' " Wolverine said coolly, yet he made no move to get out of the chair.

"What I *want,* Logan," Lensherr replied, "is your aid, as distasteful a notion as that may be."

Wolverine shook his head. "Already gave ya my answer, bub. I'm outta the hero business. 'Case ya forgot, we lost the war."

"No!" Lensherr roared. "You imbecile, don't you understand? There *was* no war where the Nazis were the victors! There are no death camps in Canada, no fleets of starships sweeping across the cosmos, no mutant ghettos! It's all a lie, a dreamscape made real by the accursed Skull and that damnable wish box!" His eyes suddenly glowed with a golden light. Electricity crackled around his body, painting the cabin in harsh blues and whites. "You *will* aid me in stopping him, Wolverine . . . even if I must force you to do so."

"Is that a fact?" Wolverine leapt to his feet, claws extended. He tensed, preparing to attack. "Don't be shy, bub. Just say the w—"

"Sit down," Magneto ordered.

He raised a hand, and with a simple gesture, Wolverine was slammed back into his chair, his claws gouging deep grooves in the floorboards. The feral mutant turned and twisted, but he could no more raise his hands than he could stand.

Beads of sweat broke out on Lensherr's forehead. It was too soon to be trying this, he knew—his body hadn't had time to heal, to throw off the effects of the neural inhibitor. But he had neither the time nor the patience for pointless conversations—not when he was in need of allies in his planned war against the Red Skull. Even if such allies included one of his deadliest enemies among their number. For now, he had to concentrate on the matter at hand, and ignore the dull aches and blinding stabs of pains that threatened to rob him of consciousness. There would be time later for rest—when the Skull lay dead at his feet, and the Cosmic Cube was once more in the hands of Magneto . . .

"What're you doin'?" Wolverine demanded.

"Your bones . . . are coated with a metal called . . . adamantium, are they not?" Lensherr answered as he labored for breath. "With the powers I possess . . . all metals are . . . mine to command. So, if

I wish that you . . . remain seated, unable to move, then you . . . have no choice but to . . . obey."

"An' *then* what? Kill me?" Wolverine snarled. "Gonna be hard t'get me t'help ya if I'm *dead,* ain't it?"

"I have no desire to . . . kill you, Logan—at least not at . . . the moment." Lensherr sat on the edge of the table, and wiped away the perspiration with the back of his hand. It was easier to catch his breath if he was off his feet. "You see, in addition to my magnetically-based talents, I possess a certain level of psychic power. It's what keeps the telepathic members of your team—Phoenix, Psylocke, your mentor, Charles Xavier—from invading my mind."

"Well, good fer you, whitey," Wolverine said with a snarl. "Must make fer one helluva party trick."

"What I plan to do," Lensherr continued, ignoring the comment, "is attempt to use it to reverse the Skull's conditioning, and restore you to the bothersome little savage I've come to know and loathe over the years." He smiled coldly. "Although, I have to tell you, distinguishing the differences between the two of you once the process is completed might be impossible."

"The only difference, bub," Wolverine replied, "will be which one'a us gets the pleasure o' killin' you."

Lensherr sighed dramatically. "My point exactly. No difference at all." He stepped forward, and placed his hand on the sides of Wolverine's head, spreading his fingers wide to encompass the top of the X-Man's scalp. The mutant overlord took a few deep breaths, then closed his eyes to concentrate. "I feel I must warn you, Logan—this may hurt. Quite a bit. Are you ready?"

"Get stuffed," Wolverine growled.

"Excellent." Lensherr paused, then: "We begin."

And with that, he sent a psychic probe from his mind into Logan's, looking for the source of the Cube-created reprogramming.

The anguished howl that was torn from Wolverine's throat could be heard for miles around.

* * *

Hours later, Lensherr stumbled back, barely able to make it to one of the other chairs before his trembling legs collapsed under him. He'd done all he could with the resources he could draw upon—the rest was out of his hands.

He gazed across the table at Wolverine. The feral mutant had lapsed into unconsciousness during the process, which was a blessing unto itself—it had finally put an end to the excessive roaring and screaming that had threatened to deafen Lensherr as he forced his way deep into Logan's mind.

Accomplishing what he'd set out to do turned out to be a greater task than he'd ever imagined. There were numerous twists and turns on the journey through the psychic plane, but he couldn't imagine there being as many divergent paths in the average mind as there were in Wolverine's. There were so many conflicting memories, in fact, that not even Logan seemed to be aware of who he was anymore. He'd twice come close to trapping himself in the X-Man's subconscious; it was only by carefully retracing his steps that he'd managed to find a path back out.

Despite his philosophical differences with his former friend, Charles Xavier, Lensherr couldn't help but feel a grudging respect for the man's mental prowess—he made this sort of work look so blasted simple! Still, the mutant overlord had always considered himself Xavier's superior, so whatever the gifted "Professor X" might be able to do, Magneto could do even better.

Sometimes, though, it just took a little longer to get it right . . .

Eventually, though, he reached the core of Wolverine—or what he thought might be the core of his being—and did his best to draw it out behind him as he withdrew from the X-Man's mind. But had he succeeded in his mission, he wondered—or just reinforced the Cube's influence? With Logan unconscious, there was no way to tell; he would just have to wait to see what developed.

And with that thought, Lensherr drifted into a dreamless sleep.

* * *

When he awoke, it was to find Wolverine standing in front of him, their faces inches apart.

"Rise an' shine, sleepyhead," Wolverine growled.

Lensherr opened his mouth to reply, then became aware of a pressing weight just under his jawline. He glanced down to find Wolverine's fist nestled there. A sense of familiarity struck the mutant overlord, and he turned his eyes from side to side—sure enough, his face was framed by two of Wolverine's adamantium claws. The third spike—the middle spike—was still sheathed, but all it would take was a mental command from Wolverine, and the remaining bio-weapon would lance out, to slice through Lensherr's skull—and into his brain.

"So," he said calmly, "have you decided which version of you is the one who gets the pleasure of killing me?"

"The only one that *matters,* ya turd," Wolverine said with a sinister smile, before his expression hardened into a teeth-baring snarl. "Now, what'd ya do with the rest'a the X-Men? An' ya better hope I like the answer, bub, or . . ." He pushed upward with his fist, to remind Lensherr of the third claw.

Lensherr stifled a yawn. "Under different circumstances, Logan, I might say, 'Welcome back,' " he commented dryly. "But since you have never been a welcome addition to my life, I'm certain you'll understand if I don't consider this reunion nothing more than a necessary e—"

"WHERE ARE THE X-MEN?" Wolverine roared.

Lensherr stared silently at his longtime enemy—at the wild look in his eyes, the flecks of spittle on his chin as he breathed noisily through gritted teeth—and softly cleared his throat. "I am more than willing to tell you, Wolverine, but you may have some trouble believing it—or the offer I am going to make. . . ."

14

"I *DON'T* believe this!"

Lady Viper's roar of outrage couldn't be heard beyond the confines of her soundproofed office, but those who witnessed her display of anger couldn't help but think of a predator that had been denied its prey.

"*What do you mean she escaped?*" she shrieked into the cell phone. She paused, listening to whoever was on the other end of the conversation—possibly the driver of the armored transport carrying Rogue, from what Jean could surmise. "An accomplice? A *mutant?* And none of you imbeciles thought to call for a Sentinel?" She stomped back and forth across the office, her free hand waving dramatically to emphasize her words. "Understand this, you slow-witted worm: You will find those two freaks, and any others who may have been involved with the escape, *tonight,* or there won't be enough of you left for your family to identify once I'm through with you!"

She snapped the phone shut; then, in frustration, threw it against the wall. Plastic shards and bits of microcircuitry rained down on the carpeting.

"Go through a lot of those?" Jean asked sarcastically. She

suddenly winced, and shot a heated glance at Xavier—the sharp pain in her head was his telepathic way of telling her to shut up.

Viper stalked up to her, and leaned in close. "Joke all you want, Frau Sommers. It's true that one of your friends may have escaped—for the time being—but she was a minor cog in the wheel, so to speak. But we still have your husband. He, at least, is being escorted by a Sentinel—I wasn't going to take any chances with the ringleader of this foolish conspiracy."

"Why do you keep calling it a 'conspiracy'?" Jean asked. "Whatever gave you that impression?"

"What would you call it, Frau Sommers?" Viper shot back. "Both you and your husband are mutants, yet you withheld that information from his superiors and the Ministry of Health. You fraternize with others of your kind, using codenames to conceal your identities." Her eyes narrowed. "Isn't that true . . . 'Phoenix'? And why hide your identities? So you can secretly plot the destruction of the Empire!"

"It's nothing like that," Jean said testily. "There's more at stake than you could ever imagine, Viper-not that you'd ever believe me. I could care less about the Red Skull and his power fantasi—"

The back of a latex-sheathed hand swept out, catching Jean across the right cheek. The blow snapped her head to the side, bouncing it off the back of the wheelchair seat. With one side of her face almost as brilliant a fiery shade as her hair, and the other aching dully, she slowly turned back to glare at her captor.

"I owe you for that," she said with a sneer.

Viper laughed. "And you accuse the Emperor of having power fantasies?" She made a grand gesture of pulling on the back of her glove to tighten its fit on her fingers. "Perhaps you should take a moment to reexamine your current position, 'Phoenix,' and then tell me who is less likely to achieve their goals: a lord of the universe, who can destroy worlds with a single command . . . or a smart-mouthed housefrau seeking retribution for a well-deserved slap in the face?" She leaned in close again. "One, I remind you, who is strapped to a wheelchair, and on the verge of a severe beating if she continues to cross me?"

"It won't always be this way, Viper," Jean said.

"Ah. Should I be expecting more of your friends to come and free you, then? But which will they be—freaks like yourself . . . or normal citizens of the Reich?" Her emerald lips pulled back in a predatory grin. "Don't think for a moment that we haven't started looking into the backgrounds of both you and the Major with a fine-toothed comb, Frau Sommers. A movement like this couldn't have gotten as far as it has without the aid of people outside your community . . . 'flatscans'—isn't that the term?" She sneered. "The one you mutants use to describe those of us not 'gifted' with abilities like yours?"

"It's not one I've ever used," Jean replied.

"At least not in polite company, I'd imagine," Viper said. "A slip of the tongue in front of the wrong people would've made us aware of your organization all that sooner. And then we might have been spared the embarrassment your husband has now brought down on all of us." She frowned. "Deceiving the Ministry of Health, allowing an abomination like him to rise to the level he has in the spacefleet—clearly, Major Sommers has some . . . influential friends in high places. But they, too, will be punished for their part in this revolution. The Empire has no use for race traitors." She folded her arms across her chest. "Soon, we'll have all the players in this little drama gathered together. And we have the professor to thank for that." She turned to glare at Xavier. "Although he failed to mention how well-informed your network might be, if its members could pull off a rescue within minutes of this 'Rogue's' arrest. I hadn't even issued the order to detain her and Major Sommers until just before the *Nuremberg* touched down."

"Because I detected no such information in her mind, Commander," Xavier replied. His eyes narrowed. "Are you accusing me now of withholding information? Should I consider myself under suspicion, simply because of my mutant status?"

There was something in his eyes, in the tone of his voice that made Viper pause. Perhaps, even without psychic abilities, she could sense the sharp increase of mental activity in Xavier, like the buildup of static electricity in the air before the onset of a major storm—Jean could certainly feel it. Or maybe she realized that she'd stepped across an invisible line of sorts by questioning his loyalty. Whatever it was, it caused the dark-haired security commander to avert her gaze, and take a step back from the professor.

"No, that's not what I meant," she said slowly, even cautiously. "I was merely suggesting that—"

"I should have conducted a more thorough search of Frau Sommers' subconscious?" Xavier asked. It was clear by Viper's expression that he'd plucked the thought from her mind. He smiled, but there was still a degree of anger evident in his eyes. "Fair enough, Commander. Perhaps my eagerness to contact Minister Zola about my discovery distracted me from completing my investigation." He cast a glance toward Jean. "I could rectify the situation, if you like . . ."

Jean ground her teeth together in agony as the psychic buildup began again. The pressure in her skull was overwhelming; black spots began dancing before her eyes.

Scott . . . she thought, just before darkness descended.

Jean, he thought, *I wish you were here beside me, right now. Then I could see the fear in your eyes as I wring your pretty little neck for betraying me . . .*

Sitting in the back of the second armored transport, Major Scott Sommers shifted uneasily on the metal bench to which he was chained. The manacles encircling his neck, wrists, and ankles were painfully tight—far tighter than they needed to be—but he refused to show any sign of discomfort to the three shocktroopers sitting across from him in the cramped rear compartment. The control studs of his visor had been disabled, preventing him from sliding open the ruby quartz lens and using the force beams contained behind his eyes. Right now, the worst he could do to his captors was fix each of them with a heated stare, and snarl.

Apparently, they didn't care for that.

"Eyes down, mutie!" ordered one of the soldiers.

"Why? Do I frighten you, private?" asked Sommers. "Afraid the monster might break free of his chains and come for you?" To emphasize his point, he rattled his restraints and lurched forward, as though attacking. He laughed as the younger man yelped and drew back.

"Calm yourself, Zumwald," said the man's superior. "He's not going anywhere. Without his raybeams, he's just another citizen." The woman—Hildebrandt, according to the nametag bolted to the breastplate of her armor—was in her fifties, with a perpetual scowl etched into her hard features. Her once-dark hair was shot through with veins of silver, and cut into a severe crewcut-the better for her helmet to fit, though right now it rested on the floor by her feet. She eyed Sommers, and flashed a wolfish smile. "Good thing your wife warned us about that visor of yours, eh?"

Sommers frowned. "She told you about that, too?"

Hildebrandt shrugged. "That's what I've heard. I understand she's been fully cooperating with the brass." She chuckled. "You know, Major, I'm not an expert, but it looks like the love has gone out of your marriage."

Sommers sneered and sat back, fuming. On further consideration, perhaps alerting the League of German Women about his wife's odd behavior hadn't been the wisest course of action to take; apparently, the talkative cow was spilling her guts to his superiors, telling them everything about him. No doubt she was hoping to cut some kind of deal that would lessen her sentence—it's what *he* would have done, were their positions reversed. Still, he was curious to know just what it was she had been doing that morning, and why. Perhaps they'd have a chance to talk about it—before he got his hands on her . . .

"Hard to believe it now," the remaining guard—Adler—commented. Like his commanding officer, he was a battle-hardened veteran whose years of service to the Reich could be seen in the creases and hard lines of his face.

"What's that?" Hildebrandt asked.

Adler nodded toward Sommers. "My kid looked up to this trash—can you believe that?"

"A lot of kids did," Zumwald interjected sullenly. He gazed at the major for a few seconds, then cast his eyes downward.

Adler shook his head, and sighed. "It's gonna break Horst's heart when I have to tell him his big hero's a monster."

"Oh, I doubt he'll be surprised," Sommers replied. He grinned slyly. "He *lives* with you, doesn't he?"

The butt of the plasma rifle the guard swung caught him in the stomach, driving the air from his lungs. Sommers pitched forward, gasping for breath, only to be brought up short by the manacle around his neck, and the short lead of the chain connecting it to the wall behind him. It almost cut off his air for good.

"If you know what's good for you, freak," warned Hildebrandt, "you'll keep your mouth shut for the rest of this trip. Nobody said you had to be in one piece when we deliver you to Lady Viper."

Gritting his teeth, Sommers drew in a ragged breath. Slowly, his breathing returned, and he eased back on the bench, staring daggers at his captors. "I am an officer of the Reich," he growled. "You will treat me with the respect afforded my rank, and—"

"And *nothing,* you piece of trash!" Adler shot back. "Didn't anyone tell you back at the spaceport, *Citizen* Sommers? You don't *have* a rank anymore. You think the Ministry of Defense would allow a *mutant* to call itself an officer, when everybody knows your kind isn't fit for command?"

"If you've heard of my exploits, Sergeant—as I'm sure you have," Sommers replied heatedly, "then you know I've proven that belief wrong on dozens of occasions. *No one* is better suited for such a position than I; the Emperor himself said as much when I was given command of the *Nuremberg.* And once he has been made aware of this travesty, he'll no doubt step forward in my defense." He smiled viciously. "And then I'll see to it that all three of you are transferred to the front lines on the next available cruiser."

Hildebrandt exchanged glances with her men, and all three burst into laughter.

"You actually think the *Emperor* is going to come to your aid?" she asked, wiping away tears. "Well, you're nothing if not confident, I'll give you that."

"Don't you get it, freak?" Adler explained. "You're an embarrassment to the Reich. If he's lucky, Emperor Schmidt won't even hear of this until long after you're put down—and by then, I'm sure, your name will have been erased from all combat records. It'll be like you never existed." He grinned. "Just another faceless mutant, dumped into a unmarked grave with all the others."

Sommers looked at each of the soldiers—at their cruel smiles, at the hardness of their gazes—and, slowly, Adler's words began to sink in. It was true, he realized. He was an embarrassment to the Reich—one who couldn't be allowed to live. Deep down, he knew he couldn't be surprised by this revelation; knew that, one day, his secret would be revealed. He'd always thought it would be one of the physicians or officers he routinely paid off who might betray him—those few who were aware of his true nature. He'd been threatened by one or two of them in the past, when they felt his . . . contributions weren't enough, but he'd settled with each of them—he'd had no choice.

But his *wife?* Who would think *she'd* turn on him so quickly? Not for the first time in recent months, he wondered what he had ever seen in her in the first place-beyond her obvious physical attributes, that is. Until recently, she'd always seemed so weak, so dependent on him, so . . . *plain* in the way she presented herself, in the way she lived. But now, suddenly, she'd developed a backbone, started skulking around for some reason or other in his absence-had even talked back to him! Where had *this* Jean Grey been hiding all this time? And if she had been following some foolish notion that she should take charge of her life *now,* why start by reporting him to the Ministry, when doing so would only cause *her* trouble as well?

Frowning deeply, Citizen Scott Sommers sat back and focused

his thoughts, trying to figure out exactly when everything in his life had gone so completely wrong. . . .

“Something is wrong,” Xavier said.

Viper turned from the window through which she had been gazing at the Manhattan skyline. “Explain.”

Maneuvering the controls of his wheelchair, Xavier rolled back from the semi-conscious Jean Grey and approached the green-tressed commander. Behind him, Jean moaned softly as he withdrew from her mind; her head lolled onto her chest.

“In conducting a deeper investigation, I'm come across some extraordinary findings,” the professor replied. He gestured at their captive. “This woman possesses more than one ego state!”

“You mean she suffers from a split personality?” Viper frowned. “That wasn't in her medical files, either.”

Xavier shook his head. “No, Commander—it's more complicated than that.” He watched the look of confusion that momentarily contorted her features, then held up a hand before she could voice her next question. “In general, a person suffering from a Dissociative Identity Disorder has undergone a series of traumatic experiences, usually during childhood, usually through repeated physical or sexual assaults, that result in the creation of a cerebral defensive mechanism that allows them to deal with the trauma. Originally, that form of escape was thought to create different ‘personalities’ that the person would adopt in times of crisis—identities separate from the core individual, with their own ways of thinking and acting and remembering. However, the Reich's psychiatric division has come to a better understanding of the condition over the years; they now know that these ‘personality states’ are simply manifestations of the same person, not separate states of consciousness.”

“So, what makes Sommers different?” Viper asked.

“Unlike ‘normal’ DID sufferers,” Xavier continued, “Frau Sommers—from what I have seen in the course of my psychic examination—has never experienced any such trauma, and, therefore, has no reason to create alternates of herself. And yet, they exist; I have made contact with them, examined their minds, as well. These other personalities are so completely separate and distinct from her own, in fact, that I would go so far as to consider them more than just submerged states of consciousness—they are living entities. Other versions of herself, to be precise."

Viper's eyes narrowed, and she stared silently at him. Xavier could hear more than the figurative wheels turning in her head as she considered all he had just said—he was reading her thoughts. Still, he concluded, it would be better if he allowed her the opportunity to voice those thoughts, if only to give her some sense of satisfaction. A way of justifying her job, as it were.

"You're saying there are two other versions of herself living in her head?" she finally said.

Xavier forced himself to flash what he considered a patient smile. "In a manner of speaking."

Viper huffed. "Preposterous."

The professor frowned, although he shouldn't have been surprised by her reaction. The military mind was often too rigid to accept unusual theories, and Viper's was no better—as he'd seen when he first moved through her thoughts. With an inward sigh, he continued. "There's more."

An eyebrow arched. Emerald lips pulled back in a condescending sneer. "Don't tell me—she's from outer space. A Kree spy, perhaps, genetically altered to live among us?"

Xavier politely chuckled, then dropped the false smile. "No, Commander, but you are not too far off the mark." He turned to glance at Jean. "Frau Sommers—or at least the woman we believe to be Frau Sommers—does, indeed, come from another world." He paused, for dramatic effect, and turned back to Viper. "Another Earth."

She scowled. "Another Earth," she said flatly. "Well, that explains everything, then."

"I'm quite serious, Commander," Xavier replied evenly. "And were you capable of peering into the deepest recesses of her mind, as I am, you would know that everything I have said is true. There are three versions of the same woman, all living in the same body, as unbelievable as that might sound, and the one currently controlling it is not from our world. As I mentioned, I have been in contact with the other entities currently occupying her subconscious. One of them is the wife of Reichsmajor Sommers, her personality submerged so another's—this 'Jean Grey'—could make use of her body. The other believes she is an acolyte of someone named 'Magneto.'" He paused. "Magneto . . ." His voice suddenly trailed off, and he fell silent.

Why, he wondered, did that name sound so . . . familiar to him? So important? Like hearing of an old friend, one not seen in a long time, but still remembered with fondness, or . . . regret? Slowly, he turned back to gaze at Frau Sommers. She had insisted during the interrogations that they knew one another, as well; he had even seen memories of a man who looked like him in her mind. But that Charles Xavier was a far different man—one of determination, of strength. One dedicated to a dream of peaceful coexistence between mutantkind and humanity. The leader of a group of men and women as dedicated to him as they were to his dream, who were willing to sacrifice their very lives in order to make it a reality-a group called the "X-Men." A man who commanded respect, even from his enemies.

He didn't exist on this world, though. The man who lived here might possess his features, but not his spirit, and fanciful dreams of universal peace had no place in the Thousand-Year Reich. They were as dead as the X-Men soon would be—by providing Viper and her people with the information from Jean Sommers'—Jean Grey's—mind, the professor could see no other outcome.

Had he *always* been so quick to condemn his own people? he wondered. So willing to betray other mutants to the Nazis in order to preserve his existence? Was his life really that important?

It was to *him,* he thought somberly. And yes, he *had* always been quick to point a finger, to notify his keepers of any thoughts of revolution he detected when he'd lived in the mutant interment camps. The survival instinct had been strong in him, then, and he did what he had to do in order to go on living. At least that's what he often told himself in the decades that followed—it made the guilt he constantly lived with a somewhat lighter burden, if only for a short time.

"Magneto?" Viper asked, shaking him from his reverie. "Sounds like another of their codenamed agents." She shrugged. "Well, he can join the other conspirators she's told us about when we start rounding them all up."

Xavier nodded. "Now, concerning her true identity, Commander . . ."

Viper sliced a hand through the air to cut short his next comment. "Don't bother me with wild tales of parallel worlds and multiple personalities, Professor—I stopped reading scientifiction by the time I reached puberty."

"Still, Commander, I feel this matter should be pursued," Xavier insisted. "From what I have just seen in this woman's thoughts, the Emperor himself may need to be informed."

Viper laughed sharply. "You want me to approach the *Emperor* with this nonsense?" She sneered at him. "Have you any idea of how difficult it is for a woman to rise to a position such as mine in this society, Xavier? Do you think I'm going to throw away everything I've fought to achieve by asking for an audience with the Emperor, just so I can spin fairy tales for him about alternate realities and a woman with three brains?"

"Not three brains, Commander," Xavier replied. "Three brain *patterns*. And I realize how difficult all this is to believe, but keep in mind that space travel and contact with alien races were considered just as fanciful, and yet we have come to accept them as part of everyday life. And the notion is not as strange as you make it sound—Minister Zola once told me of a series of experiments conducted by the Reich's top scientists during the late 1970s to mid-1980s, the purpose being to create gateways to other dimensions. Another method of expanding the Empire's borders, I'd imagine."

"And did any of these 'gateways' actually lead somewhere?"

"Not to my knowledge. But," he added quickly, "that doesn't mean that all I have told you should be so casually dismissed." He smiled. "You know, Commander, it might be best if I just showed you everything I have learned from Fräulein Grey."

"Calling her by her other identity, now, are we?" Viper asked condescendingly.

Xavier nodded. "All it would involve is you allowing me to link our minds to hers, and—"

"Absolutely not," Viper interjected. She pointed to her head. "No one gets in here, least of all some mentalist—even if he *is* the Health Minister's favorite pet mutant."

Now it was Xavier's turn to scowl. He'd tried to be patient with this woman, tried to provide her with all the information he had acquired, but she refused to take it seriously. And now she was only making matters worse for herself by sniping at him like a child.

Well, he'd seen the real reason for the Grey woman's arrival on his world, came to understand the importance of the mission she and the other "X-Men" had set out on, came to realize what might happen should they fail to accomplish their task. Yes, it all sounded like some bizarre fantasy when one stepped back to take another look at it—there was no denying it—but it all felt too real, too *true,* to be the mere fabrications of a disturbed mind. The world, the Empire, was facing perhaps its greatest crisis, but nothing could be done to prevent it unless steps were taken to bring the matter to Emperor Schmidt's attention.

And so, having reached a decision, Xavier took the figurative first step: by switching off Viper's mind.

With a soft grunt, the latex-clad officer crumpled to the floor at Grey's feet—much to the surprise of Carol Danvers. She jumped from the couch, looking in shock from Viper to her employer.

"What did you do to her?" she whispered hoarsely, then glanced at the front door. "Are you trying to get us both killed?"

"Don't be so skittish, Fräulein Danvers, " Xavier replied. "This office is soundproofed. I assure you, no one in the hall outside has heard a thing since we came in here." He gestured toward Viper. "Now, then, let us see if I can get this to work . . ."

He fell silent, focusing his thoughts on the unconscious commander, slipping through the corridors of her mind until he found what he was looking for. Beads of sweat formed on the professor's bare scalp as he set about flipping mental switches, turning psychic dials. He felt a small surge of pride as he saw the woman's fingers twitch, felt her leg muscles tighten.

And then Viper suddenly lurched to her feet, her eyes snapping open. The pupils were dilated though—evidence that she was not the one in control of her body.

"What are you doing?" Danvers hissed. Apparently, she didn't believe him about the thickness of the office walls.

Viper turned to face her, but it was Xavier's words that came tumbling out through numbed lips. "It was painfully apparent to me that the Commander was never going to bring the information I gathered to the Emperor, and time is of the essence. Therefore, I will have to do so myself—*through* her."

A soft moan caught their attention, and all three turned to look at Jean Grey. Her head had tilted back, and her eyelids were beginning to flutter open.

"I can only maintain control over one of them," Xavier explained to Danvers through Viper. "In order to place myself inside the Commander, I have had to withdraw a majority of the psychic barriers I erected within Fräulein Grey's mind. She'll be fully conscious shortly."

"Not necessarily." Danvers went back to the couch to retrieve a large handbag that sat between the cushions. Placing it on Viper's desk, she rifled through the contents, coming up with a small vial and a syringe.

Xavier had Viper shake her head. "No sedatives, Danvers. I *want* Fräulein Grey awake—we have much to discuss." He/she paused, then gestured toward the needle. "But have it ready, just in case the conversation becomes . . . volatile."

As Danvers prepared the shot, Xavier directed Viper's body to the desk. It was difficult work—he'd forgotten how to walk, in all the years he'd been confined to a wheelchair—but he managed to keep her from tripping over her feet long enough to drop her into her chair. A quick examination of her mind told him the location of her main communications set; pressing a hidden stud to the right of her seat caused a viewscreen to rise from the center of the desk. He keyed in a specific transmissions code—one only to be used in cases of emergency—and hit the SEND button.

Moments later, a man in a security uniform appeared on the screen. "Yes?"

"This is Commander Viper, in New York." Her eyes, Xavier knew, were still wide and unseeing, but the low quality of the picture being broadcast should make it difficult to tell, except on close inspection. He hoped. "I need to speak with the Emperor—immediately. . . ."

15

She'd been dreaming of empires again.

Dreaming of lavish palaces and sculptured gardens, of legions of armies marching under her banner and immense monuments carved in her image, of enemies crushed and cities burned.

So it was a bitter disappointment for Sat-yr-nin when she suddenly realized that none of what she was seeing—the throne room, the ladies-in-waiting, the viral young guards anxious to comply with her every order, the heads of her enemies perched so decorously on their pikes—was real.

And that was when the agonizing pain in her head erupted.

With a groan, she slowly opened her eyes; thankfully, the room was just dark enough for the lighting to not blind her. She attempted to sit up, but the pain in her head only intensified, and she settled back. Gingerly, she placed her fingertips to her head, and sucked in a sharp breath when they came into contact with the huge welt on her temple.

She remembered, now. Remembered finding the passage behind the throne, which led to Roma's chamber, which led to an unexpected confrontation with the Guardian's hulking captain, Alecto. Knowing he was under von Doom's thrall, she hadn't thought twice about brushing past him as he warned her that no one was allowed in the chamber—she was the doctor's ally, after all. But then, he'd had the temerity to place his hands on her—*Her!* The Mastrex of the Empire of True Briton!—like the oafish commoner he was, and she'd let her temper get the best of her. Slapping him across the face hadn't done much good for breaking his vise-like grip on her shoulder, but making a grab for his sword, so she could separate his head from his shoulders, had certainly gotten his attention. He let go of her, all right, but only so he could deliver a swift blow to her head, one made even more staggering by the weight of the big metal gauntlets he wore. The floor had rushed up to meet her, and . . .

Sat-yr-nin gazed at her surroundings, and was surprised to find she was lying on Roma's bed. Placing her here wasn't something she would have expected from a brute who had come close to crushing her skull, but she was at a loss to otherwise explain her position. Maybe it was just his addlepated way of apologizing for the assault. Whatever the reason, she'd still see his head on a pike—no one laid hands upon the Mastrex and walked away unpunished.

That, however, would have to wait. Right now, she still wanted to talk to von Doom about this reality-changing weapon he'd created.

Moving slowly, so as not to increase the strength of her headache, she rolled over to the edge of the bed and swung her feet onto the floor. Then, hesitantly, she raised herself up into a sitting position, keeping her head down and her hands placed on either side of it. Gritting her teeth, she raised her head, and was startled to discover that the bedchamber looked as though a battle had been fought in it. Smashed furniture, a broken woodcut and snapped candles—whoever forced their way in had obviously encountered the mind-controlled warrior, but what had been the outcome?

As she rose from the bed, her foot brushed against hard metal. She looked down, to find Alecto lying in a heap, a thin whisper of smoke curling upward from the nape of his neck. Apparently, not only had the mysterious intruder overpowered the guard, but they had also found a way to short out the device that made him obedient to von Doom.

Sat-yr-nin glanced around. There was no other body to be seen, so the intruder had moved on—more than likely through the open door on the other side of the room: her original destination, before the altercation. When all of this might have happened she couldn't say; to begin with, she had no idea how long she'd been unconscious. But she did, however, have a notion as to who might be responsible for the damaged room, and the sleeping guard.

"The X-Men," she hissed. "Braddock, and her insipid winged lover."

She started toward the door, then stopped, and walked back to Alecto. A quick search of his body revealed no weapons, and his sword had been taken. A pity, really, she thought—she'd been hoping to use it on him before she left. She settled for delivering a brutal kick to his face with the toe of her boot, and knocking out one of his front teeth.

Sweeping her hair back from her face—and then wincing as her hand brushed against the lump on her head—the Mastrex picked her way across the room, and stepped into the pocket dimension beyond the doorway.

"It is time," von Doom stated.

He made a final calibration to the inner workings of the machine before him, then stepped back to admire his creation. It had taken time to acquire the materials, but by sending the physician, Stanton, and the throne room guards back to the citadel on several trips, the dictator had been able to get everything he needed, even the more unusual selections on his list. As Stanton had explained, with as many levels as the citadel possessed, and as many different kinds of machinery there were to be found on them, from hundreds of worlds and dimensions, there was no shortage of equipment storage bays, or replacement parts. Von

Doom had been satisfied with the physician's responses since their last discussion; now, the man was almost *too* forthcoming with information.

The doctor was standing beside him right now, the only member of von Doom's entourage still in attendance. Being all too familiar with the ways of the so-called "super hero" community, he hadn't really expected his warrior drones to prove much of a challenge for the two X-Men pursuing him. But they would serve their purpose well enough—delaying the duo long enough to provide him time to finish his work was all he required.

And now it was done.

Softly, Stanton cleared his throat. "Um . . . Lord Doom . . . I don't wish to sound ignorant, but . . . time for what?"

"For the next stage of my plan, lackey," von Doom growled. "The stage in which Doom ascends to his rightful place . . . as a god."

"Oh," Stanton muttered, and smiled nervously. "*That* stage."

"Bring the woman over," von Doom ordered.

As Stanton walked away to retrieve the Guardian, the dictator turned back to regard his machine. It stood five feet tall, in a columnar shape with eight control sections cluttered with switches, dials, and buttons around a central core. Attached to the center by lengths of cable and fiber optics were two sets of metal handgrips, each placed on opposite sides of the construct. Von Doom began flipping switches and punching buttons, and the machine loudly hummed to life.

The squeak of hard rubber wheels caught his attention. He turned to see Stanton pushing the medical bed to which Roma was strapped. The physician brought it to a halt beside the console.

"Place the grips in her hands," von Doom ordered.

Stanton did as he was ordered, using clamps on the ends of the grips to secure them to her wrists so she couldn't just cast them aside if she awakened during the process. Completing the task, he stepped back and looked to his master.

Von Doom activated another set of controls, moving around

the console to set a sequence of dials, then toggled a quintet of switches. The humming sound given off by the machine grew louder, causing Stanton to place his hands over his ears.

"Exactly what are we—you—doing here, Lord Doom?" he asked. "Some of this equipment is familiar—parts from some of the medical equipment I gathered, and so on—but I've never seen them used quite this way."

The tyrant paused in his work. "Not that you could possibly grasp the genius that is Doom's, physician, but I will tell you nonetheless. A number of years past, in my homeland of Latveria, I once lured the alien known as the Silver Surfer to my castle with promises of friendship. The fool accepted my invitation, only to learn my true purpose: to take from him his cosmic powers, and use them to strike at the accursed Reed Richards and the other members of his insipid Fantastic Four." He raised a metal fist in the air. "And I succeeded! As none before me had ever done!" He frowned, and the fist slowly dropped to his side. "But the victory was a hollow one—for while I had absorbed the skyrider's strengths by using a device only Doom could create, I had also absorbed his weaknesses." He paused, grinding his teeth as he recalled the events that followed. "It was an energy barrier that reversed the process—one invisible to any form of detection, even those created by Doom. It had been erected by the Surfer's previous master, Galactus, the world-devourer, as a means of imprisoning him on Earth. To deny him any further chance of traveling among the stars. But when I became the possessor of the Power Cosmic, the barrier worked against me, as well. Colliding with it drained my newly acquired strength, and returned it to the Surfer." His eyes narrowed. "Such an occurrence will never happen again."

"And now you're planning to do the same thing to the Guardian?" Stanton asked. "This machine is going to drain her powers?" He pursed his lips, as though stopping to choose the right words. "Is that . . . possible? I mean, she *is* a Supreme Guardian, and—"

"Silence!" the armored dictator barked. "*Everything* is possible, lackey, when Doom is involved." He gestured toward the console. "This assemblage of parts and circuitry is crude, but should work effectively enough for the task at hand." His hands played across two of the sections, setting a final combination of relays; then he grasped the handgrips on his side of the console. "Now, we begin."

He stabbed at one last button near him, and the hum reached a teeth-rattling pitch.

And then the process began. A bright, multihued light began playing around Roma, growing brighter with each moment. As it reached its peak, when the light became too unbearable to gaze at, it suddenly flowed from her hands, into the grips. The pulse continued onward, streaking through the connections leading to von Doom's machine, then into the console itself. Without pause, it flashed upward, through the connections on the other side of the machine—and into von Doom.

The incredible power surge coursing through him initially caused him to stagger back a few steps, but he remained standing. The light grew brighter around him, even as it dimmed around Roma.

"Soon, physician!" he bellowed triumphantly. *"Soon, Doom shall achieve his ultimate destiny—and then how the cosmos will tremble!"*

Dr. Henry Stanton was not having a good day.

It hadn't started out that way, of course. But once things started happening—particularly when his former patient tried to crush his larynx for withholding information about the citadel—it didn't take very long for it to turn sour.

As the physician watched the transfer of energy going no between von Doom and Roma, he couldn't help but wonder what had possessed him in the first place to ally himself with such a madman, or with that psychotic witch, Sat-yr-nin. Actually, when he thought about it, "ally" wasn't the proper term to describe his relationship with the two power-hungry villains—"slave" was probably more accurate. He retrieved what he was told to fetch, bowed and scraped before them so neither would think he was trying to act as their equal, and therefore feel the need to remind him of his "place"—probably via swift execution—and generally kept his mouth shut unless told to speak. Not exactly the position he'd hoped to be in when he'd agreed to aid in their plot against the Supreme Guardian.

He'd *hoped* to have been promoted to the position of Chief Physician by now, one currently occupied by someone Stanton considered to be an annoying little man—a Scotsman whose name no one could remember, with a know-it-all attitude when it came to making diagnoses. A grinning jackanapes who had been given the job by Roma, even though her father, Merlyn, had been considering Stanton as the man he wanted in charge of the medical wing. The fact that the caustic doctor and the female celestial didn't care much for one another probably had a lot to do with her decision—and his, in turn, to join von Doom's campaign.

His, however, had turned out to be an awfully stupid decision; those born of anger and jealousy usually were. He had gotten his revenge on her—so what? Watching the tortures to which she'd been subjected at von Doom's hand, trying to ignore the screams that seemed to fill the pocket dimension as yet another part, another version, of her self was torn away by the multiphasic crystal technology—it wasn't how he'd imagined things would turn out. He'd thought sealing her in a cryogenic chamber, as he had done with Roma's lieutenant, Saturnyne, would have been punishment enough—von Doom would still be able to rule the citadel without interference. But the tyrant seemed to take an almost sadistic pleasure in his efforts to break the Guardian's will. And now, rather than force her to tell him all the secrets of this palace at the center of time and space, he'd apparently decided to take a different, and far more inhumane, approach, by using his infernal machine to steal her powers—and her life.

There was nothing Stanton could do about it now, though. He'd already damned himself through his selfish actions; now, all he could do was pray his master would still have a use for lowly servants—once he became a god. . . .

"God, I'm really starting to hate this . . ." Warren muttered. "You'd think we would've found Doom a few seconds after we took care of his zombie squad—but no, we're back to wandering the great white nothing again."

A more accurate description of their situation Betsy couldn't imagine. Almost immediately after the last of the mind-controlled guards had collapsed on the ground, the two X-Men had hurried to catch up with the armored tyrant. She'd even left behind Alecto's sword, so its weight wouldn't slow her down—besides, her arms were still aching from swinging the heavy blade (something she should have taken into consideration before bringing it in the first place), and she was glad to be rid of it. But no matter how swiftly they moved in pursuit, von Doom was long gone from view.

"I think it has to do with Time and Space being relative," she commented.

"Lunch time doubly so," Warren replied.

She raised an eyebrow, and playfully jabbed him with her elbow. "Thank you, Douglas Adams. What I mean is, distances probably have no way of being measured here; time, as well. It only *looked* like von Doom walked away a few minutes before we banged up his thugs—at least to our eyes—but he actually could have been gone for more than an hour. *And* he could have traveled *miles* with just a few footsteps. It all has to do with perception."

"Riiight." Warren gave a sarcastic, lopsided smile. "And everything you've just said makes complete sense to you."

"About as much sense as anything else around here," she replied.

He shrugged. "Well, *you're* the expert on this place."

She nodded. "As much as one *can* be, I suppose. And *as* the expert, I can think of only one solution for locating him."

Warren frowned. "Another cruise through the shadow realm?"

She smiled and patted his arm consolingly. "Well, it beats walking, luv. I'll just concentrate on von Doom this time, rather than Roma. That should keep us from accidentally teleporting back to that lashed-up cryogenic facility of his."

He nodded his head forlornly. "I just wish there was some kind of mass-transportation system in this pl–"

And that was when the tremor hit.

Actually, it wasn't so much a tremor, as a wave of energy that surged across the wasteland, causing the ground to twist and sway, and knocking the feet out from under the couple.

Betsy had barely enough time to realize she was going to be in some degree of pain when she woke up–before the floor smacked her in the face.

Sat-yr-nin had been stomping across the endless, featureless tundra–still fuming, still groaning from the bump on her head–when the wave slammed into her.

It swept her along in its wake, depositing her some distance from where she had been, although just how far was impossible to tell, given the limitless *sameness* of this place she'd crossed into. Regardless of distance, or even what might have been the cause of the energy wave, however, she was certain of one thing: She was in an even fouler mood than the one she'd been in when she awoke in Roma's chamber.

"Some further meddling on the part of that tin-plated fool, no doubt," she said to herself. "I just hope he hasn't gotten himself killed–although it would be just *like* the selfish brute to deny me the pleasure of killing him myself."

Picking herself up off the ground, she smoothed out the most noticeable wrinkles on her flowing white gown, patted loose strands of white hair back into place on her coiffure, and adjusted the sheath of the dagger strapped to her right thigh, close to the slit in her skirt. She wanted to look her best for von Doom . . . just before she cut out his eyes.

The wave continued beyond the aching Mastrex, across the Starlight Citadel and down through its many levels. Wherever it traveled, it left chaos in its wake. Delicate machinery exploded. Artificial gravity momentarily cut off, causing residents to go rocketing down hallways, or bouncing off the ceilings. Time momentarily froze, then resumed at twice normal speed. Accidents were widespread, destruction almost as much.

And at the bottom-most level of the structure, within a special room located there, a monitoring system connected to a cryogenic chamber shorted out, activating an emergency medical program. A pump switched on, draining the tube of suspension fluid; once the process was completed, the chamber door swung open. At last released from confinement, its sole occupant pitched forward, onto the floor.

She lay still for several seconds, then began to cough—loudly, violently. Spasms shook her body as she raised herself onto her elbows and knees. And then a veritable ocean of blue suspension fluid came flooding from her nose and mouth.

Eventually, the vomiting ended, and she collapsed onto her back, rubbing her sore throat. She stared at the ceiling for what seemed to her like hours, slowly feeling her frozen body warming, slowly regaining the ability to think straight. Images flashed through her mind: von Doom in her apartment; the attack by Dr. Stanton as he drugged her, then stuffed her inside the cryo chamber. But most of all there was the memory of the madwoman who wore her features, her clothes; who'd taken her place as the Supreme Guardian's trusted lieutenant.

Who was going to *die* as soon as she got her hands on the little witch.

Her mind filled with rage, her eyes practically flashing fire, Opal Luna Saturnyne, the true Omniversal Majestrix, staggered to her feet and lurched out of the makeshift prison, in search of revenge.

"Why do I get the feeling something like that *isn't* supposed to happen around here?" Warren asked as he rubbed his sore left shoulder.

"Because I don't think it is," Betsy agreed. She swept her lavender hair away from her eyes and climbed back to her feet. "I'd lay even money von Doom had something to do with it, though."

"No bet," Warren said, joining her. "And I've got a bad feeling it's only gonna get worse from here."

"Then we'd better hurry," she said, and took his hand. Again, a midnight-black portal opened beneath them, and they entered the shadow realm.

This time, when they stepped from the portal, Betsy had the overwhelming impression they'd just dropped into a war zone.

The sky—or ceiling—was ablaze with powerful bursts of light. The ground constantly shook from a series of explosions—some minor, some strong enough to almost knock her down. The air was tinged with the stench of burnt ozone and acrid smoke.

And right in the center of this pyrotechnic display was Doctor Doom, looking as though he was in complete control of the forces of Armageddon that raged above and around them all.

"Well, *this* doesn't look good . . ." Warren said.

The armored tyrant stood beside some sort of hexagonal control console, holding tight to a collection of wires. Power was flowing from the console into him, and Betsy turned to look at the source of the energy he was absorbing. Her eyes widened in horror.

"ROMA!" she cried.

The Guardian was strapped to a medical table that was tilted upward, her hands bound in the opposite ends of the wires von Doom held. Golden energy poured from her, into the console, and her head lolled against her chest. From this distance, Betsy couldn't tell if she were still alive.

"We should hit him now, before he's aware we're here," Warren suggested. "Knock him down, and then we can figure just what the hell he's trying to do."

"Warren," she said in amazement, "I think he's . . . draining her energy. Stealing it for himself. That might be why the citadel started shaking before—he's interfering with the natural order of things here."

"All right," he replied after a moment. "Then, Roma first. Disconnect her, and Doom's cut off from his power source. And maybe, with luck, that stops the citadel from tearing itself apart."

"Sounds good to me," Betsy said. "Let's get to it, then."

She charged forward, pounding across the floor toward Roma, now wishing she hadn't left Alecto's sword behind—it would have made cutting the wires and cables much easier. The flapping of wings nearby told her Warren was joining her in the rescue. She'd almost reached her objective—when a bolt of lightning suddenly exploded directly in front of her.

Thrown to the side, Betsy immediately rolled with the shockwave and came up standing, although she couldn't see clearly, for all the black and multicolored dots swimming before her eyes. But she could certainly hear well enough.

"So, mutants!" von Doom bellowed above the storm. "You have arrived at a most fortuitous moment—when you shall witness Doom's ascension to godhood . . . before you die!"

"Great. Like he doesn't act holier-than-thou already." A hand lightly touched her shoulder. "You okay, Betts?" Warren asked.

"Nothing a seeing-eye dog couldn't help with right now," she replied dryly, blinking rapidly to clear her vision. She patted his hand with her own. "I'll be fine."

"Okay, change of plans," he said. "You help Roma. I'll face off with Doom, try to buy you some time to get her out of here."

"No!" Betsy snapped, a little too forcefully. Watching him die once, at Magneto's hands just days before, had been almost more than she could bear; she wasn't going to let it happen again. "He's *mine."*

And before Warren could protest, she charged at the armored tyrant.

Unfortunately, she didn't get very far. A bolt of energy erupted from the palm of his gauntlet, and she wasn't quick enough to avoid it. She screamed as it struck her square in the chest and smashed her to the floor. The sensation was agonizing—like a million fire ants were crawling over her body, sinking their mandibles into her flesh. She tried to rise, only to discover her limbs refused to work; she could only thrash helplessly on the ground as the pain intensified. The green light that engulfed her grew brighter, and she screwed her eyes shut. The illumination could not be denied, though; she could see it even behind her eyelids.

A loud gasp reached her ears, and she forced her eyes to open. Warren was lying a short distance away. He, too, was suffering under a similar energy beam, wings beating feebly as he twisted and turned, mouth contorted in a silent scream.

Her mind suddenly filled with a kaleidoscope of images. She saw her life before the X-Men had ever entered it—her time as a world-renowned fashion model, then, later, as a telepathic secret agent in the British counterterrorist organization S.T.R.I.K.E. Then came snippets of her years with the X-Men—some good (especially where Warren was concerned), some bad, but all quite memorable. And there was her career as a cabaret singer in New York's Greenwich Village, just before she met Warren—

But wait. She'd never *been* a cabaret singer, had she?

No, of course not. She'd barely been able to work up the nerve to perform a time or two at Warren's mid-Manhattan nightclub; she'd certainly never made a career out of it.

So, why, then, she wondered dimly, did she possess memories of a life she knew she'd never had?

The answer wasn't long in coming. For, just as it seemed the light beam was on the verge of boring through her, it suddenly switched off.

And when she opened her eyes, there was another Elisabeth Braddock lying beside her.

"W-what . . . ?" she stuttered hoarsely. "H-how . . ."

She looked beautifully elegant, her doppelganger, even sprawled unconscious on the floor. She was dressed in a strapless black evening gown, with matching opera-length gloves; a string of white pearls adorned her neck. It was, Betsy realized, exactly the same outfit she had been wearing when she'd performed for "Emperor" von Doom, at the Washington, D.C. celebration commemorating his tenth year in power.

But it hadn't really been *her,* had it? Not the one-time fashion model, nor the former psi-agent, nor the current X-Man known as "Psylocke." It had been this woman who had sung her heart out for a worldwide audience–she knew that now. She just couldn't fathom how it could have happened–although it might explain the odd recollections she'd been having of late . . .

"Interesting," von Doom said. "Like the Guardian, and myself earlier, these mutants also harbored surrogates of themselves within their bodies. An influence of the Cosmic Cube's, no doubt."

The Cube. Of course. What else, given the current situation, could account for one person possessing two sets of memories, only to discover that she'd actually been *two* people all along? And if the Cube had fused her with an alternate of herself . . .

Slowly, Betsy turned on her side to look at Warren. There were three versions of her winged lover across from her: one, the poor unfortunate from von Doom's world, who had sacrificed himself to save his former emperor; the second, the husband of her counterpart on Magneto's Earth. In the center, barely conscious, was the true Warren Worthington III–the man she had crossed dimensions and mental landscapes to recover.

But now he was going to be taken away from her again, as she would be from him. She looked up, to see another charge of lightning building. There'd be no way to dodge it–von Doom's weapon had weakened her too much to even roll out of the way.

He'd won after all, it seemed–loosed chaos upon the Earth with his damnable Cube, then struck down Roma so he could take her place, and her power, as Supreme Guardian. And because of Betsy's failure to stop him, the omniverse—and her friends—would suffer the consequences.

She hoped they'd be able to forgive her when the end came.

16

I'M sorry, sugah, but I don't have the *foggiest* idea how I'm s'posed t'make *any* sense'a outta this mess."

Rogue ran a gloved hand through her close-cropped hair, and shrugged. "Mutant heroes, worlds where the Nazis didn't win World War II, an' the Red Skull is just some run'a-the-mill bad guy 'stead'a bein' emperor . . ." She shook her head. "It's just a li'l hard t'believe, if y'all don't mind me sayin' so."

Remy smiled. "You not de only one havin' trouble wit all dis cosmic mischief, *chere*. Parallel dimensions an' de like—dey just a bit outside de experience of a simple t'ief, too. But I swear ev'ry word o' it is de truth." The smile widened. "Ol' Gambit, he'd never lie t'you."

She smiled, too, her pallid cheeks turning a warm shade of rose. It was the first time she'd shown any emotion other than fright since his suicidal rescue attempt back on the highway. It looked good on her.

He suddenly realized how much he'd missed that smile. When he'd laid, dying, in a cell on von Doom's version of Earth, it was all he had thought about—the way it made her cheeks dimple, the way her nose wrinkled and her eyes shone so brightly. He'd regretted never having the chance to see it again once he died, and in that regret had finally found the strength to come right out and say to her what he'd so often avoided saying since they'd first met: that he loved her. They had been hard words to admit to—as much of a romantic as he considered himself, the idea of committing his heart to one woman had always been a foreign concept to Remy. But no matter how many times their relationship fractured over the years, no matter how often he'd recklessly chased after other women—whether to punish her over some stupid misunderstanding, or, more likely, as a way to punish himself—he'd always come back to Rogue.

At first, it had been difficult for him to acknowledge the possibility that they were meant to be together. Remy had never been a great believer in fate; chance was his game, and Lady Luck the card dealer. Things happened simply because they happened—you just went with the hand you were dealt, and tried to bluff your way through. No mystical forces directed *his* life.

But where Rogue was concerned, the deck had been stacked against him even before he sat down at the table. As he'd said to her in their last moments together—just before he'd sacrificed his life to give the X-Men a chance to escape from von Doom's intelligence headquarters—she was the only woman who had ever beaten a thief at his own game . . . by stealing his heart. And by admitting that to her, to himself, he had finally come to understand just how much he loved her.

Theirs had never been the easiest of couplings. Because of the uncontrollable nature of her powers, they had never been able to consummate the relationship—she was terrified of absorbing his life-force, perhaps even accidentally killing him, should their bare skin touch. It was a bizarre complication Remy had never had to deal with before—and he had known quite a few women in his time. In his younger, wilder days, he would have just shrugged his shoulders and moved on, in search of a less . . . stressful love connection.

But there was something about Rogue that drew him to her side, that made him *want* to be with her, no matter how many odd twists and turns the relationship might take. Maybe it was her naiveté that had caught his attention—she was not exactly someone you'd consider wise in all the ways of the world, and he knew all about them . . . or so he kept telling her. Maybe it was her down-home, Southern charm, which appealed to his bayou upbringing.

Or maybe it was because her powers made her feel so alone in the world, and he wanted—perhaps even needed—to comfort her. As a member of New Orleans' Thieves Guild, Remy had always been surrounded by an extended family. Rogue, on the other hand, had been cast out from her own when her powers manifested, leaving her with no one to turn to when she needed help the most. She'd found a certain degree of acceptance when she joined the X-Men, but Remy knew she still felt like an outsider, even among her own kind—able to fight beside them, able to share in their brief moments of fun, but never able to really *be* one of them. Not when she could steal their memories, their powers, their lives, with just a touch.

He could understand how she felt. Becoming a member of the X-Men had never been a direction he'd ever expected his life to take, but he'd gone along with it, if only because he was curious to see how things would turn out. Unfortunately, he'd never been welcomed with open arms into the group, and later was even suspected of betraying them to their enemies.

Yes, Remy could understand Rogue's sense of aloneness, all right. And maybe that was what drew them to one another.

They made one hell of an unusual pair, he knew: the worldly thief and the lonely Southern belle. Sharing a love that went beyond physical boundaries, finding comfort in their differences, accepting whatever cards fate might deal and making the best of them—together.

But he wouldn't have had it any other way.

"Penny fer your thoughts?" she asked, shaking him from his reverie.

Remy grinned. "Jus' glad t'see you smilin' fer a change, *petite.* T'ought maybe you'd forgot how t'do it."

Her smile faded, and a dark cloud passed behind her eyes. She shivered, as though recalling a particularly unpleasant memory. "Haven't had much reason *to* smile these days," she said quietly.

"Dat ain't hard t'believe," he replied. "What wit' de world all turned upside-down an' inside-out, an' us cut off from de rest o' de X-Men."

He rose from the metal folding chair he'd been sitting on, feeling the need to stretch his legs, and surveyed their surroundings. A room-sized storage facility in a Queens warehouse was a long way from the plush accommodations of the Xavier Institute of Higher Learning, and it only reminded Remy of how strange things had become since the X-Men returned to Earth, only days before.

As strange as the woman sitting in front of him. A woman who wore the features of someone to whom he had opened his heart only a short time ago, but who was now as foreign to him as he was to her.

He needed to find that other woman, the one who meant so much to him. Needed to talk to her, hold her, touch her. But in order to do that, in order to find her, and the rest of the X-Men, he first needed an ally. Even if it meant turning to a stranger.

"Rogue, I . . . need your help," he said slowly.

"What *kinda* help did you have in mind?" she asked in a guarded tone. "I mean, I'm grateful for the rescue an' all, but . . ."

"I need you t'understand what I was talkin' 'bout," he explained. "De parallel worlds, an' de X-Men, an everyt'in' else dat's important. I'm gonna need somebody t'show me around dis city if I'm gonna find my friends, an' it'd go easier if you knew what I was doin'."

"An' how're you gonna make me understand?"

"By makin' contact wit you," he replied slowly. "If you'll let me."

"You want *t'touch* me?" she asked, eyes wide with surprise. "That's crazy! Don't you know what'd happen if you did that?"

He nodded. "Yeah, I been down dat road before. But it still be de quickest way t'get you up t'speed I can t'ink of." He eased himself onto the chair beside her. "Please, *chere.* It's important."

She stared silently at him. There was so much hurt in those eyes. The last thing he wanted to do was be the cause of any more—but there was no other way to do it.

"All right," she finally whispered. "If'n it's *that* important. Just . . . don't hate me for what happens."

He smiled. "You, *petite*?" He shook his head. "I could *never* hate you."

Her cheeks colored, and she smiled. "Thank you," she said softly.

He nodded. "Anyt'ing for you, *chere.*"

Slowly, he raised his hand, to touch her face. She instinctively drew back.

"It's all right, *chere,*" he said quietly. "Ol' Gambit, he knows what he doin' . . ." He smiled. ". . . 'least he *t'ink* he do . . ."

She gazed into his eyes for a few moments, most likely trying to see if his expression would reveal whether it was a trick, or a trap. Then, apparently satisfied with what she saw, she slowly nodded.

Gently, he reached out, and placed his fingertips to her cheek.

It was like sticking a wet finger in a light socket.

Lightning crackled around his body, overloading his nerves, cramping his muscles. It became hard to think, impossible to move. He was stuck to Rogue as surely as a fly was stuck to flypaper, and could only hope that the contact would break before it killed him.

A wave of nausea seized him as he felt Rogue begin to drain him of his strength, his memories, his life. Her eyes turned black, with red pupils, even as his dimmed to a cool brown. He, in turn, felt her panic and horror. She tried to pull away, but somehow he found the strength to pull her closer with his other hand.

Close enough to kiss.

Their lips brushed together—

And then the change began.

It started with her body—it filled out, skin and bones transforming into solid flesh and powerful muscle. Then her hair began to grow at a lightning pace, becoming fuller and longer, until it reached her waist. The skunk-like streak that ran down the center was even more prominent now. Her face became softer, less angular.

Weakened considerably, Remy at last managed to slide away from her, and collapsed against the seat. He watched in amazement as the woman before him shifted and morphed, becoming less a stranger and more someone he knew—quite well.

"Huh," he said with some amusement. "Gambit's kissed a lotta *filles* in his time, but *dat* never happened before . . ."

And when the process ended, and she finally looked at him, the light of recognition—and shock—shone in her eyes.

"R-Remy . . . ?" she whispered.

He smiled, though the effort of forcing his facial muscles to move taxed what little strength remained. "Hello, Rogue," he said smoothly, casually. "It's been a while, *non*?" The smile broadened. "So, tell me . . . you miss your Remy while he was gone?"

She choked on her reply, and tears began running down her cheeks. She sat there, shivering, staring at him, apparently not knowing what to do next. With some difficulty, he opened his arms wide and drew her close. Grateful, she buried her face on his chest, and cried long and loud while he stroked her hair and kissed the top of her head. He could feel the warmth of her tears soaking through his shirt.

"I . . . I thought you were gone forever," she said.

Remy chuckled and rubbed her back. "You know me, *chere*. I'm like dat ol' bad penny—I keep showin' up when you least 'spect it." He shrugged. "Maybe de Big Man upstairs figured my time wasn't up yet."

"Or maybe He was afraid'a what you'd do t'his place when ya got in there," she murmured into his chest, "an' figured it'd be less trouble sendin' you back down here." She slid her arms around him and hugged him tight. "I don't really care *what* the reason is, 'long as you're back t'stay."

Remy hissed, feeling his ribs scrape together under the pressure of her overzealous show of affection. "Easy, *chere*. Give a man some time t'recover. What wit' de rescuin' and all de runnin' to-night, an' den . . ." He waved his hands in the air, trying to find the right words. ". . . what happened jus' now, ol' Remy's had one *tirin'* day."

She apologized and drew back, her face creased with concern. "Sorry," she said quietly. "I shoulda waited 'til your powers came back. It's just that—"

"It's okay, *petite*," he said with a strained smile. "Jus' lemme get my second wind, an' den I'll be happy t'give you a proper greetin'." He placed his hands on her shoulders and turned her around, so she could lean back against him. She snuggled close as he wrapped his arms around her shoulders, and he sighed. "Dis is nice, *non*? Jus' lyin' here t'gether like dis, wit'out a care in de world." A frown bowed his lips. "Too bad we *do* got a care in de world, tho'. A *lotta* worlds, for dat matter. An' we still gotta do somet'in' t'fix it."

"The Cosmic Cube," Rogue said with a nod.

"Yeah, de . . ." He paused, suddenly feeling totally confused. "*Chere*?"

"Yeah?" she asked, turning her head to look up at him.

Remy scratched the top of his head for a moment. "What de *hell* is de 'Cosmic Cube' . . . ?"

"Haven't either of you listened to a word of what I've been saying?"

Kurt Wagner—Nightcrawler—pounded his fist on the metal table in front of him. "My loyalty to the Party is beyond questioning!" he barked. "I will *not* stand by quietly and allow some . . . some *verdammt housefrau* to tarnish my good name!"

Standing on the other side of the table, Hauptmann Englande pointed a thick finger at the heavy, metal chair next to the blue-skinned mutant. "Sit down, Wagner," he growled through clenched teeth. "Any further outbursts, and I will take the greatest pleasure in silencing you—permanently."

Wagner opened his mouth to continue voicing his outrage, but paused, fist poised in mid-arc above the table, when he saw the fire burning in Englande's eyes, took note of the stance the costumed warrior assumed. One more word, he realized, and the captain would be across the table, crushing his throat in hands powerful enough to twist steel. Slowly, Wagner's mouth closed, and his fist opened. He lowered his hand to his side, then threw himself into the chair with a huff and folded his arms across his chest. He glared at a spot on the floor, knowing better than to direct the heat of his gaze at his superior.

"Preposterous . . ." he muttered sullenly.

Beside Englande, Arnim Zola sat in another chair, hands folded on the tabletop. "Not so preposterous that the Reich isn't looking into the matter, Herr Wagner," he said. "Serious charges have been leveled against you, and others of your kind. Perhaps if you just told me what your group had planned—"

Wagner rounded on him. *"I have done—"* he began, then caught sight of Englande as he took a step forward. "I have done nothing," he said quietly. He looked imploringly at the Health Minister. "I am no traitor to the Fatherland, no mutant revolutionary seeking the Emperor's destruction. My record in service to the Empire should be proof of that." He shook his head. "This is all a mistake."

"If that is so, Herr Wagner," Zola said, "then you should help us to resolve the matter, not make it worse by pounding tables and shouting about character assassinations. This is a medical facility, not a beer hall."

"I . . . apologize, Minister. I *want* to be helpful. I *want* to clear this up." Wagner drew a deep breath, then released it. "*Um Gotteswillen*, how can the Ministry of Defense take the word of . . . of some civilian trophy wife over that of an officer of the Reich? It's madness!"

Englande grunted. " 'Madness' was ever letting abominations like you join the ranks of normal men and women. You should have all been exterminated, a long time ago. Before your kind began to multiply . . . like cockroaches."

Zola waved a hand at him in annoyance. "Captain, please. You're not helping." He turned to Nightcrawler. "What would you expect the Ministry to do, Herr Wagner? When the wife of an officer as highly decorated as Major Sommers is provides information concerning a revolutionary movement among the mutant population, an investigation must be launched."

"But I have never even *met* this woman!" Wagner replied. "How can I be part of something if I don't even know what this woman looks like?"

"That is why it's called a 'network,' imbecile," Englande snapped. "You don't have to physically meet someone to be an active member in their organization." His eyes narrowed, and he leaned forward, placing the palms of his hands on the table. The metal groaned slightly under the pressure. "But you *do* know the *other* one. The black one we brought in. *The mutant.*"

Zola turned to him, one gigantic eyebrow raised in a quizzical expression. "Fräulein Munroe? How so?"

"If you recall, Minister, Frau Sommers' list of conspirators included the black as one of the revolutionaries—Nightcrawler, as well." Englande looked to Zola. "But, as for how they might know one another . . . I'm really not the one to ask." He pointed toward Nightcrawler with his broad jaw.

"What are you talking about?" Wagner asked.

"You said so yourself," Englande replied. "You thought you had met her before, but couldn't remember where." He flashed a sinister smile. "Perhaps at one of your underground plotting sessions?"

"That . . . no. It was nothing like that," Wagner said, though he knew they could hear the hesitation in his voice. "It was just . . . a feeling . . ."

"That *maybe* she looks like someone you knew before," Englande commented. It was clear from his tone, however, that he didn't believe it. "A coincidence, then."

"Something like that," Wagner admitted, staring at his hands.

The brawny captain grunted. "A coincidence that your paths should cross again on this mission, you mean."

Wagner looked up, panic in his eyes. "No!"

Englande sighed and looked to his superior. "With all due respect, Minister, I don't see the point in standing around, wasting precious time, acting as though this traitorous freak—"

" *'Traitorous'?!"* Wagner cried.

"—were one of us. Not when we both know he won't say anything we need to hear about the plans for this proposed insurrection." Englande smiled grimly. "Not when you have the means at your disposal of wringing the truth from him."

Zola paused, then cast a glance at Wagner. A sly smile creased the aged features that appeared on the viewscreen. "There *is* some work I've been doing recently—a variation on a series of psychic experiments started by the Russians during the war. Most of the test subjects haven't survived past the initial brain surgery . . ."

Wagner leapt to his feet. *"No!* I won't allow it!"

Englande glared at him. "You won't *what?"*

"I won't allow it!" Wagner repeated. "I am not some animal to be led to the slaughterhouse! I am a *man*—a decorated officer of the Empire! I have rights!"

"Not true, Herr Wagner," Zola said. "As a mutant, you have *no* rights. The laws of this monarchy were written for the true sons of Woden—the genetically pure. *Your* kind are no better than the very animals you obviously consider yourself above, to be used however I see fit—including 'leading you to the slaughterhouse,' if that is my wish." He rapped his knuckles on the tabletop. "This piece of furniture has more right to exist than you. At least *it* serves a useful function."

Wagner staggered back and grasped the back of his chair for support; the strength had suddenly drained from his legs, and it was difficult to stand. "But . . . but I am a valued member of Lightning Force . . ."

Englande laughed sharply. "Who ever told you *that?* The only value you ever had to the team was as comic relief—the freak who considered himself a human being! What a fine joke that was! And to watch your pathetic attempts to romance my Meggan!" He smiled coldly. "I must tell you, there were times I thought I'd split my uniform from laughing so hard."

Wagner shook his head. "No. You're lying. You trusted me in battle—"

"I'd sooner trust a *Skrull* to watch my back," Englande shot back. "I simply knew you would allow no harm to come to me, or Meggan, to avoid being reprimanded should you fail to protect your superiors. Acts of courage, born of fear."

Wagner trembled; his head began to ache. Why were they doing this to him? What had he done to make them turn on him so quickly? Why did they refuse to believe his innocence?

He should have known something was wrong the moment the V-wing jet touched down in Genosha. But he was so intent on proving just how wrong the African mutant, Munroe, was in her summation of his place in the Empire that he ignored the warning signs: the icy stares from the soldiers that came to meet Lightning Force; the whispered comments as he walked through the halls; the way Englande and Meggan had been ushered into Zola's office, alone, when they arrived at their meeting with the minister. If only he'd been paying closer attention—but no, he'd merely grinned smugly at the prisoner, strolled casually into the office when called . . . and been placed under arrest.

According to information Zola had received shortly before the team's arrival, Wagner was part of a plot by mutant revolutionaries to destroy the Empire—or so it had been explained to him as shackles were placed on his wrists and ankles. The ringleaders were Reichsmajor Scott Sommers and his wife, Jean—two people he had never met in his life, though he *was* familiar with the major's service record. Munroe and the remaining Lightning Force member, Shadowcat, had also been named, but theirs, apparently, were minor roles. The others who had been implicated went by codenames he didn't recognize: Wolverine. Gambit. Psylocke. Archangel. "Rogue," he was told, was a mutant "translator" who served under Sommers on board the starship *Nuremberg.* It made no difference—he didn't know any of them, and said so from the outset. But no one was listening, and he had been hustled into this cinderblock cell, to spend the next few hours fielding questions to which he had no answers. . . .

"Talk, damn you!" Englande roared, and slammed his fist on the table. The thick metal cracked along the top. "Where are the rest of your group? How many others *are* there? When do they plan to strike? How long have you been plotting against the Emperor?"

"Go to the devil!" Wagner snapped, a slight tremor in his voice.

Slowly, Zola rose from his seat. He looked at Nightcrawler, and sighed. "Very well, Herr Wagner. I had hoped we could avoid further unpleasantness, but your lack of cooperation leaves me no other choice." He turned to Englande. "Captain, escort the prisoner to the psychiatric laboratories."

"With pleasure," Englande said. He took one step, to move around the table—

—and watched in surprise as Nightcrawler vanished from the room, in a burst of brimstone and a sharp implosion of air. The chains he'd been wearing clattered to the floor.

Hauptmann Englande snarled. "So much for the loyal member of the Party . . ." he muttered sarcastically.

Kurt Wagner ran for his life through the corridors of the Ministry of Health. His career was over now—any idiot could see that—and the longer he stayed on Genosha, the better the chance of recapture. He had to find a way off the island, but that was far easier said than done. His teleportation abilities were only useful for traveling short distances, and even then he had to know exactly what his destination looked like, or he might wind up materializing inside a wall, or an object—or a person. He'd considered 'porting—or *bamf*ing as he'd come to think of it, since that was the sound made by the displacement of air during the transition—to the Lightning Force jet, but he'd been led down so many corridors and hallways and stairwells after his arrest he'd lost track of where he was. For all he knew, the jet could be one level above him, or a hundred.

An alarm sounded. He'd been expecting it from the moment he fled the interrogation room, but the loud, bleeting noise still made his heart jump into his throat. Fighting panic, he glanced up and down the corridor in which he stood—it was empty, but wouldn't remain so for long. He began trying doors, but every one he came to was locked. He considered breaking one down, but then worried that the broken lock might be discovered, and then he'd be trapped in close quarters.

He settled for teleporting to the stairwell at the end of the hall, and scrambled through the door just as the first heavy footfalls of the security forces begin ringing through the corridor.

Now came another decision: up or down? Down would take him to the lobby, and a footchase through the winding streets of Genosha was something he preferred to avoid. Up led to the landing platforms—and the jet. He paused, waiting to find out from which direction pursuit might be coming, but the ear-splitting klaxon made it impossible to determine.

Up, then, he decided. At least that way he had a better idea of where he wanted to go.

Cautiously, he stuck his head out, over the railing, and looked upward. He didn't see anyone above him—which accounted for why the bullets streaking past his head were coming from below.

Not waiting to see who exactly was shooting at him—or how close they might be to his position—Wagner *bamf*ed as high as he could go. A wise decision, because it moved him away from the guards who'd been charging down the hallway in his direction; they burst into the stairwell in time to get a good whiff of the brimstone cloud he left behind.

Wagner reappeared a dozen levels up, in mid-air. With a cry of disbelief, he threw his arms out and succeeded in grabbing hold of the railing with one hand before gravity could take hold of him. He pulled himself over, cursing the literalness of his powers—only being able to see the railing but not the steps past them was the sort of limitation that could get him killed, without anyone's help. He'd have to be more careful . . . but at least he'd been able to put some distance between himself and his pursuers.

Or so he'd thought.

A roar of air and a strong draft, like that of a subway car traveling through a tunnel, moved up the stairwell. The hairs on the back of Wagner's neck stood on end—he knew what that rush of air meant, but he couldn't help himself from looking over the railing to see it with his own eyes.

Hauptmann Englande was flying up the center of the stairwell. Their eyes met, and the captain's lips pulled back in a predatory smile.

More bullets sang past Wagner's head, both from above *and* below now. He pressed against the wall to remove himself from the line of fire.

"I'm coming for you, traitor!" Englande bellowed, still some floors away.

"You and half the Empire, it seems . . ." Wagner muttered.

He opened the door to the corridor outside, dove through, and started running again. The portal shattered behind him a moment later, as Englande crashed through it.

"Stop running, cur!" he ordered, hovering a few inches above the tiled floor. "There's no escape from here!"

Much to his own surprise, Wagner came to a halt. And turned. And smiled. An idea had popped into his head—a crazy one, to be sure, but it was the only one he had at the moment.

"I know why you are *really* angry with me, Captain!" he shouted over the annoying klaxon. "You know I am the only man capable of stealing away your woman!"

Englande laughed. "A pure-bred woman, running away with a freak like you? That will be the day!"

"Ah. But she is *not* a true German maiden, Captain, as you well know! She is of the fairy realm—a changeling left in place of a human child! She is a shapeshifter, a 'freak' like me, and yet you continue to sleep with her—in direct violation of the Eugenics Laws! I may be a mutant insurgent, but *you're* a race traitor, mein Captain!" The smile widened. "Tell me—what does she look like when *you* make love to her?"

A shadow fell over Englande's eyes, then, and he roared. He surged forward, picking up so much speed as he flew down the corridor that the walls shook.

And yet, Nightcrawler stood his ground. His foolhardy plan had to be timed perfectly, or his headless corpse would hit the floor about a split-second after Englande reached him.

The gap between them closed quickly. Englande drew back a mighty fist, preparing to deliver the fatal blow. But just as he reached Nightcrawler—

—the mutant jumped to one side, grabbed the captain's other hand in both of his own—

—and teleported.

Once. Twice. Three times. More.

Short, quick jumps down the length of the corridor, dragging Englande along for the ride. The strain on Wagner was considerable—the more he 'ported, the greater the pain he felt, like his insides were aflame. But he also knew what the process, combined with the high rate of speed at which he'd been traveling, was doing to his former team leader.

With a final *bamf!*, Nightcrawler reached the end of the hallway and released his unwilling passenger. Englande continued on, to crash headfirst into the wall. He bounced off the cracked plaster, rolled onto his back with a groan, and lay still.

Holding his sides as he waited for the pain to subside, Nightcrawler cautiously approached the captain. The man's head was a bloody mess, and his face was going to need some reconstructive surgery, but he was still alive. Wagner breathed a sigh of relief—as much as he hated him, the last thing he'd wanted to do was kill the idiot simply because he was following orders.

However, he *could* take some pleasure in knowing he'd ruined the captain's movie star looks. Meggan was far too vain to be interested in a swaggering buffoon with the face of a punching bag, no matter how godlike his physique might be.

But now was not the time to revel in the misfortunes of others. Now was the time to get out of the building, as soon as possible.

With a final glance at Englande, Wagner ran down an adjacent corridor. Somewhere around here, there had to be another fire door. . . .

17

SOUNDS like something big is going on," Meggan commented over the blaring alarm.

"Shouldn't you see what it's about?" Ororo asked. She rattled her chains. "I will wait here for your return."

Meggan sneered. "Funny girl. I'm sure you amuse all the villagers with your jokes, back at that sandpit you call home."

"There is little cause for amusement in Araouane," Ororo replied. "Not when each day is a struggle just to survive. Although . . ." She paused, and a hint of a gentle smile played at the corners of her mouth. She thought of the sandwoman, Abena Metou, and her daughter; remembered the love they shared—one that not even the hot winds of the desert could wear away. Recalled with fondness the way the girl placed her mother's bowl on her head and marched along like a little soldier, and how it had brought some levity to an otherwise oppressive day.

Perhaps there *was* a need for laughter, even in this dark world. *Especially* in this dark world, she considered.

Meggan strolled over from the only door to the small room and perched on the edge of the metal table at which Ororo sat. "Now then, Fräulein, let us talk, you and I—a friendly chat just between us girls."

"What would you like to talk about?"

The blond-haired vixen shrugged. "Oh, perhaps about the weather—you used to control it, didn't you?" She smiled coldly, but Ororo said nothing. After a moment, the smile widened, and Meggan snapped her fingers, as though she'd suddenly had an idea. "I know! We can discuss your part in this alleged mutant uprising."

"I have no part in any such thing," Ororo replied evenly.

"That is not what *I* have heard . . ."

"Perhaps you should have your hearing checked before you leave Genosha," Ororo said. "Then you might actually be able to *listen* when people speak the truth to you."

The false smile quickly curdled. "I'm going to enjoy tearing out your heart when we're done, mutant."

"You are too late, Nazi," Ororo said. "The other monsters here tore it out long ago."

The sullen tone of her voice returned the smile to the shapeshifter's lips. "Poor little goddess. You've lost everything, haven't you? Your family, your worshippers, your powers. You've been thrown into the wastelands, then shackled and abused and dragged through the halls of your enemies' stronghold. Is there no one to take pity on you?"

"*You* are the one to be pitied," Ororo replied sharply, lightly fingering the chains. There was just enough slack in them . . . "You have dedicated your life to following a man who is the personification of all that is evil, who has destroyed countless worlds and lives just so history will remember his name. A man who thinks himself a god, yet is unworthy of praise—unless it be the kind of mewling adoration he receives from zealots or sycophants."

Meggan laughed. "Spoken like a former deity . . . or a true revolutionary."

"There is *no* mutant revolution," Ororo said. "At least, none of which I am aware. But if there were, I would not hesitate to join its ranks."

"No underground movement, and yet the wife of one of the Reich's formerly most-respected officers names you as one of its members."

Ororo shrugged. "I do not know why that is. I have never met this Frau Sommers—"

"But you *have* met Nightcrawler, eh?" Ororo opened her mouth to reply, but Meggan wagged a finger at her. "Don't try to deny it. Back at the village, you admitted that you knew him from somewhere."

Ororo shook her head. "I said I *thought,* perhaps, we had met, but that would have been impossible. It's just that . . . he reminded me of someone . . ."

"Ah. Some *other* blue-skinned freak, then." Meggan slapped Ororo across the face, the sharp cracking sound echoing off the walls of the cell. "Don't try to play the fool with me, little goddess. We have you and your co-conspirator, and soon enough we will have the rest of your merry band. And once you've all been rounded up, I'm certain Minister Zola will have some . . . special treats in mind for each of you." She grinned savagely. "I hope he'll let me watch when he gets to *you.*"

"You are rather bloodthirsty, are you not, Meggan?" Ororo commented, tightening her grip on the chains. "Is that because you enjoy inflicting pain on others in general . . . or because you are jealous of the attention Hauptmann Englande paid to me during the trip here?"

Another slap, this time hard enough to leave the impressions of Meggan's fingers on her cheek.

"More one than the other," Meggan replied, leaning in close. "*You* can decide which it is later—when our session is done, and I'm ready to end your miserable life."

The chains suddenly swept upward, catching her across the face and snapping her head to one side. She staggered back, raising her hands in a weak defense, and bumped into a corner of the table. Dazed, apparently confused by the obstruction, she lowered her hands slightly and turned to glance at it, allowing Ororo the opportunity to lash out again. This time, the chain cracked against the shapeshifter's left temple; with a soft groan, she slumped to the floor.

Instantly, Ororo was upon her, searching her uniform for the key to the shackles. She found it tucked inside the woman's belt, and wasted no time in making use of it.

Softly, she crept over to the door and opened it a crack. There were no guards standing in the hall, since Meggan had ordered them away. She'd felt completely confident in her ability to interrogate her prisoner, especially when said prisoner was chained up and being questioned by a superpowered foe. Typical Nazi arrogance, Ororo thought. No wonder they had been unaware of a mutant insurrection until now . . . if, indeed, there was one forming—it simply never would have entered their minds that mutants were capable of banding together for such a cause.

She opened the door wider, and stepped into the corridor. The alarm was still sounding, so whatever had caused it to be raised was still in effect. It would make escape difficult, if the halls were filled with security personnel running about in response, but there was no way she was going to remain where she was until the emergency ended. Especially if it meant she had to stay in the same room with her tormentor.

The thought of Meggan made her look back inside the cell. The shapeshifter was still unconscious, her face bloody and bruised from the attack. But Ororo knew she would not remain insensate for long; superpowered individuals never did, when their metabolisms allowed them to heal quickly. And if she awoke and raised another alarm, before Ororo had time to put some distance between them . . .

She stepped back into the room, and closed the door. Moving quickly, she dragged Meggan behind the metal table, then grabbed the discarded chains and wrapped them around her ankles and wrists. The neck manacle was slipped around one of the table legs, then fastened around Meggan's throat to keep her from moving around. A gag was fashioned by tearing a piece of material from Ororo's clothing and shoving it into Meggan's mouth, then using the woman's own swastika-adorned headband to keep it in place.

Ororo knelt down beside her unconscious prisoner, and smiled. "Long live the revolution," she whispered in her ear.

"Revolution." An odd word to describe what was supposed to be a mission of mercy, Jean thought. How Xavier had ever come to think of it in such political terms was beyond her. Maybe presenting it that way to his superiors made him feel important—the Nazi-sympathizing mutant turncoat, proving he was of still some value to them. It was sad in a way, when she thought about it. But considering the hell he'd put her through since she arrived at his estate, it was impossible to feel any kind of sympathy toward him. She would have preferred getting her hands on a blunt instrument and demonstrating to him just how much one's head could hurt after receiving a good, solid whack on the noggin.

Of course, she'd first have to get out of her current predicament in order to do that. One thing at a time, she decided.

She paused. *Wait a minute. I just put a coherent thought together, and the professor's evil twin hasn't even said "boo." What's going on?*

And then it dawned on her: She couldn't feel Xavier in her head.

That was a surprise. He'd been spending so much time in there she'd half expected him to set up an apartment in her subconscious. He would have had to share it with a couple more versions of herself, though . . .

Jean shook her head a tiny bit to dismiss that notion. Images of *Three's Company* episodes aside, she needed to focus on taking advantage of the situation. With Xavier no longer poking around, his psychic barriers had weakened, and that meant she could think clearly again. The drugs in her system had apparently run their course, too, which left her with only the nagging throb at the back of her skull, where Danvers' blackjack had connected.

That should be the worst *of my problems, as Mom always used to say,* she thought. *A couple of Tylenol can take of that later—right now, I need to worry about my "hosts."*

She opened her right eye to a narrow slit. Nothing new to see there—she already knew what her chest looked like. Slowly, she rotated her head—hopefully, just enough to make it look like she was still out of it. Through the strands of red hair that had fallen over her face, Danvers rolled into view. She was standing near Viper's desk, nervously chewing on a thumbnail as she stared past Jean, toward the front door.

Hope this doesn't mean someone's standing behind me . . .

For a moment, she considered probing the area telepathically, to learn if there was another presence in the room. But the realization that its use would alert Xavier to the fact she'd woken up halted her. She wasn't ready to confront him—not just yet. Not until she'd had time to regain her strength. Her only option, therefore, was to just hope nobody was there and move on.

She opened her eye a little wider, and caught sight of the syringe and bottle lying on the desk, close to Danvers.

And right there is exactly *the reason why I didn't just sit up straight when I started to wake up. I've had one too many "naps" imposed on me during this mission already; I'd like to stay conscious at least long enough to try and* complete *it.* The corner of her mouth curled up in a brief smile. *But that needle* does *give me an idea . . .*

Jean tilted her head back, ever so slightly, to get a look ahead. What she saw made her stomach turn over, and sent a chill up her spine.

Viper was standing on the far side of the room, facing a giant viewscreen that must have been hidden behind the wall; Jean didn't remember seeing it before. And projected on the screen was the image of a blood-red death's-head, with eyes that burned with hate. But this was no icon Jean was looking at; rather, they were the grotesque features of the Emperor of the Fourth Reich. A madman who held the powers of Creation—and destruction—in his hands, via the properties of the cosmic wish box he now controlled.

The Red Skull.

"Am I to understand, then, Commander, that the Empire has been . . . invaded by a group of mutants from an alternate world," the Skull was saying, "here to prevent the world from being destroyed?"

"Yes, Your Majesty, as Professor Xavier has explained to me," Lady Viper replied. "By a threat greater than any the Empire has ever faced."

His eyes narrowed. "And you *believe* this story?"

She paused. "Yes, Your Majesty. That is why I thought it imperative that you be informed, as soon as I was notified." She turned to point at Jean, who quickly shut her eyes. "In fact, I have one of them here now; another of her group is en route from the spaceport."

Something was wrong with Viper; Jean could feel it. Her movements were too stiff, her verbal responses too slow. It was as though the words were being chosen for her, and her body was being controlled—

Like a puppet on a string . . . she realized.

Now she understood why Xavier had vacated her mind—he was too busy setting up shop in another. She let her head roll to the other side so she could look out through her left eye. Xavier sat motionless in his wheelchair, hands gripping the ends of the armrests. A thin sheen of sweat was beaded on his brow, and his facial muscles twitched noticeably. It was taking a great deal of effort to do what he was doing—so much that he'd had to release his hold on Jean.

I wonder if Viper slapped him, too, and he just lost it. Doesn't explain why he's playing ventriloquist with her, just to have a conversation with the Red Skull, though.

"What is the name of your prisoner?" the Skull asked. "I do not recognize her."

"She calls herself 'Phoenix,' Your Majesty," Viper replied. "The one arriving shortly is her husband: 'Cyclops.' " She paused. "You may know him better as Reichsmajor Scott Sommers."

Cautiously, Jean opened her eyes again. The Skull's lipless mouth curled downward. "Are you telling me, Commander, that one of the most respected officers in the Reich . . . is a *mutant?"*

"It would . . . appear so, Majesty."

"Unacceptable!" the Skull roared, and pounded the large, oaken desk at which he sat. *"UNACCEPTABLE!"*

Viper nodded solemnly, though stiffly. "I understand your disappointment, Majesty, but this threat—"

" 'Disappointment'? *'Disappointment'?!"* He pointed an accusatory finger at her. "A genetic aberration has penetrated one of the highest levels of the Empire, has somehow managed to keep his true nature a secret during all the time he rose through the ranks, was given the honor of commanding a starship, and you consider it a 'disappointment'? No, Commander, this is far worse—it is an insult to my genius! A black mark on all I have created! A flaw in an otherwise perfect gem!" He slapped the desktop with the flat of his hand. "Have the mutants exterminated—both of them! Immediately! I will not tolerate their existence one moment longer! And when you find the rest of the group, do the same to them!"

"But, Your Majesty, what about—" Viper began.

"Immediately, Commander!" the Skull bellowed.

That sounds like my cue, Jean thought.

Gently, she reached out telekinetically and grabbed hold of the sedative-filled syringe on the desk.

"She's awake!" Xavier suddenly cried out. Even as he spoke, Viper collapsed to the floor, his hold over her broken, the connection severed.

"What—?" the Skull said. "What is going on?"

Jean snapped her head up, and sent the syringe hurtling across the room. Xavier lurched back in his chair as the needle penetrated his neck, and the plunger was rammed home. He groaned loudly and toppled forward, dropping in a heap to the floor.

"Commander Viper, what is happening?" the Skull demanded. "Where are you? Answer me, damn you!"

Even as the professor was falling, Jean turned to see Danvers rushing at her, blackjack at the ready. Using her mind, Jean *shoved,* and sent her crashing into a wall. Danvers slipped to the carpet, unconscious.

Jean now turned her attention to the straps binding her. A few seconds of telekinetic manipulation, and the clasps popped open. Jean blew out a sharp breath, and began rubbing the circulation back into her tired limbs.

"You! Mutant!"

Startled, Jean looked up. The Skull glared at her through the viewscreen, his blood-red features filling the frame.

"Where are you going, X-Man?" he asked.

"Then you *do* know who I am," she replied.

"I recognized your ridiculous codename," he admitted. "But without your gaudy costume, you are just another faceless drone—less than a drone, given your genetic impurities."

"Ow. I'm so insulted," she said dryly. *Careful, Jeanie,* she warned herself. *Remember, he's got the Cosmic Cube in his possession. He could turn you into a statue, or inside out, if he wanted to. All he has to do is think about it . . .*

"Have you come to destroy my empire? To put an end to my 'villainy' once and for all?" The Skull huffed loudly, and waved a hand in a dismissive gesture. "Bah! You costumed cretins are disgustingly predictable!"

"So are super-villains." Jean raised herself from the seat of the wheelchair, wincing slightly at the pins-and-needles sensation that ran through her legs. "But, no, we haven't come here to destroy your precious empire, as much as I'd like to see happen the 'mutant revolution' everybody kept talking about. We're more concerned with the *source* of your empire."

His eyes sparkled with dark mirth. "Ah. You're here for the Cube, then. And how did you propose to take it from me, you and your little band of subhumans?"

Jean paused. She was on deadly ground here—one wrong word, one insult that pushed him too far, and she'd be praying that killing her would be the *worst* he'd do to her. "I . . . was hoping you would hand it over."

The Skull stared at her for several long moments. And then he burst out laughing. "I retract my earlier comment. Unlike your heroic associates, you, woman, are *not* predictable. How refreshing." The laugh faded, and he eyed her closely. "You do not fear me, do you?"

"What I fear," Jean replied, "is what will happen to the universe if you *don't* surrender the Cube."

"Indeed." The Skull sat back in his chair, and rested his chin between the thumb and forefinger of his right hand. "Then this 'threat' Viper kept mentioning—"

"Is all too real. And it's only going to get worse."

"Would it have anything to do with the flaw I detected in the Cube?" Her look of surprise was confirmation enough for him. "Then you should cease your worrying, mutant, for I have already addressed that problem—and corrected it."

"No . . ." Jean whispered. "How could you . . . ?"

"Because only the Red Skull has touched the face of Eternity! Only the Red Skull has journeyed to the depths of the Cosmic Cube, and seen the power that is his for the taking!" he crowed. "Only I—who have been as one with the cosmos—could do what those bunglers von Doom and Magneto failed to do: master the Cube, and thereby master the universe!"

A lump formed in Jean's throat, and she swallowed, hard. *Well, this is certainly an unexpected turn of events. I don't know if I should be happy that he's managed to halt the reality-cancer—or terrified that he's achieved total control over the Cube . . .*

"So, you come from a parallel world, do you?"

The change of topic caught Jean by surprise. "What—?"

"How did you get here?"

"I . . . I'm not sure," she replied, just a little too quickly. "Some big machine we had to step through—looked like a circular gateway. I'm not very technical . . ."

"You lie poorly, mutant," the Skull snapped, "and I have no patience for word games—*or* for conversing with you any longer through a television screen."

The change was startling. One moment, Jean was in Viper's New York office; the next, she was standing before the Red Skull. Teleported across an ocean in less than a heartbeat, by the power of the Cube.

Oh, Jeannie, she thought, stepping back from his desk, *you are in* so *much trouble . . .*

"Now, then, X-Man," the Emperor growled as he rose from his chair, "the choice is simple: Tell me what I want to know—or prepare to die. . . ."

18

I'M not dead.

Not exactly the most original thought one could have upon first awakening, Betsy considered, but given the fact she hadn't expected to *ever* wake up again, it seemed the most appropriate.

She opened her eyes, and found herself staring at the floor. She couldn't remember how she'd gotten into that position—had the lightning bolt struck close to her and tossed her a few feet, or did she roll out of the way and come to a halt this way? Probably the latter, since she didn't *feel* like she'd been electrocuted.

Groaning slightly, she rolled onto her back and sat up, tossing back her head to get the hair out of her eyes. Maybe she should consider a shorter hairstyle, she thought. It would certainly be more practical in combat situations . . .

She surveyed the area. Von Doom and his lab coat-wearing lackey were nowhere to be seen—much to her surprise, but not to her regret. Nearby, the other Betsy was still unconscious, which was all right with her—the last thing she needed right now was coming to terms with the fact that she had been living in another woman's body—and mind—for the past month. Across the way, Warren was beginning to revive, and Roma . . .

"Roma!" Betsy shouted. She leapt to her feet and ran to the Supreme Guardian. The goddess was slumped forward on the medical table, the restraints digging into her body.

Betsy released the braces supporting the table, and lowered it to a horizontal position. Then she set about undoing the straps.

"Roma? Roma, can you hear me?" Betsy asked. She grabbed the Guardian by the shoulders and roughly shook her. *"Roma!"*

"I . . . live . . . Elisabeth . . ." came the weak response. The dark-haired goddess slowly opened her eyes and looked at her. "But not for . . . much longer . . . if you continue to . . . assault me . . ."

"Oh. Sorry." Betsy immediately released her and took a step back. "I didn't mean to get so physical—"

Roma waved off her apology. "Nonsense. Your concern for . . . my well-being . . . is greatly appreciated."

Apparently nursing a major headache—judging by the way he was rubbing his temples and moaning—Warren staggered over to join them. He looked around in confusion. "Hey . . . where's Doom?"

"He . . . and Stanton . . . have departed . . ." Roma whispered.

"They left? Just like that?" Warren asked. "What happened to him getting ready to kill us?" He paused. "Uh, not that I'm complaining, of course."

Roma shook her head. "At times . . . the powers of . . . a celestial being . . . elevate its bearer . . . above such . . . petty considerations."

"You mean he just didn't think we were worth the effort of killing." Betsy grunted. "Typical super-villain. He steals the powers of a goddess, but not her wisdom. I'm surprised he didn't hang around to tell us all about his grand scheme for ruling the omniverse." She shrugged. "Well, his oversight will be our advantage . . . hopefully."

Roma struggled to sit up; Betsy lent her a much-needed hand. "We must . . . return to the . . . citadel . . . immediately."

"You shouldn't try to move around just yet," Betsy cautioned her.

"I . . . am weakened, Elisabeth," Roma said, her voice sounding just a bit stronger, "but I am not infirm. It *is* true that the human, von Doom, has caused me considerable pain—but what he has stolen from me is only a small portion of the power I possess." She swung her legs off the table and, using it for support, stood on her feet. "Though I may not be whole until all the aspects of myself that were torn away have been returned, still am I Roma, daughter of Merlyn." She tilted her head back proudly, a determined expression now set on her face. "Still am I Supreme Guardian."

A soft moan from the floor caught their attention, and all three looked to its source.

Betsy's alternate was starting to revive.

"She must not know of this place," Roma said gravely.

Betsy looked at her in shock. "You're not going to *kill* her, are you?"

Roma gently placed a hand on her shoulder and smiled weakly. "No, but it would be best if she did not see a duplicate Elisabeth Braddock standing before her when she awoke, or that she ever learn of the existence of the Starlight Citadel—if anything still exists by the time this day is through." The hand on Betsy's shoulder tightened as the Guardian began leaning on her for support. "Please . . . help me over to her . . ."

Both X-Men supported her as she walked the short distance to Elisabeth, then aided her in kneeling beside the groggy woman. Roma lightly touched her on the forehead; a warm light played over Elisabeth's features, and she settled back. Warren picked her up and carried her to the medical table.

"She will sleep now," Roma explained as Betsy helped her to her feet. "With luck, she will remember nothing of these wretched events when she awakes."

"Except that she's lost the only man she ever loved . . . the one who died in my—her—arms . . ." She turned to Warren. "What about your other counterpart? The one from Magneto's world . . . ?"

Warren shook his head as he walked back to join her. "He's . . . gone, Betts."

"Oh," was all she could say. She couldn't think of anything else.

"The strain of division, no doubt," Roma said. "His body could not handle the effects of the multiphasic crystal accelerator. It is a wonder that both of *you* managed to survive the process."

"Cold comfort in that," Betsy said quietly. "*We're* still here, but we've lost *two* lives already."

"And an even greater number may soon be lost, Elisabeth," Roma said gently, "if the chaos unleashed upon the omniverse is not put to an end."

Betsy nodded. "You're right, of course. It's just . . . I wish I could have done more for them. For everyone."

"Hey." Smiling warmly, Warren wrapped his arms around her waist from behind and drew her close. She placed her hands on his and leaned back, feeling comfort in the warmth of his body. "We've *all* felt that way at some point, Betts—wanting to do better, cursing ourselves when we can't. Thinking what we could have done differently, replaying it over and over again in our heads until it all becomes a blur . . . No one ever said being an X-Man would be an easy job, and it's not—take it from a founding member. Every day we put our lives on the line, without a second thought for our own safety, because we know that we're doing something *good*. Because people count on us. But we can *only* do the best we can."

"But sometimes that's not good enough," Betsy said.

"True," Warren agreed. "But we're not gods, Betts. We're not perfect; we have our limitations, just like any other person. And we can't expect to save *everyone* in a crisis, no matter how hard we might wish otherwise." He gave her a small squeeze. "You can't save the universe all on your own, Betts; Lord knows other people have tried before you, and failed. It's just too big a job." She felt him kiss the top of her head. "But if you want to try—okay. But you don't have to shoulder the burden alone. Not as long as you have *me*."

Betsy tilted her head up to look at him; at the caring eyes and the warm smile. She reached up to touch his face and gently stroked his cheek, her fingers gliding over the sandpapery, day-old stubble growing there. He was right, she knew.

"Thank you," she said softly, and kissed him.

"The reward makes it all worth the effort," he said, nuzzling her cheek with the tip of his nose. Then, with a smile, he turned to the celestial being standing before them. "Umm . . . About that 'gods' comment, Roma . . . no offense meant."

"None taken," she replied pleasantly. "Just be grateful my *father* was not present to hear it." Her smile faded. "But now, my friends, we must go. Time grows short, and only Order and Chaos know what madness the human von Doom will unleash upon the cosmos, now that he possesses the power of a Supreme Guardian."

Warren snorted. "Between that Knights of the Round Table reject and the Cosmic Cube, it's a wonder the cosmos is still *around.*" He frowned. "Just wish I knew who had their hands on the damn thing *now*. . . ."

From a corner of the room, Leonard watched quietly as the Red Skull advanced on the redheaded woman who had just materialized a moment before. Obviously, his master had tapped into the power of the Cosmic Cube, and used it to transport her across the Atlantic Ocean, bringing her from New York to Wewelsburg Castle in less than a heartbeat. Knowing that the Skull was able to do so without having to hold the device—a feat he had seen him do on other occasions—reminded the young Nazi of just how in control of everything the villain was . . . although the revelation that one of the Reich's outstanding officers was, in actuality, a mutant showed that even the all-mighty Emperor was capable of overlooking the smaller details in his creation. Not that Leonard was ever going to bring it to his attention—he might be a weak man, in the Skull's opinion, but he certainly wasn't a *stupid* one.

"Now, then, X-Man," the Skull growled, "the choice is simple: Tell me what I want to know—or prepare to die . . ."

Leonard started. *She* was one of the X-Men? He'd heard about them—renegade mutants who were always causing some bit of trouble somewhere in the world—but he'd always thought of them as freaks and grotesqueries, like the ones who were always being shipped off to Arnim Zola's labs on Genosha. He never thought any of them could look so . . . well, so *hot.*

But if she really *was* a mutant, maybe he was looking at an illusion—a mental picture she was generating around herself—and her good looks were just in his head. Or maybe she was in some kind of transitional phase, like a butterfly, only in reverse, and at any moment, she might degenerate from a beautiful woman into some gnarled hag, or a boneless lump of flesh writhing on the carpet.

Still, until that happened, he didn't mind scoping her out. It certainly beat looking at the Skull's face.

"You already know everything you need to," she replied. "The Cube is a danger to the universe—"

"Yes, but *how* do you know this?" the Skull asked. He snarled. "This nonsense of you traveling from another dimension to bring dire warnings—I do not believe it! You are of *this* world, are you not?"

She hesitated for a moment. "Yes."

"Then, why were *you* not affected by the Cube?" She fell silent, and he eyed her warily. "Because you were not *on* Earth when von Doom first activated it," he concluded, and nodded, agreeing with himself when she didn't answer. "Yeeesss . . . That would explain a great deal . . ." He stepped back and began walking around her in a slow circle, arms folded across his chest. "But where *were* you, then, when the transformation occurred? Another dimension, as Viper mentioned? Perhaps. And yet . . ." He halted in front of her again. "And yet you *knew* that the Cube was involved. You *sought* the Cube—to reverse the process, yes?"

"Yes," she replied, glaring defiantly at him.

"But, how was that possible?" He stepped closer. "Who told you of it? What prompted you to go offworld?"

"No one told us about *anything,"* the woman replied. "And as for why the X-Men weren't on Earth when everything changed . . ." She paused. "It has nothing to do with this situation."

"No," he said, and thrust a finger in her face. *"No.* You are lying, mutant!" His eyes began to glow with a golden light, and the woman flinched.

"W-what are you . . . doing . . . ?" she gasped, placing a hand to her forehead. "Stop it . . ."

"Tell the truth, and I shall consider it," the Skull replied. "You hurt only yourself by feigning ignorance." The glow brightened, just a bit, and she gnashed her teeth. It was clear to Leonard that the Skull was increasing the pressure—using the Cube to squeeze her head, or something like that. He wondered just how much she'd be able to take before it exploded.

"Now, then," the Skull continued, "who told you to leave the planet before the Cube was activated?"

"N-no one. We were asked to . . . help a . . . friend." The woman compressed her lips together and moaned sharply. "Leaving when . . . we did . . . it was just . . . a coincidence . . ."

"And the universe runs on such whims of fate, does it not? But *where* did you go, hmmm? *Who* was this 'friend' who could transport you across dimensions? *What* was so important that it took you away from Earth?"

She gasped and suddenly stiffened, the glow from the Skull's eyes now enveloping her body. Even from where he was standing, Leonard could see her eyes roll back in her head.

"What are you hiding from me, mutant?" the Skull purred. "What is it that prevents me from—Ah. Now, I see . . ." The light in his eyes flashed brightly—

And then two other versions of the woman suddenly peeled away from her, and dropped, unconscious, to the floor.

"Interesting . . ." the Skull said.

"Daaaamn . . ." Leonard muttered.

One was dressed in the clothes she had been wearing just a

moment ago—white blouse and black leather skirt. The other was attired in some kind of maroon and purple bodysuit, with matching gloves and boots. But it was the third woman—the one still conscious—who captivated his attention.

She wore a bright green bodysuit, with golden thigh-high boots and long gloves. A golden sash encircled her waist, resting low on her hips. Her hair tumbled around her shoulders in a fiery mane, framing the bird-like design emblazoned on her chest.

"Welcome, Phoenix," the Skull said.

Slowly, the woman regained her feet, then looked down at herself in amazement. "I'm . . . free," she said, and turned to the Skull. "But . . . why did you do that?"

"Because your mind was cluttered with useless thoughts," he snapped. "Yours, and those of your duplicates, which I detected as I made my way into your subconscious. The information I seek is buried in the depths of your mind; obtaining it simply required removing the blockage. And now that I have cleared the way—*I shall have it!*"

His eyes suddenly blazed again. Phoenix cried out and clutched her head.

"Get . . . get out . . ." she moaned through gritted teeth. *"Get out, damn you!"*

"Stop fighting me, mutant!" the Skull ordered. "Your mental powers are considerable, but they are as *nothing* compared to those of the Cosmic Cube—or the one who commands it!" The light intensified. *"Open your thoughts to me! Give me that information!"*

The woman screamed, and dropped to her hands and knees. Seeing the sadistic grin on the face of his master as he strengthened his assault on her mind, Leonard pressed against the wall behind him, as though he could conceal himself within the paint.

"Yeesss . . ." the Skull hissed, eyes closed as though in ecstasy. "I see it now . . . a gleaming palace at the center of reality . . . one to which all dimensions are joined . . ." He grinned his death's-head smile. *"That* is the next prize to be won—a challenge worthy of the Red Skull! To rule not just one, but countless dimensions! To reach my hand across Eternity, and know that billions upon billions of subjects tremble in its shadow! *To be master over all of time and space!"*

His brow suddenly furrowed; the smile faded. "But how to *reach* this wondrous edifice? Why do I not see *that?* I sense the power that sent you hurtling across infinity, but not a way to return to its source . . ."

He opened his eyes, and the light faded. Groaning loudly, Phoenix collapsed at his feet, breathing hard. He'd released her, Leonard realized, and eased forward from the wall.

The Skull frowned as he gazed at Phoenix. "The information is incomplete. You only possess a small part of the puzzle. I need the rest of the pieces–the ones that must lay hidden in the minds of your team members." His lipless mouth pulled back in a disturbing smile. "And I know *exactly* how to go about acquiring them. . . ."

INTERLUDE(S) VIII

SO, you got a plan fer gettin' t'the Skull?" Wolverine asked.

"Not at the moment, Logan," Lensherr admitted. He glanced at his traveling companion as they tramped through the moonlit woods, saw the frown that creased his weathered features. "Really, Logan—I only just escaped from a concentration camp last evening. I have been beaten, bloodied, and bruised, shot at and mutilated. My body is weak, my powers still recharging. What would you have me do?"

"Droppin' dead right in front'a me would do fer a start."

"Beyond that."

Wolverine snarled at him. "I think you've done enough already, ya piece o' slime. We had a deal, back when Doom had the Cube—"

"Yes, yes," Lensherr interjected. "I'm well aware of the terms of the agreement I reached with your leader, Cyclops. In exchange for my cooperation, you would have the chance to try and reverse what von Doom had done to the planet."

"An' ya went back on yer word, bub," Wolverine said.

Lensherr shook his head. "Not true. You imbeciles *had* your chance, as we'd agreed, and you failed. Therefore, it was necessary for me to step in."

"By orderin' yer acolytes t'attack us, an' then snatchin' up the Cube fer yerself."

"Oh, come now, Logan! Did you actually think I would simply stand around and allow the means of achieving ultimate power to slip from my grasp?" Lensherr snorted. "You, almost as well as Charles Xavier, should know my motivations clearly enough by now."

"I know ya all right, Magnus," Wolverine countered. "I just expected *better'a* ya."

The comment took him by surprise. "You insolent little thug! How *dare* you!" he bellowed.

"How dare *I?*" Wolverine snapped, rounding on him. "*I* ain't the one who went screwin' around with the flamin' Cube, bub! *I* ain't the one who stabbed the X-Men in the back, when we was tryin' t'fix what yer old buddy Doom messed up! An' *I* ain't the one who allowed the Red Skull t'get his scummy hands on the Cube so he could turn the whole flamin' planet into a stinkin' Nazi slaughterhouse!" His lips drew back in a feral snarl, and he pointed an accusatory finger at Lensherr. "There were billions o' people across I-don't-know how many dimensions who were countin' on us t'get the job done, an' because o' *you,* an' *Doom,* an' the *Skull,* all'a them—an' *us,* too—got a good chance'a never seein' another day!" He looked at his long-time enemy in disgust. "How dare *I?* Where the hell did *you* ever get the idea you could play God? All ya know how t'do is cause misery an' destruction—oh, yer *real* good at *that,* ain't ya? An' fer what? So ya can rule the world, like you've always dreamed?" He spat on the ground, near Lensherr's feet. "*That's* what I think'a yer dream, ya piece o' filth, *an'* yer high-an'-mighty attitude."

He stomped forward, getting right in Magnus's face. "You wanna go on thinkin' yer better'n me? Fine. But when I'm done with the Skull—if the world hasn't totally gone t'hell by then—you an' me, we're gonna *finish* this, once an' fer all. An' *then* we'll see who the better man is."

"Oh, indeed we shall, Logan," Lensherr murmured with a snarl. "I look forward to the outcome . . ."

And then, without any warning, they disappeared in a flash of light.

Hundreds of miles away, high above the streets of New York, in an office belonging to the commander of the city's security forces, a heavily sedated man groaned in his sleep and rolled over.

Slowly, the eyes of Professor Charles Xavier began to open. His body felt stiff, his thoughts still cloudy from the powerful drug. But there was something different about him, now: a determined set to his jaw that hadn't existed before; a fire that burned hotly in his eyes; a hard-won triumphant smile that came to his lips.

"At last . . ." he whispered. "I'm . . . *free* . . ."

And then he vanished in a burst of light.

The last person Nightcrawler literally expected to run into—or wanted to see—as he tore through the corridors of Ministry of Health headquarters was Ororo Munroe. He was certain the feeling was more than mutual.

Getting to the landing area had turned out to be more difficult than he'd expected—mainly because someone had obviously figured out where he was heading, and dispatched the majority of the security forces to keep him from climbing any higher in the building. He'd tried making his way through the ventilation system, but the airflow tunnels had apparently been designed to prevent such a situation; no doubt other mutants in the past had tried escaping in just such a fashion. That left him with two choices: the elevators, and the stairwells. The former had a certain appeal, because he could climb through the roof hatch in one of the cars and climb up the shaft. The latter meant another chase in a tightly enclosed area, with bullets whizzing all around him.

He had some success with the elevator shaft, until he must have tripped a hidden sensor somewhere along the way. Then the door on the floor above him had been wrenched open, and some fool with a flamethrower had tried to burn him. Wagner teleported behind the man and gave him a shove, catapulting him into the shaft. When he struck the top of the car a few moments later, his screams of agony over his broken leg were all the proof Nightcrawler needed to hear to know he hadn't killed him. But any sense of relief had been quickly replaced by thoughts of self-preservation as more doors slid open on higher floors, and soldiers started rappelling down the shaft.

Well, at least someone had turned off the damnable klaxon. It was bad enough being chased through a building by an army without having to deal with a splitting headache.

Another mad dash through an adjacent stairwell later, and he had tumbled out onto the sixtieth floor to catch his breath, knowing his pursuers weren't too far behind him. Not for the first time, he wished that the designers of this facility had had the foresight to have maps placed on each floor; a small sign stenciled with YOU ARE HERE in bright red letters on a grid would have done wonders for his sense of direction.

It was as he whipped around a corner at the end of the hall that he collided with another fugitive. The impact sent his stylish sunglasses flying through the air, to smash against a framed blow-up of the Emperor.

"Bright Lady preserve me," said a familiar voice. "You!"

Picking his dazed head up off the floor, Wagner looked at the feminine obstruction that had brought him to a halt. "Fräulein Munroe!" He sneered. "What an unexpected surprise. It's so rare that one bumps into an alleged co-conspirator these days."

"So, *you* are the cause for the alarm!" she said, using the wall behind her for support as she regained her feet. A sly grin crept across her exquisite features. "What happened, Nightcrawler? No longer a valued member of the Reich?"

"Thanks to you and your cohorts," he replied. "I hope you're pleased with the results of your slanderous remarks."

"To a degree," she admitted, "though it was no fault of mine. This woman they kept mentioning—"

"Frau Sommers."

"Yes. Apparently, she is under the impression that she knows us."

"That seems to be happening more often these days," he remarked sarcastically. He grabbed her by the wrist. "But now is not the time for sorting through our memories for previous encounters. We must go—now."

They turned toward a door leading to another set of stairs. But before they could move, the corridor filled with a dazzling light.

And when it at last faded, they were gone.

"You sure this is such a good idea, Remy?" Rogue asked, her voice heavy with uncertainty. "I mean, breakin' into the main headquarters of the city's security forces? It's crazy—an' suicidal, if ya don't mind me sayin' so."

"Well, dat's de place dey was takin' you to," Gambit explained, "so it makes sense dat dat's where we'll find Cyclops. All we gotta do is sneak in an' break 'im out—but quiet."

" 'Quiet.' Right," Rogue said. "Quiet like the way you got me outta that armored car on the highway?"

Remy smiled. "Dat was an accident. But I didn' hear you complainin' 'bout it after I did it."

"Well, I . . ." She paused, then smiled, too. "I wasn't *myself* then, sugah. Otherwise, you woulda gotten an earful."

"Den I should be grateful for small favors, *non*?" he said, and grinned.

Not waiting for a reply, he quickly stepped past her and flung open the door of the storage chamber.

Rogue tossed him the oversized trenchcoat he'd loaned her. He caught it in one hand, then held it out to her. She shook her head. "You keep it; it'd just wrap 'round my legs while we're flyin'." She smiled wryly. " 'Sides, y'all look down right underdressed without a big coat on."

Remy nodded in appreciation and slipped it on. He paused as something in the pockets thumped against his legs. He reached in, and came out with four packs of cards: two of playing cards, one of a collector's edition commemorating "Great Moments in Reich History," and one of a child's well-thumbed "Go Fish" set.

"I found 'em in one'a the cartons, when I was rootin' 'round 'em before," Rogue explained. "Thought y'all might need some ammunition, for when ya get an urge to blow somethin' up." She grinned broadly. "An' I *know* how y'all get some mighty *powerful* urges when it comes t'that kinda stuff."

"Among *other* t'ings, *chere*," he said slyly. He extended his hand toward her, and she stepped forward to take it—

—and they both suddenly vanished in a burst of light.

The armored transport containing *former* Reichsmajor Sommers pulled into an underground parking garage just off Forty-fourth Street and Lexington Avenue. The trip through Queens, and across the Fifty-ninth Street Bridge into Manhattan, had passed without incident—no fear of a rescue attempt by mutant revolutionaries this time, not with a Sentinel hovering overhead.

The vehicle continued south for two blocks, down a side passage, to come to a halt beneath what was once known as the Chrysler Building, but had since been designated the New York headquarters of the Ministry of Defense. As the vehicle parked, the doors to a bank of elevators opened, and a squad of heavily armed soldiers poured out to meet it.

One of the soldiers moved to the back of the transport to open the rear doors, as the others took up firing positions. Their orders were simple: If Sommers had broken free, kill him before he could use his powers; if he were still shackled, escort him up to Lady Viper's office, where he would join his wife.

The doors swung wide. To the disappointment of most of those assembled in the subterranean space, the prisoner was *still* a prisoner, chains clanking as he struggled to his feet. Sommers paused at the edge of the top step, and stared at all the guns pointed at him.

"An honor guard? For me?" he asked sarcastically. "And here I thought I'd fallen out of favor with the Empire."

The youngest guard riding with him—Zumwald—gave him a savage push from behind. "Out, freak!" he barked.

Sommers tumbled from the vehicle and landed awkwardly, as the chain between his ankles made it difficult to keep his balance. Nevertheless, he was able to right himself before he fell flat on his face. Snarling, he turned back to the young soldier.

"You should be more careful about whom you touch, private," he said. Zumwald gazed at him blankly. "Don't you pay attention to the notices from the Ministry of Health?" Sommers flashed an icy smile. "You never know what sort of unpleasant diseases we filthy mutants might be carrying."

Zumwald started, and stared at his hand. He'd removed his padded gloves during the ride from the spaceport, complaining they made his hands too sweaty. Now it was clear he wished he'd never taken them off.

"I should have that examined immediately, private—you wouldn't want to grow a third arm, or an extra mouth, would you?" He laughed at the look of horror that transfixed Zumwald's face, then turned to the soldiers clustered around the area. "I believe I have an appointment with your commander." He drew himself to his full height, chin tilted upward in a defiant gesture. "Inform her that Reichsmajor Sommers is here to see her, and—"

He never got to finish his pronouncement. There was a sudden flash of blinding light in the dimly lit garage; when it faded, he had disappeared.

The chains he'd been wearing clattered noisily to the asphalt.

Cautiously, one of the soldiers stepped forward, waving a hand out in front of him, as though expecting to come into contact with a mutant suddenly gone invisible. When nothing happened, he slowly reached down and picked up the chains, then looked at his fellow warriors.

"All right," he said. "Who wants to explain this to Commander Viper. . . ?"

19

THE first indication Linda McQuillan—Captain U.K. of Earth 794—had that something was *very* wrong aboard the Starlight Citadel was when the very man she and the rest of the Captain Britain Corps had been hunting for hours came strutting down the main promenade, as though he owned the place.

Of all the bloody cheek . . . she thought.

The second indication was that he was accompanied by that annoying, self-important Dr. Stanton from the medical wing. He didn't appear to be a hostage, though; in fact, he seemed to be acting as an escort.

"Not good . . ." Linda muttered. "Not good at all . . ." She tapped the comm-link button on her helmet. "Central, this is Seven-Nine-Four U.K. You're not going to believe this. . . ."

Stanton glanced around nervously as he and von Doom walked along the promenade. He saw the startled expressions on the faces of the people they passed—he was certain they matched his own.

Von Doom obviously noticed. "Is there a problem, physician?"

"Umm . . . well . . ." Stanton fumbled, looking for the right words. "Do you really think it's . . . wise to be doing this . . . er,

Lord Doom? I mean, walking around so openly when you're being sought by security?"

"Stop your quivering, worm," von Doom snapped. "This day, you walk with a god."

Stanton nodded, head bobbing up and down as though attached to a loose hinge. "Oh, yes," he mumbled. "The powers of the Guardian, and all. I forgot about that . . ."

"For too long has Doom remained in the shadows." He waved a hand at the hundreds of representatives of humanoid and totally alien-looking races milling around them, yet giving both dictator and physician a wide berth. "Now it is time for these rabble to meet their new lord and master—and learn to fear him . . ."

"HALT!" ordered a loud feminine voice.

Striding purposefully down the walkway toward them was an attractive young woman dressed in a bright, Union Jack-decorated uniform. A shock of white hair stuck up from the open top of her helmet/mask. The distinctive outfit identified her as a member of the Captain Britain Corps, and Stanton recognized her as Captain U.K., who had been one of the warriors who originally brought von Doom to the medical wing for observation when he arrived on the citadel.

Not bothering to acknowledge Stanton, she walked right up to von Doom and seized his arm in a powerful grip. "Victor von Doom, I am placing you under arrest for the cold-blooded murders of Captains Wales and Commonwealth," she stated in an authoritative tone. "If you resist, I shall have no choice but to use force."

"You *dare* lay a hand upon your god?" von Doom growled.

"Oh, so now you're a god, are you?" Captain U.K. sneered at him. "I hate to tell you this, 'Your Almightiness,' but the position was filled a long time a—"

And then she was suddenly airborne, careening wildly across the promenade, to crash against a wall. There were cries and shouts from the bystanders around her, and they began running in all directions.

"Well, I can't say that *that* was unexpected . . ." Stanton muttered.

"You *will* respect me, woman!" von Doom bellowed. "You will *worship* me—or you will *die!*"

She lurched to her feet, and glared at him. "If I choose the latter, does that mean I won't have to listen to your rubbish any more?"

Standing behind von Doom, Stanton sighed, and shook his head. "Now, *that* wasn't a very wise thing to say . . ."

As if in response, the armored tyrant roared, and raised a gauntleted hand at his costumed enemy.

Leaning against the wall, Linda tensed, waiting to be thrown around again like a doll. But that didn't happen. Instead, a circular opening appeared in the palm of von Doom's glove—and it began to glow with the build-up of an energy charge.

"Oh, bloody hell!" she cried.

The first beam passed over her head as she ducked low, and then she was diving for cover. More blasts quickly followed, and the windows of shops around and behind her exploded as the accelerator energy violently separated their atoms. Patrons, visitors, and workers were sent flying, and debris rained down on the promenade as fire alarms began sounding.

Crouched behind a sweets cart, she stabbed at her comm-link. "Central, the subject is armed—I repeat, *armed*—with an energy weapon! I need backup! What—?" She paused, and sneered. "No, I *don't* know how he obtained one, you idiot, and I'm not about to bloody well ask him! Now, stop talking and—*Damn!*"

The beam detonated the spot on the floor where she was—or just had been, if she hadn't seen von Doom targeting her again. She took to the air, this time under her own power, and sped straight at him, hoping to knock him off his feet before he got off another shot.

But she never reached her objective. Because with a simple flick of von Doom's wrist, she suddenly found herself outside the citadel—and hurtling through the swirling, destructive currents of the space/time vortex.

"Oh, my God . . ." she whispered—and then she was swept away.

"At last, all the players have been gathered together, and our drama nears its final act."

The Red Skull looked about the room, obviously quite pleased with what he saw. Enveloped in a golden glow, suspended a few inches above the carpeted floor of his office, was a group of costumed men and women, most of whom Leonard did not recognize—not counting the redheaded Phoenix, of course. The rest, he figured, must be other members of the X-Men, although he found it hard to believe that its roster would include a middle-aged bald guy and someone who looked old enough to be his grandfather.

But it was not just the X-Men who were gathered in this office. Scattered across the floor, like discarded rag dolls, were a collection of unconscious variants of the mutants—including one that could only be Reichsmajor Sommers himself—that joined the two alternates that had been torn away from Phoenix. Did *every* mutant have an extra body or two they carried around inside them?

The only group member who apparently didn't have a duplicate was somebody named "Gambit," although, according to the identification found on him, the uniform he wore belonged to a worker named Remy Lebeau, who was a clerk at Kaltenbrunner Spaceport in New York. The Skull had mentioned something about being unable to separate the X-Man from the lowly clerk, but had then moved on.

There were two more costumed women, both as attractive as Phoenix. (Was *every* female mutant as good-looking as these three? If so, Leonard reflected, he might have to change his opinion of them as a whole.) One was white, with a skunk-like streak through her brown hair, wearing a green-and-yellow bodysuit decorated with an "X" on the left breast, yellow boots and gloves, and a beaten-up leather bomber jacket. The other was African, with a mane of white hair that fell to her waist, and who possessed no discernable pupils in her eyes—the sockets were filled with a disturbing, overall whiteness. She wore a shoulderless black leather outfit, with a pair of immense pieces of material joined loosely to the sleeves; they almost looked like wings. "Rogue" and "Storm," respectively, the Skull had called the women.

Beside the black woman was something that looked like an honest-to-God blue-skinned demon, complete with fangs and pointed tail and ears. Leonard recognized him as "Nightcrawler," one of the members of Lightning Force. But since no one else from the team was present, he assumed it meant that, in the "real" world, the German-born mutant lived among others of his kind. It made sense—a lot more than the notion that a subhuman like Kurt Wagner would be trusted to work alongside his genetic superiors.

Next to Nightcrawler was a short, thuggish-looking guy in his forties, wearing a yellow-and-blue costume with a ridiculously large set of points jutting up from the sides of his mask. "Wolverine," the Skull had called him, and Leonard could understand the reference: the guy certainly looked hairy enough—and mean enough—to be mistaken for a wild animal.

Then there was "Cyclops." His dark Nazi uniform replaced by more colorful blue and yellow spandex, it was difficult for Leonard to see just how anyone could have overlooked the man's mutant nature—the visor covering his eyes should have been a clue, considering he never took it off. From the worried glance Phoenix had given him when he materialized beside her, Leonard imagined they must be a couple, maybe even married. The thought of intimacy between freaks—even ones as handsome as these two—made the young Nazi a little queasy.

Or was that *jealous,* because he could see just how deeply in love they were?

On the other side of Rogue was Gambit. Except for Rogue, the other mutants had acted like they'd seen a ghost when he'd first appeared, teleported to the castle like the rest of them via the Cosmic Cube. Why they should have had that reaction was unclear, and the Skull hadn't seemed particularly interested in pursuing the subject.

The baldheaded man in the dark business suit was Professor Xavier—Leonard had seen him on the viewscreen during the Skull's video teleconference with Lady Viper. He also remembered him as the idiot who'd tried to stop the Skull from stealing the Cube, back when the white-haired septuagenarian next to him—Magneto—had possessed it.

Magneto. Shouldn't he be dead by now? Leonard wondered. He'd seen with his own eyes how deeply the Skull had rammed his obsidian blade into the mutant overlord's chest when he made his play for the Cube. Had seen how much blood had poured from the wound; had heard him take his last breaths. And yet, there he floated, healthy once more, looking quite formidable in his maroon-and-purple outfit, light playing off the gleaming metal of his gladiator-style helmet.

But *why* should he be so healthy? Did the Skull *always* let his enemies go on living, even when they were at death's door? Wouldn't it just be easier to let them die, so they wouldn't have a chance to strike back at him later?

Perhaps, Leonard reflected, that was why the Skull had always been defeated in the past. That overriding sense of vanity the man possessed; that illogical need to crow of his triumphs to his enemies, to let them know he could kill them *if he wanted to*—it had always been the cause of his downfall. Perhaps it would be again.

And would that be such a *bad* thing if it did? Leonard had to admit it: he'd had his fill of death and misery. He had seen what a world controlled by the followers of Adolf Hitler would be like, and it was nothing like the fanciful visions he'd created in his mind of all-powerful Master Race leading mankind into a new Golden Age. No, this was a miserable, dark, horrifying place, filled with suffering and torture, despair and anguish, human monsters and madmen who imagined themselves the saviors of their race, and—

And now, he just wanted things to go back to the way they'd been . . .

"All right, Skull," Cyclops said. "You've brought us all together–now what?"

"Now, mutant," the Skull replied, "you give to me the knowledge of this 'Starlight Citadel' your lovely wife was good enough to provide." He reached out a gloved hand and caressed Jean's cheek. Her lips drew back in disgust. "Each of you has retained a tiny portion of the power used to transport you back to Earth. By wresting them from your minds, I will be able to retrace the route you traveled, and lay the foundation for a new empire–one that will stretch from the dawn of Creation, to the end of time itself, and across infinity!"

"And humans say *I* have delusions of grandeur," Magneto commented drolly.

"Silence, Jew!" the Skull barked. He stomped over to his longtime rival for world domination. "I know not why you arrived here with the others–perhaps the Cube recognized your taint from when you held it, and summoned you–but, in a way, I am pleased. For now you shall bear witness to the moment when the Red Skull threw off his Earthly bonds, and began his ascendancy to godhood!"

With a triumphant grin, he put out his hand–and the Cosmic Cube suddenly appeared.

"The Cube . . ." Magneto said in hushed tones. His eyes glittered with desire.

"This cannot be good . . ." Storm commented.

"Uh-huh. I t'ink we in for a world o' hurtin' now, *mon braves*," Gambit said.

"Oh, yes," the Skull replied. He placed both hands around it, coveting his hard-won prize. His eyes began to glow with a harsh light. "Yes, you are. . . ."

20

"THIS is ridiculous."

It hadn't taken Sat-yr-nin long to realize she was never going to locate von Doom in this . . . whatever it was—wasteland, limbo, cosmic storage facility that lay beyond Roma's bed chamber. It might look like a flat, unbroken plain, but she could swear she'd been cresting hills and descending into valleys during her journey—either she was imaging things, or the true design of the landscape was undetectable by the naked eye.

Eventually, she gave up the search, and started looking for an exit. She'd noticed how her skin began to tingle when she walked in a particular direction; it grew stronger the farther she advanced. The sensation was akin to the one she'd experienced when she passed through the door leading from the Guardian's chambers—therefore, it stood to reason that the pins-and-needles effect was an indication that she was getting closer to her point of entry.

The journey back went a great deal faster and easier than the one going out, now that she had a guide of sorts to direct her. In not time at all—or what felt like it as she walked through this blank-featured neverland—she had located the doorway.

As she gripped the knob and turned it, an idea came to mind. Perhaps chasing after her errant ally had been the wrong way to approach confronting him about the Cube. She *was* the Mastrex of an empire, after all—armored imbeciles like the self-proclaimed "Doctor" Doom should be seeking *her* counsel, not the other way around. Let him come to her when he had finished doing whatever it was he was doing back there in limbo. She would wait for him in the throne room—to test out the fit of the high-backed chair, and maybe even think of a truly inventive way to kill him . . . before he had a chance to kill her.

Sat-yr-nin grinned wickedly and opened the door. Alliances were such fleeting things, she thought—especially when neither party could be trusted . . .

So focused was she on her plans for revenge that she never realized someone was standing just to one side of the door in the Guardian's apartment—until something cracked against her skull, plunging her into darkness.

For Betsy and Warren, finding their way from Merlyn's pocket dimension back to the Roma's apartment was a simple task. All it required was another trip through the shadow realm, with a small power boost from Roma to allow them passage through the transduction barrier that kept the featureless landscape from coming into direct contact with the citadel—for safety reasons, she had explained.

Before they'd departed, Betsy gave a brief account of her encounter with the mind-controlled Alecto, and the damage that had been done to Roma's belongings. She'd just wanted to prepare the Guardian for what she was going to see when they got there, and Roma said that she understood, But when they stepped from the portal Betsy had created, they were greeted by a sight none of them could have prepared for.

There were two Saturnynes in the room.

Both were attired in the same flowing white robes; both possessed a fine mane of snow-white hair. The sole difference between them came from the fact that one was wide awake and free to witness the arrival of the X-Men and their celestial charge, while the other was unconscious, bound and gagged with strips of torn bed sheets, and tossed onto a pile of large throw pillows on the floor.

Roma looked stunned. *"What is the meaning of this?"* she asked angrily.

The version of the Majestrix still standing looked equally surprised by the sudden appearance of the trio. She dropped to one knee, and inclined her head. "Forgive me, m'lady. I wouldn't have normally barged in, unannounced, like this, but knowing that your life was in danger—"

The Guardian's stern expression faded, replaced by a gentle smile. "Saturnyne? Is it really *you,* my friend?"

The Majestrix raised her head. "Yes, m'lady. I apologize for not getting here sooner, but I was unavoidably detained by . . ." She gestured toward her restrained surrogate. "Well, you can see for yourself."

"Indeed," the Guardian said, and gestured for Her Whyness to stand up. Roma walked over to her lieutenant and gently placed her hands on the woman's shoulders. "I am pleased to know you are well, my friend."

Saturnyne seemed genuinely touched by the Guardian's sentiment. "Thank you, m'lady," she said. It was one of the few times Betsy could ever recall seeing the woman smile.

"Come," Roma said to them all. "We must away to the throne room."

Warren pointed to Sat-yr-nin, who moaned softly through the folds of her thick gag. "What about her?"

"She'll keep—until she can be placed back in stasis," Her Whyness replied with a malicious smile. She turned to Roma, and the smile immediately evaporated. "Umm . . . about the torn sheets, m'lady—"

"There *are* greater concerns this day, Saturnyne," the Guardian replied.

"Indeed," the Majestrix said, nodding in agreement.

With a final glance at the prisoner, and a quick check of Alecto—who was still sleeping off his rather violent encounter with

Betsy's psi-blade—they hurried to the throne room . . . in time to meet von Doom and Stanton as they entered from the hallway.

Warren sighed. "Is this guy like a bad penny, or what?"

"You are too late, woman!" the tyrant shouted triumphantly to Roma as he ascended the throne. "Doom has won! And there is nothing that you, or anyone else, can do to stop him from laying claim to his destiny—to rule infinity!"

And that was the moment, as fate would have it, when what could only be described as a multi-dimensional missile streaked into the east wing of the citadel, and exploded.

The structure tilted crazily as the projectile continued through level after level, room after room. Artificial gravity cut off, and the vacuum rushed in to fill the hole created by the impact. Hundreds of residents and visitors were sucked into the vortex, never to be seen again.

And matters were only going to become worse.

In the throne room, everyone but Roma and von Doom were thrown to the floor by the explosion. Alarms sounded, and the shadow creatures that lived in the depths of the chamber began screaming in agony.

"A reality breach!" Saturnyne cried. "M'lady—"

"Yes, Saturnyne—I know," Roma said.

"*I* don't," Warren commented. "What does it mean?"

"It means the citadel has been opened to the vortex," Saturnyne explained curtly. "It means the transduction barriers protecting us from the forces of time and space have fallen, and the temporal energies now threaten to rip us all apart, if the damage is not repaired."

Warren blew out a sharp breath. "Man, things just keep going from bad to worse around here, don't they . . . ?"

"What is this?" von Doom roared as the citadel continued to shudder. He pointed an accusatory finger at Roma. "What have you done, woman?"

"I have done nothing," the Guardian answered. "But I fear we may learn the cause of this disaster soon enough."

And then, as if on cue, the floor of the throne room erupted, and the projectile finally came to rest. The chamber filled with smoke, and the burnt, ozone-tinged stench of spent energies. Betsy coughed violently: her eyes watered, her lungs were burning. But through the choking haze she could see a figure moving about—one clad in gleaming armor.

But it wasn't von Doom.

"I have arrived!" the figure proclaimed, stepping from the smoke. And as he moved into the light of the chamber, his identity became clear to all.

"The Red Skull . . ." Warren said hoarsely.

Staring in wide-eyed horror at the scarlet-hued death's-head that cackled madly before her, and the Cosmic Cube that he clutched tightly in one hand, only one thought came to Betsy's mind: "This is very bad. . . ."

21

"DIS is bad, people—*real bad!*"

No truer words could have spoken, Jean thought, even if they *did* come with a heavy Cajun accent.

The ground bucked and heaved, like a bull released from its pen at a rodeo, and all the X-Men could do was lie flat on the office floor and try to ride it out. Anything not bolted down—which meant just about every piece of furniture and decoration—tumbled and twisted, bounced and bumped around and against the group, eliciting a variety of groans, gasps, and colorful expletives from the heroes as each object made contact.

Well, Jean thought as she dodged a marble statue of Winged Victory that ricocheted past her head, *in a strange way, as bad as things may be, it certainly beats having someone digging around inside your brain . . .*

The Skull had squeezed the last bits of information about the citadel from his prisoners, leaving them too weak to do anything more than hang limply in the Cube-generated field that suspended them in the air. The process had been especially hard on Xavier, who, like Jean, had initially struggled to keep the Skull from invading his mind. But the grotesque villain would not be denied; in time, the professor, too, surrendered his piece of the puzzle.

And then, with the parts of the location finally collected within the Cube, the Skull simply vanished in a burst of light.

A moment later, the X-Men came crashing down onto the carpet, the hold over them released.

"Some host *he* is," Rogue said sarcastically as she sat up. "Didn' even say 'good night' before runnin' out on us."

"Let us just hope, *mein freund*," Nightcrawler said, helping Ororo to her feet, "that he has not—what is the expression?—'stuck us with the bill'?"

That was about the point where the first tremors began.

"I *hate* it when ya say stuff like that, elf," Wolverine muttered. "It just puts a jinx on the whole flamin' thing."

"There are times when I am in complete agreement with you, Logan," Kurt replied with a sigh. "Especially in this case, since I appear to have left my wallet in my other costume . . ."

The floor lurched again, and this time the quake created a fissure along one wall. It started at the base, then began working its way up. Chunks of stone fell as it reached the ceiling.

"We have to evacuate!" Scott yelled. Using the Skull's executive desk for support, he raised himself up, then pointed to the group's unconscious doppelgangers. "Let's get these people out of here! Move!"

Rogue, Ororo, and Jean were the first to respond, because their powers allowed them to fly over the shaking floor. Jean telekinetically grabbed hold of her alternates; Rogue did likewise. Ororo, however, was momentarily brought up short when she saw that one of her duplicates was wearing a wedding band. Jean didn't have the heart to tell her the poor woman was married to Doctor Doom—the thought that, in another lifetime, she might have willingly devoted herself to that tyrant would only haunt Ororo for the rest of her days. Her surprise lasted only a moment, though, before she focused on the task at hand.

"Hey! What about me?" asked a panicked voice.

A man in his early twenties stumbled toward them. He wore a dark gray uniform and black leather jackboots, his blond hair cut short, in the style worn by most young Nazis.

"You're the Skull's assistant!" Jean said. "I saw you skulking in the back of the room when he brought me here."

"Er . . . yes ma'am," he said sheepishly. Another rumble shook the building, and now pieces of the ceiling began raining down. He looked up, wide-eyed, then turned back to Jean. "But, could we talk about this when we get outside, though . . . ?"

Amazingly, Magneto—*Magneto,* of all people!—used his powers to shatter the room's outer wall, then gathered together the Skull's assistant, as well as the rest of the X-Men and their counterparts, in a protective magnetic bubble, and floated them away from the castle. The three women quickly joined them, and set their charges on the grass, just as the ground finally settled.

"Hey!" Gambit said, and pointed to the stronghold. "Does everybody see dat, too?"

As one, the heroes and villain turned to look.

There were three versions of the castle standing before them—but not separately. They overlapped in a phantom-like state, changing size and design from one moment to the next, becoming solid, then fading. It was difficult to look at the effect for long without feeling a dull headache.

"I believe we are seeing what happens when the Cosmic Cube has been removed from Earth," Magneto said. "Without its energies to sustain the illusion, the world is returning to normal."

" 'Normal'?" Jean said. She pointed to their alternates. "You think three versions of the same thing is normal? Don't you understand what's going on here?" She waved a hand around; the effect the castle was experiencing had spread across the countryside. The landscape looked like a picture taken out of focus. "This isn't an illusion—this is all real! All these worlds, all these people, are real! I learned as much from communing with my . . . other selves. And from what I could piece together, I think I've finally figured out what the flaw in the Cube is: It's not changing the world, it's finding other versions from the multitude of choices in the omniverse—and laying one on top of the other!"

Lensherr started. "But that would mean there are—"

"Yes! Three different Earths, all trying to occupy the same space!" Jean concluded.

"An' us caught right in the middle of 'em," Rogue said. "As usual."

"And without the Skull to control the situation," Jean continued, "the reality-cancer created by the Cube is going to start spreading again."

Scott nodded grimly. "Which puts us right back where we started from . . . only in an even worse situation."

Lensherr suddenly turned to the professor. "Charles, where is my daughter? Where is Anya?"

Xavier paused, then shook his head. "I . . . don't know, Eric. When the Red Skull transformed the world—"

"You *swore* to me, Charles!" Lensherr roared. "You *swore* you would protect her! You *swore* you would keep her safe from the monsters running this planet!" He grabbed Xavier by the lapels of his jacket and hauled him to his feet. "You *lied* to me, Charles. You kept telling me that, in order for reality to be stabilized, *nothing* I created with the Cube had to remain—friends, family, the very world itself. But that wasn't true, was it? If Phoenix is correct, that world has always existed—one where my daughter never died!" The hardness in his eyes subsided. "Don't you realize what that means, Charles? I could have had her back! I could have held onto the piece of my soul that was torn from my breast long ago, when the fire consumed her." The steel suddenly returned to his gaze, and his lips curled back in a snarl. *"BUT YOU LOST HER, DAMN YOU!"*

"Let 'im go, Magnus," Wolverine growled, and clasped a hand on his shoulder. "I ain't gonna say it twice."

Lensherr turned his head to glare at him. Dark eyes flashed

within the depths of the battle helmet, and the feral mutant was sent hurtling across the lawn. Wolverine bounced once, then rolled to his feet—and triggered his claws.

"That one ya get fer free," he said, holding his lethal bio-weapons at the ready. "Now, *I* get one."

The mutant overlord relaxed his grip on Xavier, and let him slide to the grass. Then he turned to face his adversary.

"What of all your bluster about dealing with the Red Skull first, Logan?" Lensherr asked.

"Skull ain't here, bub," Wolverine replied. He smiled coldly. "Means *you* get t'move t'the front'a the line . . ."

"STOP IT! BOTH OF YOU!" Cyclops shouted. The two men came to a halt, and looked at him. "We don't have *time* for this nonsense, damn it! We have to do something about this!"

"And what would you have us do, Summers?" Lensherr asked. "Create a new Cube before the world comes to an end? I don't believe we have the luxury of time to work out the specifics."

"So, you'd rather spend your last moments engaged in some senseless brawl?" Scott replied. "What happened to the great man of peace, who fought so hard to unite humanity and mutantkind?" Lensherr started to reply. "And don't say it's one of your other selves I'm talking about. *You* were the one who held the Cube, Magnus; *yours* was the will that directed the dream."

The mutant overlord halted. "You . . . are right," he finally said, then turned back to Xavier. "I . . . am sorry, Charles. I should have realized the Cube would affect you as well. Like the rest of us, you were trapped within your alternate. There would have been no way for you to learn of where Anya was placed in this hellish world." He looked past the professor, toward the uniformed man standing a few feet behind him. "But there *is* someone, I believe, who might know . . ."

Lensherr raised a hand, seized him in a magnetic grip, and yanked him across the short distance. Eyes glowing with rage, the mutant overlord seized him by the throat. "*You* are the Skull's lackey. You would know where the location of prisoners is recorded. Tell me where I might find my daughter—or your master will have to find a new whipping boy."

"Erik—don't," Xavier said.

The X-Men leapt forward to intervene, but Magneto formed a magnetic bubble around himself and his prey. The heroes' strongest blows simply bounced off.

The Nazi's eyes bulged from his head as Lensherr tightened his grip. "I . . . don't know what . . . you're talking about . . ." he gasped. "The Controller . . . didn't tell me . . . anything . . ."

"How unfortunate—for you," Lensherr replied. "To die so young, and so ignorant . . ."

"Wait. *Wait!"* the man screamed. "What . . . what's her name?"

"Anya Lensherr, you miserable worm. Her name is Anya Lensherr."

His victim started gazing from side to side, then up and down, as though searching his memories. "I know that name . . . I . . . I've heard it somewhere . . ." Then a nervous smile lit his features, and he looked to his costumed assailant. *"I know!* I know where she is!" He waved a hand toward the valley below—and a collection of military-style buildings there. "She's at the camp! I saw her!"

"Are you certain?" Lensherr asked through gritted teeth. He closed his hand again.

"Yes! *YES!"* the Nazi cried, his face turning an unhealthy shade of red. "She—she's in the band!" He whimpered. "Please . . . please don't kill me," he whispered.

Lensherr sneered in disgust. "You are not even worth the effort." And with that, he lowered the magnetic bubble and tossed the man to the heroes. "Here, X-Men—do what you wish with him. I have more important concerns."

He took to the air, then, and sped toward the concentration camp.

The ground began to tremble—another earthquake created by the trio of worlds shifting positions.

"What do you want us to do, Professor?" Scott asked.

"There is not a great deal we *can* do, given the circumstances," Xavier replied. "And yet, we must do *something,* if only to help ease the suffering of those few we can aid—before the end comes." He gazed at the distant figure of Magneto as he swooped toward the valley, purple cape flapping behind him like great wings. "Perhaps Erik has the right idea . . ."

"Now yer talkin', Charlie," Wolverine agreed.

Xavier nodded. "Come, X-Men—let us do some good."

And with that, they hurried to join Magneto in liberating the camp.

No, they couldn't save the world—not this time. But then no one ever said being an X-Man would be an easy job.

They could only do their best.

And sometimes that was enough.

The throne room had been transformed into a war zone, in just a matter of seconds. Having realized who it was that invaded "his" sanctum, von Doom roared in anger, and lost no time in attacking his hated rival.

The sides were evenly matched, however. Von Doom might possess the powers of a Supreme Guardian, but the Skull had those of the Cosmic Cube to call upon. The result was that a lot of destructive energy was being unleashed, but it was the Starlight Citadel—and those trapped aboard it—that would end up being torn apart, not the two combatants.

Grabbing hold of Roma, Betsy and Warren retreated from the battle to a safer position, outside the throne room. "Safer," though, was a relative term, since there was really nowhere to go to escape from this cosmic Armageddon.

The main doors flew open, and the Captain Britain Corps came charging past them, only to come to an abrupt halt as they saw what was happening. It was clear they had no idea how to respond to this bizarre crisis, but it didn't stop them from launching themselves into the fray, if only to protect the Guardian as she withdrew.

"I'm not sure they're going to be enough, Roma!" Betsy shouted over the din.

"Nor do I, Elisabeth," Roma admitted. "Yet, I am not strong enough to intercede, despite my powers."

"Well, is there someone else you can bring in?" Warren asked. "Some other security team you can call on that's in the citadel?"

Roma shook her head.

"What about their associates, m'lady?" Saturnyne suggested. "The X-Men?" She paused. "If they weren't destroyed by the Skull already, that is."

Roma gazed at her lieutenant for a few moments, then: "Yes . . ." she replied. "Yes, there may be a way . . ." She turned to Betsy and Warren. ". . . but it will require your assistance."

"Just tell us what to do," Betsy said.

Roma nodded. "Both of you have experienced the effects of the Cosmic Cube, and both of you have journeyed to and from the infected Earth. It is possible, therefore, that your contact with the Cube's energies will allow me to penetrate the barrier that has prevented me from seeing events on your world, and reach your teammates." Gently, she placed the tips of her fingers against their foreheads. "I need you to concentrate on your friends. Picture them in your thoughts, feel them within your hearts. Focus on all they are, all they mean to you—and summon them."

Betsy stared at the Guardian standing before her, then beyond. She could see the swirling energies of the vortex in her mind, hear the song of the Cube as the Skull drew upon its vast cosmic power. She closed her eyes and thought of the X-Men—the people who were always there for her, who stood by her in some of her darkest hours. The people who had saved her soul when she'd almost made a fatal decision on von Doom's world. She loved them all, cherished their friendships, wished more than anything that they could be with her right now, when she and the universe needed their help so badly.

And when she opened her eyes, the X-Men were there.

They glanced at their surroundings, obviously surprised to find themselves suddenly back at the citadel. Wolverine noted the war raging between the Skull and von Doom, and turned to the Guardian and her entourage.

"Somebody call fer backup?" he asked.

"Wow . . ." Warren whispered.

Betsy glanced at him, and smiled. "That, luv, is truly an understatement . . ."

22

THERE was no time for a proper reunion. Once the situation became clear to the X-Men, they immediately moved to assist the remaining members of the Captain Britain Corps who were still standing. There weren't many—most hadn't lasted long against the kind of energies being cast about by the two villains.

The Skull charged the throne, apparently outraged that he'd already been beaten to the seat of power. The dictator responded by hurling bolts of black energy at the invader, but the Cube's power was more than a match for them; under the Skull's control, it absorbed the discharges, then fired them back at von Doom. The tyrant deflected the bolts, and they exploded against a wall—one extremely close to a certain pulpit-like stand . . . and the delicate slivers of quartz contained there.

"The crystals!" Roam shouted. "If they destroy the crystals, all is lost!"

That was all the X-Men needed to hear before they attacked, Betsy and Warren at their side. They had literally gone through hell to protect the omniverse from the taint of the flawed Cube; they weren't about to let two of the villains who had so selfishly abused its power destroy the remaining dimensions in some cosmic territorial firefight.

The chamber shook as Storm created a miniature weather system high above, then summoned down bolts of lightning that struck their enemies time and again, without success. Rogue, and Wolverine tried a more physical approach, but their strongest blows only bounced off the protective barriers that had formed around the combatants. Cyclops's eye beams, likewise, were ineffective, as were the kinetically-charged playing cards thrown by Gambit. And yet, despite the intensity of the attack, neither villain turned their attention toward the costumed men and women who kept trying to reach them.

"It is as if they do not even know we are here," Nightcrawler observed.

"They don't," Jean said. "Their thoughts . . . They're so far removed from what's going on around them, so focused on their hatred for one another, that nothing else exists for them."

"Well, at the rate things are going around here," Warren said, "that might not be too far off the mark. If this place comes down around our ears, the *only* ones who'll still exist will be those two."

"Then we'd better do something to get their attention, people!" Cyclops ordered.

They launched another attack, pooling their resources with those of the recovering Captain Britains—and slowly, they began to crack the barriers.

Von Doom's, surprisingly, was the first to give, and Betsy couldn't help but wonder if perhaps Roma had something to do with it. Maybe the power he'd stolen was finite, and would have needed recharging. Whatever the reason, the armored dictator suddenly found himself cast down from the metaphorical heavens he had sought to claim, reduced once more to the lowly status of just another human being—one who was quickly swarmed over by an army of Union Jack-clad warriors.

The X-Men, meanwhile, focused their attention on the Red Skull. He stumbled back under the attack, the heel of his boot catching on the lip of the very pit he'd created when he'd made his entrance. Unfortunately for him, his startled reflex to regain his balance instinctively caused his clenched hands to open—and the Cube to fall out of his grasp.

"NO!" he cried.

Without thinking, he twisted around and made a desperate jump to retrieve it, apparently too surprised to simply call it back to him.

But it was Betsy who caught it, leaping over him to wrap her hands around the device. Warren swooped in and caught her around the waist before she could fall, then deposited her on the far side of the pit.

The Skull, however, was not as fortunate. He plummeted into the pit, and continued falling. All the way to the bottom of the tunnel—and into the void that swirled beyond the walls of the citadel.

"Roma—I have the Cube!" Betsy called out.

"Then make use of it, Elisabeth!" the Guardian replied. "Return to Earth and undo the damage that has been wrought! Put matters to right, before it is too late!"

Betsy stared at her, then the Cube. "But the flaw . . ."

"There is no time, Elisabeth!" Roma shouted. "You must go—now!"

She was right. There was no more time. No time to think of an alternative solution; no time to contemplate what calling upon the Cube's powers would do to her.

There was only time for a brief glance at Warren. She wanted to say so much to him, but all she could do was mouth "I love you" as she listened to the song of the Cube, tapped into its energies—

And then she was hurtling across infinity.

Leonard Jackson sat on the grass, watching the world come to an end.

In the space of only a few hours, he'd lost everything, including his beliefs—and, soon enough, his planet. He'd been abandoned by his master without a second thought, left behind so the death's-headed Controller could chase after some fairy tale castle in the sky. And with him had gone the Cosmic Cube—the only glue that had been holding together the pieces of his mad dreams. As for the others who'd fled the castle with him, Magneto was down in the valley, tearing apart the concentration camp in search of his daughter, and the X-Men had simply vanished.

He was alone now, more alone than he'd ever been in his entire life, with no one to mourn him when he'd gone. No one to ever know he'd existed at all, actually. He'd never make his mark on history now, he reflected—he'd just be another nameless statistic, lost among the billions of people who were going to die as the overlapping Earths vied for the position of dominant reality.

He'd been such a fool, thinking he was helping to change the world for the better when he'd only been making it worse. And as he sat there, watching the worlds tear themselves apart, he wished there was only something he could do to fix all this—better yet, to have prevented it from ever happening . . .

And that was when, as if on cue, the attractive Asian woman in the blue latex outfit suddenly appeared beside him.

This was it, then. The moment she had been dreading ever since von Doom had offered her the Cube, what seemed like a million years ago now. The moment when she would have to make the ultimate sacrifice, if she were to stabilize the realities.

Betsy looked around. She had no idea where she'd landed, but it was more than likely someplace close to where the Cube had last been stored. And since the Red Skull had been the last person carrying it around, she figured it could only be the German countryside.

She experienced a severe bout of vertigo as the ground rumbled, and she came to the startling realization she was looking at three different Earths. They were layered one on top of the other, like some mad three-dimensional picture seen without the special glasses.

"All right," she muttered, trying to psyche herself up for the task. "Let's get this over with . . ."

She closed her eyes, and opened her psychic senses to the Cube. It sang to her, as it had on von Doom's world, promising power beyond imagining. Why save the world, it seemed to whisper to her, when she could make one of her own? Why settle for a hero's sacrifice when she could be worshipped as a goddess?

She fought the temptation. There was too much at stake; too many people counting on her to do what was right. The Cube wanted her to draw upon its cosmic energies? Then so be it.

She concentrated, and made a wish–for worlds to return to their rightful places, for the fabric of time and space to be repaired, for the chaos to end.

And then it felt like her soul had been ripped from her body.

The Cube seized her in an iron grip, reached deep inside her, and began drawing out every ounce of energy she possessed. It became hard to breathe, and now the feeling of vertigo she'd experienced before became constant. She was growing weaker, even as a powerful light began to surround her. She could feel something happening, but it was taking so long . . .

"Let me do it."

Betsy started, and turned to face the young man in the Nazi uniform who was suddenly standing beside her. For a moment, she wondered how he'd been able to get so close without her being aware of his presence, but then she focused on the fact that he was holding out his hand. He wanted her to give him the Cube.

"No," she said. "You're one of . . . the Skull's men . . . I'd sooner . . . give it to . . . Magneto . . ."

"You don't understand," he insisted. "I want to do this. I *have* to do this. I allowed all this to happen. I should have done something about it sooner, but . . . but I thought . . . I thought I was doing something *good*. I didn't know it would be like this! I didn't know about the deaths, or the experiments, or what the camps were really like–it was all just stuff in history books, y'know? It wasn't *real.* But this . . ." He ran a trembling hand through his hair, and shivered. "I just didn't know . . ."

"And what is . . . *your* wish, if I gave you . . . the Cube?" she asked.

"My . . . ?" He paused. "To fix what I helped to break. To put an end to the hate and the pain and the suffering that went on, while I stood by and watched, and did nothing. To make things right again." He held out his hand again. "Please . . . let me take it."

She thought about saying no, thought about refusing him. But then she looked into his eyes, telepathically touched his mind, and saw the goodness in the heart of this scared, confused, misguided young man. A nobility of character that the Red Skull had refused to see, equating compassion and understanding with signs of weakness.

"You'll . . . die," she gasped. "It will only work . . . if it . . . absorbs your life . . ."

His hand never wavered. "That's okay. I always wondered what'd it be like to die a hero."

Gently, she placed the Cube in his hand, and immediately her legs began to wobble. The Cube had put a considerable drain on her own life. He helped her sit on the grass, then stepped back.

"Thank you . . ." she began.

"Leonard," he replied. "Leonard Jackson."

"Thank you, Leonard," she said, and smiled. "Thank you."

He smiled, too, and clasped the device to his chest, fingers laced around its sides. The light grew brighter, and waves of energy began to flow from the Cube, some spreading across the land, others rising high into the night skies, until they shone from horizon to horizon like an aurora borealis. The wind intensified, whipping to near-hurricane like speeds, and Betsy had to flatten herself on the ground to keep from being blown away.

And still the light grew stronger. It was difficult to look right at it, and Betsy was forced to shade her eyes with her hand to see what was going on around her.

The ground was shaking, and she had trouble focusing her

vision—it still appeared as though there were three versions of the same castle wavering in front of her. But then, slowly, the structure began to stabilize, shifting from three images, to two, then to one.

"It's working," she whispered. "He's doing it . . ."

She turned toward Leonard. The light had taken on a ball-like shape around him—a cocoon of cosmic energy. And somewhere within its depths, a good man was dying, allowing the Cube to drain away his life so that three worlds—and a multitude of interlocked dimensions—would have a chance to survive.

Remember me, she suddenly heard him say in her thoughts.

I will, Leonard, she promised. *I will. Always.*

The ball of light rose high into the air. It hovered miles above the land; then, without warning, it exploded, filling the night sky with the brightness of a miniature sun. Betsy gasped and turned away—

And when it faded, both Leonard Jackson and the Cosmic Cube were gone.

The winds subsided; the ground turned on its side for the last time before drifting back to sleep. And as the Earth returned to normal, Betsy rolled onto her back and looked up. The night was ablaze with stars—so many it was almost hard to believe the sky could hold them all.

And somewhere beyond them, she knew, waited a man she'd gone to hell and back to be with, whose love for her was as powerful as the cosmic forces that had threatened to tear them apart. A man she so desperately wanted to be with right now—and soon would be, thanks to a selfless young man . . . and the simple wish he'd made.

23

THE trip back to the Starlight Citadel went much smoother this time, now that the reality-cancer was in remission, and the crystal containing the life-force of Dimension 616 had been recovered from beneath the grillwork in the throne room, where Sat-yr-nin had dropped it. Betsy materialized in one of the debarkation suites—possibly the same one she kept popping into, although they all looked alike to her—a short time after the crisis was averted, and wasted no time in falling into Warren's welcoming arms.

But a proper welcome would have to wait, he explained. Roma had wasted no time in assembling a hearing in the throne room, judgment to be immediately passed on the two remaining parties responsible for almost destroying an infinitude of realities: Doctor Doom and Magneto.

Taking Warren's hand, Betsy set off at a quick sprint for the sanctum. She wanted a front row seat for this . . .

"Victor von Doom," Roma said.

Alecto and one of his men stepped forward, pushing the boisterous dictator before them. Without his stolen powers, or the makeshift weapons that had been stripped from his armor, he didn't present as much of a problem to the security staff.

Von Doom came to a halt before the Supreme Guardian. There was still quite a bit of damage left to be repaired in the throne room, but Roma had been adamant about dealing with the cause of the multidimensional tragedy in her sanctum. Betsy imagined it had a great deal to do with Roma proving to herself that no one was just going to barge into her home and expect her to accept the situation.

"Victor von Doom," Roma stated, "you are accused of the disruption of the space/time continuum, the near-destruction of three planetary systems, and the loss of countless lives, across a dozen or more dimensional planes. You have expressed no remorse for your actions. As Supreme Guardian, I therefore consider you a danger to all life." Her eyes began glowing brightly. "In conclusion, for your crimes against the omniverse, as well as your heinous assault on a celestial being, I sentence you to—"

"Your Majesty?"

The light dimmed, and Roma turned in surprise to look at the X-Men, who were standing quietly off to one side. Her gaze fell on their leader. "You wish to speak, Charles Xavier?"

"If I may."

Roma fell silent for a few moments. She rested her chin between thumb and forefinger and frowned, obviously taking some time to contemplate the request.

"This is highly irregular, m'lady . . ." Saturnyne cautioned.

"These are highly irregular circumstances, Saturnyne," the Guardian replied. "Very well, Professor."

Xavier nudged his hovering wheelchair forward. "Your Majesty, as unusual a request as this may be, I ask that you not execute the prisoner."

The throne room was filled with startled cries, and loud gasps of surprise. Even von Doom seemed surprised. Roma gestured for silence, then nodded for Xavier to continue.

"I realize the chaos he unleashed with his device, and the agony he has caused you personally, Your Majesty, but surely an enlightened being such as yourself is above the need for revenge?"

A wisp of a smile played at the corners of Roma's mouth. "You have never met my father, Charles Xavier."

"Mitras wept!" Saturnyne exclaimed angrily. "M'lady, we shouldn't be standing here discussing the fate of this tin-plated egomaniac! He should be executed immediately, his atoms scattered across the vortex, and the matter brought to a swift end!"

"*Someone* feels the need for revenge . . ." Ororo commented.

"Yes," Betsy replied. "But can anyone really blame her? I'd be enraged too, if somebody attacked me in my own bedroom, drugged me, and stuffed me in a freezer."

"Speakin' of human popsicles," Rogue said, "did they put Satyr-nin back on ice?"

Warren nodded. "Yeah. And Stanton, too. Roma's leaving it to Saturnyne to come up with a suitable punishment for him."

"I could almost feel sorry for the poor man," Nightcrawler said. He paused, then shook his head. "Well, no—not really."

Betsy turned her attention back to the proceedings.

"Saturnyne *does* have a point, Charles Xavier," Roma conceded. "While he lives, Von Doom will remain a constant threat to the omniverse. His kind never learn from their mistakes; they only create new ones."

"You *dare* speak of Doom that way?" the tyrant shouted. "Alien witch! I should have destroyed you from the outset—"

"Silence!" Roma ordered, her voice rumbling like thunder across the chamber. Much to everyone's surprise, von Doom actually did as he was told, and ceased his protestations. A wise move, Betsy thought. The Guardian turned back to the professor, and gestured toward the dictator. "You see that of which I speak, Charles Xavier."

"Then grant me a boon, Your Majesty, for all my students and I have accomplished this day. If von Doom's knowledge of the Cube, and the citadel, put the omniverse at risk, then simply remove that knowledge from his mind. Render him incapable of creating another such device."

"The best way of doing that would just be to kill him . . ." Saturnyne mumbled.

"It *could* be done . . ." Roma considered. "But he will only return to creating havoc on your world if he is sent back."

Xavier nodded. "A necessary evil, Your Majesty, if it means sparing his life. Von Doom may indeed continue his insufferable attempts at world domination, but there have been and always will be noble men and women to stand in opposition to him. To counter his evil acts with those of great good. To balance the darkness with the light."

Roma sat back on her throne, deep in thought.

"Very well, Charles Xavier, it shall be done as you have requested. Knowledge of the Cosmic Cube and the Starlight Citadel will be erased from the prisoner's mind, and he will be returned to your Earth. What becomes of him beyond that point will be entirely up to you—and your X-Men."

"No!" von Doom roared. "You cannot do this! You *will not* do this!"

"Remove the prisoner!" Saturnyne ordered. She didn't bother to hide the icy smile that lit her as von Doom was led away.

"Mark this day well, Guardian!" the tyrant shouted. "The day you made an eternal enemy of Victor von Doom! Let your minions do their worst—Doom will yet prevail! And then he will return—and destroy you all!"

His vows for revenge were still ringing in the air when he and his handlers exited the throne room and turned a corner.

"Nice li'l speech he had there on the way out," Rogue said with a smile.

"I'm glad t'see he's takin' de verdict so well," Gambit commented.

Roma turned to the next cause for concern. "Erik Magnus Lensherr."

Magneto stepped forward, carrying his helmet in his hand. He walked ahead of his guards, and bowed sharply when he stopped before the Guardian. Then he held his head up—proudly, almost defiantly, Betsy thought. Ready to face his punishment.

"You, also, have caused serious injury to the fabric of space/time through your selfish actions." Roma paused. "However, Professor Xavier has already told me of your intention to surrender the Cube, and how you were prevented from doing so through the intervention of the Red Skull."

Standing near Betsy, Wolverine grunted. "There he goes again, with that bleedin' heart routine. First Doom gets off 'cause o' him, now Magnus?" He snarled. "We're gonna have t'have a little talk, me an' him, when we get back home."

"What's wrong, Logan?" Cyclops asked. "Disappointed you didn't get another chance to lock horns with Magneto?"

"This ain't the time or place fer grudge matches, Summers," Wolverine replied. His eyes narrowed. "But it's like I told that dirtbag: I *know* him. It ain't gonna take 'im long t'start makin' trouble fer us again—you can bet on it. An' when that happens, I'll be comin' fer him . . ."

Across the aisle, Lensherr raised an eyebrow, and looked with surprise at his one-time friend. "Charles?"

"Your reasons for possessing the Cube were noble ones, Erik—although dangerously misguided in their execution," Xavier said. "'No one is fit to be trusted with power. Any man who has lived at all knows the follies and wickedness he's capable of. If he does not know it, he is not fit to govern others. And if he does know it, he knows also that neither he nor any man ought to be allowed to decide a single human fate.' " He smiled when he realized Magnus couldn't place the source of the quote. "Sir Charles Percy Snow."

Lensherr chuckled. " 'Ah, but a man's reach should exceed his grasp, or what's a heaven for?' "

"Robert Browning," Betsy whispered to Warren.

"I knew that," he said. She glanced at him, and raised an eyebrow. "Classical education, remember?"

Xavier sighed and shook his head. "Erik, we really should talk about this . . ."

"Another time, Charles," Lensherr said. "We will always have time to sit and discuss our dreams. And what to do about them." He looked back to Roma, and bowed courteously. "Your Majesty." And then, turning on his heel, he strode from the room, followed closely by his guards.

"And what of the Red Skull, m'lady?" Saturnyne asked.

"For now, I am content to leave him where he is," Roma said.

Betsy was surprised. "In the vortex? But isn't that . . . well, dangerous?"

"Have no fear, Elisabeth. Contact with the Cube, and others like it, has charged his body with just enough cosmic energy that no harm will come to him. He will simply drift wherever the temporal currents take him."

"Actually," Betsy said, "I was concerned more for the vortex . . ."

"Excuse me . . ."

The voice was deep and sonorous, reaching all parts of the throne room so that everyone heard it. The assemblage turned to gaze at the main doorway, the portal still swaying on broken hinges, from when von Doom had forced his way in. Standing there was a man well over six feet tall, with an enormous bush of brown curls that looked more like a party wig than natural hair. He was dressed in a baggy gray suit and matching overcoat, and a wide-brimmed brown hat rested at a rakish angle on the back of his head.

"I just wanted to stop by for a moment," he explained, matter-of-factly, "and return one of your errant patrol officers before I inspected the medical facilities for any damage."

He stepped aside, to make room for a Union Jack-garbed woman with a shock of white hair poking out from the top of her helmet.

"Captain U.K.!" Betsy said.

Linda McQuillan walked up the main aisle, removing her helmet as she addressed Roma. "I apologize for not reporting sooner, Your Majesty, but I was . . . unavoidably detained." She cast a heated glare at von Doom's back as he was led from the chamber.

"You see," the man said as he strolled up behind her, the dark-brown tones of his voice echoing in the vast space, "I was just on my way here, when I found your charming captain adrift in the vortex. So, naturally, I had to stop and see if I could provide any assistance and—well, here we are." He turned to the costumed warrior. "Well, I really must be getting on to the infirmary." He shook her hand and grinned. "It was a pleasure to meet you, Captain. We should do this again, under better circumstances. Feel free to drop by the medical wing any time—I make an exquisite cup of Darjeeling." And with that, he turned on his heel and proceeded toward the door.

"Just a moment! Come forward!" Saturnyne snapped. "Who the devil are you?"

"Oh, I'm terribly sorry," he said, and began walking up to the Majestrix. He snatched the hat from the mass of curls and jammed it into one of his pockets. "Didn't I introduce myself?"

"No, you did not," Saturnyne replied

"Ahh," he said, nodding sagely. "Well, I'm the Chief Physician." He smiled, revealing an oversized set of gleamingly-white teeth, and grabbed the Majestrix's hand. He began pumping it furiously. "It's an honor to meet you—again . . . 'Your Whyness,' isn't it?"

"Let *go* of me, you fool!" Saturnyne said, and snatched back her hand. "*You're* not the Chief Physician! You look *nothing* like him!"

The man's large eyes bugged out even further, and his mouth fell open in astonishment. "What? Are you absolutely certain?"

"Of course I am! He's—" she held up a hand level with her collarbone "—about this high—"

The man pointed to her hand. "That high?"

"Yes." She gestured toward her head. "And he has less hair . . ."

"Less hair? *Less hair?*" He frowned, and pulled at his lower lip in agitation. "Dear me. Dear me . . ."

"And he talks with a Scottish accent."

His expression suddenly brightened. "Really? Highland or Lowland?"

"What difference does it make?" Saturnyne replied. "The bottom line, you grinning imbecile, is that you *are* not—*cannot* be—the Chief Physician!"

He smiled, then spread his arms wide and simply shrugged. "Well, what can I tell you, Majestrix? I'm just not the man I used to be . . . or will be . . ."

It took a bit of explaining, but the situation was eventually made clear to one and all—much to Saturnyne's consternation, and Roma's amusement. A bio-scan of the new arrival revealed that he was, indeed, the man he claimed to be, although the Supreme Guardian appeared to be the only one not surprised by the news; why that might be, she wouldn't say.

Still, she went on to say, his appearance on the citadel was a timely one, for she had need of a doctor—not for herself, but for a very special patient.

The omniverse might have been restored to something of its former self, but there was still one bit of business left to attend to. . . .

24

NOW, you sure dis won' hurt none, right?"

Roma gently smiled as she looked at Gambit. "I can make no promises, Remy Lebeau. What I must do is a difficult task, performed only once before, to my knowledge—and then only by my father."

"Well . . . dere's a first time for ev'ryt'ing, I s'pose," he mumbled. "Jus' wish it wasn't de first time for *you,* too . . ."

She patted him consolingly on the arm, then gestured for him to lie on the table before them. Remy paused, and looked across the chamber. On the other side of a protective wall, watching him through two-inch-thick glass, stood his teammates and Saturnyne. Led by Roma, the group had descended into the depths of the Starlight Citadel, to a darkened chamber that not even the Majestrix knew existed. The Guardian had ominously commented that this was where her father, Merlyn, used to conduct some of his more . . . exotic experiments.

"Don't you worry none, sugah," Rogue said to Gambit through an intercom speaker mounted on a wall, her voice sounding strained. "I'll be right here when y'all wake up."

"We *all* will be, Remy," Scott added.

"Dat's good t'know," Remy replied with a nervous smile.

"'Cause ol' Gambit, he ain't never been too crazy 'bout operations."

He climbed onto the table and lay down on his back, lacing his fingers together on his stomach. He fidgeted for a few moments, obviously trying to make himself comfortable, then turned to look at his friends one more time. Betsy saw his eyes lock with Rogue's, and the look they shared. Then he flashed a warm smile, and turned back to Roma.

"Let's get dis over wit' Your Guardianship," he said. "Dere's a certain *fille* I promised t'take to a Harry Connick, Jr. concert, an' Remy Lebeau *never* goes back on his promises to a lady."

Betsy heard Rogue's tiny gasp. And then the Southern belle softly chuckled.

"He remembered . . ." she whispered.

"Very well," Roma said. "Then, close your eyes, and we shall begin."

Remy did as he was instructed, and Roma placed a hand to his forehead. There was a brief flash of light, and his body suddenly relaxed.

"He sleeps," she explained to the X-Men. "I would not want him conscious for this procedure." She looked at the team as she spoke, but her eyes fixed on Rogue. "Perhaps you should wait in one of the suites that has been prepared for you until this is finished. The next stage may be . . . difficult to observe."

"With all due respect, Yer Grace," Rogue said huskily, "I told Remy I was gonna wait right here fer him—an' I *never* go back on a promise."

Roma nodded. "Very well."

She turned to the shadows of the vast chamber, and gestured. The Chief Physician stepped forward, carrying a circular object that looked like an oversized glass ashtray. It was actually the projection unit for a powerful, sterilized stasis field—a large, glowing ball of energy that contained a collection of relics that brought audible gasps from the mutant adventurers. Even the battle-hardened Wolverine, Betsy noted, was taken aback by what he saw.

There were scraps of cloth—black and maroon material, brown leather—floating in the field, along with bits of skin and hair and brain. A finger, severed from a hand. Pieces of bone, including part of a spinal column. And a single eyeball, still attached to its stalk.

This, then, was all that remained of Remy Lebeau—the true Lebeau, not an alternate version who lived on a world under fascist rule. The X-Man, the thief, the rogue, known as Gambit. All that remained of the man who had selflessly given his life so that his friends could escape from captivity.

All that remained of the man Rogue loved as deeply, Betsy knew, as she herself loved Warren, or Jean loved Scott.

Rogue shuddered as she watched Roma take possession of the field projector and its precious contents, and Jean gently placed her hands on her friend's shoulders—to give comfort, to give strength.

"I . . . I'm okay," Rogue said hoarsely. It was clear to all, however, that she was anything but.

Gambit's remains had been obtained by members of the Dimensional Development Court, under Saturnyne's watchful eye. The recovery team had journeyed to the world once ruled by von Doom's elderly counterpart—Earth 892, to be precise—and sifted through the rubble of Psi Division Headquarters until they located the few elements now in Roma's possession. There had been other, larger parts, but, as the Majestrix had explained to the X-Men, they were unusable—tainted with the techno-organic virus that had been killing Remy before his heroic sacrifice. Still, she had said encouragingly, what they gathered should be more than enough for the Supreme Guardian to work with.

Roma moved over to an immense machine, the top of which was lost in the shadows of the ceiling. She placed the field projector on a flat, table-like surface, just beneath a collection of what looked like small broadcast dishes.

"The first stage will be to reconstruct his body, using these elements as the basis." She punched a code into a small keypad beside the machine, then stepped back. "While the bio-fog begins the process, I must retrieve the part of your friend that *cannot* be regenerated—the part that resides within this body he borrowed."

"Are you talking about his soul?" Scott asked.

Roma said nothing. Instead, she walked back to Lebeau and placed her hands inches above his chest. She closed her eyes, and her palms began to glow.

"The machine," Ororo said. "Something is happening . . ."

As one, the group stared at the stasis field. It was hard to see, but something was moving in the bio-fog—the pieces of Remy Lebeau had begun to swirl around, slowly at first, then faster, until they became just a blur.

And then something began to form—a skeleton. Bits of bone grew larger, became skull and vertebrae, femurs and sternum, ribs and ilium. Then the rest took shape, joining together as the stasis energy guided them to their proper places. The field expanded to fit the structure growing within it.

"Amazing," Xavier said.

"A miracle," Nightcrawler breathed. Betsy was surprised by the reverent tone in his voice.

Across the chamber, the Chief Physician walked over to the machine to check the readings. "The skeleton is complete, Your Majesty."

"Initiate the second stage," Roma commanded. Her hands continued to hover over the alternate Lebeau's body, but now a silvery glow surrounded him.

The doctor entered a new code. The fog thickened, obscuring the skeleton from view. When it cleared after a number of minutes, organs and nerves had appeared.

"Begin stage three," Roma said. The glow around Lebeau intensified and centered around his chest. Slowly, a ball of light began to rise, and Roma cupped her hands around it, as though to hold it together.

"Oh, my God . . ." Jean gasped. "Is that . . . is that Remy's soul?"

...olled down Rogue's cheek, to splash against the collar ...jacket. "It's . . . it's beautiful," she whispered.

...he fog billowed again, and now skin and muscle and hair ...ere regenerated. A familiar face took form. And then the swatches of material that floated above the body settled onto it—and began to spin into clothing. A costume, boots, gloves, an ankle-length coat—all were restored, in the space of seconds.

The machine suddenly powered down, and an ominous silence filled the chamber. The doctor stepped over to inspect the final readings.

"The process is complete," he reported.

"Then, open the field and stand aside," Roma replied.

The physician did as ordered, and the Guardian grasped the ball of light—the soul of Gambit—that floated above Lebeau. Moving quickly, she crossed the short distance to the costumed body, and raised the soul above her head.

"Let there be a joining!" Roma shouted. *"LET THERE BE LIFE!"* And she plunged the silvery ball deep into the chest of the reconstructed body.

And then it—he—screamed.

It was a cry of pain and despair, of great loss and even greater gain, of life and love and hope and joy.

It was the cry of rebirth.

And when the last echoes had faded in the great chamber, Remy Lebeau opened his eyes and took his first breath—and smiled.

Roma did, as well, and glanced toward the observation room. "The reclamation was successful," she said. "He is whole again."

There were sighs of relief, then, mixed with tears of joy; even Saturnyne was affected. Rogue was the first through the door, half running, half floating, to join Remy, and throwing her arms around him as he sat up.

"He will be weak for a short time, so he should rest," Roma told the group.

Tears streaming down her cheeks, Rogue turned to face her. "I'll make sure he *stays* in bed," she said, wiping her nose on the sleeve of her bomber jacket, "even if I have ta strap 'im down t'make 'im stay put." She smiled, and started crying again. "Thank you."

Roma placed a hand on hers, and gave a gentle squeeze. "For all the X-Men have done for the omniverse this day, friend Rogue, I could do no less, in turn, for you."

As Rogue turned her attention back to Gambit, Saturnyne approached the Guardian. "I'll see to it that the X-Man's counterpart is returned to his proper Earth, m'lady."

"Thank you, Saturnyne," the Guardian replied. "Right now, though . . ."

They stepped back, then, and allowed the X-Men to cluster around their comrade.

As Betsy watched Rogue and Gambit, and felt tears well up in her eyes, she felt a hand slip around her waist, and smiled. She turned to look at Warren. Then she put an arm around his waist and drew him into a kiss that would never last long enough.

He was right, she realized. She couldn't save the universe all by herself—none of them could. But they didn't have to. Not as long as they had each another; not as long as there was a shoulder to lean on when the burden became too great.

They'd put their lives on the line to save countless billions this time—billions of sentient beings who would never know them, never know of the sacrifices they'd made, the agonies they'd suffered along the way. And she knew that tomorrow they would go back and do it again. Because they were doing something good. Because people counted on them. Because they were committed to doing the best they could.

Because that's what being an X-Man was all about.

And sometimes—*sometimes*—that was good enough.

25

ROMA exited the Life Chamber, feeling—well, she didn't know exactly *how* to describe how she felt. Satisfied? Elated? Emotional states were such an alien concept to beings like her father and herself—so many to sift through, so many she didn't understand—it was difficult to pick the one that best suited a given situation.

Physical sensations, however—now, *that* was something she had come to understand quite well. Her head and body ached, even more so after undergoing a painful process of her own: the restoration of the aspects of herself that had been separated by von Doom. Being subjected to the rays of a multiphasic crystal accelerator, even one handled by an expert, rather than a power-hungry tyrant, had been no less agonizing with her alternates going in, than they had coming out. If she never came near another such machine again for the rest of her immortality, she decided, it would be too soon.

"Well done, Your Majesty," the Chief Physician said, suddenly beside her. He grasped her hand and shook it vigorously. "Merlyn himself couldn't have handled the reclamation process any better."

She raised an eyebrow, amused by the notion of a cosmic entity being congratulated by a lower life-form for performing what amounted to a difficult, yet altogether minor, task. "You are pleased with my efforts, then, doctor?"

"Yes. Oh, very much so." He nodded sagely, and tapped the side of his nose with an index finger. "In my humble—yet extremely expert—opinion, Your Majesty, I would say you possess the makings of a fine surgeon."

The eyebrow climbed higher. "You do."

"Indeed, I do," he insisted good-naturedly. "And I think such fine work as yours should be rewarded." He smiled broadly, all teeth and curls, and reached into the pocket of his surgical scrubs for a small paper bag. "Would you care for a jelly baby . . . ?"

INTERLUDE IX

THE walk through the desert had been an arduous one, but it gave him time to be alone with his thoughts.

Now, as he crested a dune in the first light of day, Erik Magnus Lensherr stopped to look at the village before him. Once it had been a thriving oasis, but over time the sands had begun washing over it, stripping it of color, of life. And yet, there was still life to be found here.

A door opened in one of the mud-brick buildings, and a dark-skinned woman emerged. From where he stood, Lensherr could not make out her features, but he knew who she was by the colorful blanket she wore—and the large bowl she carried in one hand.

"Good morrow, Abena Metou," he said pleasantly to himself, testing his use of the language. The pronunciation still sounded a little too stiff for his liking—still too phonetic, as though he were reading it directly from the portable Berlitz guide on his Palm Pilot. But he had learned the meaning of patience here—a lifetime ago, it seemed—on another world; he could do so again. The words would come with time.

She would not recognize him, of that he was certain; in this world, the "real" world, they had never met. But that would change.

Behind her walked a child—a girl no more than three or four years old. Her daughter, Jnanbarka. Watching her, an image suddenly popped into his head, and he reached into the back pocket of the tan cargo pants he was wearing. He pulled out a thin metal case and opened it. Inside was a faded, worn black-and-white photograph of an eight-year-old girl. Her dark hair was cut into bangs that framed wide, joy-filled eyes and a big, gap-toothed smile. Even now, decades later, he could still remember how excited she had been when the Tooth Fairy generously rewarded her, the night before the picture was taken.

It was one of the few truly happy moments in his life that he could recall, for there had never been another after the night she died in the fire. The night when Magneto vowed to the heavens that he would punish the world for the death it had caused—a punishment that he had never tired of administering.

Until now . . .

He smiled gently. "Anya . . ." he whispered.

With a sigh, he closed the case and put it back in his pocket. The sun was a little higher in the morning sky now, its light blending the purple of night with shades of pink and lavender, gold and orange. A new day was starting, and with it the struggle between humanity and mutantkind would begin again, picking up where it had left off before the Cosmic Cube had turned the world upside down. A new day of misery and intolerance for his kind. A new day of pain and suffering and blinding hatred.

Would his efforts to change that situation—however misguided or villainous they might seem to the world at large—ever make a difference? he wondered.

He had to believe that they would—that they did. He had only to look into his mind's eye for the proof: To see the world his alternate had built. To know of the peace that had finally been established between races. To know that a man could put hatred behind him and build a family, and in doing so regain his soul.

To put hatred behind him . . . Now, *there* was a challenge for Magneto, he reflected. A challenge like none he had ever faced before. One that relied more on strength of character than strength of will. One, perhaps, that would make him the man he always thought he had been.

The notion appealed to him.

It would be interesting, he thought, to go forward in time a hundred years or so, and see what became of his life's work, of the paths he chose to walk down. Would he be idolized as a great peacemaker, or vilified as one of mankind's greatest enemies? Would he, too, have found a way to bring man and mutant together, like his counterpart, or would he have returned to his old ways, and once more sought to make *Homo superior* the dominant species on the planet? So many questions to be answered; so many choices to make . . .

" 'Had I but worlds enough, and time . . .' " he said, and shook his head with a knowing grin.

He would never find out, however, unless he started down the first path, made the first choice. After all, he considered, a journey of a thousand miles begins with but a single step . . .

And with that thought comforting him, he took that step.

The first step on the path to salvation.

EPILOGUE

A NEW day dawned.

The sun rose high and warm above the Yucatan Peninsula, that South American landmass that separates the Gulf of Mexico from the Caribbean Sea. It would be another hot and humid day, as it had been yesterday, and would be again tomorrow. But the breeze that blew in from the East was a welcome change from the soaring temperatures, and the water was cool and inviting.

Sixty-five million years ago, it's believed, a comet or asteroid struck the Earth here, near what is now the village of Chicxulub. The effects of the impact—firestorms, tidal waves, skies choked with dust and dirt for years—were probably responsible for wiping out every dinosaur in existence, as well as quite a other animal and plant species, and bringing to a close the Cretaceous Period.

Mankind thought it impossible that a disaster of such magnitude would ever happen again; if it did, however, there was no doubt in anyone's mind that the human race would never survive.

But the means of creating global destruction did not have to come from space, as anyone who lived in a world of superpowered men and women could tell you. Not when not a day went by, it seemed, without someone threatening to unleash nuclear

Armageddon, or open a mystical portal that allowed murderous Elder Gods to stalk the land, or detonate the planet's molten core. Why worry about comets and meteors and asteroids, when there were *people* more than capable of destroying the world, with just the push of a button, or the flick of a lever—

Or by making a simple wish.

No, the means of creating global destruction did not have to come from space—not if one looked long and hard to find alternatives. Not if one knew *where* to look for them.

And yet, on this beach where the hand of fate had struck the fatal blow against the world's great thunder lizards, there were no pieces of space debris to be found, nor a button or lever in sight. There were only golden sands and colorful rocks, glistening seaweed and faded driftwood—

And a tiny shard of a wish box that had tumbled from the sky the night before.

A shard that sparkled with the promise of dreams yet to be realized. . . .

Take this kiss upon the brow!
And, in parting from you now,
This much let me avow—
You are not wrong, who deem
That my days have been a dream;
Yet if hope has flown away
In a night, or in a day,
In a vision, or in none,
Is it therefore the less gone?
All that we see or seem
Is but a dream within a dream.

Edgar Allan Poe
A Dream Within a Dream